SLEEPER ASSASSIN

THE METALIST'S JOURNEY, BOOK 3

KD LUMSDEN

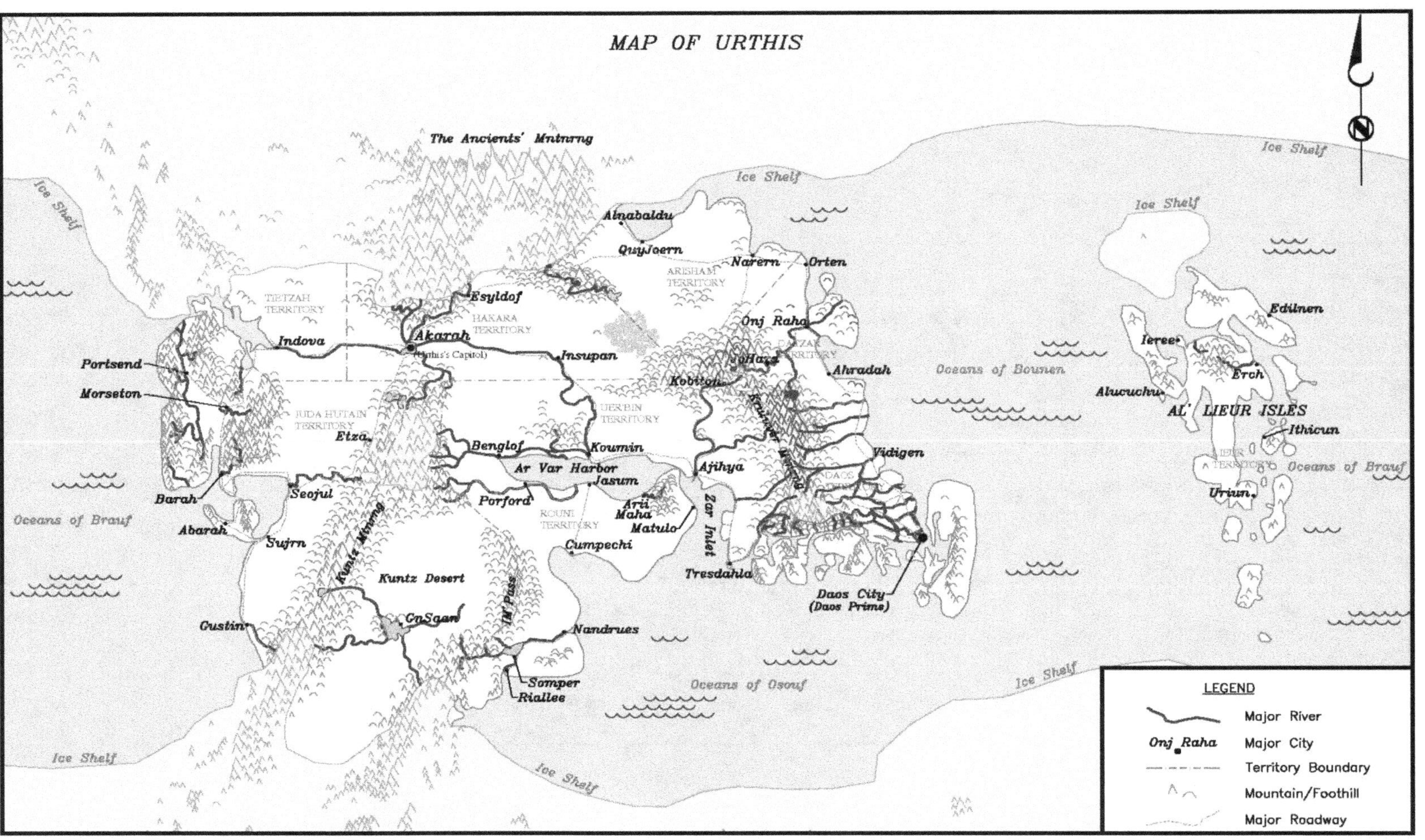

MAP OF URTHIS
N
The Ancients' Mntnrng
Ice Shelf
Ainabaldu
QuyJoern
Narern
Orten
TIETZAH TERRITORY
Esyldof
HAKARA TERRITORY
ARISHAM TERRITORY
Akarah
(Urthis's Capitol)
Indova
Insupan
Onj Raha
SoHara
Kobitoh
Ahradah
Oceans of Bounen
Portsend
Morseton
JUDA HUEIAIN TERRITORY
UERBIN TERRITORY
Etza
Benglof
Koumin
Ar Var Harbor
Jasum
Ajihya
Vidigen
Barah
Seojul
Porford
ROUNI TERRITORY
Arii Maha
Matulo
Zar Inlet
DAOS
Abarah
Sujrn
Kuniz Mtnrng
Cumpechi
Tresdahla
Kuntz Desert
In Pass
Daos City
(Daos Prime)
Gustin
GnSgan
Nandrues
Somper
Riallee
Oceans of Brauf
Oceans of Osouf
Ice Shelf
Edilnen
Ieree
Erch
Alucuchu
AL' LIEUR ISLES
Ithicun
Oceans of Brauf
Uriun
LEGEND
Onj Raha
Major River
Major City
Territory Boundary
Mountain/Foothill
Major Roadway
Ice Shelf

THE METALIST'S JOURNEY
Book 3 ~ Sleeper Assassin
Book 4 ~ Land of Cannibals

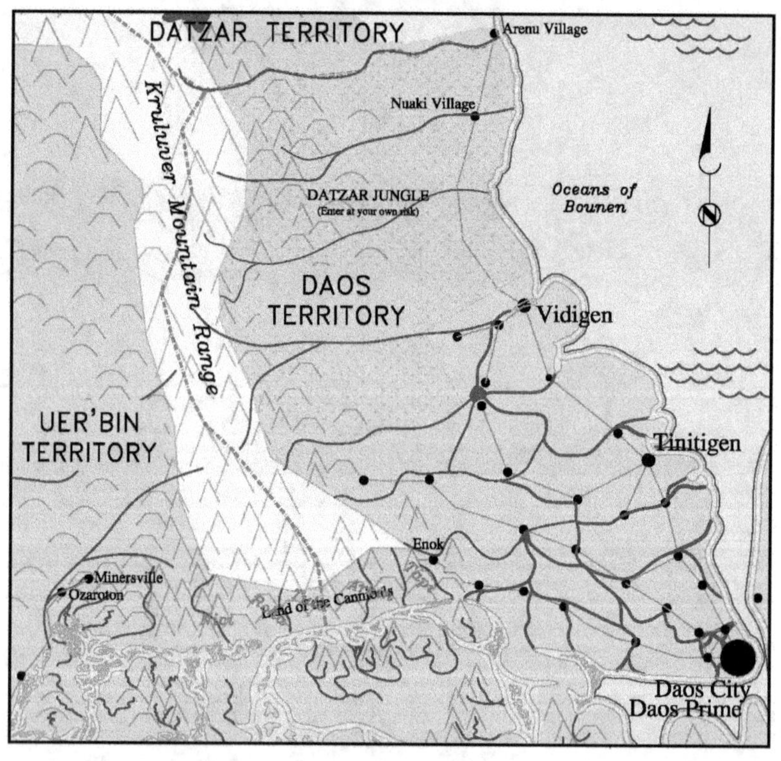

CONTENTS

1

<u>Arenu Village</u>

Metal twangs vibrated across the courtyard.

Awake, Irwin tossed in his bed, unable to ignore the clanging and banging from the nearby forge. Metallic songs from the hot metals, only he could hear, sang in his ears and tingled down his spine. To him, every type of metal had its own song, and his body longed to absorb them all.

It was barely light, but there was no going back to sleep. The dog, curled up between the ration boxes in the back of the wagon, whined in his sleep. That was Irwin's best friend, Kipp, in his canine form—a clever and useful trick of the Clan-Duin species. The scent of freshly baked sweet rolls did not wake the always hungry Kipp with his keen sense of smell. Yet Irwin's stomach grumbled and pulled him from the music of hot iron.

He lay still on his bed in their makeshift home on the back of their wagon.

If I go for sweet rolls, I will be confronted, and the baker will not sell to me.

What about last night and that belligerent dockhand's attempts to provoke me?

That was quite a spectacle he had caused. But now anyone present in that saloon knows not to mess with me.

Or it might have given the locals more freedom to provoke. Ugh. I do not want to be incited, but this is what life is like for everyone of Talent when around Mortals. It does not matter what I do, I will be judged. Although I look Mortal, I still smell like Death.

His stomach grumbled louder and more painfully.

I really want one of those sweet rolls!

He swung his legs off the bed and heard jubilant voices echoing around the courtyard through the wagons' canvas cover. "Oh, Arrol!" Loud laughter followed the cry.

Quickly, he shimmied into his pants. Arrol was the Eunuch Irwin met upstairs in the Gritty Titty Saloon last night. So even if word had not spread about last night's incident with Batton, he would most likely be safe with his new friend. He and Arrol had shared little conversation, but their embrace had been emotional for Irwin.

Securing his pants, he climbed through the front portal of the covered wagon, over the seat, and landed bare foot on the cobbled ground. Arenu Village was a port of call, made from Erthin ingenuity. There were shell mosaics along the upper fortress walls and inlaid colored stones providing pathways for visitors to follow. Without looking back, Irwin moved like a ghost across the square toward the two Eunuchs and an unknown shrouded person.

He called out, "Good morning, Arrol."

Arrol stopped and turned. His painted lips curved into a smile. "The morning is good, thank you—Samuel, is it?"

Irwin smiled at the Eunuch; happy he recalled this alias name.

"You're up early."

"As are you." Irwin glanced toward the forge where an Erthin worker stoked a fire, turned back to Arrol. "I figure a person who works at night would sleep late."

"On the contrary, we take naps day and night." Arrol made a delicate hand gesture toward his friends. "This is Ron, and that is Jorge."

Jorge, the shrouded one, stood behind Ron's shoulder, keeping himself hidden. Something was different about Jorge—he emanated a low, vibrating, magnetic pulse. "Good morning, Ron and Jorge. Are you going to the bakery?"

Arrol sang out, "Of course! Only the best sweet rolls."

"Do you mind if I join—"

Arrol grabbed Irwin's arm, entwined it with his own and yanked him along. "Of course you may join us. The more the merrier, right ladies?"

In a husky, but effeminate, voice, Ron said, "Our friend Jorge is visiting from Nuaki Village. He's an Empath, one of the rarest of all creatures. That's why he lives there." Ron rubbed Jorge's arm.

Jorge's silky teal robe prevented Irwin from seeing too much of him. But as he moved along with Arrol, he caught a glimpse of Jorge who seemed to resemble Kipp.

Must be the shadows beneath the hood.

"You are from Nuaki Village?" Irwin wanted to talk to Jorge, but the Empath dropped his head. "Yes."

"Oh Jorge, you can be more cordial than that." Ron elbowed the Empath.

The metal from the forge kept on calling to Irwin. His heart pounded. Droplets of sweat ran down his back. And as they walked past, he saw yet another mixed-blood, Erthin/Clan-Duin smith who was hefting several rods of metal into an iron bucket at the edge of a cast iron pit. The Erthin waved his hand across the low-burning fire, and flames rose to the top, heating the iron cauldron and its contents until it glowed. Mesmerized—he had never seen this trick before.

Arrol whispered close to his ear, "Kol, the smithy, is quite a handsome brute. He's very strong, too, but can be gentle."

"I am not looking at Kol."

The metal heated faster than he had seen at any other forge; probably because the fire was under the control of Erthins. The metallic tunes shifted, and a new sound hurt his inner ear. He winced, shook his head, and ignored the high-pitched squeal as best he could.

Arrol winked at him. "Sure you weren't."

"Samuel, honey, you should never play cards. You're not a good liar!"

"Lying around here is a death sentence," said Jorge from beneath his hood.

Irwin felt his sweltering backside turn into a cold sweat.

They sauntered into the cozy bakery. The smell of fresh-baked bread filled the room like the scent of new spring flowers on Irwin's childhood mountaintop. He was reminded of his old life and the caves where he grew up—all the misery wrought by his father—even the pain and heartbreak when his father left him for dead by the side of a road. Mortally injured by his father's blows, he was dumped and deserted to die alone.

An apprentice baker was brushing a honey glaze across sheets of hot sweet rolls. Irwin snapped out of his daydream and examined the young man behind the counter; guessed him to be the same age as he was, but scruffy and missing several teeth.

This apprentice was lanky and part Clan-Duin. His light brown hair hung over his brown eyes. His soft features hinted to Mortal, but Irwin sensed that the apprentice held yet another power. They all approached the front counter. "A bag of goodies for ya fellas?"

Arrol leaned across the counter. "You know what we want, Hank!" He winked. "Give it to us."

Hank glanced over his shoulder at the doorway into the kitchen, then back at Arrol. "Oh, I'll give it to you," he winked back. "Who's this new fella?"

Arrol pulled Irwin close. "He's mine. This is Samuel."

"Are you the Mortal everyone's talking about?"

"I am no Mortal."

Hank looked at Irwin's hairless chest, and then all the way up and down. "You're too pale to be anything else—unless you're a Telepath."

"I am no Telepath! I am Erthin."

They all chuckled.

"What about Corporal Teigahn?" said Irwin. "He appears Mortal yet lives in Nuaki Village."

"Teigahn's an ass of a Telepath," replied Arrol. "Telepaths don't count. They just blend with the rest of society."

Ron said, "I thought Teigahn said he's Coterie."

"Oh, he's Coterie," Jorge said. "He'll boast that he's full Capritian, too, though no one really cares."

Arrol said, "Probably why he gets along with all those rapists and murderers in Nuaki."

Hank nudged Jorge. "Only the worst of the worse live in Nuaki Village, Jorge, so why are you there?"

"I plan on going to Nuaki Village," Irwin said.

"Why?" Arrol coughed.

Irwin did not look at Arrol, but above his head, and smirked. "What if I am the worst of the worst?"

Arrol petted Irwin's arm. "You're too tender to be all that bad, Samuel."

Hank offered Arrol a bamboo plate with an assortment of sweet rolls. "Can you take time off now?"

Taking all this in, Irwin wondered what Arrol wanted from Hank.

Hank looked back at the kitchen. "No, I can't. Nadire wants me to get all these done right now. He found me screwing around yesterday and has been spurring me all morning. He's an ass."

"Maybe a drink later." Irwin noticed a familiar, seductive look in Arrol's eyes.

"Yeah, maybe." Hank stiffened. Nadire pounced like a cat into the display room. Sweat poured from the old man's brow, already splotched with flour. "You owe a silver," Hank said, no doubt hopeful someone would pay.

Irwin formed a silver coin in his hand, pulled it from his pocket and gave it to Hank.

Arrol led the small group into an alcove with a large open window and a view of the forge and even the Gritty Titty Saloon.

Irwin studied the Saloon's towering windows and front door. Arrol shuffled into a seat next to him. "Many thanks, Samuel. That was a gracious gesture." He looked tenderly at Irwin.

Irwin's back was to a stone wall. He could see through the doorway into the bakery's display room. Jorge and Ron joined the table. Jorge pulled back his hood, exposing short, greasy yet curly, brown hair that complimented the same color eyes. He was like Jyn, the barkeep—Daosian in appearance. His yellowish skin was freckled with white spots. His jawline and cheeks were pock-marked, and he squinted, scrunching up his oval face. Jorge was lanky—seemed overly conscious of his posture. He sat so straight it looked painful.

Arrol and Ron stared at Jorge.

Arrol stuttered, "What happened to you, Jorge?"

"What do you mean ...?" Jorge looked at his speckled hands and arms. "What's going on? How is this possible? You shouldn't be able to see my physical form." He looked at Irwin through his gangly fingers. "Nothing has changed with me," he said, and pointed one of those fingers at Irwin. "You're the only thing different here. This is you. It must be. How are you doing this?"

"What! I am not doing anything. Why do you think it is me?"

Great! Something else my power can do. I hope I do not seem evil.

"You have to be doing something." Jorge glared at him; suspicion drooling from the side of his mouth. "I've done nothing different in my routine, except meet you—sit near you." He pointed again, his fingers curving like the claws of a bird. "You must be doing this to me. Somehow, you're making this happen!"

"I do not understand. What am I making happen?"

"We can see Jorge." Arrol said. "Not that we couldn't see him before." His gaze rested on Jorge. "I told you Jorge is an Empath. He's got the ability to be what you desire, or whom you desire to see. Most of the time, when I see Jorge, I see myself. When Ron looks at Jorge, he sees who he desires right then. But somehow, we're able to see who you desire, Samuel."

"This is not what I desire."

If that was the case, he'd look like Kipp.

Arrol brushed his brown-skinned hand across Jorge's pale face. "Remarkably bizarre. I would've never guessed you to be Daosian. Oh, Jorge, I can't imagine what it's like for you to not see what we all see. But we still love you."

The Empath turned and placed his hand on Ron's arm who backed away as soon as he saw the face, the hands, and the rest of him.

"Ron, what do you see?"

"Well, you've got dark circles under your thin shaped eyes; your cheeks are gaunt and high-boned, and your nose is fat and long. Your pigment isn't pleasant with your hair color." Ron sounded earnest, almost solemn. "And your hair!" He touched Jorge's knotty hair. "It's the tightest of curls. I wonder why we see this. Is this what you desire, Samuel?"

Irwin shook his head, embarrassed and sorry for exposing Jorge.

"I accept you for you, Jorge. You know that." Ron's face was red hot.

Jorge wove his fingers together on the tabletop and stared at Irwin. "What's your Talent, Samuel?"

"I-I am Erthin."

Arrol fluttered his hands. "You're no Erthin, honey! My guess is you're one of those hidden treasures, like Jorge. You can tell us your Talent, Samuel. We're not ones to gossip or judge." They all lowered their voices to whispers and bent in closer to each other across the plate of buns.

"I have been told I am a Healer Erthin." Irwin watched Ron and Jorge, hoping they would buy his lie.

Ron, eyes on the tabletop, said, "You don't smell Erthin. If you smell like anything, you smell like Death."

Do not panic.

He knew not to tell anyone about his powers. So, he made a knife appear, pretending it had been stashed down the backside of his pants. He laid his arm across the tabletop. Meanwhile, his leg shook under the table.

"All I know I can do is regenerate instantly." The blade punctured the skin on his forearm. He had done this trick many times, repeating the same words. It was the best way to keep gawkers from asking the same questions about him and his powers.

People do love a spectacle.

Blood spilled from his arm splayed open on the tabletop. He pressed hard and deep, tearing muscles and tendons. But as the blade drew along his forearm toward his elbow, the puncture healed as they all watched—the gaping wound was now closed. He placed the bloodied blade on the tabletop. Only a few dribbles of blood remained on his arm. His flesh was whole again.

Ron pushed back from the table. "Whoa!"

"WOW!" Arrol jumped back too and drew his hands to his face.

Jorge's eyes bulged even wider. He did not look away, unlike the others—clearly measuring Irwin. "Be cautious in the south. Nuaki Village is the type of place where your Talents will be challenged."

Irwin put the blade away, pretending again to stash it in the backside of his pants—his skin reabsorbed the metal knife. "I am not too worried about that. Nuaki is not my final destination."

Arrol leaned closer to Irwin. "You're not going to Daos, are you?"

"Yes, I am."

Arrol gripped Irwin's wrist. "Don't go!"

Although Arrol was Clan-Duin, Irwin was wary of too much contact with anyone. He gently pulled away from the grasp.

Ron agreed with Arrol. "Daos is a dangerous place."

"It's possible you could go through all of Daos without being identified as Talented," Jorge said. "You appear Mortal, even though you've shown us you're not. If you don't call attention to yourself, you might not be bothered."

Ron asked, "When did you find out you could heal like that?"

"More like, *how'd* you find out?" Arrol said.

Irwin looked at the faces around the table and took a sweet roll from the bamboo plate. "I was born this way." He pulled off a bite of the glazed bread and shoved it into his mouth. "I have never been sick or hurt beyond repair."

"Oh, honey, you've been hurt." Arrol sensed the lie. "You might not have physical scars. How you were with me last night tells me you come from the same sheet of fabric we do. What's your story Samuel? All we did was cuddle, but because I'm Clan-Duin, I heard your silent crying, felt your despair. It's all right, Samuel. We've all cried. You're among friends. You can tell us anything."

Irwin persisted in silence, trying to keep his mind and his leg still.

Jorge stared. "There's something more powerful than regeneration going on here. You say you're Erthin, but what you're doing is more than Erthin energies." He pointed his sweet roll at Irwin. "And if you weren't affecting me like you are …."

Arrol turned to Jorge. "So, what's your theory?"

"Well, his power affects me without so much as a touch—as though my power is affecting everyone without me touching them. But his power appears to be proximity based."

Arrol eyed Irwin. "What happens if you two touch?"

He is from Nuaki Village. He could be a Telepath. Or linked to one. It is possible, but I will break that spell.

Should I allow contact?

Why not? What more could go wrong with my morning?

Humoring the Eunuchs, he reached over and touched Jorge's hand. Nothing. "That's what I thought," said Jorge. He stood, shifted off the bench. "How far must I be before you stop affecting me?" Jorge took one step back, then a second—a third.

One last step, and Irwin saw Kipp standing there instead of Jorge. "How the …!"

"About time I got to look at something so handsome." Arrol winked at Jorge.

"As they have said, I'm an Empath. I appear as the one person you desire to see the most—a dead relative, family member, lover. Some see archrivals. Everyone is different.

"You see what you want to see in me. I can tell by someone's reaction what type of emotion has been invoked. I then gauge how to interact. I can tell if the person you see me as is friend or foe. I can tell if they boost your confidence or slander it.

"By your reaction, Samuel, the person you see is someone you enjoy. A lover or close confidant, perhaps? This person holds your hand but won't hold you. And because of that, you shy away."

Irwin squirmed while the Empath, appearing as Kipp, gazed at him intently.

"You look at me and then you look at Arrol."

Seeing Kipp and hearing him speak with Jorge's voice disturbed Irwin's soul. *Jorge is a rarity.*

"In time, your affinity for this person will change. Everything in life changes, and you must learn to accept that."

Spellbound, Irwin implored, "How did you find out about your Talent, Jorge?"

Jorge stepped back toward the table, changing back to his real self, and took his seat next to Ron. Irwin felt the magnetic vibration Jorge secreted cease the moment he stepped near him. "Well, Samuel, much like you, I was born this way." He chomped absently on his sweet roll. "My mother and I lived on a pirate ship. She kept me safe until one day I was taken away. The pirates who stole me brought me here, but I ended up in Nuaki Village.

"They trained me as a *Shayot*, but I was never allowed to leave. Unlike any of the others. Nuaki Village is where I will live until the day I die."

"If they do not allow you to leave, then why are you here? Why go back?"

"I couldn't go anywhere if I tried. Not looking like ...." His hands dramatically moved across his chest.

"Was your mother an Empath?"

"No. She was a pirate. At least that's what I remember of her. I remember her crying when I was taken. But she did nothing." Jorge stared at his food.

"She was a whore," Arrol chuckled, "just like all our mothers."

"No, she wasn't." Jorge spat. He ran a hand through his thick brown curly hair.

"Do you know if there are any others like you out there?"

"No." With heat in his eyes, Jorge sighed and said, "I am the last of my line."

"You'd love it if you were the last Empath, but I don't think you are. There are many people on Urthis. Maybe there's a whole commune of Empaths somewhere you don't know about."

Jorge rolled his eyes at Arrol, swallowed the rest of his roll. "Samuel, what about your family? Do you know them?"

"I lived with my father until half a year ago." He felt safe to confide that much. "I am a Gypsy now."

Ron chuckled, his mouth still full. "You're no Gypsy."

"Why would you willingly go to Daos?" asked Jorge.

"To sell my wares and see the sights."

Arrol touched his hand. "What are your wares?"

"I am a cutlery specialist."

His thoughts wandered back to the mountaintop—back to the only place he had ever known until the night his father had lost his mind, his senses, and, when it was all over, left Irwin to die. He had been like a wild boar on the kill. His father possessed only half of Irwin's Talents—the half that could turn certain metals to silver pieces, the part that could go crazy when there was too much metal around him—too much chaos from the singing of nearby metals. His father and his grandfather and great grandfather had taught him to work all kinds of ore. It was easy for him to pose as a cutlery man, to make and fix knives along this unexpected journey. He watched a flock of seagulls scatter toward the ocean as someone walked across the courtyard. He might never see his cave or his father again. And that made him sad until more seagulls fighting for a catch outside the bakery brought him back to this table full of new friends.

2

<u>Sweet Rolls</u>

"**C**utlery Specialist? Daggers and knives?"

"Yes."

Arrol's eyebrows arched. "Don't tell me that wagon is your forge?"

"No. My merchandise was made in my hometown." Will they detect this fib? "My plan is to travel around Urthis—sell my wares and see the sights of our magnificent land."

Jorge's light brown eyes sparkled. "You're touring the world?"

"For almost six moons now." His knees began to itch.

"Speaking of travel," Ron changed the subject. "Did anyone see the Uriun trade ship yesterday?"

"Yes. Wasn't that exciting to see it moored outside the harbor?" Arrol said. "The seamstresses bought reams and reams of fabric from those pirates—all different colors and patterns. They always buy the best silks. We should get enough to make more robes." Arrol winked at Jorge who was still studying Irwin.

"Oh," Jorge turned to Ron, "I would love to get enough fabric for another sarong." He elbowed Ron, who was avoiding eye contact with the Empath. "Maybe we could get some matching slippers out of the deal."

Arrol agreed, "Oh, now that sounds fun." He turned to Irwin, whose attention was on the forge. "Samuel, why don't you buy some fabric for Daos-style clothing? They wear very specific garb. All the men wear the same pants and vests. We'll get you suited up and ready for your journey southward. Does anyone want another sweet roll? I'll buy the next round."

"I'll take another." Ron gazed out the window. "It looks to be another glorious day. Let's take advantage of it."

"I agree! Since I'm leaving tomorrow ..." Jorge leaned his chin on his hand and stared at Ron. "... is there anything you want to do with me today, Ron?"

Ron's eyes dropped. "I'll have to think about it."

Arrol stood and straddled the bench. "Jorge, Samuel, I'm buying this time. Either of you want another roll?"

Jorge's response was distant and muffled. "Yeah."

Irwin's focus remained on the forge and the ringing metal. "Yes, please, and thank you."

Arrol put his hands on Irwin's shoulders and squeezed. "I'll be right back."

His body tensed.

Ron didn't say anything until Arrol was gone. "You don't like Arrol, do you?"

Every muscle in his body turned to a knot under Ron's scrupulous Clan-Duin eyes. "I am not used to so much touching."

But if he was Kipp ....

"Yet, I get that you seek it," said Jorge.

He felt uneasy around these two. "I have never met anyone quite like you three."

"Arrol and I have known each other since we were young. We were bought, castrated, and forced to work on ships. Being gelded does something to you. It changes your mentality, your outlook on life. If I had to do it all over again, I'd have made myself a gelding from day one. I'd much rather be a woman, but here I am in this body. What can a boy do?"

Irwin could not picture Ron as a woman, but he could easily see Arrol as one.

"I am glad to be a boy. I would not want to be anything else."

Jorge chirped, "Why did you say boy and not man?"

"Because I am still a boy in many ways. You are a boy too! Ron just called himself a boy."

"Ron is a young child trapped in a man's body. I was a boy," Jorge said, "but then I became a man. That was a long time ago. Looking into your eyes, Samuel, I can see you became a man a while ago too." He held Irwin's eyes. "Did your father call you boy? Did he not think of you as a man? Is that why you left?"

I hope Jorge is not linked to a Telepath. His demeanor did not change when I made contact. So why does he want to know about me? Perhaps it is his nature.

"That was one of the reasons."

"What was the other ... the other reason you left your father? Was it abuse or something else?"

Irwin hated thinking about the abuse at his father's and his grandfather's hands. The nightmares had finally stopped—he had not thought about Saryh's death in a long time. And yet, the pang of regret was fresh. The vision of Saryh's bloody body flung across the bed after his father sliced her throat was seared into his brain. He made a fist under the table.

He opened his mouth to speak, but Jorge jumped in. "Oh! He left you."

Irwin admitted it in front of these new friends. "My father is a murderer and a liar—not trustworthy at all. But he is dead now so …."

Jorge said, "It looks to me like he was also an abuser and a taker. He gave you nothing, so you owe him nothing. I'm sorry for inquiring about your father, Samuel. I was just curious, that's all."

Why is he so curious when he already seems to know more than I have told him?

Arrol returned with more sweet rolls and set the plate down. "What did I miss? You're all so quiet."

"It turns out that Samuel's father is a murderer."

"What?!" Hands to his lips, Arrol stared at Irwin. "You don't say?"

"Yes, he is, and that's the end of that." Jorge changed the subject. "I would like to go to the beach today—play in the surf, be naked and enjoy ourselves. You like that idea, Ron?"

"Sounds like a perfect afternoon," Arrol said, licking the ends of his fingers after plucking a roll from the plate.

Ron glared at Irwin. "Will you be coming along, Samuel?"

Noticing Ron's angry Clan-Duin stare, Irwin tried to be cool, to remember once again that he and Kipp had agreed that he would go undercover as Samuel here. "No. But thank you for the offer. Hauss and I have a few things to do today while we are still here."

It is hard to remember to call Kipp 'Hauss'.

"You should come shopping with us before you go," said Arrol. "Be prepared for Daos. There's much you don't know about those people and their sense of dress. If you don't fit in, then you'll stand out, and that can be deadly."

Jorge asked, "Your friend—is he the Mortal?"

"I am the one they speculate as Mortal. My friend is Clan-Duin."

"Clan-Duin? Well, he's as good as dead if he stands on two legs in Daos," said Jorge. "He's better off in his animal form there—a dog or a bird, not a cat. They eat cats. They're considered a delicacy to Daosians."

"Reams and Seams won't open for a few hours," said Arrol. "After this, you wanna take a hot bath, go shopping … then to the beach?"

"Sounds good." Ron rang less than enthusiastically, still trying to ignore Jorge's appearance. At least, that was how it seemed to Irwin.

Everyone fell quiet; the only sound was that of chewing, finger licking, and an occasional hmm-hmm.

Irwin's attention drifted again from the bakery to the forge. He tried to ignore the chorus of metal, but the songs were so loud. Before he could squirm in his seat, he caught sight of three Telepaths pacing toward them from the wharf. He watched until their long shadows spread down the courtyard like dark snakes as they passed the forge. Eyes straight ahead; their footsteps fell like sudden rain; dark clothing billowed in their wake. One of them wore a robe with red and gold embroidery—a matching sash fluttered as they all walked to the tower. Only one of the Telepaths was a mixture of powers—a wind Erthin; it was he who led the procession.

The one with the red and gold frock noticed Irwin and the others looking out. He turned toward the bakery window.

Everyone at the table looked at the last of their sticky buns. The three Telepaths quickened their pace across the square.

"Who was that?" Irwin asked.

Arrol made a face. "Who's who?"

"The Telepaths."

Jorge shrugged.

"I don't see any Telepaths," Ron said, spewing breadcrumbs from his lips.

"You mean the men at the forge?" Arrol leaned across Irwin to see who might be there. "Only Erthins and Clan-Duins work there."

"Telepaths prefer simple work," said Ron.

"None of you just saw those Telepaths? There were three of them. They looked right in this window."

"I saw no Telepaths, Samuel," Arrol replied. "I see Kol working, and Fritz, and Barret over there in the corner."

Irwin slumped and held his head in his hands. "Huh, I guess I do not know what I saw. I am tired."

"You must be," said Arrol.

I bet that was Admiral Ubic. And he used his telepathy on these three. There is no other explanation.

The resonating sound of a hammer hitting metal echoed throughout the courtyard. Everyone but Irwin flinched at the twangs. The metallic melody filled his body, called for him to mold it. He resisted the urge.

Arrol stood. The others scraped their feet, preparing to rise. Jorge pulled up his hood; stepped back from the table and from Irwin. The Empath's body morphed into its enigmatic appearance.

"Thanks again for the morning meal and conversation," Irwin said, and followed the trio into the large courtyard.

Ron and Jorge chatted quietly; Arrol engaged Irwin. "Keep yourself out of trouble, Samuel. Maybe consider staying here in Arenu. If you like playing at the forge and selling metal wares, this place might be perfect for you. Much trade happens here and with people from all over Urthis." Arrol sounded pensive, and Irwin remembered how Arrol had held him in his sorrow and confusion while Kipp was with a woman—one of his most tender experiences. He could still smell the incense, hear tiny bells jingling, and feel his tension subside.

"Well, if you change your mind, or if your partner and you want to enjoy the beach and get away from here before you head south, feel free to come up to the second floor. You know where my room is. We'll be around until midday." Arrol hugged Irwin, who could not bring himself to reciprocate. "Hopefully, I'll see you later, Samuel." Then Arrol joined his friends, heading for the saloon and a nap.

Irwin watched the two Eunuchs and the Empath return to the strange environment in which they lived and worked.

They are something!

The large forge area was perfectly proportioned for the gargantuan Erthin and Clan-Duin crossbreeds who worked there. Two enormous fireplaces mirrored each other with a fire pit blazing in between; there were benches and an array of tools; there were high ceilings with chains and pulleys attached to presses and hoists. There were barrels that collected rainwater; they were tapped with faucets and wooden pales were stacked below. This place was a wonderland for any smith.

Beyond the heat and molten metal, there was a cordoned off room where raw materials were kept. He heard all the unused metals sing to him. The door to the storage area was open. Hundreds of pounds of iron, lead, silver, copper, nickel, and many more precious metals were so close he could feel the fire in his belly. He innately knew how heavy each type of metal was and where it was located in that hidden storage space.

He studied one of the smith's forceful hammerings against a metal rod, over and over. Sparks flew this way and that. He watched the hot piece of metal flatten—ever so slowly—from the smith's vicious blows.

The Clan-Duin smith who tended the forge was thick with weight and muscles. And while he applied a reserve of pressure and force, he received no instant reward for his hard work.

It will take that blacksmith all day to make that shaft of iron into anything useful.

The same task would take Irwin but a moment—all he needed was an idea of what to create.

Irwin watched the smith work for a while, until he felt tired again. He knew that once they set out for the next leg of their journey, there would only be erratic sleep for him and Kipp. He turned toward their covered wagon.

He tried not to disturb Kipp as he climbed onboard and slipped inside. But Kipp's nose was always on, and so he morphed into his two-legged self and turned over. "Mmm, sweet rolls." He licked his lips and opened his brown eyes. "You bring me some?"

"No. But I can if you want."

"Wait! You went and got sweet rolls and weren't heckled? No one convoked you?"

Irwin nodded, smug.

Kipp yawned, stretched his arms, and stood up. He scratched his bushy hair; yawned again. "How long have I been asleep?"

"It is barely dawn, Kipp. Only a few hours." He sat on the bed and yawned. "It was nice, though. The young man working the counter this morning was not the same one as yesterday, and he did not heckle me. No one did."

"Ummmm. I'm hungover." Kipp rubbed his head and face, licking his lips. "Sweet rolls sound good. Would you mind getting me a few?"

"Of course. I will return soon." He moved from the bed and climbed through the wagon's front portal.

This time, he had to wait in line. There were more locals awake now. Most of them were ladies from the saloon, although a few Erthin sailors bantered back and forth while they waited for a fresh baked good. It took Irwin longer than he had thought, but no one was cross with him or looked at him as though he was strange.

When he finally stepped back through the bakery door and into the courtyard, Kipp bounded toward him. "I did not think there would be so many people." He handed the wrapped goodies to his drooling Clan-Duin friend. "I got eight."

Kipp tore open the hemp-cloth packaging, pulled out two steaming rolls, and stuffed them into his mouth.

"Yum. Thanks," Kipp said, crumbs all over his lips and cascading down his hairy chest.

They walked back to the wagon, and after finishing a few more of the treats, Kipp said, "I passed out last night."

"Indeed, you did. You were snoring and whining all night long. Which made it hard for me to get any sleep."

"Sorry 'bout that. Usually happens when I drink too much. Well, this is the last time we'll be getting drunk for a long time, so it was worth it!" Kipp pressed his eyes with the palms of his hands, one at a time. "Oh, my head."

"Maybe you should rest some more. We have little to do today except bathe and get our clothes laundered."

And talk with Admiral Ubic.

"I think it's stupid that we're not allowed to leave today. Now we'll be days behind Yace."

"Remember Kipp, the Oracle put it this way: 'wary travelers travel warily together. Those who are alone, die that way'. Even Jyn advised us to travel with the men from Nuaki Village. I would rather ride with someone who knows the land, especially if there are Uoala and Arlos, or whatever they are called out there."

"I don't trust any of them. It's absolute horseshit!"

Poor Kipp, nothing but Yace.

They had been chasing after her and Dephen Ishik for three moon cycles since her kidnapping. "Kipp, I understand." Irwin put his hand on Kipp's shoulder. "I know how you feel."

Kipp huffed and shrugged the hand from his shoulder.

"We must stay positive."

"Says you."

Irwin moved his hand to Kipp's forearm to keep the all-important contact, to keep any Telepaths from overhearing their conversation through the Clan-Duin's mind. He whispered, "We will leave tomorrow; early. If we keep to ourselves today, there should be no harm."

Kipp was visibly angry again. "What about Yace? If we don't save her—"

"Look, Kipp, we knew this might happen. And if we try to force things—it will not work in our favor. We must be patient."

Several Telepaths dressed in long-sleeved white tunics exited the tower and headed toward them. Had those blue-eyed, pale-skinned, blonde-haired men just eyed Irwin and Kipp as they passed by?

Phew! They are heading for the bakery.

Irwin tracked them, watched them step into line. "Even Alio told you the Datzar Jungle is a dangerous place. Take a deep breath and stay calm, please. It is better to travel that jungle in numbers."

Kipp shrugged, and Irwin gazed out across the courtyard.

I wonder what the people of Arenu Village are saying about me.

"No one else said anything to you?"

"No, not really. Everyone in the line was with someone else. There were faces I recognized from last night at the saloon. Maybe they remember Jyn's intervention with Batton. No one tried to heckle. It was nice." He sensed Kipp was focused only on the bakery.

"Good. You seem to be in a better mood than yesterday. Time with that Eunuch helped, didn't it? By the way, how long have you been up?"

"Since daybreak. That was when I went to the bakery the first time."

"I still can't believe they served you!"

"Well, I was not alone."

"Really?" Kipp's brown eyes were studious. "Who were you with?"

"The Eunuchs let me sit with them."

"Eunuchs took you out to breakfast?"

"I woke up to the smell of those sweet rolls and ringing metal. And then I heard Arrol—the gentleman from last night ...." His face still felt warm. "Anyway, they invited me to sit and talk while we ate sweet rolls."

"Why would they do that?"

"Sweet rolls! Need I say more?"

"I hope you didn't say anything that will hamper our mission south."

"Nope. Everything I said was calculated."

Kipp rolled his eyes.

The sun was making its way higher into the clear blue sky. There was a soft breeze that brushed their hair around as they meandered back towards the square. They could have been on the old mountain top during a summer day, except for the presence of the ocean and the seagulls flying and screaming overhead.

"Arrol was telling me," He spoke briskly, before Kipp could cut in, "that we will want to change our clothing for Daos. That way, we do not stand out."

"What? Daos! They know we're going to Daos?"

"I told them that Nuaki Village is not our final destination."

"Why? They don't need to know anything about us."

"It is part of the plan." Irwin reached for Kipp's arm again.

"They don't need to know if we're staying or going. Dang you and your stupid plans." Kipp rolled his eyes again, the way he did when he was frustrated. "They're gonna dress us?" He pulled away from Irwin's touch. "I thought we knew what we were doing. You're the knife salesman, and I'm your aloof Clan-Duin assistant, remember? No one needs to know more than that. And we don't need any help from a bunch of Eunuchs. If I wear the appropriate garb, we're fine."

By the time Kipp had enjoyed some sweet roll and they were back at the front of the wagon, they each climbed on board. Kipp took the driver's seat where he could enjoy the breeze. Irwin straddled the seat and inched into the covered wagon.

"Jorge was quite specific when he said that you will want to remain in your Clan-Duin form. He also said that you are as good as dead if you are seen on two legs."

Kipp said nothing, but Irwin felt his rage.

"Have you ever seen, or met, an Empath before?" He felt smitten to have met someone as unique as himself.

"An Empath?"

"Yes. Have you ever even heard of them?"

Kipp shook his head.

"Well, Jorge is an Empath from Nuaki Village. He lives there because he is unusual, and get this, he can appear to be whomever you desire to see."

"Whomever I desire?"

"Yes. I imagine if you were to look at him, you would probably see Yace, or maybe your mother. It depends on who you want to see at that moment."

"I would?"

"Yes. Whoever you desire to see is who you see when you look at him. But if I get too close to him, his powers stop working and he appears ... well, he appears Mortal."

Kipp's tongue slapped against the roof of his mouth, making a clicking sound. "Was that part of your plan?"

"Well, no. And I did try to deflect speculations of my power."

Kipp raised an eyebrow. "You tried?"

"I did! I showed them my power for instantaneous healing and explained that I do not know more than that."

"And they bought that story?"

"It is the only story I have."

"Maybe we should come up with another one. A better one."

"Why? We will be gone by tomorrow morning."

"Are you sure about that?"

"Yes."

I must be. If they try to keep us from leaving ... I do not know what I will do. I do not want to resort to violence.

"You look like you've something else to say."

Irwin yawned and yawned again. "I want to lie back down for a while."

"Inside the box, or out?"

"Why?"

"I'm hoping to have some flat-on-my-back bedtime."

"That is fine. I will probably sleep better if I am in the box, anyway." Irwin pulled back the blankets enough to lie beneath them. His body sank into the substantial metal lockbox, a cool reprieve from the sticky air that hung thick in Arenu Village. And Kipp laid on top of Irwin's sanctuary to catch his own nap.

3

A Bath And A Pretty Lady

Sometime later, Irwin surfaced from his hidden bed in the metal box. Kipp was gone. He figured the Clan-Duin was taking advantage of the hospitable landscape—the village of Arenu was made specifically for those with Talents. He remade the bed and heard what sounded like a skirmish beyond the wagon's canvas walls.

Muffled voices turned to shouts. He poked his head out the front of the wagon. Fists were flying against flesh. Back and forth, slaps and smacks. Before he could get a better view, he sensed the fight was turning deadly.

He heard sounds of snarling and spitting, like animals, and moved to the back of the wagon, where he could get a better look. Irwin drew back the canvas opening and saw more and more people gathering. Two Clan-Duins, one feline and the other canine, were fist fighting, but their abilities were equally matched. So, as if in a dream, they both took on their animal forms. The canine was thick chested, with long legs and gnarled teeth. The feline was smaller, but well-built and with amazing reflexes and fluid movements.

The feline tried to slice the canine as he dared to chomp the cat's swift-moving paws. From where Irwin was perched, he could see both fighters batting and swiping at each other.

More onlookers crowded in. At least fifty men and women were wagering bets. Shouts of money-bids rang around the circle; people were betting on death. Beyond the bellowing bookies, some cheered, and some scorned the fighters.

He jumped off the wagon, and scanned the faces, searching for Kipp, but did not see him. The oohs and aahs were followed by a hard body-against-body slam. The canine Clan-Duin flew through the crowd toward Irwin. The crowd parted as the unconscious body tumbled away from the fighter's ring.

The bruised and bloodied canine came to a rest at Irwin's feet. He lay lifeless on the cobbled ground. The feline transformed back into a thick-headed Clan-Duin with large shoulders and a square jaw. He was bruised, cut-up and bloodied, but still alive.

That cat glared and hissed at those who continued to watch. He grabbed his orange sarong from the ground and wrapped it around his midsection. He spat in the direction of his dead opponent. The deceased canine's body slowly transformed into a two-legged Clan-Duin, blood pooling around his head.

Irwin stepped back; several villagers came, and each grabbed an arm or leg and dragged the cadaver to the barnyard. Everyone crowded in to retrieve their winnings from the bookies and then scattered in all directions. The fun was over.

He looked down at the small puddle of blood, knowing that before long, it, too, would be cleaned up. Kipp's shadow edged up to Irwin's feet. He looked up to see his friend holding lunch.

The sun had reached the top of the bowl of blue sky. He felt rejuvenated, especially after the excitement of the fight, but he was sorry to have slept so long and wasted so much of an important day.

I need to talk to Admiral Ubic!

He heard sea birds overhead and glanced up to watch them soar.

Kipp offered him a cooked crab leg. "This place is amazing. I wish there were more places like it. Everyone knows everyone. These are fresh by the way. I was told they were caught fifteen minutes before I bought them."

"Thank you, Kipp." He eyed the crab's thick pincer leg.

"You break it here and just start eating the meat." Kipp demonstrated how to eat the crab leg. They walked beyond their wagon to enjoy the juicy crab. They stood near a stone mosaic of fish swimming toward the Saloon's main entrance. They slurped and smacked their lips, enjoying the fresh, sumptuous treat. "I tried to get here as fast as I could; did you see the fight?"

"Yes. It was over quick."

"I really wanted to see it."

"Where have you been?"

"Around. I stopped at the bakery for more sweet rolls, but they were sold out. Then I went back to the Oracle to see if she could contact Yace again. There was no luck with that. Then I sat in the Saloon hoping for a meal, but instead I talked more with Jyn. Man, she's a fun one. I wish she were a servicing woman. We'd have a good 'ol time.

"Oh, and your friend—Arrol, was it—asked for you. Those Eunuchs wanted to take me shopping. They also invited us to go to the beach. I think they believe we're lovers. Hey, if that's what they wanna believe, let them. But I'm not joining in."

"Did they go shopping already?"

Kipp stared at Irwin. "Not that I know of. And why do you care? We can find Daosian style clothing on our own, Irwin. We don't need men who enjoy acting like women to tell us how to dress. It's as bad as having Yace around."

"I just figured they would know more. I mean, they live here. They interact with people who journey to and from Daos all the time. They do not want us to get killed."

"You positive about that?" Kipp pointed at the pool of blood. "Didn't you hear all the men betting on death? I heard them all the way from the markets. Irwin, you need to understand that there was no recourse for that fight. No one around here cares if we live or die; it's every man for himself.

"Those Eunuchs are lucky to live in a place that allows them so much freedom. I've met Eunuchs who've had much less." Kipp rubbed his arms as if he were cold.

"I believe you have been thinking about Yace too much again."

"I told you I went to the Oracle to see if she could summon her." Kipp's lips flattened. "Yeah! I need to know if she's gonna be all right. I don't trust Nonbry, and I don't trust the Telepaths here, either. And you've been acting odder than usual. I'm guessing it's because you're holding things back from me, which is probably good—though you said you wouldn't." His nostrils flared, and he seemed to be turning things over in his mind. "Yes, I'm angry we're still here. I wanted to leave after resupplying yesterday, just like you." His jaw was clenched and the veins on his neck bulged. "We know where Dephen is going. We need to stop him. Staying here gets us nowhere."

Irwin pulled out the last bite of crab meat and savored the buttery taste. "You know what I think? I think we need baths!"

"I was hoping you'd say that!" Kipp cackled and started off in the direction of the bathhouse.

Irwin glanced at the wagon. "What about our clothing?"

"I already took those sacks of dirties. I also fed the animals and mucked the stalls." Kipp paused in stride, waiting for Irwin. "Oh, and I found a handful of coins in your trousers while you were sleeping." They both stopped as a Telepath strode past, heading toward the tower. Kipp turned and started to walk away. "That's how I paid for the food and a few other things."

"If you need money, just ask."

"Now that you're up, I don't have to."

Kipp guided Irwin to the bathhouse, located on the east side of the Saloon. Lacey and colorfully dyed curtains blew in and out of upper windows; linens were hung on a line strung between buildings. A blue dress caught Irwin's eye.

That is Yace's color.

A lump snuck into his throat.

The double doors into the Bath House foyer were open wide. It was much cooler inside, a welcome reprieve. Chairs and benches lined the wall, but the place was empty of patrons. Kipp had been here earlier and the middle-aged Clan-Duin woman remembered him. She was kneeling before one of the woven chairs, darning a tear in the fabric. She looked up and gave them a big bucktoothed smile.

Slow to get to her feet, the woman finally stood with a hunched back. She was short and her dark blueish-gray eyes lingered on Irwin, possibly attempting to telepathically assess him.

"This is your friend?" she asked, looking him up and down.

"Yeah. This is Samuel."

"We serve no Mortals here." Her eyes bounded between Irwin and Kipp.

"He's no Mortal."

"I am Erthin," said Irwin.

"Haha! You're too pale. You have no red hair, no green eyes! Breathe me some fire, produce rain, whip my hair around." Her hands were expressive, and her chin pushed forward.

Irwin could have made a fire roar from his hands, or even rainfall. He chose to keep knowledge of those powers hidden. Instead, he used the same old ruse. He again pulled out a knife from the back of his pants—or it would seem to the old woman—and stabbed his forearm. The knife slid through his flesh from wrist to elbow.

Kipp always seemed impressed by Irwin's gracefulness and manipulation of his metal. He didn't wince, although it always hurt—the puncturing of skin, muscles, tendons, and sometimes bones; but the pain was momentary. Immediately, and before the woman's eyes, the wound healed.

"Well, that's a Talent," she gasped. "We will allow you to use of our facilities for three silvers each."

"Three silvers each!" Kipp pointed toward the ocean. "You have water all around and hundreds of Erthins at your disposal, but you charge three silvers for a hot bath?"

"Four for you, if you're not careful."

Irwin placed his grounding hand on Kipp's shoulder. Kipp flinched. But they both took a deep breath. He produced six silver pieces. Arguing with a local would get them nowhere.

She studied the Metalist as he dropped the coins into her outstretched hand. She sniffed and sneered at him like any Clan-Duin would. "Follow me."

She smiled at Kipp, yet frowned at Irwin.

She is trying to antagonize. A classic Telepath trait.

They dipped through curtains separating the cool entry room from the steamy laundry. They followed her up four flights of stairs and down a long, narrow hallway. Every twelve paces there were doors mirroring one another. She led them to a room around one more corner.

The bathing chamber was open to the sky, yet climate controlled just like the rest of this enormous bathhouse. The Erthin spells at work were ingenious. Soldiers patrolling catwalks surrounding the village could see into the roofless bathing rooms. A few loomed overhead. The interior walls were made of bamboo stalks, thick and tall, and designed for privacy between rooms. Vibrant green leaves rattled as a soft breeze came through. Even the benches and clothing pegs were made of bamboo. A solid stone bathing tub rose from the slab floor. Murmuring voices wafted from the other rooms. Distant giggles echoed, but no one could truly see one another, except those on the catwalks.

These Erthin spells are marvelous. I wish I had time to study them all.

"This is your bath," the woman said.

Kipp squawked, "There's no water in the tub."

Picking up an hourglass from a small shelf outside the door, she turned it over and said, "Your attendant will be here momentarily." She closed the door.

"That was rude." Kipp pulled a hip-bound satchel bag from under his pants. "I brought the soaps and a brush." He paused and then confessed, "Jyn told me all their attendants are exotic. They'll scrub our backs and massage us."

"Thank you for remembering the soaps." Irwin stared at the empty tub. "You know, I could fill this."

"Why? We'll have an attendant. And she'll be here any moment." Kipp pulled his pants off and heaped his clothing on the bench. "It's their job to attend to us!"

There was a knock on the bamboo door. Kipp jumped to open it. Their pretty bathing attendant had arrived! He moved excitedly out of her way as she entered the room. The woman was a tall, black-skinned beauty. Her light-hazel eyes held flecks of amber, her eyelashes dark and long. Her buoyant brown-reddish hair made her half a head taller than either man.

"This is Samuel Irwin, and I am Hauss Kipp." Kipp was embarrassingly excited by this beautiful woman.

A long purple and pink sarong was wrapped tight around her body. She acknowledged Kipp with a nod. She gripped a bucket full of water and said rather brusquely, "I am Roq. I am here to fill your bath. No more."

Kipp licked his lips. "I thought we got massages and back scrubs."

"If you want that, you pay more," said Roq, still arrogant in her tone, Irwin thought.

"Pay more?" said Kipp. "We paid six silvers to take a bath!"

"You paid only for water."

Kipp balked, "For four silvers I can get bedtime with a whore!"

Roq's eyes flashed. "You did not pay for any other services, so what you get is what you get."

"They weren't joking when they said the women in the baths are fiery." Kipp pouted and stood next to the empty tub.

Irwin felt weary of this strange-looking woman. He took several steps back from the tall beauty, feeling her Erthin energy radiating. It was then he realized Roq encompassed all the powers most Erthins wished they could summon; earth, fire, air, water, and spirit—she could do it all.

An Elementalist!

But there was also something else about Roq, something he had never seen or felt before. When he peered into her hazel eyes, he saw a hole of black energy that shadowed her iris. That dark energy pulled him toward her. He resisted.

Roq moved closer to Irwin, her eyes on his; she tossed the bucket of water into the tub. She wove her hand over the stone bathing tub, water molecules instantaneously replicated—bubbling and filling the empty space. She turned away from the tub and placed the empty bucket outside the room—closed the door. This was her routine. It was obvious she had filled bathtubs hundreds, if not thousands, of times and never paused her pace. She returned to the tub just in time to stop the cold running water. Her feet did not miss a beat—she never spilled a drop.

She looked from Irwin to Kipp. "I assume you want it hotter than cold?"

Kipp said, "Medium hot, yeah. Right?" He glanced at Irwin.

"You know, we will pay for your time if that is what it takes for you to soften your attitude." Irwin made a golden piece appear from out of nowhere and handed it over. His eyes dashed to take in Kipp's reaction; he noticed a telepathic change in Roq—how she now held herself, the way she walked; she appeared stiffer than before.

In a monotone voice, she said, "Thank you."

As if hypnotized, she took the coin and went to the door. Roq's motions and movements were drawn-out as she set the coin on the shelf next to the hourglass.

During the time her back was turned, Irwin and Kipp spoke to one another with their sign-language.

Kipp motioned first. *'Something happened there.'*

'Yes. Under telepathic control.' Irwin answered in their silent language.

'Touch her.' Kipp responded.

She turned, and they stopped.

Irwin was nervous about touching her, so he climbed into the cool tub. "This feels good." He laid back.

"Are you fooling?" Kipp's arm was in the water. "It's too cool for my liking." He turned to see Roq take off her long swath of clothing. "I would like it ... ahh .... Wow, you're mesmerizing."

Roq had no physical scars, but she did have piercings and hoops through her nipples, belly button, and her ears and nose.

"Aha." Kipp was stunned by her beauty. "Can you warm the water, please?"

"Yes, I can." Roq stepped close to Kipp, brushing against him; she bent over the tub's edge. She looked at Irwin too. He was trying to ignore her.

Kipp looked Roq's backside over, and giddily glanced at Irwin who shook his head. He did not want Kipp to act on impulse.

Kipp grinned and asked, "So what all did that gold coin just buy us, Roq? Do you know?"

Seductively, she turned, luring him in with her words. "Whatever you want."

Kipp gasped, palpably erotically hungry for this woman. "Whatever I want?!"

"Yes."

"Could we go a round of foreplay?"

Irwin knew exactly what Kipp was thinking. "Hauss, we are here to wash up, not dirty ourselves more. Besides, what did you say last night about genitalia?"

"But Irwin, I've never—I don't wanna disrespect you, Roq, but I've never seen a woman like you. Your soft dark skin, those hazel eyes, and your smell." He inhaled and his eyes rolled back in their sockets.

Irwin ignored Kipp's slip-up with his name. "Your instincts want to take over here, Hauss. All you really want to do is lay claim," he said, noticing the drool on Kipp's lips. "Resist the urge, my friend. Remember, Yace is waiting for you."

Her body was nearly touching Kipp's. "I can always start with massaging your back," she said. Kipp shuddered.

"Get in the tub, Hauss." He did not want to watch, or be a part of, any more debauchery.

We are supposed to be taking it easy, not riling up the natives.

"Clean up before you get your dog on; at the very least, you owe Roq that much."

"You're right, Irw-Samuel. I do owe Roq that much." Kipp stepped into the pool.

Irwin reached out and touched Kipp's forearm. He jumped. Their eyes locked. "Just checking," he said, releasing his friend.

Kipp chuckled at the sensation.

4
ROQ

Roq's hands reached for and summoned Kipp to lie back in the warm pool. She said nothing and began massaging his shoulders. Kipp groaned, releasing his tension, relaxing into the warm water.

Irwin watched Roq push on his friend's shoulders and upper back. After a long time of her kneading and rubbing, he asked, "So, Roq, where are you from? What is your story?"

"You want to know how I came to be here?"

"As my friend here said, he has never seen a beauty such as you. And I never knew skin black-as-night existed until meeting you."

Kipp said, "Hakra. He's black. Like you."

"Are you related to Hakra, Roq?"

"I do not know Hakra. Who is he?"

"You're lucky to not know Hakra, or what he stands for," Kipp mumbled.

"From what I understand, Hakra has black skin like yours, but blue eyes," Irwin said. "He is seen as a godly person to most."

"He's no god," said Kipp. He gazed lustfully up at Roq. "You look nothing like Hakra."

Roq giggled.

Irwin watched her hands work Kipp's muscles. "Of course, I never really noticed skin color until it was brought to my attention."

Only attitudes and insults.

After a long pause she said, "I come from a place so far away, you cannot get there by walking, or horseback, or ship even."

Did her eyes darken just then?

There was a long pause, and then Irwin asked, "How did you arrive in Arenu Village?"

"How did I arrive?" Roq repeated the question several times—as if trying to summon a story. "Pirates. They brought me here. They traded me and two friends for supplies. My friends were sold, but I was allowed to stay. The people here see my potential and they keep me safe."

"And your friends?"

"They go. I do not know."

"Do you think she could be related to Hakra, Kipp? Maybe a long-lost relative?"

"No. She looks nothing like him." He smiled at her. "You're a beautiful flower compared to Hakra, Roq."

Irwin continued to press. "What about before the pirates? Do you remember your family, or the place where you grew up?"

"Not really, no."

Kipp moaned. "You need this too, Irrrr ... ahh. Yeah, right there. Ooh ...."

Not wanting to feel hands on his body, Irwin reminded Kipp, "You were the one holding onto the reins all that long journey. You need to be massaged."

"We should have done this yesterday." Kipp said, exhaling.

Roq said, "We were very busy yesterday. Today is much better for relaxing."

"Ahhh, yeah, today." Kipp's body was so relaxed he sank into the water.

"Yes, I agree. Today is a better day to be here."

She asked, "What about you two?"

"Huh?" Kipp snapped out of his reverie.

"Your story? Where are you from?"

"Oh, our story is boring," said Kipp.

Roq looked at Irwin. He watched her work out knots in Kipp's upper back and shoulders. "We come from the north, heading south to sell my wares."

She raised a curious eyebrow. "What are your wares?"

"I am a cutlery specialist. I have knives and swords for sale."

"You have knives and swords for sale? Are you a smith?"

"Yes. I can also do minor repairs on minor items." Kipp chuckled and Irwin added, "I have tools in my wagon and can make small repairs to almost anything."

"You must be rich, making money selling knives and swords."

"My family has a forge in a small village about the size of this one," he lied. "Over the years, I have made many knives and swords that I sell so I can roam this grand planet."

He could see Kipp snickering at his story. He kicked Kipp with his toe under the water. Startled, Kipp sat up and Roq dug into his pectoral muscles. He groaned and winced from her hard knuckles, but relaxed again.

"You should really allow her to massage you, Irw-Samuel."

"I don't bite," Roq said, smiling. "Many say I am good at what I do."

"I bet you are, but I am quite relaxed." He laid back, closed his eyes.

Kipp made a sound as if he was going to speak, but kept quiet. Roq slipped into the tub. They giggled and whispered. Then the moaning and groaning commenced.

Irwin tried to ignore all the extraneous dripping and splashing sounds, tried to enjoy his well-deserved soak—until the water began heating up.

Roq was sitting on Kipp's lap, facing him. The two were entwined in passionate kissing. The hot water began vibrating. He was certain this was all Roq's doing.

Not wanting to be a part of, or interfere with, what they were doing, Irwin stepped out of the bath, allowing Kipp and Roq privacy. He retrieved the brush and soap, scrubbing all the days of dirt and grime from his body. By the time he was fully soaped, Kipp and Roq were finished. She stepped out of the tub.

"I can scrub your back if you wish." She moved toward him, but Irwin returned to the hot tub to wash off the soap.

Kipp stepped out of the tub. "You can scrub my back." She came to his assistance, but her eyes drifted toward Irwin. Using the same soap and scrub brush, Roq helped clean Kipp.

"How about my chest?" Kipp guided her soapy hands. "Now between my legs." He groaned as she cleaned his body. "Yeah, make sure that is cleaned too."

Roq giggled.

"Are we about done here?" Irwin did not want to listen to Kipp talk Roq up any longer.

"Are you sure you don't need anything else cleaned?" She asked Irwin, "I am very good at what I do."

"Yeah, you are," said Kipp, his goofy smile beaming.

"No, thank you." Irwin was curt this time.

"Irw-Sam, you should allow her to at least massage your shoulders."

He glared at his friend for not remembering to use nicknames.

Without warning, Roq placed her hands on Irwin's tense back. He tried to move, tried to deflect her touch, but they made contact—and disappeared.

It was pitch black. He heard his breath but saw nothing—not even his own hands. He felt for his face and eyes and extended his arms out toward the void. "What the ... where am I?" He could not stop shaking.

"They're coming." She was there. Her voice vibrated, echoing in the darkness.

"Roq?"

Her words flew to him, "Don't believe what you hear."

"Roq, where are you?"

"Don't believe what you hear."

"Roq?"

She repeated herself several more times. "Don't believe what you hear."

"What do you mean?"

"Don't believe what you hear!"

"Roq, what is going on?"

She whispered, "Don't respond." Her words reverberated in the hollow of the dark void.

"Roq!" Fear turned his belly, gripped his chest. "Where are you?"

Her voice crackled with fear, "Everywhere. Nowhere. Get out of here. They're coming!"

"Roq? What is going on? Where are we?"

The abyss was silent. Then she began screaming. "Roq. Roq! Stop. Stop!" Irwin felt himself rushing. He did not know where he was, where Roq was, or where to go. Though his instinct to flee had taken over, he forced his feet to stop. He shouted again, "SHUT UP!"

The screaming stopped.

Roq whispered, "There is someone here," her words still echoed and rose with fear. "Someone is here. Someone is here. Safe. Am I safe? They're coming. They're coming. They're coming for me. They're coming for me!" Her screams were terrifying.

"Roq, I am here!" Irwin shouted, frantic to find her—and himself.

"You're here? You're here? I am here. Here? Here I am." She stopped shrieking and only her thoughts echoed. *I am here. Here am I. I am here. Here am I.* She appeared like an apparition, kneeling at his side. A bright white light radiated from her palm. She pushed her hand toward him. Her mind spoke loudly while her lips quivered. *Take it. Take it. Take me. Save me. Take me out of here.* "I do not belong here."

"Where is here?"

"I am here. You are here." She looked like a crazed creature.

"Yes. I am here, Roq. But where is here?"

"You are here?" She looked at him. Her eyes grew and her furrowed brow relaxed. "You are here!"

"Yes, I am here. But where is here, Roq? Where are we?"

"You are here!" She stared at him, wild and scared. "Take my hand." He was wary, but she pleaded, "Take my hand. TAKE MY HAND!"

He grasped her palm, and they teleported out of the darkness.

5

<u>A Fight To The Death</u>

As quickly as they flashed out of one plane of existence, Irwin and Roq were back in the baths.

Kipp gasped.

Roq was on her knees, quivering. Her hazel eyes on Irwin, their handhold tight.

"What in holy Hakra just happened, Irwin?"

He dropped contact with Roq and backed away. "I do not know. What did you see happen?"

The naked woman—huddling against the stone tub—began screaming again.

"What in the name of Hakra did you just do, Irwin?!"

"What did I do?" He pointed at Roq. "I did nothing. She touched me!" He covered his ears. "She did this! I do not know what happened."

"I'll tell you what happened. You two disappeared."

"We what?"

"Or you became invisible. Or something."

"We were not invisible."

"Then you disappeared. You both went somewhere, but then you came back."

"Disappeared?"

"Yes!"

"How is that possible?"

Kipp put his hands over his ears. "Can you silence her?"

"What? I am not going to kill her."

At the top of her lungs, Roq screamed again. Irwin knelt at her side. "You are alright, Roq. We are back. We are safe."

"I don't think this is gonna end well." Kipp jumped out of the tub and grabbed his pants while surveying the ramparts above them.

Irwin pleaded, "Roq, listen to me, you are going to be alright. We are back from the darkness. Everything is going to be alright. Open your eyes. Look at me, please. Roq, please, look at me."

"Dang me. I'd hate to think your power did this," Kipp said, pulling his pants all the way up.

Roq breathed heavily in and out; then she caught her breath, coughing and gagging. She stared at the door. "They're coming." Over and over, "They're coming."

"Who are *They*, Roq?"

"I think she's talking about the soldiers up there." Kipp pointed up to where Clan-Duin and Erthin soldiers looked as though they were closing in on the three of them.

Irwin could feel the men with their metal weapons hiking up the stairs, racing down the hallway. The Erthins stationed on the rampart were readying themselves for battle—charging up their powers. "There are also soldiers coming to the door."

Kipp tied the hip satchel around his belly and slid it down into his pants. "What are we gonna do?"

"Stay calm." Irwin remained at Roq's side.

"Stay calm? Are you foolin' me?"

"Kipp, no one will hurt us, and we will not hurt others. Remember, we have done nothing wrong."

"Her screaming might make people think otherwise, Irwin."

Footfalls halted outside the door. Kipp looked from the door to the shadows of men along the catwalk.

"You know we're surrounded, right?"

"Yes, I know." Their relaxing bath time had turned so stressful, so quickly.

One hard knock resonated. Irwin jumped and grabbed his clothes.

As the door opened, Irwin secured his pants around his waist. "You're both coming with me." The woman who had brought them to this room stood outside with a force of a dozen Erthin and Clan-Duin men and women.

"Why? We have done nothing wrong," Irwin said.

"Why is your attendant on the floor, naked and screaming?"

"I think you know why," he said. He believed this woman had been in control of Roq the whole time until the beauty touched him, releasing her from the telepathic hold. That was when her power of teleportation took hold, transferring them somewhere else.

Erthin and Clan-Duin soldiers filed into the small room.

The telepathic woman remained at the door. "You've been convoked."

"Oh, I have? By whom? You? One of your men?" He heard Kipp gasping.

"Escort the *Mortal* to the circle. The Clan-Duin can follow. Bring Roq to me."

"Samuel." Kipp stepped away from the two Erthins who tried to grab his arms. Two Clan-Duins roughly picked up Roq who appeared to be catatonic. Kipp growled, "What are you gonna do to her? Don't hurt her!"

The Telepath held an evil eye on both men. Irwin saw what she was planning on doing to Roq. "She is going to lock Roq away in her mind again." He raised his voice. "I want to speak to Admiral Ubic at once."

The woman said, "After the fight."

"I know Admiral Ubic wants to speak with me."

She waved a cautionary finger in the air. "Not until after the fight."

He closed his eyes. "Of course. They wanted something like this to happen."

Four sets of hands grabbed and pulled his arms to lock his hands in metal shackles behind his back. He chuckled.

They think they can contain me.

"About time I was challenged. Let me guess, I will be fighting only Arenu's best fighter!"

"Correct!"

The Telepath stepped out of the way, allowing the prisoners to exit the bathing room. He smiled as he was roughed up, pushed along. Slowly, the iron shackles were absorbed into his flesh. None of the gruff men surrounding him noticed what he was doing, even as they descended the stairs.

By the time they exited the building, Irwin's hands were swaying at his sides as he walked—voluntarily going along with these soldiers.

Once they stopped, one of the men realized the cuffs were gone. "Hey, what happened to your shackles?"

Irwin lifted his hands before his eyes. "Huh? Where *did* they go?"

"No really, where'd they go?"

"You don't think he's got powers, do you?"

A few of the soldiers stepped back while the rest pushed Irwin into the fighting circle. It was the same place as the earlier fight. His escorts took positions around the inlaid stone ring.

Half a dozen Telepaths exited the wooden door at the base of the enormous lookout tower. Locals began arriving from across the village. It was obvious that word had been sent out telepathically that the Mortal had been challenged.

He saw Kipp surrounded by Telepaths and Erthins.

Do not panic, my friend. Remember what Alio taught you. I am afraid they will hear his thoughts. Be thoughtful, Kipp, please.

He inhaled and closed his eyes.

I do not want to fight. Maybe I can intimidate.

He then allowed the recently absorbed metal to flush across his skin.

"Not Mortal," was murmured throughout the amassing crowd.

The Telepath named Donnolin shouted, "No powers!"

How hypocritical! In the last fight, powers were used! How can one use no powers in this fight? They would not even know if I was Talented had I not just shown my hand.

His skin gleamed in the sunlight, and Irwin turned to see the large gathering of locals. His silvery eyes gazed at the faces.

Fine, I will play by their rules.

He saw the cheese merchant from yesterday placing a bet with the local bookie.

He said he would bet on me—and if I win, I get a small sack of silver!

He glanced at Kipp and withdrew from the metallic facade. He shouted, "No powers."

The locals squeezed around the inlaid stone circle. They studied him until the snorting sounds of his opponent stole the show. An enormously tall, thick-bodied hybrid Erthin/Clan-Duin, with muscles upon muscles, stomped and announced his appearance. The crowd parted. And when his opponent stopped at the edge of the circle, he snorted at Irwin.

Irwin felt scrawny in every way next to this giant man.

He towers over everyone. How am I going to get out of this?

His adversary flexed his muscles; his tattoos bounced as if alive.

With heavy breaths, the hybrid fighter readied his body for the fight—making himself appear even larger than before. Irwin could feel that this partial Erthin was an earth mover, but did not seem very strong with that ability. Instead, he used his brutish Clan-Duin powers to puff up his body and intimidate.

The big fighter threw the first punch.

Being wiry and nimble had its advantages. Irwin jumped out of the way of the first powerful throw. He could feel his opponent's iron-laced blood moving and heard the wind as the fist just missed his head. A second throw, and again Irwin felt the breeze. He darted side to side, backing toward the onlookers.

The Erthin grunted as he lurched forward trying to grab Irwin. He was quick to drop to his hands and knees. Irwin scrambled between his opponent's thick legs. He shuffled along the edge of the crowd but was pushed toward the fighter. Slowly, steadily, a chant began to rise. "Barnst! Barnst!"

Barnst smiled, hearing his name shouted over and over. His thick jaw muscles flexed, and he threw another punch, barely missing Irwin again. The Metalist toyed with Barnst, hoping to tire him.

They danced.

Irwin averted many throws, but Barnst made contact with his left eye and temple. He felt Barnst's fist slide across his face, leaving no mark, but Barnst broke Irwin's left cheekbone denting his face. But no one saw any physical damage—his body instantly healed the contusion. The hit threw Irwin back into the crowd, and they pushed him toward the center of the ring.

He wiped his face, looked for blood, but there was none—only pain from the breaking of bone. Shaking off that hit, Irwin continued to tap around Barnst. He deflected another punch, moving with it, spinning around, trying to find a better spot to fight from.

They jabbed back and forth, but Irwin did not make contact. Barnst tagged him in the gut and Irwin was pushed back. He moved away before throwing a punch at Barnst's face.

Irwin finally made contact, but Barnst reacted to the punch as if he were a pesky fly. The larger fighter carried on, swinging with both arms. Again, he tried to hit Irwin's face, backing him into the crowd. The locals tossed the Metalist toward the menacing fighter who swung again but missed. The momentum of his own force made Barnst stumble. His arms flailed toward the crowd. They parted enough for him to swing around and come back to Irwin—it was clear no one wanted to become an extra casualty.

Back and forth they danced, just missing one another, until Irwin noticed Barnst slow to catch his breath. In that split moment, he initiated a hard-hitting attack. He was not as strong or as forceful as Barnst. But sometimes, the small precise hits produce the most damage. He congealed metal around his bones and joints beneath his flesh—aiding in the hardness of each hit dealt.

He sped around the ring and hit Barnst in all the right spots with his blunt Metalistic force. A hit to the neck first, then Irwin twisted away to tag Barnst in the same spot on the other side of his neck. He delivered a hit to the temple and moved before Barnst could smack back.

Irwin raced behind the bulking fighter, readying to hit the opposite temple, but Barnst predicted that maneuver. He put his arm up to defend and Irwin instantly changed his tactic. He jabbed Barnst's lateral muscles along his ribcage. The experienced fighter moved to deflect and turned with a violent swing, trying to hit Irwin with both fists. Again, Irwin jumped away.

By this time, the crowd was roaring, chanting for Barnst to "Kill the Mortal! Kill the Mortal!"

He threw another hard blow to Barnst's head. He switched up his pattern and approach. He hit low and then high. This tactic might have looked haphazard to the onlookers, but Barnst fell forward.

Blood trickled out Barnst's nose and he went down onto one knee. Again, Irwin's metal coated knuckle bones made contact with Barnst's face, chipping away at his flesh. When the giant Erthin man saw his own blood, he grunted and stood tall. His eyes were angrier, as were his swings. He fiercely tagged Irwin several times, breaking his upper left ribs and right cheekbone.

Irwin was down on his knees, out of breath and in pain. He flushed metal under his skin, wrapping broken ribs and protecting his facial bones. The pain from fusing broken bones was always worse than breaking them. Straining, Irwin breathed through the pain and slowly rose. He was light-headed but aware of Barnst looming close, readying for another attack.

He felt Barnst's iron laced blood flow as an arm swung toward his face. Irwin ducked out of the way from another flying fist, fell to the ground, but rolled to safety. In that same moment, Barnst tripped over his own feet and now both men were on the ground.

The crowd's chanting never ceased. "Kill him! Kill him!"

They were eagerly waiting for either man to finish off the other. No one cared who lived or died at this point. They all wanted to see blood.

Irwin staggered to his feet and looked at the Telepaths encircling Kipp. They were all wide-eyed, studiously waiting for him to kill Barnst. The crowd was heated and more bloodthirsty than ever.

He glanced down at the blood smeared across his body. Irwin felt his many broken bones mending and bit through that pain; ignoring the tender bruises and the torn muscles that were also mending. There was a cut above his right eye as wide as his eyebrow, but already only blood was smeared across his forehead—that cut healed. He had a broken wrist but flicked that hand and everything popped back into place. All the villagers witnessed his instant regeneration, and their chanting quieted.

Barnst would not regenerate as fast as Irwin. He gasped for breath, spit up blood, and was noticeably angry at being on the ground again. But it was obvious to everyone that the well-suited fighter was having a hard time steadying himself; he did not rise—seemed to be waiting for Irwin to inflict more pain.

The Metalist stood back from Barnst, hands up in the air, showing his surrender. "I am done with this fight," Irwin shouted at the Telepaths. "I will not kill this man."

From beyond the shouts and heckling taunts, he heard Kipp yell. "Finish Barnst, Irwin! Finish him!"

Once more, Donnolin spoke over everyone, insisting, "If you don't kill Barnst, he'll kill you."

"I am done with this fight!" he declared. His arms were as tall as they could get.

Barnst recovered and slowly stood. He caught his breath and appeared ready to go another round.

Again, they sparred.

Both fighters stumbled around the circle a few times, tired, but they made contact once more. Barnst initiated and Irwin defended, knowing he could not get away from the giant man. It seemed that all of Irwin's hits had no effect on his opponent. And the moment Barnst slugged him, several of Irwin's mended ribs broke again.

The wind was knocked out of his lungs and Irwin was on the stone ground once more. It was cool against his hot flesh. His eyesight blurred, but he felt Barnst's approach and rolled away.

Irwin scrambled across the ring before bounding to his feet. Unfortunately, that quick motion pulled at the muscles around his broken ribs. He winced and put his hand down guardedly. He was sure he now had five broken ribs and just as many torn muscles. He held his breath and pushed through the pain as he had always done.

Everyone was anxious. Barnst's name echoed around the crowd and the Erthin moved to attack. Irwin stood still, a perfect target. From behind him, Barnst lunged, and Irwin moved away from the flying fists. He took that moment to collect himself and concoct a brutal attack.

Barnst moved and Irwin counteracted, going for the jugular on the left side first. Then he circled twice—punching Barnst in the same spot repeatedly. He danced in and out, zigzagging, tagging Barnst two more times in the neck. Every hit was precise and caused debilitating blows to the oversized Erthin. Irwin was done fighting. He wanted to end this shenanigan.

Barnst lunged toward him again, but all those hits had already taken their toll. The copious man staggered before his eyes rolled back into his head. Barnst's body fell sideways, convulsing as it tumbled. He hit the inlaid stone floor, and his head bounced. Barnst was unconscious, barely breathing.

Although he was not proud of what he had done, Irwin stood victorious in the fighter's ring. He kept himself alive and had not killed anyone, yet. All the villagers' eyes were on him. He ignored the crowd and looked only at the Telepaths. He knew they were the key to his and Kipp's release.

Two of the larger Erthin soldiers stationed along the edge of the circle stepped out. They went to their fallen brethren, checking Barnst's condition. One of them shouted, "He's still alive!"

"Finish him," said the oldest Telepath. "That is the way." His blue eyes followed Irwin.

All the spectators waited to see how Irwin would kill Barnst. There were many ways he could finish him off, but Irwin didn't want to. "Killing an innocent is not my way."

Again, Kipp shouted, "Irwin!" He then recalled how different the culture was inside Arenu and Nuaki Villages—it was not the same as the rest of the world.

This is not how I want this to go. I do not want to kill this man, but I have to. That is the rule. Fine. What shall I show these people? They are here for the show. Be humane, make it quick and easy. I shall summon him into me. That will be an excellent demonstration of my power. The best way to honor Barnst.

He closed his eyes, bowed his head, and lifted his hand, twisting it in the air using his Metalistic and newfound Coterie power to annihilate Barnst from existence. The Erthin's body instantly burst into millions of molecules, pulling apart, floating like bubbles on the wind, swirling around Irwin, and was then absorbed into his skin.

I must always honor those who I do not wish to kill. All I can do is to be humane. I just want to be a peaceful person! I can only hope this demonstration is impressive enough to make anyone else think twice before wanting to fight me.

The crowd went silent upon witnessing the exciting dance of Barnst's execution—his body assimilated into Irwin's. No one in Arenu Village had ever seen a power like his. There were many startled faces.

I hope I never have to do that again.

He could now feel Barnst's power, adding to his collection of Erthins. Although he had not been a powerful Earth Erthin, he knew Barnst's life had been snuffed out prematurely.

Irwin had caught his breath, but his lungs still heaved. He tried to hold back a sob.

I really want to be a peaceful person, but those I find myself surrounded by do not want that outcome.

Eyelashes fluttered open and three sets of cool-blue telepathic eyes were trained on him. No words were exchanged as soldiers swarmed and pushed Irwin and Kipp along, out of sight from the natives.

He felt his silver coins in his best friend's pocket only a few strides behind. The two were shuffled beyond the thick wooden door at the base of the enormous red tower, filed down a wide curving hallway, and then each was taken into a separate windowless room.

Irwin was pushed into a room filled with men. Kipp was left alone.

6

MEETING ADMIRAL UBIC

A long wooden table and straight-back chairs filled the room. Thin strips of copper hung in the far corners holding large candles radiating a golden hue, and a bright lantern swung over the table. Two pitchers of water and drinking glasses on the table's center—*how convenient.*

Admiral Ubic was seated at the far end. He wore a dark blue tunic with a red sash—adorned with golden thread. Irwin recalled seeing him walk through the courtyard that morning. The old man had not watched the fight.

Lieutenant Bejorn and Corporal Teigahn each sat at the Admiral's side—wearing matching dark green attire—Irwin recognized them from the Saloon from the night before. Those two had watched the fight. The Admiral held two pieces of paper—hand-drawn sketches and words he could not make out.

All eyes were on him.

In came two more Telepaths, four multi-powered Erthins, and two Clan-Duins. Two of the four Erthins turned and left the room. He felt them standing guard beyond the closed door. The other two Erthins pushed him toward a vacant chair. He gave them both sideways glares. Had they not just seen what he was capable of?

Admiral Ubic motioned, "Have a seat." He summoned his telekinetic power and pushed the chair away from the table without moving himself. "Please." The Admiral looked at him as though he would make Irwin sit if he had to.

Keep calm. Stay neutral. Let what they say slide off my back. Remember, do not be offended by others. They do not know me, and I do not know them.

He took the seat.

He looked at Lieutenant Bejorn, feeling a slight fluctuation in the Erthin's power. The Lieutenant was an Elementalist. He could feel all of Bejorn's power turned on, ready to erupt.

I wonder if Bejorn is intimidated by me. He exudes an electric force unlike any other Erthin I have met, except Roq.

"I am Admiral Ubic. You met Corporal Teigahn last night." Admiral Ubic went around the table, introducing his cohorts. "Lieutenant Panili and Captain Muslid escorted you here from the fighting ring."

The Lieutenant and the Captain—both Telepaths—took seats opposite one another; they left an empty chair between themselves and Irwin. No one wanted to be too close to him. Muslid's eyes leveled on Irwin, glaring. Panili appeared more relaxed and did not gaze at him for long.

"Lieutenant Bejorn, you've also met. And these are our resident Warden apprentices." It seemed the Admiral was trying to either put him at ease, or flex conjoined power, but the introductions did not change his stoic expression.

There fell an awkward and empty silence until Lieutenant Bejorn said, "That was quite a show of power out there, young man."

Captain Muslid, eyes narrowed, asked, "What type of creature are you?"

They all leaned forward, awaiting his answer.

He looked at each of them and said, "Erthin."

Everyone chuckled.

One of the Wardens standing behind him muttered, "A weak Erthin, maybe."

Irwin was eager to ask the many questions boiling in his mind, but he felt there was protocol to follow. He sat back in the chair, trying to remain calm—stoic like Ubic. There was a lot of metal in the room, several types.

Everyone has metal on them—no one is protected. I could kill them all if I wanted to. Breathe.

Muslid jeered, "You're no Erthin."

Keep calm; be polite.

Snapping his fingers, the candles in the corners of the room extinguished, as did the overhead lamp. He reignited them. "Lieutenant Bejorn thinks I might be an Elementalist, like him."

Bejorn said, "I believe you're more than you say you are, but you don't feel all that powerful."

Muslid asked, "What are your powers?"

I am not telling you.

"All I know is that I can regenerate instantly and perform a few Erthin tricks."

"What you did to Barnst was not an Erthin trick," Bejorn said.

Muslid interrupted, "What about the metal?"

He played dumb. "Metal?"

"Before the fight, you coated yourself in metal—obviously an intimidation tactic taught to you," Muslid said. "But it didn't work."

He flushed metal across his skin. "Oh, this? This is how I usually look. Most people I meet prefer a more Mortal appearance." The metal receded into his pale skin. "So I will sustain this look for you."

Admiral Ubic did not smile. "We know you've multiple powers, Samuel. We all know what you're capable of. The destruction to the Hall in Onj Raha and your escapade in Ahradah has shown us much about you and your abilities."

Muslid slapped his hands against the table. "Why'd you take the Gypsy dog?"

He folded his arms and sneered at Captain Muslid. "I took no Gypsy dog."

"The Gypsy dog was following a female Telepath," Muslid said, "but now he follows you. What did you do to his mind?"

"Captain," snapped Admiral Ubic.

"What!" Muslid shouted and snarled. "You want to know why too!"

There was a telepathic exchange: eyes moved, faces wrinkled, snorts and muffled sneers were directed toward Irwin.

I wonder what they are saying to one another. Hopefully, Captain Muslid is being reprimanded.

Lieutenant Panili caught his attention. "How did you come to meet Kipp Hauler?"

"Why do you care?"

Again, the Telepaths spoke to each other mentally, eyes darting, nostrils flaring. After a long quiet, two papers floated his way. Admiral Ubic asked, "Do you recognize either of those two men?"

On each paper there was a drawing of a man and written details. He glanced at the images. "No."

"Huh," Admiral Ubic stared down his long nose at Irwin. "I figured you would. You look very similar to them. Of course, by now, they'd be old. Perhaps one is your grandfather or great grandfather."

He looked over the pictures once more, Edger Sampson and Edwin Sampson. *Papa Edwin!*

"I have never met anyone with the name Sampson."

"Do you know anyone named Edger, or Edwin?"

He remained silent.

Admiral Ubic pointed toward the flattened parchments. "Your last name might have changed, but your resemblance to those two brothers ...."

His great grandfather appeared older than he was in these hand drawn images, but younger than Albert. They had hairy faces and long hair—never allowed during his lifetime. "I do not know these people."

Lieutenant Panili said, "Perhaps they died before you were born, but we believe you're related to them."

"Then why do you care if they are dead?"

"Just answer the question," said Muslid.

Lieutenant Panili pressed, "What about your father?"

His eyebrows narrowed and his voice deepened. "What about him?"

Muslid accused, "He's the one who killed all those people in Kobiton, isn't he?"

Shit, they know about that too? Of course they do. They are Telepaths. Keep calm.

"Yes," Irwin replied quietly. "He killed the whore and the soldiers, and I was witness to it all."

Muslid prodded, "Why didn't you stop him?"

"You think I could have stopped that man?"

"Did you try?"

This time Lieutenant Panili and the Admiral chided their telepathic brethren, "Captain." More secret talking. He watched eyes bound between faces as the Telepaths chattered among themselves without a sound. Bejorn stared at him.

"What about your mother?" asked Panili.

"She is dead. I never knew her."

"Do you have any siblings?"

"No."

Panili huffed, "Do you have any aunts or uncles?"

"Not that I know of."

"What do you know?"

Irwin leaned toward Panili. "Why do you want to know about my family?"

Muslid spoke up, "People like you are not trustworthy."

Admiral Ubic's eyes flew to his underling.

Muslid's head spun like a top. "What?! They aren't. What he did in Onj Raha proves that."

"What I did in Onj Raha was not me," he said, still feeling remorseful.

"We all know it was you," Muslid scoffed.

Admiral Ubic spoke over Captain Muslid. "There were many lives extinguished that night, and all of them saw you working for Death. We know you're a powerful man, Samuel Irwin Miner. What you did in Onj Raha proves it."

Hearing his full name was like fingernails across his backside. He winced, trying to contain any outward movements. His eyes dropped, and so did his shoulders.

"What happened in Onj Raha was beyond my control. If things could have gone some other way ...."

"Some other way," Muslid laughed, "like not killing two hundred and eighty-six people?"

Two hundred and eighty-six. Shit.

He lowered his head again.

"Over a hundred of them were Erthins," Muslid added.

He knew exactly how many.

I absorbed one hundred-seventeen Erthins that night.

Bejorn said, "There is no denying that you're more powerful than any of us." Several men made sounds in their throats or scraped their chairs around.

I am no better than my father—quick to snap, quick to kill.

Bejorn said, "You can tell us your powers. We won't judge."

"All I can do is instantly regenerate, and a few Erthin tricks, like the light thing. I am not all that powerful."

I cannot let them know I am a monster. Too late for that. They already know.

"You turned Barnst into tiny pieces!" Muslid's voice rose. "That's not a power any of us have ever seen. And that's not the first time you've done that either. That's how you killed the Erthins in Onj Raha and Ahradah, isn't it?!"

"He could be Elementalist, if properly trained." Bejorn said to Admiral Ubic. "I feel that he encompasses all Erthin abilities, but he's obviously weak."

"Hey, Bejorn," Muslid asked, "are you sure what he did to Barnst isn't an Elementalist power?"

"No, not that I know of."

Lieutenant Panili leaned toward Bejorn. "What about the power to manipulate metal? Is that an Elementalist trait?"

Bejorn shook his head, kept his eyes on Irwin. "Harnessing metal like he does is not an Erthin power ... that I know of."

"I've noticed he can harness metal in many ways," said Muslid. "Like how his handcuffs disappeared before the fight today."

Corporal Teigahn spoke, "IThinkWhatHeDidInAhradahWasMoreImpressive."

Muslid looked at Teigahn. "That's when he helped that woman on dead-row escape."

"Yes. And took all the soldier's swords."

Wow! The PCP knows a lot about me.

He kept a humble posture, and did not interrupt the conversation.

"Yes," Lieutenant Panili said. "He revealed much of his powers that night."

Muslid asked, "But how are you manipulating the Gypsy dog? He must be telepathic too, right? Or are you Coterie?"

"His name is Kipp, not Gypsy dog."

Muslid glared, "No, it's Courtyard Sitter."

What was Muslid trying to incite?

Admiral Ubic addressed Muslid, "Captain, you may leave."

"Sorry, Sir...it won't happen again," Muslid pursed his lips.

"I am not manipulating Kipp," Irwin said. "That is what a Telepath does. I am no Telepath."

7

TELEPATHIC MANIPULATIONS

The air was static and dry. Candlelight danced in each corner of the room—a spark of energy snapped between Irwin and Lieutenant Bejorn. The Elementalist flexed his powers like a cock in the ring. "What'd you just do?" Bejorn pointed accusingly at Irwin.

"What did I do?! Whatever that was, it was all you, Bejorn."

Bejorn leaned forward. "Do you know your powers?"

"No."

Captain Muslid snarled, "That's a lie."

"No, it is not."

"Deny, deny, deny."

Admiral Ubic raised a pale eyebrow and his voice over Muslid's. "Why does Kipp Hauler travel with you and not Nonbry's Gypsy band?"

Of course they know about Nonbry. They overheard the Oracle's conversation just as Nonbry speculated.

They were all looking at him, waiting.

"Why do you care?"

Ubic's eyes peered into Irwin's. "For years he's been seen with Nonbry's Gypsy band. He's also been seen with a young female Telepath who goes by the name of Yace Yellsen. Since your time in Onj Raha, the young woman has vanished, and you've kept Kipp Hauler close."

"Why do you care about either of them? We all know that without being part of the Gypsy band, Kipp would most likely be a PCP soldier and Yace would be used as a Talented female is. Most of you would not care about either, but for some unknown reason—"

"It's my prerogative to care about those who've entered my domain," said the Admiral, rubbing his chin and sneering at Irwin. "That Clan-Duin of yours has never traveled far from her." His blue eyes were trying to telepathically probe, but

Irwin's Metalistic power would not allow it. "What are your motives for having Kipp Hauler with you?"

Muslid demanded. "Did you kill her and take hold of the Clan-Duin's mind?"

I do not like how they know so much.

"No. I met Kipp in a tavern in Onj Raha after he left Yace behind with her father. We are traveling together now, seeing the world, selling my wares."

Muslid laughed, "That's a Gypsy lie!"

"Why do you care that Kipp is not traveling with Yace or the Gypsy?"

"You were seen with them long before Onj Raha," said Muslid.

Lieutenant Panili added, "She's not been seen since Onj Raha. She was with both of you at that time."

Muslid snapped, "Did you kill her?"

"No. And as far as I know, Yace is alive."

"How do you know?"

"Because we have been following her trail since Onj Raha." He could see no one believed him.

Ubic leaned in, hands folded on the table. "Why have you told people you're heading to Daos?"

"Because Daos is south of Datzar." Irwin stared at the Admiral. "Once again, why do you care?"

"This is my domain!" said Ubic. "And I don't appreciate liars."

"I am not lying." He saw those old telepathic eyes fishing for information. "I am guessing you heard something from the telepathic world?"

Beyond what Nonbry said last night.

"That you should be locked away for crimes committed against the Public Constable Patrol and those loyal to Hakra," said Muslid.

Ubic hissed, "People with Talents shouldn't travel into Daos Territory. You're as good as dead the moment those people know what and who you are."

"I know."

Ubic pressed, "Then what's the real reason?"

Irwin took a moment to measure his reply. "You want to know the whole truth? Dephen Ishik."

Muslid grumbled, "Who's Dephen Ishik?"

Ubic considered the name. "Dephen Ishik." He paused, then said, "I've not heard that name in a long, long time. He's been dead for years."

"Has he?"

The Admiral's eyebrows furrowed, and his eyes again pierced Irwin's. "I met Dephen Ishik many years ago. He was old then. He frequented this port many times before his death. I'm sure that Dephen Ishik has been dead for at least five years."

"How sure?"

Panili growled, "You don't speak to the Admiral in that way."

Ubic asked, "How do you know of Dephen Ishik?"

"I figure you already know the answer, since you seemingly know so much about Nonbry's Gypsy clan. If you must know, Dephen Ishik is Yace Yellsen's father."

The Admiral chuckled.

Muslid leaned forward. "You do know that lying to a Telepath is a death sentence here."

"What about Ishik's decree?" Irwin asked.

"Ishik's decree. How do you know of Ishik's decree?" Ubic twisted a gold ring with a ruby inset on his middle finger. "Sounds like another Nonbry story."

"If someone put a bounty on my head, I would fake my death. And that is exactly what Dephen Ishik has done."

Ubic laughed. "Those Gypsy have filled your head full of nonsense. That's what they do. They take naïve Talented people, such as yourself, and telepathically manipulate them to suit their needs."

"You think they manipulated me?"

"Of course they did!" Muslid said. "They got you to destroy the PCP Hall in Onj Raha and slaughter hundreds of soldiers! Then you made a fool of the Hall in Ahradah by freeing their youngest Talented female murderer."

Ubic snarled, "Muslid! Button it!"

"What would the Gypsy have to gain by manipulating me into killing all those PCP?"

Muslid spoke again, "Gypsy loath PCP. They hate anything having to do with Hakra too."

Ubic ignored his underling's outburst. "What do you know about the Gypsy, Samuel?"

"That they are here to help people who have been hurt by the PCP and Hakra. They protect the most helpless of Talented people, and they do not enforce Hakran propaganda."

They all laughed.

Ubic said, "We don't force Hakran propaganda here, my dear Samuel."

"Elsewhere it is by PCP and loyalists."

Panili regarded Irwin. "Those Gypsy have filled your head full of something, that's for sure."

Ubic continued to press, "Let me ask you again, Samuel Irwin Miner, why do you think you're heading to Daos?"

"Dephen Ishik." He knew he would be laughed at again. "He kidnapped Yace Yellsen and is using her powers."

The men around the table resumed their laughter.

"Kipp and I have been chasing them since Onj Raha."

"First you say he left her for you; now you say you're chasing her," Muslid barked. "Which is it?"

The Admiral again leaned closer. "Your friend Kipp seems to believe Miss Yellsen is in the carriage bound for Nuaki Village. Is that how you are getting him to follow you by manipulating his heart?"

"No. I know she is not in that carriage, but Kipp believes she is."

Muslid grumbled, "He's gotta have telepathic abilities."

"Yace and Dephen left the carriage back at Lady Gretchen's house. Then they took a ship and sailed here, enjoyed a rowdy night at Das Grits Tits, and then continued on.

"I know you all heard about it. The two whores who were broken—that was all Dephen. He has been using Yace's body to do whatever he pleases. He broke the whores so he could take their minds and see through their eyes. He has done it before."

Muslid shouted, "He's a liar!"

"Sounds like a bunch of nonsense," Panili said, glancing at the Admiral.

"Dephen used his Coterie powers, somehow inserting his mental presence into Yace's body. He has placed traps for me and Kipp ever since taking her from Onj Raha. And with her powers, he can camouflage himself."

None of the men believed his story and were having a gay old hoot. Irwin huffed, "All I know is that Dephen Ishik is playing us for fools and apparently there is no Telepath in all Arenu Village wise enough to see that."

Muslid, Panili, Teigahn, and Bejorn kept on snickering. Even Ubic's lip was upturned until Irwin finished describing how Dephen had taken over Yace, and that they could not be Talented enough to know about this fact. Ubic did not appreciate this chide.

"You're a fool Samuel Irwin Miner."

"No. You are," he said, unable to contain his wrath.

The enthusiasm among the officers in the room cooled.

"I was told there would be wise Telepaths here; that you are all competent and highly trained and would be able to see the manipulations created by Dephen Ishik."

Teigahn stumbled into the conversation. "IThinkHe'sBeenManipulated-ByTheGypsy."

Muslid added, "I don't believe a word you're saying."

"He does appear turned around," Bejorn said, looking at the Admiral.

"You all believe I have been manipulated by the Gypsy, when it is you who have been turned around by a master Coterie."

"Definitely Gypsy lies." Muslid rolled his eyes.

Now Irwin pleaded, "Did none of you see the fiery red head all the men have been talking about? Did none of you notice that she is being controlled by another being from within her mind? How could you be so blinded by a Coterie? I thought you were powerful enough to see through fake facades." He waited for someone to reply, but no one spoke. "Do none of you care that there is a powerful Ishik on the loose?"

Ubic's voice boomed, echoing off the stone walls. "You'll be going to Nuaki Village tomorrow morning with Corporal Teigahn, Lieutenant Bejorn, and the rest of their unit."

"Perhaps you do not understand the severity of this situation, Admiral Ubic, Sir," Irwin's voice strained. "Dephen Ishik is planning on assassinating his brother, the Emperor of Daos. And he is using his powerful daughter to do so."

Panili, slack-jawed, asked, "Where are you getting your information?"

"This guy's a dumbass!" Muslid snorted. "If I had to bet on someone being bent on assassinating the Emperor of Daos, I'd place my monies on him."

"I thought Telepaths were smart!" Irwin felt like crying.

"You've fallen into a Gypsy trap, Samuel Irwin Miner," Ubic said. "We believe the Gypsy have manipulated your mind and sent you on as a Sleeper Assassin—someone who doesn't know they've been manipulated and is bent on murdering as many as they can."

"That is a lie."

Muslid pushed his finger into Irwin's face. "Then you're a cold-blooded murderer."

"Muslid." Ubic glared at the man and then returned his attention to Irwin. "You'll be going to Nuaki Village. Once there, you will live out the rest of your days in exile."

"Exile? What if I choose to leave?"

Shaking his head, the Admiral said, "Should your name come up in the lottery, you'll be allowed to travel here, but only here."

"Why am I being exiled?"

"You're a Sleeper Assassin, Samuel Irwin Miner. A puppeteer'd goon." Ubic seemed to be losing all patience. "You can't be allowed anywhere else but with your own kind."

Puppeteer'd goon? What is the Admiral talking about?

"Were you sent here to kill us too?" Muslid continued.

"I do not want to kill." Irwin slapped his hands on the table. "And I am not an assassin!"

The Wardens behind him took that as a hostile threat; turned on their Erthin powers and tried to suck the air from his lungs. Their spells boomeranged and they could be heard gasping for breath. One of the two Erthins fell to his knees, sputtering, choking.

Irwin said, "Release your spells and you will be able to breathe."

Bejorn was clearly amazed. "How are you doing that, Samuel?"

"We should kill him now, Sir!" Muslid barked, striking the table with his own fist.

"Contain yourself Muslid," said Panili.

He could hear the two struggling for breath. He repeated, "Let up your spells." He turned to see them on their knees. "Attempting to harm me will only back-fire."

Ubic said, "How interesting."

Panili appeared to be in a panic. "This shouldn't be allowed, Sir."

Muslid chanted, "Let's kill him! Let's just kill him!"

"Alright, fellas, listen to Samuel. Withdraw already," Bejorn instructed while visibly containing his enthusiasm.

The Erthins let up their spells and could breathe again.

Just in time.

The room fell eerily silent. The men looked at Ubic who was mentally speaking with the others, all the while glaring at Irwin—perhaps annoyed he could not read the Metalist's mind.

Ubic broke the silence. "You're a young naïve man, Samuel Irwin Miner. And you've been blinded by the Gypsy's power over you. This story about Dephen Ishik and Yace is something they want you to believe. None of it's true. Do you know why the Gypsy sent you as a Sleeper Assassin? Because you're expendable."

"Then why is Kipp with me?"

Muslid pointed another accusing finger. "You stole him!"

"Maybe he is expendable too," Panili remarked.

"You killed the girl first, then took the Clan-Duin as a prize."

Irwin spoke over Muslid's outburst. "Where do you get your information, Admiral? Is it other PCP Telepaths, or was it relayed through Lady Gretchen?"

Muslid beat the tabletop again. A water glass crashed to the floor. "You get a thrill from killing those you don't like, don't you?"

Irwin understood Muslid was there to be the over reactive Telepath; Panili wanted to know about his family—as did Admiral Ubic. He could see the game these men were playing—he decided to show a card. "Did you know that Lady Gretchen is related to Dephen Ishik? He went to her because he knew she could help him get rid of me. Did you know she poisoned me and turned Kipp into a pig?"

"We can't trust this assassin's mouth!" Muslid was revved up again.

"If anything, Yace Yellsen is the Sleeper Assassin." Irwin said with confidence. "Dephen has taken her body, and he is using his cunning and his Coterie gifts to slip into Daos and find the Emperor. They stowed away on a boat, came here to rile you all up—and it worked! And now she is on her way to the Emperor's palace in Daos to kill him."

The room quieted again. No one was laughing. Muslid watched the Admiral; he appeared to be almost groveling. Irwin watched another long exchange of silent communication and then felt Bejorn's eyes trained on him. "You are not privy to their conversation, are you?"

Bejorn said, "Muslid's an ass." The soldiers behind him snickered and snorted. "He deserves what's coming."

Irwin noticed something about the telepathic conversation. He could see the way each Telepath looked at one another; they were being thoughtful about their conversation, and all the while studying him.

He said, "They are not talking about Muslid."

Panili said, "We never finished our discussion about your father."

This again?

"What do you want to know?"

"Do you know where he went after Kobiton?"

"As far as I know, he is dead."

"How sure are you of that?"

In my heart, "Fairly sure. He left me for dead by the side of the road; then later I found his donkeys. He never leaves them behind," he lied. No one needed to go looking for his father; and if they did, they would not survive. "His heart was weak. He complained about it hurting from time to time. It most likely stopped working."

Albert's heart stopped working long before I was ever born.

Panili fished for more information. "And what about your mother? Aunts and uncles, cousins, or other relatives?"

"As I said, everyone in my family is dead. My mother died when I was born. And my father has been dead half a year. I am the last Miner alive."

"How about your grandfather?"

"I do not know of my grandfather."

Although he is dead, they do not need to know about Jebadia.

"So, you and your father lived outside of Kobiton for how long?"

"All my life."

"What did you mine?"

You should already know this answer.

He stared through Panili. "Coal."

"How often did you visit Kobiton?"

"I have only visited there a dozen times."

My life has changed so much since my last visit.

"So, your family lived in the forest?"

"We lived in the mountains." He remembered the chilly air, the star-filled sky that looked like snowflakes in the night. "In a cave that no longer exists. Thanks to my father."

I am so thankful to be six moons removed!

"Sounds like a dull existence," said Panili.

"It was."

Admiral Ubic and the other Telepaths mentally returned to the room. He said, "You believe Dephen Ishik faked his death, lived in Onj Raha, then stole away in his daughter's body to assassinate the Emperor of Daos?"

"Yes."

Ubic examined the palms of his hands and said, "He was nearly a hundred years old when he died five years ago."

"Dephen Ishik is rich. He had healers keep him alive."

Ubic tittered, "That sounds like a Gypsy story."

"This is not a Gypsy story."

"Why, then, would Dephen Ishik search for his bastard children?" asked Ubic. "From what I understand, like him, they're all dead."

"To turn any one of them into an assassin." Several men chuckled again.

Panili chimed in, "Please tell us again why you think he wants to kill his brother."

"Revenge. Dephen Ishik wants payback for all the evil things his brother, Somer, did to him over the years."

Ubic raised an eyebrow. "You believe he wants revenge on Somer? Why? Somer is as old as Dephen, maybe older. What you're telling us makes no sense. And there's no proof." He sat back, smoothing over the hand-drawn pictures of Irwin's great grandfathers.

More laughter. They all seemed eager to please Ubic. Irwin was ready to use his powers to provoke, but that was what Muslid wanted. "Why do you think an extravagant carriage was sent here?"

"Ahradah headquarters sent it along as a decoy," said Ubic. "They knew you'd follow it—it's made of metal."

Muslid jeered, "You like shiny things, don't you?"

"Then why send the carriage on to Nuaki Village?"

"We sent it, knowing you'd follow," said the Admiral.

"Is that what you were told?"

Ubic responded first, "Yes." Several others agreed.

"By whom?"

Panili replied, "Ahradah headquarters, of course."

"You believe that was the Ahradah PCP speaking to you?"

"They were the ones who caught you!" Panili said.

"I was never caught."

"Yes, you were," said Panili. "You were caught trying to free a dead-row prisoner, a young woman by the name of Avarian Dometree. The soldiers escorted you here, using the carriage as a decoy."

"How absurd."

"That young woman you freed horrifically murdered her whole family," Ubic said. "She was sentenced to die the next morning."

"She did not kill her family."

"Did you do it?"

Irwin glared at Muslid. "Dephen Ishik had her family killed and used her as a ruse for Kipp and me."

Hilarity again. They were having fun.

Muslid rolled his eyes, "Clan-Duins *are* stupid."

"If you know about Avarian, Admiral, then you know she looks just like Yace. That was why she was used by Dephen Ishik—a distraction for Kipp and for me. I believe Dephen knows where all his children and grandchildren are. He is a powerful Telepath and Coterie. He is not above manipulating us all."

Ubic stood. "You'll be escorted to Nuaki Village at daybreak."

"Sir, are you blind to this manipulation? Or did he pay you off? I know that Lady Gretchen was asked by Dephen Ishik to kill me and Kipp. She confessed it after taking Kipp's mind and poisoning me, believing I would soon be dead."

Ubic was openly agitated. "Lady Gretchen's dead because of you."

"She was instructed to tell you that we never made it to her house. She planned to tell you after we were dead. But then I recovered from her poison, and from being buried alive, and I killed her."

Muslid barked, "Lies!"

"Lady Gretchen would do nothing of the sort," said Panili. "She knows those who come by land are supposed to come to us first."

"I believe she sent you the message about me and about the carriage right before I killed her. Or maybe Dephen did it after. That is why the carriage continued here—a ruse for everyone. And you all fell for it."

Ubic grumbled, "More Gypsy lies."

"I know I angered Dephen when I killed his cousin. I believe that is why he took those ladies at the Saloon. He wanted extra eyes and ears on me, and all of you, too."

"You're a Sleeper Assassin," Muslid said. "That's why you're going to Nuaki."

"This is all part of Dephen's plan." Irwin could see the massive mental manipulation happening, and these men were a part of it—they, too, wanted to be rid of him. He did not want the conversation to be over, but Ubic strode around the table, away from the discussion. "Sir, please, you need to understand the urgency of—"

"I don't listen to Gypsy lies."

What did I say that angered him so much?

"I am not lying, Sir. Lady Gretchen was going to get rid of us for Dephen. He did not want me to come here and tell you what I know. But after I killed Lady Gretchen, Dephen manipulated the situation so that now you will lock me up. He has been trying to thwart my efforts at rescuing Yace ever since he overtook her body in Onj Raha."

Ubic waved his hand as if trying to shoo away Irwin's words. "Do with him as you wish, Lieutenant Bejorn."

He wanted to lock the door—to keep the Telepaths' attention until they understood, until they believed him. "Sir, please, there is no time to waste. Something bad is going to happen to the Ishik regime!"

One of the Erthins opened the door for Ubic, who was followed out by Lieutenant Panili, Captain Muslid, Corporal Teigahn and the other guards. Only Lieutenant Bejorn remained with Irwin at the table, smiling artfully. He reminded Irwin of someone, but he could not place who.

8

<u>Lieutenant Bejorn</u>

Irwin sat with Lieutenant Bejorn. Neither spoke. Bejorn—light-olive skin tone, curly, wild red hair, and hazel eyes—was something to behold. He could not help but be curious about the man. To be an Elementalist was unique, and Irwin was curious to know more.

Bejorn spoke first. "Do you know how you did what you did to those Wardens?"

"Kind of."

After another long pause, Bejorn asked, "And how, exactly, do you manipulate metal?" Irwin remained silent, apparently unnerving Bejorn who said, "We can do this the easy way, or the hard way."

Irwin folded his arms. "Am I being held here against my will?"

Bejorn smiled. "You're coming with me and Teigahn tomorrow."

"That is not what I asked."

"Yes." Bejorn turned on all his Erthin powers. "You're not allowed to leave this room until tomorrow."

The spark of energy bit them both again.

"Why do you keep doing that?"

"I'm flexing my powers," said Bejorn.

"You might not want to do that while I am present."

"Why? What'll you do in return?"

I will kill you.

Irwin softly replied, "Nothing. I just do not want my powers to react to yours. I will not be in control of what happens."

"That's what you said about Onj Raha, but I believe you were in control that night."

"I did not know what I was doing. I wanted only to save my friend and find Yace."

"Was that the first time you ever used your Erthin powers?"

"I did not know I had Erthin powers then."

"But you knew you had the power to manipulate metal and instantly regenerate."

He held still.

"Your father revealed much to the PCP during his escapade in Kobiton. I think you knew he had that metal power. When did your power to manipulate metal come to you?"

"Recently."

"How recent?"

"This year."

"I'm not buying it."

And I will not tell you anything other than lies.

"I do not know what you want from me."

"Honesty."

"I am being honest."

"Ha! I think you've been able to access your powers for longer than a year."

Irwin did not respond.

After a while, he decided to probe Bejorn. "Last night, you said you could harness all five elements equally. Were you always able to do that?"

Bejorn grinned. "By the time I was thirteen, yes."

"Thirteen? Impressive."

"I came to live in Nuaki Village at five years old," Bejorn said. "They take gifted boys, sometimes girls, and train them to be loyal warriors, or *Shayot*. If they're lucky enough, they'll get to be Wardens."

"Children are allowed to live in Nuaki Village?" He was confused. "I thought that is where the worst of the worse live."

"We're not all that bad." Bejorn chuckled. "That's not to say there aren't wicked men living in Nuaki Village. Bad people live here too; they live everywhere. There's no way to avoid the evils of the world."

A shiver darted down the center of Irwin's back. He thought about the children's stolen innocence. "The *Shayot* must fear for their lives around such menacing men."

"On the contrary, they learn much from the adults in Nuaki Village."

"They learn to think like murderers and rapists?"

"They learn to be smarter than them, yes." Another long silence lingered between the two; then Bejorn asked, "So, do you know how to use all five Erthin powers?"

"Kind of."

"Well, you can use the snap technique for fire; that's a good start. Have you tried that with wind yet?"

Irwin placed his hand flat and pushed up a bout of wind to spin around in his palm. "I can summon wind." He considered his small twister. "And I can replicate water." He motioned to a cup half-full of water. The twister moved around one hand, while the other pushed the water to percolate and fill the cup to its rim.

"I'm impressed you can harness two powers at once, especially since you're untrained."

"I have practiced with water and wind more than with fire."

"What about earth?"

"I have not tried much with earth."

"Hm. What you did to Barnst isn't an Erthin trick—that I know of," said Bejorn. "Although, I've never tried a stunt like that. It's possible that it's a different type of Erthin spell. How'd you do it?"

"Not anything other than open myself up ..." He said while turning on this magnetism. "... and connect with earth elements." He played with his powers, pulling on Bejorn's hand.

Bejorn yelped, and his left index fingertip began to separate from the finger. Bejorn roared, "What are you doing!?"

"I am so sorry! Like I said, I do not know what I am doing." But he did know; intentionally removing Bejorn's fingertip.

"Argh!" Bejorn pulsated his power toward Irwin, trying to match his energy level. "Oh, I think you do."

"I am so sorry." He withdrew his energy and kept his head down, groveling—as he would have done with his father.

Bejorn used his own power to heal the top of his finger. "Don't try that again!" The Elementalist studied his fingers, making sure he had fully healed himself.

Irwin looked at Bejorn. "Maybe you can show me how to manipulate earth without hurting others."

Bejorn grimaced. "Hm. How well do you heal?"

"My body regenerates instantly. Why do you ask?"

"Every time?" Bejorn was clearly disbelieving. "Do you heal without a glitch every time?"

"Some injuries take longer than others. But I have had every bone in my body broken at least once."

Bejorn grumbled, "I'd like to see how well you can heal."

"I do not think that would be a good idea. I do not know how to control my abilities very well. I would not want to hurt you."

Bejorn chuckled at this insinuation. "I could kill you where you sit. Your abilities don't scare me."

I could kill you too.

Irwin leaned back in his seat. "I would feel safer to battle you out in the open. I would not want to bring the tower down."

Grabbing a cup of water, Bejorn placed it down in front of him and tapped his fingers on it. "What, no close quarter hand-to-hand combat?"

"No. I have never been taught."

"Ha! You were taught how to fight. That spar with Barnst was quite impressive."

"I learned that type of fighting from my father. That is how he beat me."

"Those moves were not taught to you from avoiding thrashings. No. You moved like a combatant. You were studying Barnst's moves. You calculated how to counteract his brutality. I've trained that way all my life. No, sir. You were trained to fight, trained by a *Shayot*, weren't you?"

"I do not know how to fight. I only know how to defend myself against my father and others."

Bejorn cackled. "You're gonna try to convince me you learned all those moves while being beaten as a child? Now I know you're lying."

"I am not lying. I was beaten within a toe-length of death many times. I learned from my family's brutality. And that is why I do not like to fight. Too many people get hurt."

"That might explain a few things."

They studied each other. Irwin leaned forward, grabbing one of the full glasses, he drank it down. He waved his hand over the cup to refill it. "Why are you here, Bejorn?"

"You don't want me here?"

Irwin did not respond.

"You're wondering why I am here in this room watching you?"

"Yes."

"Someone must make sure you stay put."

"You think you can stop me from leaving?"

"Yes. I can, and I will."

Irwin scratched his head and leaned back in his chair once more.

I should just kill him and leave. Then what? They will have the place surrounded the moment I leave the room, and then I will have to kill them all. So much death and destruction on my hands.

"When you put it that way, I guess I will stay put."

Bejorn broke a long stretch of silence. "How long have you been able to instantly regenerate?"

"Since birth."

"So, you *did* know you have Erthin powers!"

"I did not know that was an Erthin power until someone pointed it out. I always thought it was part of my other power."

I should not have said that.

"Your other power meaning your metal power?"

He was slow to answer. "Yes."

"And your father has that power too?"

"Yes. He was quite strong with it."

"Did he use it often?"

"He seldom used it around me." Irwin did not care that he was outright lying to Bejorn. He knew the man across the table was not a Telepath, only an Elementalist.

"So, you've always known about the metal power," Bejorn pressed, "but you've only been able to use it for a year?"

"Yes."

"You seem to know how to use it well."

"It comes more naturally than my Erthin powers."

"I've met no one who could harness metal."

"Neither have I. My father was the only one."

"What about your grandparents?"

He shook his head. "No one other than my father. But his primary power was his ability to berate and beat me until I was bloodied, inside and out."

"Did he ever talk to you about your mother?"

"I know nothing about my mother other than she died right after I was born."

"Do you know what killed her?"

"From what I understand, women die often from childbirth." Irwin's vitriol was thick.

They measured each other, each man wondering what the other's next move would be.

Irwin broke the silence this time. "You say you were adept with your Elementalist powers at thirteen?"

Bejorn smiled, and raising the glass of water to his lips, he sipped it slowly. "Yes, I was the youngest Erthin ever to pass all the tests, and the only one who could use all five powers equally at such a young age."

"Is one power easier to work with than the others?"

"Fire is undemanding; if you have a temper; fire is easily ignited by anger. Wind came next for me; the ability to blow people over is now my strong suit. Then healing and earth. But water ... water was the hardest." He laughed. "At first I had a hard time turning it off once it came on."

Irwin nodded. "I had a hard time the first time too, though it seems easier than earth."

Bejorn was visibly curious. "Have you tried healing others?"

"No."

"Well then, when we arrive in Nuaki Village, we can start a rigorous training regimen. We'll work those abilities to your advantage."

"I would like to learn how to heal others."

"You know, it's quite possible that your metal ability is your earth power," Bejorn said. "Metal is a basic element, and most elements are moldable to earth-harnessing Erthins. So maybe you are simply stronger with metals than any other Earth Erthin."

"Could be."

"Although it doesn't exactly explain how you were able to do what you did to Barnst," Bejorn drummed his fingers on his cup before taking a sip. "We could test you, of course. In Nuaki, we have rooms to play in, fields we can tear up." He laughed again and added, "We'll have a fun ol' time!"

"We could." Irwin struggled to keep his reserve. A silence filled with curiosity and distrust hung in the air between them. Irwin did not have to look at Bejorn to understand what he was up to. The man was like a curious old hen pecking around the barnyard with his red crown of unkempt hair.

Finally, Bejorn said, "I would like to talk with you about your metal powers—your ability to make counterfeit coins."

"I do not make counterfeit coins."

"Oh! So, you just happen to always carry hundreds of pounds of coins on you?"

"Yes."

"Don't lie."

"I am not lying. Before I arrived here, I had about a hundred pounds of silver. Now I only have about twenty. I've spent much of my cache in the markets and at the Saloon."

Bejorn was sarcastic again. "You don't say. How'd you get so rich?"

"Mining coal. It pays well. I saved and saved so I could take a journey."

"Sounds like another one of those Gypsy stories."

Would anyone miss you, Lieutenant Bejorn, if I killed you right now?

He studied the older man whose jaw slacked with exasperation. "What do you want to know about me? You obviously are here to question me and to hinder me from leaving this room. But why are you here, and not a Telepath?"

"If we're going to be traveling together, I need to know that I can trust you in the jungles of Datzar."

"You think I might slit your throat?"

They eyed one another. Bejorn snapped, "Yes, I think you would."

"You can leave," Irwin told Bejorn. He did not want the Elementalist in the room anymore. "I will stay here and wait for morning, as the Telepaths wish it."

"No, you won't. You want to leave now?"

You are correct.

"I am not in any mood to harass or provoke. I will stay. As requested," Irwin said. Meanwhile, he imagined himself stabbing Bejorn's face and chest.

"How about this ..." Bejorn said, "... order us some food from Das Grits Tits!"

He shifted in his seat. "How would I do that?"

"With your telepathy, of course!"

"I am not a Telepath, nor do I appreciate the insinuation that I am anything like them."

"Fine." Bejorn waved his hand as a sort of dismissal. "What would you like to eat?"

"A platter of their cheesy bread, please."

"What, no pork pie?"

You mean Clan-Duin pie.

"No, thank you."

"Suit yourself!" Bejorn said and rose from his chair and left the room. Outside the door, two Erthins stood guard. "Make sure this remains closed up tight," the Elementalist said.

Irwin heard him hustle down the hallway.

9
<u>WHAT TO BELIEVE</u>

Kipp sat alone in another room not far away. The last he had seen of Irwin, a gang of Erthins, Clan-Duins, and Telepaths were hauling him around a corner down the long corridor and then they were all out of sight. Irwin could be dead. You couldn't trust these Telepaths. He wiped a tear before it could trickle down his cheek. If Irwin was dead, Kipp could not keep chasing Yace and Dephen alone. She would be lost to him forever—she may already be.

Time dragged on. The chair in which he slumped was hard and his back ached. He put his feet up on the table and waited for something to happen. After a long time, there was a loud click. He jumped. Had he been sleeping? The door flew open. A draft of air filled the small musty quarters. Donnolin flew in on the tailwind of the breeze. "How are ya holding up?"

The man left the door open and Kipp saw an Erthin escort out in the corridor. He stood, feeling a rush of anger boil from the base of his spine. "Tell me why I'm here! Where is Samuel?"

"Calm down, I'm not here to interrogate you, so don't get huffy." The Telepath snapped his fingers, and two females entered. Obviously, Clan-Duin, they both had long, flowing dark hair, glistening eyes, and dark, lustful feline features. Both wore tie-dyed dresses of bright yellows, deep oranges, and blood reds. Looking into one woman's eyes, he saw that each eye was a different color—one green and one blue.

Donnolin motioned for them to put the trays of food—fruit bowls, sweetbreads, a cube of cheese with a knife sticking out of it, and dried meats—onto the table. The one with two different eyes placed a carafe of wine and one of water in the center. There were silver goblets for drinking, intricately glazed dishes, and delicate utensils. Probably also silver, he thought. He looked up at the women.

Donnolin's voice cackled. He looked pleased with himself. "You'll be here for a while, so I thought I'd accommodate your needs."

Kipp ignored Donnolin and watched the women move around him, felt them swish their garments against the sides of his legs. Finally, he looked up at the Telepath and asked, "Donnolin, right?"

The man nodded.

Anger bolstered Kipp's confidence. "What are your superiors doing with me and with Samuel?"

"I don't know. I'm not privy to that information."

Donnolin approached Kipp; his face close enough, Kipp could smell the man's breath.

"You could listen in, can't you?"

"The nice thing about stone is that it muffles telepathy."

"No, it doesn't. I know better." Kipp searched for a reaction in Donnolin's face, perhaps a movement of the body. He knew well that Telepaths could hear a person talking or thinking, no matter where they were.

"How do you know this?"

"My girlfriend's telepathic."

"I've heard of worse combinations. Lizel here is half Clan-Duin, half Telepath. Arelia is half too but doesn't look it."

Lizel winked her blue eye at Kipp. "It works out fine for me, but children of half-bloods tend to be used as minions by more powerful Telepaths."

The other said, "Crossbreeding with Telepaths can bring about the mutant factor where we appear Clan-Duin in every way but have keen telepathic abilities. Some of us become isolated from our pack, and if we're found out, we're attacked or killed."

Why are they telling me all this?

Donnolin picked up a wine goblet and took a slow sip. "How do you like it in Arenu?"

"It's alright. I mean, it's nice to be around my own kind. I don't have to worry about walking three strides behind anyone. Or being picked up by PCP for not wearing the right clothes."

Lizel said, "That's why we live here." She sat next to him, picking from a clump of grapes, chewing each slowly as she eyed him from the corner of hers.

"You're Telepaths. That's why you live here."

"Why have you been traveling with a Mortal?" Donnolin wanted to know what he most likely already knew.

"He's no Mortal. And we're touring the land so he can sell his wares."

Donnolin chuckled. "That's not what I heard."

"Oh! Then you know we've been chasing my girlfriend who's possessed by a Coterie?!"

Both women giggled. "If she's running away from you, there's probably a reason she doesn't want to be with you. She mustn't love you. But don't worry, there are many beautiful women here in Arenu Village." One of them rubbed the back of his neck with her fingers.

Kipp kept quiet, folding his arms across his chest. He felt no desire for these women. He wanted Yace. He wanted to know that Irwin was safe and that the two of them could continue.

He turned his head away from the contact on his neck and, and like fireflies in the night they all vanished as quickly as they had appeared along with the food and wine. There was no trace of their smell. He sniffed. He listened for any sound, but heard none.

He raised his fists, kicked back the chair and raced to the door, slamming his body again and again against it. "Let me out!" He beat the palms of his hands against the hard surface.

His anger boiled over; he kicked and punched at the air. After this burst of seething rage, he realized he was uselessly spending energy; all in vain. The Telepaths had him in their net. He wiped the spit falling from his mouth.

"I hate this," he muttered. He knew he had to clear his thoughts, to focus, to keep the Telepaths away. But he couldn't think straight—so angered by the situation. The light had dimmed, and he could barely breathe. He was tempted to take on his canine shape, but he knew the Telepaths were monitoring him. "How dare you try to control me, assholes!" Then it struck him to test the doorknob.

The handle turned, and the door swung open, knocking him backward with the force of Irwin's entry. Irwin then shut the door and backed into the room, turning to place his hand on Kipp's shoulder. "We are in trouble."

"No shit. There're Telepaths everywhere trying to get into my mind."

"We have to abort our mission, Kipp. We are risking our lives, and for what? You think Yace will want you after all this? After everything she will have gone through. She will be broken. She might even die, and we would not know it until too late. We cannot save her, Kipp."

"But you're the one who is supposed to save her, Irwin! We can't quit now. You've been telling me we're so close. Have you been lying this whole time? Or did they really fuk with your mind?" He held his gut as though he was about to vomit. "You've been telling me over and over not to quit, but now *you're* gonna?"

"Those Telepaths out there, they told me their plans. They are going to make me into a puppet. I cannot guarantee your safety, Kipp. You are better off leaving me and Yace behind!"

"You can't mean that!"

"I am sorry, Kipp, but this will not go well for any of us. I do not see myself living past tonight."

"You told me you can't die. But now you can?"

"I cannot guarantee anything right now."

"You've gotta have a plan."

"My only plan is to get you out of here. And when I say out of here, I mean, get you out of Arenu Village."

"You'll open the southern doors?"

"No. The Datzar Jungle is not a good place to travel alone. You must go north for Nonbry," he said, determined to make Kipp understand. "Rescuing Yace is now beyond our control. Only Nonbry can save her. You need to bring Nonbry back here."

"But I thought ... I thought the Gypsy couldn't continue south because of what you did to the Hall in Onj Raha."

"Nonbry was overreacting. They can continue on to the south, but not north. North is not an option for the Gypsy now." Irwin gripped Kipp's shoulders. "This is up to you. I need you to do this for me. You need to get Nonbry and the rest of the Gypsy down here."

"I'm not sure about this, Irwin. Getting Nonbry ... it'll take many moons just to convince him to come this way. There's gotta be a better way."

"I need you to do this. Only Nonbry can save her now."

"It's hard for me to believe you can't help. It'll take many moons for Nonbry and everyone to get here. By then, Yace could be .... There's gotta be a better way, Irwin. I know, do what you did in Onj Raha and get us out of here."

Irwin shook his head.

Kipp felt the weight of the situation press on him until his back ached.

"It would take too long to get the horses, and we would be stopped. And all the carnage. No. I cannot. Please understand. It is easier if you go north. I will not be able to leave. Not without a fight. And you know I do not want to fight. But I do need you to be safe, Kipp. And I need you to go get Nonbry. He will have to retrieve Yace."

"Nonbry said you're the only one who can save her!"

"Only Nonbry can save her now."

Kipp's voice shook; he crouched low and growled. "How badly did they mess with your mind, Irwin? You almost sound like you want to stay."

Irwin opened the door, revealing a barren passage. There were no guards, only bright lanterns hung from the low ceiling.

Kipp stepped up to the door's threshold and peered out. He sniffed at the air, listened. He turned to speak with his friend, but Irwin had vanished, just like Donnolin and the women and food.

10

<u>KIPP'S ESCAPE</u>

Kipp yelled and slammed the door. "This is shitty. Fukin' Telepaths. I'm onto your mind games." He started back toward the table but turned and returned to the door; it was still unlocked. Softly, he opened it again; scanned the hallway, noticing two Erthins stood guard. He shut the door, and after a few breaths, opened it again. Now two Clan-Duins stood guard. "This is all make-believe." He glanced over his shoulder. "I'm still sitting in that chair, staring at the wall. They've got my mind. Shitty asshole Telepaths!"

He resumed his leaned-back position—feet on the table. He mumbled and grumbled, trying to hold his thoughts still. "I hate being telepathically manipulated."

Soon he fell asleep.

Kipp!

He heard Yace's voice echo from the depths of his mind, of his soul.

Kipp, blink if you can hear me.

Yace called to him from between the dreaming world and reality.

"Get out of my head, lousy Telepaths."

No Kipp, I'm going to get you out of here.

"That's what Irwin said." He wasn't fully awake and unsure if he was in a distorted reality created by the Telepaths.

She appeared before him as a translucent apparition; glowing blue dress, matching eyes, and cascading blonde hair.

I cannot exist here for long. There are many strong Telepaths in this place. I need you to listen, Kipp. Do not think about what I say.

"I'm not gonna listen to anything you have to say."

Kipp. Take those coins Irwin made, the ones in your pocket, and place them against your temples. They can get you out of all this telepathic chaos. You need to get somewhere safe. The best place is that metal box-bed Irwin made. That's the only place you'll be safe from them.

He did not want to believe her, but then again, he did.

Please Kipp. Irwin can't help you now.

If you stay, they will make you go north. They want you to bring Nonbry and the rest of the Gypsy back here. Don't do it; it's a trap.

Now is the time, Kipp. Do not falter. If you do, no one will save you. And you'll be sent off as a ruse to bring Nonbry and the others into a trap from which they'll not be able to break free.

He stuffed his right hand into the pocket, found the coins. Pulling out the silver pieces, he moved them around between his fingers—hesitant, not sure of anything.

"It won't hurt to try."

Without thinking, he placed the coins against his temples. Yace disappeared, and the room brightened.

He wanted to chase after her, but he knew that was not possible. So, he walked to the door—coins pressed against his head. He knew not to think, but could not help wondering if this was a dream or a trick. He tested the latch.

The door was really unlocked, and he pulled it open. A Clan-Duin soldier sat still, possibly sleeping there in the hall—eyes half closed. He opened the door more, fearing the creak would wake the guard, and there sat another on the other side of the doorsill. Neither moved, as if overtaken by a sleeping drug.

He held the coins firm on his temples, using the side of his foot to prop the door open. Neither soldier appeared to have heard. Both looked almost like stone statues in a garden. He held still. Held his breath. He snuck past the spellbound Clan-Duin guards—coins tight against his temples. The door swung shut but did not latch or alert soldiers. With no more than a few long strides, he was at the front door he had come through earlier.

Kipp looked back. Both guards were still staring ahead, still motionless.

He pressed the coins against his head with one hand again. His fingers were long enough to hold the coins in place while opening the front door with his other hand—a good thing, he thought, to have long fingers, and they made nice paws when he needed them. Kipp peered out the sliver of opening.

The evening sky was darkening. Stars appeared. He neither heard nor smelled anything of note. Murmurs of people conversing while eating outside; and the usual odor of dead fish filled his nostrils. A flock of gulls had gathered on the edge of the far roofline. Like him, they seemed to be holding their breath.

He slipped out of the tower, holding close to the shadows, trying to steady his breath as he scurried along, keeping his senses on full alert. He climbed on-board the wagon without looking back. Holding the coins in place, he stretched his legs over the front seat and into the enclosed wagon-bed. He straddled ration boxes, bags, and barrels, and without losing his grip on the coins and without falling over. He found the covered bed.

Once on top of the bed, and hidden from view, he listened to people come and go from the tower and move around the village square. He figured they were on their way back to their living quarters, or maybe somewhere within the courtyard for a bite. The aroma of freshly cooked food wafted in his direction. It was coming from the Saloon. The smell of fresh meat, bread and cheese and ale filled his nose. His mouth watered and his stomach growled.

He waited, coins still pressed hard against his temples, until the boisterous sounds from the Gritty Titty Saloon died down. He longed for Irwin to emerge, but he knew the Telepaths had him, probably still grilling him—messing with his mind as only Telepaths can do. Besides Irwin, Kipp had no thoughts other than food and sleep. He moved from the bed and arranged the blankets down where he usually slept in his dog form. He took the coins off his head, placed them on the exterior relief created on the lockbox, and opened Irwin's secret chamber.

After relieving himself in their pisspot, he took two flasks of water and some rations and slipped into the casket. Once inside, he felt safe, protected by Irwin's metallic box from all telepathy, from those telepathic devils. "I hope I'm not still sitting in that dang room," he thought. Had Yace really been there in his consciousness? Were the Telepaths still holding him mentally hostage?

11

<u>STAYING COOL</u>

Lieutenant Bejorn returned to the chamber carrying a large platter of food and a carafe of ale.

He must be pleased to see me still here, as I promised.

Irwin felt no inclination to engage in any more conversations with Bejorn, nor did he want to get drunk.

Bejorn set down the cheesy bread, a bowl of fruit, and smoked salmon strips. The Elementalist left—probably sensing the Metalist's irritability—taking with him a large pork roast slab with steamed carrots and potato chunks and, of course, the ale. Irwin was contented with his time alone and the tasty food. He was more than certain his food had been laced with something, but it only affected him in one way—he craved more.

For the rest of the night, he sat isolated in the room that sometimes glimmered with candlelight and sometimes spun dark.

He could have left at any time but chose to play their game; aware that any transgressions would be met with death. The cost of living here, or in Nuaki, was high.

At one point, bored, he moved around the small space. He tested the door—it was unlocked—and he thought about opening it but did not want to startle the Erthins standing guard outside. He did not feel like provoking the people of Arenu Village anymore, especially the Telepaths. Instead, he found a semi-comfortable position in a chair, placed his feet on the edge of the table, and fell asleep.

By the time Bejorn returned the following morning, a paraffin smell lay thick in the room. Candles had melted during the night. The Lieutenant appeared well-rested, a smell of sweet rolls on his breath. "Time to get going. We'll want to collapse that canopy on your wagon before we leave."

There had been a change of guards outside the doorway. One Clan-Duin and one Erthin stood like statues—like the sentries they were meant to be.

Bejorn kept one step behind Irwin. "I took it upon myself to supply you with breakfast this morning. Hopefully, you'll enjoy the sweet rolls waiting for you on the driver's seat of your wagon."

I hope I am not stuck with this man the whole way.

Bejorn remained close on Irwin's heels.

He is already irritating.

The Lieutenant followed him out the main doorway and into the morning air. The smell of saltwater and fishy odors permeated Irwin's sense of smell, and he thought sadly of Kipp. The sun had not breeched the horizon, but a few rays of light were already signaling another warm, bright day.

Irwin went to his wagon and walked around it, inspecting the exterior and interior.

"What are you doing?" Bejorn bellowed.

"Making sure none of the locals messed with my property." He noticed the blankets had been tossed onto the floor, exposing his long lockbox.

Bejorn stepped beside Irwin, catching a glimpse of the gleaming bed. "Is that where you keep all your coins?"

Irwin covered the box and the bed with the blankets—secretly studying his metal box. He felt Kipp and those two coins inside.

"Your wagon cover. Remove it, posthaste."

Irwin raised his hands, and the canvas cover collapsed around him. All he had to do was to absorb the metal and redistribute it throughout the wagon. The canvas fell into his hands, and he folded it.

Bejorn watched as he pushed the canvas into a square, and then another. He appeared baffled by how fluid the wagon cover dismantled—so easily, so quickly.

"It is all in the wrist," said Irwin.

A second wagon rolled through the portal from the stable yard into the main courtyard of Arenu Village. Corporal Teigahn sat next to a thirty-something Clan-Duin who held the reins. Dressed in a short pale-green and blue sarong, the Clan-Duin was dark-skinned, muscular. He had a full head of dark hair, no wrinkles, and some might say he was well built. He smiled at Irwin.

The Clan-Duin pulled the wagon to a halt next to Irwin's. "Good morning, fellas; ready for a ride?"

Bejorn chuckled, "Yeah, I'm ready to leave this place."

"HowLongWillItTakeYaOverThere?"

Irwin still did not understand Teigahn, and he did not respond. He placed the folded canvas on the bed. He looked up to see Jorge leading Bodi and Roper. For a second, he could have sworn that Jorge looked like Albert—angry to be pulling horses.

He shouted, "Do you need any help, Jorge?"

"No," Jorge snapped.

Bejorn was climbing up onto Irwin's wagon, but paused and asked, "How'd you know Jorge?" He looked down at the Empath who was attaching the horses to the wagon.

Jorge glared at Lieutenant Bejorn, said nothing, and kept on with his work.

"We met yesterday morning at the bakery," Irwin offered.

Bejorn harrumphed at Jorge who kept silent. He looked back at Irwin. "All your gear tied down?"

"Yes."

"The canvas and blankets?"

"I am not worried about the contents of my wagon."

The Clan-Duin on the other wagon grumbled, "He looks Mortal. Why's he coming to Nuaki?"

Teigahn chuckled, "HeWillWishHeWasMortal. Orders."

Irwin muttered, "I need to get my Jennies."

Lieutenant Bejorn grunted. "Jennies?"

"Are you referring to those little creatures with the tall ears?" Jorge looked at Irwin.

"Yes. They are donkeys, but the females are called Jennets or Jennies; Jacks are boys."

Bejorn said, "Perfectly sized for being in a mine, perhaps."

"I will go get them," Irwin said and moved to jump from the wagon.

"Unless you're gonna put them in your wagon, it's best to leave them here."

"I am not leaving them," He jumped down.

"They can't be pulled behind," Bejorn insisted. "They'll get eaten."

"Then I will make space for them."

From his perch, the Clan-Duin said, "I don't think you understand. We need to leave right now."

Everything inside Irwin's wagon had metal on it, in it, or around it. All he had to do was move his hands and summon the boxes and barrels closer together. Several slid on top of one another, stacking high and creating a seatback for the driver.

They all saw what Irwin had done and were silenced.

"I will be right back." He went to retrieve his donkeys.

The Clan-Duin said, "Pfft. A bit pushy, I'd say!"

"HeAndJorgeWillGetAlongJustFine!" Teigahn chuckled and slapped his partner's back.

"I'd like to know what he plans to do with those donkeys." Both men chortled, and their jubilation echoed after him.

Irwin had learned to keep his calm and not take offence from heckling by people who did not know him. He hustled to gather Jenn Jenn and Nee Nee and return. The donkeys did not need lead lines, and they were so glad to see him. They followed close behind Irwin, back to the wagon.

When they got to the wagon, he pointed at the open wagon-bed and commanded, "Jump up." One-by-one the donkeys sprang up into the confined wagon bed. He fastened the tailgate, strode to the front of his vehicle, and climbed on board.

Everyone, including Jorge, stared at Irwin as he took a seat next to Bejorn.

"That's impressive!" The Lieutenant remarked. "You train them yourself?"

Irwin said nothing and stared ahead, waiting for the signal to depart.

"Now, are we ready to go?" The Clan-Duin glanced over at them—Bejorn nodded.

Teigahn raised his hand, whipped it around, and shouted, "Yahoo!"

As the verbal cue was expelled by the Corporal, Lieutenant Bejorn moved his hands around, lifted them up, and a wagon-sized hole opened in the southern stone wall of Arenu Village. The wagon bed creaked, and the wheels rattled against the cobbled surface. Once on the dirt roadway, the wagon would not be as noisy. Lanterns hanging from poles on the wagons were lit for the light they would need as they neared the gnarly jungle corridor. There would be no other light to guide the way, and Irwin felt a pang of trepidation, harsher than he had before. He watched the shadows of the lanterns swaying in the dusk-like surroundings as they slowly made their way into the jungle.

The Clan-Duin and Corporal Teigahn's wagon led the way through the brief passage toward the dark jungle. Jorge sat atop covered ration boxes on the rear of Teigahn's wagon. He was facing Irwin—appearing as Albert. Irwin tried to ignore him as he ushered his own horses into the dark corridor, reins slapping buttocks, trying to ignore Jorge.

After both wagons rolled through the passageway, Bejorn turned, moved his hand, and closed the portal. They had left Arenu Village and were now venturing into the jungle—no hope of return once the entryway was sealed; no place to turn around, no way to maneuver back into the sanctuary of Arenu Village. They were southbound—on their own—until they made it to Nuaki Village. Their pace was fast.

The sight of Jorge appearing as Albert faded into grandfather Jebadia—angrily eyeballing Irwin who blinked, trying to think of someone else, but those wrathful eyes would not stop staring. Each swaying lantern made shadows, made objects in the distance seem to move; animal sounds echoed in the darkness.

It was early in the day, and the jungle was awake. Irwin was not sure if he should worry. He knew nothing about the animals in Datzar Jungle except what he overheard Kipp and Jyn talking about the night prior. They spoke of vicious beasts: alligators, apes, jaguars, and rhinoceros that roamed this place. He remained vigilant and took cues from the men with whom he now traveled.

"I don't get it. You no longer mine, but you keep donkeys. Why?" Bejorn started a conversation. "You think you'll want to go back to mining?"

Irwin shrugged, said nothing, not wanting to chat with this man.

"There can't be much to mine. I mean, well, coal is valuable, and so is iron. Jamal knows more about metals than me. But why mine? It's not a suitable existence, especially for a child." Bejorn kept on. "You grew up in a cave? I can't imagine—did they let you outside? Did you get to see sunlight? I mean, you're quite pale, not from around here type of pale."

Just like yesterday.

Irwin tensed. He felt the Elementalist charging his power.

The air between them snapped.

"That tickles." Bejorn chuckled. "What about you? Does it tickle?"

He really wanted to ignore Bejorn.

I wish I was in my box.

He noticed Jorge intently watching something behind them. The Empath pointed at moving foliage just beyond the backside of Irwin's wagon. Bejorn turned to gauge the situation. It was nothing.

As he turned his attention frontward, Bejorn picked up the conversation again. "We try to keep this section of road clean. It's bad if drivers have disruptions or delays. Everything we do is based on a schedule."

"What about the road south of Nuaki Village?"

"It's rarely traveled."

"People do not travel north from Daos?"

"Not usually," Bejorn sighed. "I heard you journeyed through the nomad lands in a moon's time. That's unheard of! Only those who are chased travel at that fast rate through there. You can kill a horse going that far that fast. But it means your horses are fit for the hard and fast journey to Nuaki. When we travel, we go quick."

Bejorn paused, but not for long. "We have running races from Arenu Village to Nuaki. When we train the *Shayot* to run long distances, we make them race from village to village. For us drivers, we can make the trip in four days if we have enough men for rotations.

"The *Shayot* are expected to run the distance in one day and night by the end of their training. No sleeping, only running. The first few tries can take up to ten days."

"Ten days? How far apart are the villages?"

"About two-hundred kilometers. But the *Shayot* contend with a lot of hazards along the way. So, they're trained to avoid confrontations. However, we lose a few every year."

"How do you lose a *Shayot*?"

"There are many creatures in the jungle that enjoy a good pursuit and a harsh confrontation. Many *Shayot* perish during their training.

"I'll say this, being *Shayot* isn't easy. It requires extreme self-discipline. There are many years of hard physical feats, all of which take incredible use of one's abilities. That's why we are valued leaders when we finally reach adulthood. It's said that if a *Shayot* can survive in the jungle of Datzar, they can conquer the world."

"Do you know if Dephen Ishik was a *Shayot*?"

"I don't know. But every *Shayot* Nuaki's ever hosted—all their personal information is kept in a book. And there are many of those books in the Nuaki library. Names, pictures, stories, fact, fiction, it's all there. The librarians could help you find that information. We have articles from a thousand years past stowed in the vaults." He puffed out a chortle. "We have books so old they were written before the night rained red and Urthis became Urthis. They speak tales about how this world evolved—interesting indeed, and it's all been translated by scholars of the ancients!"

Irwin held the reins tight, chewed on the inside of his cheek, trying to tune out Bejorn. But the blowhard went on and on about nothing that mattered to anyone but himself. Irwin was busy keeping his horses from moving too quickly. They were all but nose-to-tailgate with the other wagon. He was still trying to ignore Jorge perched on that lead wagon-bed displaying Edwin's elderly face.

He missed seeing that kindly face.

I wish Great Grandfather Edwin had lived longer.

Jorge was a distraction. From Edwin, to Jebadia, then Albert again—his shifting appearance was maddening. He tried not to appear disturbed, tried to think of Kipp.

Now I know why Jorge lives in Nuaki. I wish he would lie back. I do not want to look at you anymore, Jorge. Lay down, please.

He ate half of the sweet-rolls, and he knew Kipp could smell them—plenty of air holes in the metal box. He wrapped two and placed the packaging under the blanket on the lockbox. With his Metalistic powers, he lowered the sweet rolls into the box. He would have to wait to hear Kipp's story.

How did he wind up in that box?

Lieutenant Bejorn kept on with his boisterous, one-sided conversation. He talked about *Shayot*, and alcohol, food in general, and then apples specifically. Would there be no end? Bejorn ranted on and on about apples—all different types and their uses. He then argued—with himself, apparently, that Nuaki Village needed more apples.

Irwin laughed to himself as the Lieutenant voiced his opinions about this and that. He noticed Jorge also snickering.

Bejorn might be an Elementalist, but he has a secret power—talking people to death.

A stop at the first river crossing, and Kipp pushed the lid off the lockbox and stood—startling everyone. "Man, do you ever stop talking?"

Lieutenant Bejorn stopped in mid-sentence, swung around, and stared at Kipp. "Where'd you come from?"

The donkeys bellowed as if answering for Kipp. Irwin inserted himself between Bejorn and Kipp. "He is with me."

Bejorn jumped to the ground. "We know he's with you. But he's not supposed to be here."

"HeIsSupposedToBeHeadingNorth.   IThoughtTheAdmiralMadeSure-OfThat!" Corporal Teigahn rushed toward them. "INeedYouTwoToGetDown."

"This should not have happened." Bejorn spoke menacingly.

Kipp, too, jumped from the wagon and dropped his pants to relieve himself.

Irwin followed his friend, standing protectively between Kipp and the men from Nuaki Village. He tried not to smile.

After he was done peeing, Kipp whispered, "Just incinerate them and let's go."

"That is unnecessary," his voice low so only Kipp could hear. "There is only one way to Daos, and that's through Nuaki Village. Your plan is not well thought out."

Bejorn asked, "So that lockbox of yours is also a stowaway chest?"

Kipp kept a hand on Irwin's shoulder and whispered, "Snap him out of existence first."

He might have taken Kipp's suggestion if no one else was around, but there were three others—and one was telepathic. He put his hands up in a defensive posture—Kipp breathing on the back of his neck. "My friend here is on his own mission, Corporal."

"ThatIsALie."

"The fact that Kipp happens to be here at the same time as us is mere coincidence."

"Good save." Kipp whispered, then spoke out, "That's right! I just happened to be here just now." He smiled nervously at both commanding officers. "I'm heading south to find my beloved. It's peculiar that we'd find each other here at this moment."

Bejorn spat, "I saw you come from the lockbox. You didn't just appear from out of the sky."

Irwin stepped in. "You are correct, Lieutenant. That box is a stowaway chest as well as a lockbox."

And it is one-hundred pounds of metal that I could use against you right now.

"Yace?" Kipp gasped, his eyes bulging.

Jorge and Jamal jumped from their rig and detached the horses from the lead wagon. When Kipp laid eyes on Jorge, he thought he saw his beloved Yace. The empath was walking a horse out into the tall grasses along the river's edge.

Irwin placed his hand on Kipp's chest. "That is not Yace, Kipp. That is Jorge."

Bejorn spoke to Teigahn, "What should we do about this?"

The Corporal scornfully eyed Irwin. "OurTimeHereIsLimited. GetThose-HorsesOutAndEating."

"How the ...?" Kipp whispered, clearly baffled.

"That is Jorge, Kipp. The Empath I told you about."

"Empath?"

Bejorn looked at Kipp, "You can't journey with us, Clan-Duin."

"His name is Hauss Kipp," Irwin said, placing himself between Kipp and the others.

Bejorn smirked, "I thought it was Kipp Hauler."

Irwin did not back down. "He has my protection, and he is coming with me. If you do not allow that, then—"

"HeCanTravelToNuakiWithUs. HeJustCannotStayThere. That'sAll!"

"What was that?" Again, Irwin struggled to comprehend Teigahn's jargon.

Bejorn explained, "Teigahn says Kipp can ride with us."

"Good! Good to know we agree." Irwin said, noticing Teigahn study him as Admiral Ubic had.

Teigahn said, "HaveThemGrazeTheirHorses."

Bejorn clapped his hands. "Our time here is limited, but we always allow the horses a reprieve; the next stop isn't until tomorrow." He looked at Jamal and Jorge hand-grazing their animals. "Unhook your animals, let them have a few bites."

"My donkeys, too?" They were bellowing from the back of the wagon.

"Yes," Bejorn waved his hand, "Hurry."

They unhitched the horses from the wagon and let the Jennies down from the bed. Both Jenn Jenn and Nee Nee trotted toward the horses. The grasses were as tall as the Jennies—only their ears protruded above. It was a relief to be in the sunlight again. The river roared past like a bold creature, and the wild oats and wheat grasses danced in the warm breeze.

"I'm sorry Irwin. My plan was to keep hidden as long as possible. But all the jostling and nonstop jabbering ...."

He patted Kipp's backside. "I am glad you used the box for what it was intended."

"Did they fuk with your mind like they did with me?"

"No." Irwin could see the tension gather in Kipp's chest. The muscles around his jaw spasmed.

As they approached Jamal, who by now was deep in the grass, he puffed out his chest. "Another Clan-Duin." Kipp reciprocated the Clan-Duin gesture but said nothing.

Kipp was drawn to Jorge who looked like Yace to him.

Irwin squeezed between them and close to Jorge. Everyone all at once saw the Empath as he was: yellow skinned, curly brown hair with matching eyes, and larger than normal nose and ears.

Jamal sputtered, "Holy shit!" He stepped back.

Corporal Teigahn yelled out, "What in Hakara?!"

Kipp, too, was startled. "Irwin?"

Jorge knew what had happened and scoffed, angered that Irwin's powers had once again transformed him. He thrust the lead-lines at Jamal and ran toward Corporal Teigahn, once again reflecting each man's thoughts and dreams.

Jorge shouted to Teigahn, "Don't report this!"

"WhatJustHappenedThere?"

"That was all him!" Jorge pointed at Irwin.

"ExplainToMeWhatHappened."

Jamal tossed Kipp his horse's line and raced toward the heated conversation, probably figuring it might explode.

Jorge said, "I don't know how to explain what happened." He pointed at Irwin. "But he's got a power over me."

Bejorn eyed Irwin. "He better not have power over you!"

Teigahn glared at Irwin too, then engaged Jorge in a quieter tone.

Irwin and Kipp stood close to each other, near the grazing horses. "Why don't you seem surprised about this, Irwin? What the fuk just happened there?"

"When I ate breakfast with the Eunuchs and Jorge, I affected him for the first time. All I can say at this point is that only in close proximity to me is Jorge's true flesh seen." He rubbed the back of his neck. "It is truly bizarre."

"I don't remember you telling me about it!"

"I told you about Jorge."

"You didn't tell me that happened."

"Actually, I did. When Jorge is close to me, like you are, everyone can see him for himself. And then when he is ..." Irwin took two strides backwards. "... this far away, he is that Empathic creature we see now."

"Ah! That's right. Now I remember. But ... your power does that?"

"Yes, unfortunately."

Kipp whispered, "Plan still the same?"

Irwin's hand landed heavily on Kipp's shoulder. He did not want Teigahn overhearing. "Yes. We are going to save Yace."

"The Telepaths tried to trick me. They wanted me to get Nonbry. They had you come to me and tell me that only he could rescue Yace."

"They know a lot about Nonbry, you, and Yace. We need to let Nonbry know the next time we talk to him."

"How are we gonna get out of this and away from these guys?"

"Remember the Oracle's words? Wary travelers travel warily. Those who are alone, die that way."

"You can't be serious! We're gonna stay with these asses?"

12
<u>MONSTERS EVERYWHERE</u>

High-pitched screams and low-pitched roars emanated from the depths of the jungle. It felt like creatures were coming after them from all sides where they stood frozen in the tall, waving grass. The air vibrated when a swarm of black monkeys flushed forth from the thick foliage along the river. Screeching, hooting, beating chests, and tearing at tree branches. Small faces framed in shocks of hair, their long arms dragged across the dirt along the road, kicking up dust as they danced and swayed and made offensive gestures. The ruckus was deafening, and the horses danced sideways and back and forth. They snorted and whinnied—ready to run or rear up. Irwin and Kipp held the lines and stroked their animal's sides—gleaming from the heat of the sun. Composed, the donkeys kept busy munching trails through the high grass.

Corporal Teigahn shouted and waved his hand. "RoundUpTheHorses. BringThemBackToTheWagon."

Jamal clarified. "Bring the horses back!" He yelled. "We're leaving, now!"

Lieutenant Bejorn appeared from the far side of the wagons, where he had slipped away to relieve himself. He tossed fireballs toward the wall of agitated monkeys who kept their distance on the other side of the waterway, and their cries bounced off the wall of jungle along the southern embankment.

The donkeys did not want to leave the luscious grasses. Bellowing, Nee Nee charged at a few angered monkeys who were descending into her tall grasses. Jenn Jenn followed her sister's lead.

A few monkeys who jumped into the grass were chased off. It was apparent to everyone that it was difficult to scare a donkey. Nee Nee and Jenn Jenn were no strangers to intimidating beasts. Jenn Jenn spun around kicking, while Nee Nee raced forward, teeth out, trying to bite. They were willing to fight for more grazing time. It had been a long time since they had enjoyed such a thing.

"Girls, come on!" Irwin shouted, but they did not listen, and he did not blame them, but he had to get them to safety.

"Get the horses hitched!" Shots of fire continued to leap from Bejorn's hands. "Get those donkeys loaded!"

Jorge and Jamal each grabbed a horse. Irwin noticed once more that they had been trained to hitch up in record time. Their skills, and the now calm of the horses, were uncanny. Neither man faltered, gladly taking help when given by those they did not know. Irwin and Kipp were also used to hooking up without a minute to spare. They all worked together while Bejorn held ground with his fire.

Teigahn shouted, "LoadUp. GetGoing."

Jamal chuckled as he swung his leg up and jumped on board the lead wagon. "Go find the *Arlos*, Jorge!"

Jorge glared.

Teigahn shouted over Jamal, "No. SamuelWillGo."

Irwin stiffened hearing his alias. Jorge glanced in his direction. "You want Samuel to go?" Then he eyed Teigahn.

"Yes."

Why would he have me lead in place of Jorge?

Kipp buckled the last attachment to the horse he was working on. They wanted to be on the same rig, not separated, but they would have to be patient and wait a little longer.

Jorge climbed onto the lead wagon and assumed his sentry position. He watched Irwin step past, heading toward the river.

Teigahn called out, "Hurry!"

Kipp shouted at the donkeys when they reached the back of the wagon, "Load up, girls!" They both jumped into the wagon bed. Kipp secured the tailgate. He took a seat and picked up the reins. Bejorn was still behind the wagons train, waiting for them to move—keeping the angry monkeys at bay. Once they were rolling again, he climbed onto Kipp's wagon.

Irwin walked past the first wagon, trying to ignore the watchful eyes. He stepped into the water ahead of the small caravan. It was warm, murky green, and alive with fish and hidden reptiles. He made his way across the warm green water; the sun blazing the top of his head.

The lead wagon lurched, springs squeaking as it bounced over rocks and descended into the slow-moving river. It was summer, and the water was low.

Even at the widest spot, the wagons would only be submerged up to their axles. There was a stone roadway beneath the running water, flat and smooth for driving across. Aquatic life thrived undisturbed in the rest of the river bottom. Irwin stepped into the stream, and his smell kept the alligators at bay; they swam away from the rolling procession.

Once on the other side of the river, after the second wagon cleared the water, both wagons rolled on, and Irwin jumped up to catch a ride.

"SamuelWithMe." Teigahn ordered. "JamalSleeps."

Jamal smiled broadly at being relieved of driving duty. He stepped across the seatback, maneuvered across the covered rations boxes, and laid next to Jorge. He folded his hands under his head and appeared to fall asleep.

Hesitant to take the assigned seat, Irwin climbed up next to Teigahn—slowly—and glanced back at Kipp. He did not have to drive, thankfully, but sitting next to the only known Telepath of the group was unnerving.

Wagons creaked and rattled while the horses snorted and bobbed their heads as they trotted through the ever-thickening jungle.

Irwin could hear the one-sided conversation Lieutenant Bejorn was having with Kipp. He felt sorry for his friend.

Please do not do anything brash, Kipp.

He glanced over his shoulder and looked knowingly at his disgruntled friend. Bejorn finally quieted down.

Irwin watched the serene landscape pass by—tangled vines; large slick leaves; brilliant flowers of all kinds of sizes and shapes left a blanket of aroma for them to travel through. He felt the quiet creatures that lined the corridor—colorful birds fluttered and swooped from tree to tree; snakes with bulging eyes dangled from vines. Reptiles and amphibians were camouflaged, but he could hear their boisterous chatter. Rodents raced across the road, skittering this way and that to escape the marching hooves.

Now the sun was hidden above the canopy of the jungle. Although each wagon held a bright lantern, the jungle ahead was a dark void. The horses kept on and into its sweltering depths. It was good to feel the rhythm of the wagon again.

Corporal Teigahn spoke slowly, pronouncing each word so Irwin could understand him. "Warmth you seek?"

He jumped at the sudden sound of a voice. He had been daydreaming, allowing his imagination to wander. He cautiously replied. "Yes."

"Found it, have you?"

"Yes. Although it is very humid here."

Teigahn chuckled and raised his hand. "Telepathically speak. Easier for me." And he moved the hand toward Irwin's.

He pulled away. "I dislike being touched."

"You slept with Eunuch?"

Ugh! Is there anything they do not share?

"What I do in my personal time is personal. I do not understand why you pretend to care about me. All your people want to do is manipulate, invade minds, and influence thoughts and ideologies." He glared. "You intimidate, instigate, one-up those who you believe are less-than. Do you think you are above everyone else? Do you ever think about how other people feel when you are like that?"

Teigahn was calculating something when Irwin decided to make contact with his hand lying still between them. He cleared his mind of everything except for one event—visually pronounced—a horrific event experienced as a teenager under grandfather Jebadia's rule. He played that memory over and over in his mind's eye while mentally speaking to Teigahn.

You need to let go of your want to command me. Whatever knowledge you have of me will be limited. I am not a pawn to be played, nor am I a person to be reckoned with.

He let go of the Corporal's forearm.

Teigahn gripped the reins tighter. He sat rigidly, staring forward for a long time. "*Rar Joeaput*. Reason. Acceptance. Respect. Judgement. Openness. Engagement. Actions. Power. Understanding. Truth. *Rar Joeaput*."

"*Rar Joeaput*?"

"Reason with head, not heart. Emotions ruin thoughtfulness. Be accepting of all, even Mortals. Respect earned by all. Give respect, get respect. Judge not unless open to judgement, be open of self and others." He inhaled, stifling a yawn with his hand, and his brown eyes scrutinized Irwin. "With eyes, mouth, we engage; actions speak too, be thoughtful of all communications. To have power, you accept defeat. We are all imperfect—accept that. On understanding all I say, be true to you. *Rar Joeaput*."

That is a non-answer.

He slowly responded. "I think I understand."

"Nuaki basic rules," said Teigahn. "You try to intimidate. I am unamused. Your word is weak, much like your power."

Irwin set his eyes forward.

He is trying to provoke. Just smile and nod and keep quiet. If Teigahn knew what all I could do ….

"We have a forthright conversation." Teigahn offered his hand once more.

"You are not touching me. And we are done conversing." He flared his nostrils and looked back at the jungle.

He heard Lieutenant Bejorn chuckle.

I wish I was riding with Bejorn.

He looked over his shoulder and saw Kipp's brown eyes transfixed on his horses' backsides, obviously trying not to look at Jorge, and trying to ignore Bejorn. He didn't notice Irwin staring at him.

"When is the next stop? My friend looks ready to fall asleep."

Teigahn said nothing, but then he saw Bejorn signal Kipp to take a sleep break.

Ugh. Hack telepathy.

"I am going to sleep too."

Teigahn snapped, "No."

"Why not? Jamal and Hauss are!"

"Attacks."

"I will not attack anyone."

"No. Uoala, or Uere, or Enoo."

"You are afraid of monkeys, jaguars, and rhinoceroses?"

"Yes."

"But why do I have to stay up?"

"They fear you."

Irwin harrumphed loudly.

You think that keeping me awake keeps them away? Ha! It is my smell, not my alertness, that keeps them at bay—foolish telepathic mind games.

Occasional shards of light through the overgrowth faded to complete darkness. The horses' hooves thumped on the packed dirt road, and the nocturnal beasts came out, and daytime creatures went to sleep.

Traveling through the night at a good pace, they crossed two small streams before daylight ascended. Irwin leading the way across each time. During the night, the Corporal and the Lieutenant switched sleeping spots with Jamal and Kipp. This allowed Irwin time to be mentally comfortable; he would rest himself soon.

He sat next to Jamal who fondled the reins, breathing in and out of his mouth loudly. He never really inhaled through his nose, but did snort and huff a lot while keeping watchful eyes on the road ahead. During their time together, Jamal never looked his way, even when being stared at.

He does not like me.

It was not until dusk on the second day that the animals could walk around freely, be apart from their heavy loads. Ever since the donkeys showed their aggressive side, they were given the option of being inside Irwin's wagon or walking behind the caravan. Often lazy by nature, the donkeys preferred the back of the wagon where they were secured and watched after. They enjoyed the nighttime, indulging on the grass.

The six travelers stopped along the southern side of the second wide river crossing. A fire glowed near the bank for light and to keep hungry predators at bay. This was considered the middle mark of their journey to Nuaki Village. The well-used camping spot provided an elongated swath of open land that hugged the river's edge. They found the grazing area upstream from the campsite, but all around them were marshlands. This was the perfect spot for the animals to rest.

Before lying down for the night, everyone ate freely from the ration boxes and drank from flasks of cool water or the cheap liquor Bejorn seemed willing to share. Once full, it was time for some to catch some rest. Irwin and Jorge were elected for sentry duty while others slept between the small fire and the two idle wagons.

Jorge was closest to camp and stood with his lantern dangling from a wooden pole. Upstream, Irwin was closer to the horses standing in the tall reeds away from his lantern light. He was to watch the river and the river's edge. He watched and listened and enjoyed the solitude.

What will we do when we find the carriage and Yace is not with it? Kipp will lose his mind. I must be supportive of his decision to follow it, but I know better than to believe she would be there.

What about Nuaki Village? How will we get out of there if they deny us passage south? Peacefully, I hope.

He thought of an earlier exchange with Teigahn.

I need to be tactical with my words around Telepaths—come up with some stories. I hate lying. I have not forgotten the beatings from father and grandfather....

Now I understand why the Gypsy make up stories. But truth gets you further than lies. Oh, Papa Edwin. Why should I be truthful with any Telepath, any PCP, I do not know? They are just waiting for me to slip up.

I cannot sit next to Corporal Teigahn again. Those eyes give me shivers. He is just doing what a loyal Telepath does; watch over me. More like he is trying to figure out the best way to cook me!

He was bored watching for alligators all night long. He played with two perfect spheres, dancing them across his palm—practicing mindfulness and patience. He also used those metallic spheres to slice intruding alligators. He had killed two, and their bodies were already being eaten by other alligators upstream. He stepped toward a third intruder, daring to slither between him and Jorge.

Jorge asked in a loud whisper, "Why are you coming this way? You should stay over there."

"You think the men would like alligator for breakfast?"

"We eat alligator all the time." Jorge said.

"Huh? I have never had it."

"It's kind of tough meat, depending on what part you eat. I think the tail tastes best, although I enjoy fried alligator fingers." He licked his lips. "Alligators aren't easy to kill. It takes two or three Clan-Duins to kill one. For Erthins it's a little easier—they just drown them."

"Not easy to kill?" He chuckled and raised the tail of an adolescent he had just slain. "This one died quickly."

Jorge glanced over his shoulder at the camp. He was supposed to be watching for alligators approaching those who slept, but was curious to see Irwin's prize. "You killed one? How? You've no weapons."

"I have killed three, actually."

"Three, but I didn't see you. How'd you ... with no weapons?"

"I have powers, you know."

"But I didn't see you," Jorge sputtered. "How'd you ...? I was ... I was told you didn't know your powers well." He leaned over to feel for the knife secured to his thigh. "I was also told you're not allowed to have anything metal."

Irwin smiled but did not respond. Instead, he levitated the metallic spheres above his head. They glistened in the lantern's light.

"How the ...." Jorge's eyes bulged. "Your-your powers are amazing, Samuel."

"That is how I feel, but your peers do not see me that way." He nodded toward the sleeping men. "They think I am a threat. And your reaction to me changing you're outwardly appearance yesterday—"

Jorge raised his voice. "I don't appreciate you disarming me."

"Neither do I! I keep finding things out about my power that I never knew. Trust me, I do not want to take your power away from you. Quite the opposite. I want to promote your abilities, not deny them. Your uniqueness is what makes you, you!"

"Uniqueness is not tolerated in most places," said Jorge.

"Yes, I have noticed that."

"You enjoy traveling?"

"It is better than being stuck down in a dark cavern for days, mining to pay for your next meal."

"You're a miner? I thought you said you were a Cutlery Expert, or something like that."

"I am now. Less than a year ago, I was a miner. For my whole life, until recently, my family mined coal. We traded it for food."

"I take it you did not enjoy the work?"

"It was not work a child should be forced into."

"I agree with you on that!" Jorge swatted away a flurry of mosquitoes near his face. "They had me mucking stalls at four."

"Mucking stalls at four years old?"

"Yeah." Jorge rubbed his neck, nervously looking toward the river. "The barn is the best place for me. Keeps me out of sight of most the men in Nuaki, because—really—none of them like me."

"Not even the men you travel with?"

"These guys are the least of my concern," Jorge said. "Yeah, they push me around and tell me what to do, but they're nicer than most. I wish I could leave, but I'm not like anyone else. I can't just walk out without people noticing me, if you know what I mean."

Putting up his hand, hoping Jorge would not move, he whispered, "Stay there." Another alligator slid from the water, slithering silently through the tall reeds toward Jorge.

"I hear it! Where is it?" Jorge cried. He was scanning the surrounding tall grasses, reeds, and dark shadows when Irwin released his metallic orbs into the air. They flew with precision to their target. Straight through the eyeballs, rattling around the small cranium. His metal carved the alligator's brain into a paste before exiting through the nose.

After a stillness filled with fright, he said to Jorge, "You are safe now. He, or she, is about eight strides this way of you."

Jorge remained still. "Where is it?"

"Right there," he pointed. The body was only a few feet from Jorge.

"I don't see it," Jorge said. "How'd you see it?"

"My light." He pointed over his shoulder at the bright lantern. "They glisten."

"Your lantern. It's higher!"

He just smiled.

"And your light seems brighter. How is that?" Jorge kept on looking for the alligator; then he knelt to inspect the body. "Holy shit! How'd you kill it? Where are the eyes?" He gasped, "How'd you do that?"

"My orbs." He summoned the spheres to swirl around before landing on his outstretched hand.

"What are-are you telekinetic?"

"No. Not that I know of."

Though, anything is possible at this point.

"Wow, what's that?" Jorge pointed at what was left of the brains leaking out of the alligator's nose.

"I cleaned out his skull."

"Wow! I'd hate to be on the receiving end of your wrath." Jorge shuddered. "You know, you should ask to ride with Jamal."

"I already did. He does not like me."

"Yeah, he said you smell like death. He wants to know why you're traveling with us."

"My smell." Irwin rolled his eyes. "Clan-Duins hate my smell. Not even the monkeys liked it. Hauss told me they were curious, but scared of me. It is probably why alligators run from me too. Clan-Duins call me Death."

"That's mean."

"It is ignorance, nothing more."

"Still, you should ride with Jamal, get him talking. I think you two have a lot in common. He works at the forge, loves playing with metal. He's the youngest Master Smith ever to work in Nuaki, and he doesn't like the Telepaths either."

"He is not afraid to engage them."

"It's only because we have to." They both stared at the bloodied alligator.

"So, I understand why you live in Nuaki. Even Lieutenant Bejorn and Corporal Teigahn have their reasons. But why Jamal?"

"He's one of those unique orphans, like me." Jorge chuckled again. "You'll have to ask him about his upbringing. He loves telling the story."

"He will not talk my ear off like Bejorn, will he?"

Jorge said, "He might, but he enjoys quiet time too."

"When I rode with Jamal last night, he breathed out his mouth, the whole time—made choking and growling sounds, and sneered a lot. I am not sure I should ride with him."

"You probably know Clan-Duins can be standoffish. Of course, you could warm up to him by cooking a leg." Jorge pointed at the dead alligator. "We don't have time to pit cook a whole one. But a seared leg for breakfast ..." He hummed and nodded. "... I'm sure Jamal would enjoy that."

"Clan-Duin stomachs." Irwin made a face.

"It's the easiest way to get them off your back, that's for sure." Jorge said, studying the body. "How will you remove the leg? My blade's not big enough, and you don't have a knife."

"I can cut it off." Irwin produced a large blade.

"Where was that hiding?" Jorge blinked.

Irwin knelt next to the small-sized beast. "Which leg is better to eat? The front legs look easier to cook, but we would need both to feed everyone. Hm. The back one looks like it would feed us all, but you said the tail is better for strips of meat."

Jorge looked from the alligator to Irwin. "The front legs."

13

JAMAL'S STORY

Irwin set up a metal spit and skewered the front legs of his alligator kill. Then he cranked the rotisserie—made sure they would cook evenly—and summoned more heat to the fire. He stood proudly contemplating the meal, inhaling the aroma of the alligator legs as they began to cook. He did not realize a potential flaw in the plan. Bejorn rose from his sleep as though he had been stung. "What is the meaning of this?" He bolted toward the high dancing flames. "Why did you stir up the fire?"

"I am making breakfast for everyone. Sorry. I did not mean to wake—"

"You're supposed to be guarding, not cooking!"

"Jorge is guarding. I will return to it soon; I just wanted to get these on the fire."

"We eat rations. We don't have time to cook."

"And you told me that you would sleep most of the night. These should be ready by the time you wake up later."

Bejorn frothed with anger. "We eat from the ration boxes."

Bowing his head, stepping back from the fire, Irwin took the one-down position. "I did not mean to anger you, Lieutenant. I only wanted to make breakfast."

"We don't need a large fire either," Bejorn said, asserting himself once more over Irwin.

Teigahn was groggy. "MaybeWeShouldGetGoing." He rolled over and crawled to his feet.

Kipp and Jamal remained on the ground, no doubt ready to return to sleep.

Bejorn stepped closer to Irwin. He puffed out his chest and folded his arms across it. "I am done with your antics."

Irwin felt Bejorn trying to snuff out the fire but did not allow it to happen—stronger with fire than he had let on.

He wants to kill me; I see it in his eyes—same as Father's.

The angry Lieutenant pulled again for the fire to cease; camp lights flickered, but Irwin sustained their glow. The two men's eyes locked.

Steadfast, Irwin snapped his fingers and stole all the light in the camp—even the light from Jorge's lantern and his own hanging from its rooted pole across the meadow. Total darkness—only starlight reflected off nearby rippling water.

"I am done with you believing you have power over me," Irwin spit his anger at Bejorn and tightened his lips. Snapping his fingers, he re-sparked the lights.

He heard Kipp gasp and held back the urge to look at him. He kept his eyes steady on Bejorn, itching to defy the older and well-trained Elementalist. He waited for him to instigate a fight.

"Don't give me a reason to kill you, outsider," said Bejorn.

The air between the two sparked as they flexed their powers. Irwin smiled, knowing he had the upper hand.

Bejorn's jaw muscles tightened. "We're leaving now. Get the horses!"

Jamal looked at the fire, the meal simmering above the fiery flames. "What about the legs?"

"We're wasting time." Bejorn snapped; then he shouted, "Jorge, bring the animals. We need to get moving."

"AlrightYouSonsOfBitches. GetGoing," Teigahn ordered. He was at Bejorn's side, a hand on the Elementalist's chest. He whispered to Bejorn, his head close to the Lieutenant's ear.

Irwin held his ground and waited for Bejorn to make a move toward him.

I could kill you where you stand. Please, press me!

He was ready to handle this situation just as his father would, but sustained his restraint better than his father ever could. He watched Bejorn and Teigahn calculating their next move. Their eyes narrowed, and they looked around the camp, chattering softly.

Teigahn is talking to Bejorn about how to handle me. I can almost see the telepathy transpiring between the two.

Spit flew from Teigahn's lips when he shouted at Irwin, "Go get your animals!"

He wanted to stay put; he did not want to fall prey to Teigahn's telepathically laced words. Yet an impulse to leave—if only because the telepathic Corporal was there—took over. The two scrutinized him. He could read them both.

I know that look. Teigahn is controlling Bejorn right now. He wants me to walk away, because he knows it will get out of hand if Bejorn is mentally present. Then maybe I should.

He turned to retrieve a horse and hustled toward Kipp.

Kipp barked, "What're you trying to prove?"

"Bejorn needs to know not to provoke me. So does Teigahn."

From behind them, Jamal raised his voice at Bejorn and Teigahn. "Just cook them. You're Erthin!"

Bejorn said, "We have rations. I don't wanna have this discussion, Jamal!"

"Fuk you Bejorn, you think that just because you're...." Their argument became inaudible, but then Jamal shouted, "But it's fresh! Just cook it up!"

Kipp chided Irwin, "I don't wanna get killed because of you."

"You will not get killed because of me." Kipp's brow furrowed. "Trust me, I can handle Bejorn."

"I trust you," said Kipp, glaring at him, "But you seem to be getting more and more flippant—like Yace."

"I am not intimidated by men like Bejorn. Besides, I am more comfortable with my newfound powers. There is nothing they can do to harm me."

Unless they killed you. That would kill me.

They walked together toward the horses across the meadow. Kipp whispered, "So where's the rest of the alligator?"

"Over there." He pointed toward the location of the sliced-up body.

Jamal shouted, "Why?!" They stopped, turning to hear Jamal shout, "Not the river!"

Kipp sniffed the air. His nose found the parted alligator, now being consumed by a larger one near the river's edge. The hungry alligator hissed at Kipp. He backed away from the hostile beast, bumping into Irwin. "You killed just the one?"

"I killed four, actually," he said, sauntering away from Kipp toward a grazing horse.

Jorge swatted at bugs swirling around his face, addressing Kipp as he approached. "Samuel saved me from that alligator. I'm sure it was coming for me!"

"That young beast was looking for a quick meal," Irwin said, haltering a horse. "You probably would have heard him right before he attacked."

Jorge said, "You heard him first."

"I saw him moving."

Kipp looked nearly speechless for once. "I can't believe you killed four!"

"You should have seen it," Jorge kept up the account. "He poked out the eyes and made brains come out its nose; then blood oozed from the mouth and ear holes." He passed Kipp the lead for one of the horses.

Kipp gazed off into the dark jungle. "I wish I could've seen it."

Grabbing the last free horse, Irwin haltered it and then summoned both toward the wagons. Jorge walked on ahead with one giant black horse at his side.

Kipp moved slowly, allowing his horse a few more bites of grass.

They walked side-by-side; Irwin whispered, "They are trying to keep us apart. They do not want us to talk."

"I've noticed," Kipp said. "We need to sign."

Irwin nodded, and they led the horses back to the wagons, rigging them for another day's drive.

Jamal had convinced Lieutenant Bejorn not to throw the partially cooked alligator legs into the river.

The angered Elementalist watched Irwin walk through camp and glared with resentment. Bejorn had extinguished the fire and was now cooking the alligator legs with his Erthin powers. Each wagon would have a leg to share for that day's driving.

Kipp turned to Teigahn, "Can I sit as sentry on your wagon, Sir?"

Teigahn took his time and then nodded. "Bejorn. Jamal. Samuel. YouAllTogether. SamuelNap. Jorge. Kipp. WithMe."

Irwin was beginning to understand Teigahn's speech, his odd version of slang. He shouted to his donkeys, "Girls, load up!" Each Jenny grabbed a large mouthful of grass and trotted to the wagon, leaping and chewing.

Jamal climbed on-board Irwin's wagon—assumed the driving position.

Irwin clambered up and sat next to Jamal, but Bejorn snapped, "You sleep."

Again, the air between the two sparked.

"Hey, if you're gonna fight, do it now on the ground," Jamal growled.

"I have no qualms with the Lieutenant. He did not appreciate my gesture for a fresh breakfast." Irwin smiled at Jamal and climbed over the front seat. He would find comfort in his metal bed.

Bejorn held the hot metal skewer jabbed through the steaming alligator leg. His lips twisted. "They're cooked all the way through." He glowered at Irwin. "How you were going about it was all wrong. Alligator is best cooked in a pit over coals wrapped in banana leaves; then you leave it for a day to steam. It's hot, by the way," he said, passing the meal to Jamal.

"Then cool off the skewer," said Jamal, his tone bitter. He refused to take the leg.

Bejorn thrust over the alligator leg anyway, and then stepped up onto the front seat. He continued to lecture Irwin. "Alligator legs can take more than half a day to cook the way you were doing it. You need proper temperature and cooking conditions. Which you had all wrong. Next time, think before doing something stupid like that."

Jamal fondled the reins and muttered, "This is gonna be a fun ride."

Teigahn waved his arm from his position on the lead wagon, inciting the others to proceed. All four massive black horses stepped forward, and the wagons lurched, creaking and rocking as they made their way back into the dreary jungle.

The swaying and rattling of the wagon lulled Irwin to sleep.

He woke at someone's touch. It was already mid-morning, although the jungle did not give away any hints.

He yawned.

This is not fair. I do not feel like I slept at all.

He changed places with Lieutenant Bejorn.

I believe they are trying to deprive me, catch me off guard.

Are you sure? Maybe you are just tired of the journey.

What more is there to be sure of? Kipp and I are not allowed to be near each other without someone close by. Someone always comes in and makes small talk or tells us what we should be doing. I am always sitting next to Jamal, Teigahn, or Bejorn; never Kipp and never Jorge. Why not Jorge? He fears me. No, he just does not know me, that is all.

Maybe they told him about me. No, I imagine Jorge is on a need-to-know basis about me, unlike everyone else from Nuaki Village. He is just scared. Or maybe-maybe that is how Teigahn and Bejorn want it. This all feels like telepathic manipulation.

Nevertheless, Teigahn accepted Kipp's proposal for sitting as sentry.

Kipp signaled a *'ready-to'* sign!

Kipp moved across the wagon-bed, dangling his legs over the tailgate. He was smiling the way he did when he was feeling sneaky. They could talk uninhibited now using their secret sign-language.

Jamal rode along quietly, eyes forward, ignoring Irwin. He kept the horses from putting their noses on the lead wagon's tailgate—they were close enough for Kipp to walk across.

The jungle's underbrush whipped at their faces, hanging lower today than before. The lantern lights flickered, and the constant hum of wildlife held a musical quality that droned on and on.

Jamal had been silent since they started out. "Hauss told me about your undertakings with the cutlery and such."

Irwin jumped when Jamal spoke. He looked at Kipp, a look his friend would recognize as a rebuff.

"He did, did he?" Irwin rolled his eyes at the thought of Kipp revealing any information about the two of them.

"He said you're a cutlery specialist."

"Ah, yes. That is what I do."

"I also heard you do other things with metal, like absorb it into your skin."

"You must have seen me fight Barnst?"

"No, I was busy. But I heard you killed him with fancy maneuvers no one's seen before."

Irwin chuckled to himself. "You could say I am a magnet to Erthin powers and metal."

"Huh." The sound of the horses' hooves on the roadway grew louder again when the two stopped talking. After a short way, Jamal asked, "How'd you find out about your powers?"

"I was born with the ability to instantly regenerate. Everything else I am learning as I go." He rubbed the back of his neck. "I hear you have an interesting story about *your* powers."

"Who'd you hear that from?"

"Jorge."

"Jorge actually talked to you?"

"While on duty last night, yes."

"Huh. He told me he didn't like you."

"That is what I thought too. I feel you dislike me too."

"Hauss made you sound harmless. But after all I've seen and heard, I understand why Jorge fears you."

"Jorge fears me?"

"I've smelled it on him." The wagon rolled on for a while and then Jamal said, "No one here is harmless. We all have self-preservation in us."

Irwin noticed Kipp flipping hand signals when something flopped into their wagon—a large black snake. Irwin leaped for it and as he was about to throw it over the side, it bit him—sinking its fangs into a tender spot on the inside of his arm. He yelped out in pain. He felt venom being pushed under his skin, his blood absorbing it, processing it. The fang marks didn't heal right away either. The holes became red, then turned black.

Jamal gasped, "You gotta get the venom out of you! That was a black jungle snake. They can kill quicker than any bite I know of."

Irwin could feel the venom moving in his blood. He put his mouth to his arm, trying to suck out whatever venom was still there at the surface of the puncture. His arm ached more than it ever had from a bite, and he'd had plenty. But he said nothing, not wanting to draw more attention to himself. This almost reminded him of Lady Gretchen's poison. He would have to keep alert, suck the poison out if he could, but his body would have to process the rest. He felt dizzy.

"You gonna be okay, mate?"

"Yes. He only nicked me."

The wagon rattled on before Jamal broke the silence again. "My life started with self-preservation," he said, thumbs caressing the leather reins. "I knew from the beginning I was different." He inhaled, held it, and then exhaled. "From the moment I was born, I knew. I remember that day—vividly. The horror in my mother's eyes, and everyone else's in that room. To be born a kitten instead of a two-legged baby; imagine."

"You are Clan-Duin."

"As far as I know, all Clan-Duins are born two-legged. That's not to say we can't be a part of a large litter, you know, several siblings born at the same time."

"Do you have siblings?"

"No."

"What is a kitten, exactly?"

"A cat."

"A mountain cat?"

"No. Smaller, like a barn cat—that's what they're called on the west coast. Or house cat. But I was small, just a baby; a kitten."

Irwin measured with his hands so Jamal could see, and he nodded. "I have never seen a cat that small."

"Real kittens are smaller than I was, but I grew little those first few years."

"I cannot imagine." He stared at Jamal.

"I was thrown away—out a window and into the garbage. I can still hear my mother wailing. Being Clan-Duin, you are treated as garbage most of the time anyway, so that was my first life lesson."

"What a shitty lesson, and on the day you were born."

"Life is full of lessons. We're here to learn."

I agree.

Irwin tried to imagine: "A kitten," he said.

"Yes, a four-legged, furry, black-haired, partially blind, drinks-too-much-milk kitten. Good thing I came into this world as a kitten, though. Dogs are eaten in many places along the west coast. But cats are used as rodent control." He reached for a flask hidden by his feet and pulled off the cork with his teeth.

After his mouth was moistened, Jamal continued his story. "I remember everything from that day. I cried out for the longest time, meowing and meowing, and she heard me. A sweet little girl rescued me—stole me into her bedroom and kept me there secretly for many moons. She fed me scraps of her food and brought me goat's milk and rice milk—nurturing my growth. She was the only mother I ever had, and she was only eight years old.

"When she slept, I learned how to be two-legged. I studied her every day—practiced to be like her every night. She never knew I was Clan-Duin, only—as I grew—a larger than usual cat. From the beginning, I could walk on four legs. Two were harder to master at first, but by the time I was about six moons old, easy."

Irwin was mesmerized.

"In the beginning, I could only shift from a kitten into an actual baby. I kept to my cat form until I was about two years; it was about then I realized I could become any animal I saw—not just a cat.

"So, while the girl was learning lessons, or out doing good deeds, I practiced changing into all different types of birds. They are more commonly seen in cities than any other creature, except perhaps butterflies or moths." Jamal paused. "Anyway, I would follow her. I watched over her. I felt a responsibility to her because she had saved me."

"Did she ever see you following her?"

"She saw me, but I was never me, the cat she loyally adored."

"So, you were mutable from the beginning?"

"Yup."

"That is so interesting." Irwin studied Jamal, tried to imagine what he had been through.

"That girl took care of me for about six years."

"You pretended to be a house cat for six years?!"

"Yes."

"And she never knew what you were?"

"Nope."

"Then what happened?"

"She was married off at fourteen to a creepy old man who already had several kids, but his previous wife died, and he wanted more. It was really ...." Jamal sighed and stared off into blank space—what was he remembering?

"I feel sorry for women," Irwin said. "The lives they have to live."

Jamal was quiet.

"Did you follow her?"

"Yes, I did. But I didn't like what I saw. That's when I went out on my own. I took voyage on ships, usually as a stowaway cat, but I pillaged as a stowaway boy would, eating all I could whenever I could. I was about eight when I was discovered stealing bread in Tresdahla. The PCP soldiers who caught me realized I was not the usual type of Clan-Duin child," he chuckled. "I gave them a hard run of it, but they were PCP ... and smart!

"They called me a Child of the Tygeress and sent me to Nuaki Village for training. I'm one of those rare orphans who just happened to be noticed under the right circumstances and sent to the appropriate people for training."

"Child of the Tygeress?"

"I have the ability to be whatever I want, animal wise. I can be a hummingbird, a rat; I can transform into an elephant's body and then walk away like a lizard in three blinks of an eye."

Irwin stared at Jamal, waiting for more.

Jamal passed the reins to Irwin and began instantaneously changing among body shapes and types—the two-legged person he first appeared to be morphed into an iguana. His pale-colored sarong now covered him. He stepped out from underneath the piece of clothing and morphed into a skunk.

Beady black eyes stared up at Irwin who held his breath, astonished by what he was witnessing. Jamal's ability to mutate between creatures appeared flawless. Staying in black and white fur, his body grew, changing once more into a giant panda bear. He remained in that bear's form for an instant—Irwin blinked—then Jamal reappeared as himself, pulling his sarong across his midsection and tying it at his hips.

14

DEATH AND DESTRUCTION

I rwin's and Kipp's mouths hung at what they had both just witnessed.

"Very few are as fluid as me," said Jamal.

"That is amazing."

"I prefer to be a teacher, as opposed to a soldier," Jamal took back the reins. "Besides, I tend to provoke those who think they have authority over me. It's fun challenging the *Shayot* to be that creative."

"I was told Hauss was the right type of Clan-Duin," Irwin whispered. "His totem is canine. But I have seen him turn into a pig."

"A pig?"

"Yes."

"Was that at Lady Gretchen's?"

"Yes."

"Hauss told me what you did at Lady Gretchen's place—freeing all those Clan-Duins."

"Yes, I did that," he tried to sound unaffected.

"I would've enjoyed seeing that." Jamal snickered. "And you think I'm impressive? You've the ability to ground out mutations!"

"No. I can only ground out the telepathic spell that twists one's mind, making you believe you are a pig, or a goat, or a chicken."

"How positive are you on that?"

"Lady Gretchen made all those children, women, and men—all those Clan-Duins—believe they were the animals they appeared to be. All I did was ground out her spell."

"What if your power does more than that?"

He rolled his eyes, measuring his effect on Jorge. "It is possible."

"You think you could ground out a Clan-Duin's shifting abilities? You know, turn 'em two-legged, or keep them from turning into four?"

"I have never tried." He was interested, yet soured, by the proposal. He took the reins from Jamal again and then watched the Clan-Duin shift into his cat form. Grouping all the reins in one hand, Irwin placed his free hand on Jamal and flexed his magnetic field.

Nothing happened.

Jamal waited for something to transpire before returning to his two-legged body. "Apparently your powers don't work on me?"

"Apparently not."

"Interesting."

"Indeed." Irwin felt glad he couldn't accidentally change any Clan-Duin he met. Yet being able to prohibit Jorge's energy—disarming the Empath's physical appearance—saddened him.

Jamal's eyes drifted to the roadway after taking the reins again. "Did you know that almost all who end up at Lady Gretchen's abode are 'Children of the Tygeress'? That's why they're turned into food. Of course, those who can't change are assimilated into her gruesome bunch of wranglers. Though some are sold as slaves to passing trade ships. I thank you for destroying that Witchtress of a woman."

"It was my pleasure to rid Urthis of Lady Gretchen. She was a vile woman indeed." Irwin flashed a hand signal of anger at Kipp.

The wagon rattled on, their conversation subsided, and then Jamal said, "Did you know that most Clan-Duins who have one totem have singular eye colors? You won't see any flecks or types of discoloration in their eyes. And they're usually light in color, either a solid green, amber, or brown. Although, I've seen solid dark brown eyes too. Now, Children of the Tygeress have different color eyes—a tiny fleck or discoloration reveals their mutation. And they can have any color eyes, except blue, or anything with bluish hints; that's a Telepath in disguise."

"I have learned that lesson," chuckled Irwin, thinking back.

"Our eyes need to be colorful so that they can change as fluidly as our body."

Irwin listened to Jamal but studied Kipp's brown eyes. He had examined them before—up close when he wasn't aware—noticing flecks of green, amber, and brown.

"Usually our powers come gradually, starting with the totem of our parents, like canine." Jamal pointed at Kipp. "But then our abilities progress. As we get older, we learn to change the color of our hair, structure of our bones, muscle shapes, even skin pigment—if properly trained."

"I noticed your eyes have all the colors."

"I was born with flaxen eyes, but they turned gray over time. They tend to stay that way, most of the time, but they change when I do." With a lighthearted chuckle, Jamal pointed at Kipp. "I'd appreciate my life being spared when you decide to kill everyone else."

"Huh?"

"That's what Hauss just signed. He said he wants you to spare my life."

He knows what we have been saying!

Trying to remain outwardly calm, his heart pounded. "How do you know he is not swatting flies or scratching his arm?"

"You are using *Shayot* language. It was invented several hundred years ago to secretly communicate without using their powers."

With a few flicking hand gestures, Jamal told Irwin, *'Everyone in Nuaki Village knows these signals.'*

Great. Now what do we do?

"I've been watching you two talk for a while. You're both quite versed with the signs. How do you two know it?"

Irwin flashed a message to Kipp to stop speaking with his hands. "Hauss taught it to me."

"And who taught him?"

Not wanting anyone to overhear their conversation, he grasped Jamal's arm and leaned in. "The Gypsy."

Jamal looked at the firm contact on his biceps. His steely eyes met Irwin's. "And who taught the Gypsy?"

"I do not know."

"Did they rescue a rogue *Shayot*?"

Irwin shrugged.

"It's happened before. Occasionally, a *Shayot* will runaway." Jamal's attention drifted back to the horses, and he tightened the reins, then momentarily grabbed the brake. "It's not easy being *Shayot*; much is expected of them. Some are not ready for that type of responsibility. That sign-language is only used by *Shayot* and those of us who teach it. And it's not supposed to be used outside this jungle."

Irwin fell into a silent stupor. So did Kipp.

After a while Jamal said, "It really doesn't matter to me, but I'd definitely refrain from using signals in Nuaki."

I hope he does not tell Teigahn.

Jamal sniffed loudly at Irwin's fear. "You're not in trouble for knowing it. It's just surprising that someone who was not raised *Shayot*, or from Nuaki Village, knows the language."

Irwin felt the life in the jungle oppressive. His arm ached where the snake had bitten him, but he kept the discomfort to himself. The bite marks were healed over by now, but the poison, that was a different matter. That would take time, and he was beginning to feel sick to his stomach.

The wagon rattled on. After a while, Jamal asked, "You've said you're a cutlery specialist. Where're your wares?"

"In the box under our bed."

"What all do you have in there?"

Nothing.

"Short knives, long swords, pots and pans, buckles, hooks, nails, you name it, it is in there."

"Hinges?"

"Yes, I have some of those."

"Levers and pulleys?"

"It is possible. I have many metal wares I have been trading for food and such."

"All that fits in there, along with Hauss?"

Did he just figure out my lie?

They looked at each other but said nothing.

The wagon rattled over rocks; branches scraped his face and his shoulders. He ducked, heading toward another dangling snake, recoiling, shaking his throbbing arm, and holding his gurgling stomach.

"Would you consider yourself a Smith?" asked Jamal.

Irwin rolled that title around in his mind. "Yes."

"Did you make all those items you say you have?"

"Yes."

"Huh. I'll see if we can get you working at the foundry."

"Foundry?"

"Forge, foundry, smith shop—the work is all the same." Jamal patted Irwin's back. "You might be out of shape for work now," he laughed softly. "But we'll get you into shape, that's for sure."

"Thank you for the offer, but I am not staying in Nuaki Village."

"Where else would you go? South to Daos?"

"Wherever my wagon and horses take me."

"That's not what I heard. I heard Nuaki is the end of the road for you."

"Of course; that is what you have been told. But I have better things to do than to be held prisoner in a place where I do not belong."

"Held prisoner ... don't belong," Jamal chortled. "HA! You belong there as much as I do!"

Irwin pressed his lips again on the spot where the snake had sunk in its teeth, and rubbed his arm, keeping his mind clear of thoughts.

Jamal held the horses back; the wagon halted. They were riding too close to the lead wagon. Irwin leaned over the side and vomited.

"Yeah. There ya go! That'll make you feel better."

Irwin agreed, hoping all the venom had gone over the side.

The wagon lurched forward. Jamal said, "I heard you killed some PCP."

After a few hundred feet, Irwin asked, "Did they tell you how many?"

"No."

"I only killed three."

"Only three," Jamal's tone was filled with sarcasm. "Really?"

"Well, four if you count Barnst."

Ignoring the two-hundred eighty-six Erthins, Clan-Duins, and Telepaths slaughtered in Onj Raha.

"That is not right. I did kill a few of Lady Gretchen's men, and her, of course." He counted a few extra fingers. "Twelve. No, thirteen. I almost forgot to count Lady Gretchen." Sweat trickled down the back of his neck. His skin felt like hot coals in a campfire. He doubted Jamal believed any of his words at this point.

"Does that number include all those you killed in Onj Raha?" Jamal's voice dropped. "I heard you blew up the Hall."

Of course he knows. Damn Telepaths.

"Well, if you add in all those PCP the number is closer to three hundred." He frowned.

Three-hundred and two to be exact.

"Three hundred! Wow, I've only killed a handful of men. And I was young and stupid then. Dancing with Death isn't something most men can do without a heavy heart." They nodded simultaneously.

"I do not like to kill."

"You've killed three hundred, and you don't like to kill. As a Clan-Duin, I commend you for ridding the world of Lady Gretchen. But if you don't like it, then why do it?"

"Lady Gretchen was the only one who truly deserved to die," he said, feeling that deep pain of remorse again.

"Oh, did you hear? There's another Telepath moving in, taking her place!"

"That is not surprising." Irwin's eyes fell to the foliage, away from Jamal's stare.

"Did you know I've met Lady Gretchen?"

"You did?"

"Twice. The first time I was brought to her as a dishonorable *Shayot*."

Irwin was floored by the idea and forgot about his shame. "Twice? How did you live through the first time?"

"I'm smarter than the average Clan-Duin. I don't fall for telepathic manipulation—which is why I ended up there a second time. I defied Admiral Argustos. You should know, by the way, he doesn't tolerate dissidence. He runs a tight fortress—strict rules of engagement. He boasts it's for the safety of all, but he's about control like every other Telepath."

"I believe controlling people is a telepathic weakness, not a strength. To me, it is like grasping at sand, or the wind. It is fleeting." Again, Irwin kept a keen eye on the low-hanging jungle ahead.

"Corporal Teigahn isn't as bad as most of the Telepaths in Nuaki."

"He still wants to control," Irwin muttered, hatred in his gut.

"Hey, we all want some sort of control. You can't tell me you don't."

"I do not want to control people; I want them to be free."

"Ha! Good luck with that." Jamal slapped his knee. "None of us are truly free."

"Do you believe that?"

"Freedom, real freedom, means you're responsible for yourself—everything you do. Do you know how many are not ready for that? All of us."

"I do just fine."

"Says the guy who killed three-hundred men and women."

His shoulders slumped.

Why did I leave my mountain home? For warmth? What a stupid reason.

"Hey, don't feel too bad about the kills. They're all replaceable."

"Hauss said the same thing. PCP are morbid."

"Yeah. Yeah, they are. Wanna drink?" Jamal pulled out his flask again and took a long swig.

"No, thank you."

"There're worse offenders in Nuaki than you—just so you know."

"Bejorn told me." Irwin was soon lost in thought, his eyes on the trees. "What I want to know is why you are there?"

"Because I don't wanna live anywhere else. I kind of like the place, even if the hierarchy has Telepaths on the top and Clan-Duins on the bottom. At least we get time with a woman every so often. As a whole, the village is self-sustaining and pleasant."

"Yes, Bejorn told me about it in great detail."

"Oh man, he can go on and on."

They both laughed and the tension that had built up in Irwin subsided. He was having fun for a change.

"Did he tell you about our cider?"

"Yes."

"You'll have to try some when we get there. Nuaki's been making it since the beginning of time," Jamal smirked knowingly. "We export it from Arenu. It's world renown!"

"The cider?"

"It's the only alcohol we make."

"I thought alcohol was not allowed in Nuaki Village."

"We're not allowed to bring any in, but we do anyway in small quantities." Jamal gestured with his flask. "The cider is our only export. Sometimes we sell our apples, but that's when it's been a good year for the fruit. We use the cider to trade for clothing, or lye, or metal—you know, things we can't or don't make.

"Argustos doesn't allow us to trade our alcohol for alcohol. But those of us who go on these runs, we bring back a spirit or two from the saloon or the wharf." Jamal tossed down another swig.

"Huh. Lieutenant Bejorn said alcohol was not allowed in Nuaki because it riles you all up."

"Yeah. There are rules about alcohol consumption. First off, we're not allowed to drink before dark. That doesn't mean we don't do it from time to time. And we can't get visibly drunk, you know. No stumbling, falling, or other belligerent acts. That'll earn you three days in the brig. But after a run to Arenu, contraband is shared among friends."

This does not agree with what Bejorn admitted. I wonder where the truth is being blurred.

After a time, Jamal asked, "Did you trade any of your metal in Arenu?"

"No. I did not know I could. Nor would I want to ruffle any feathers. It is bad enough that I appear Mortal. Very few people in Arenu Village seemed to appreciate me. Most of the vendors did not want me in or near their shops or to smell me. I was heckled a lot."

"Your smell's something else."

"It is always my smell that gets me in trouble with Clan-Duins. Erthins try to use their powers against me, but that never goes well for them. And Telepaths, they cannot hear my thoughts, which irritates the shit out of them." He sighed until he yawned. "There are days when I feel better suited to live with Mortals."

"That's probably why *They* want you to live in Nuaki Village."

"That is one of their motives, yes," Irwin said, raising an eyebrow. "It seems that no one likes me. I get it, I guess." He shrugged and swiped at his hair, feeling something crawling in it. "I know I can be coarse sometimes."

"How does Hauss stomach you?"

"He barely tolerates me. There are days when I wonder. I mean, I was born into an extremely volatile family. My grandfather and father became violent over nothing. I could easily have wound up being like them, but it takes a lot of energy to be angry and want to constantly fight."

Jamal's eyebrows lifted. "You don't like to work hard?"

Tapping his forehead, Irwin replied, "Smarter, not harder."

"I'll admit your smell threw me off the first time we rode together. And the stories I was told—and what little I've seen, like that trick with stacking your ration boxes. But after talking with Hauss, I can see you're not like what everyone says you are, even if you've killed three hundred people. That's not to say that you don't deserve to live in Nuaki. Hauss, on the other hand, he's not—how do I say this without it sounding offensive—he's not special enough."

Kipp could be heard scoffing.

Jamal called out, "Sorry mate! But you're not Talented enough to be worthy of living in Nuaki Village."

"I disagree," Irwin said, and his voice rose. "If you could see him in action, Jamal. I believe Hauss is a Child of the Tygeress. He is as quick to change as you are, especially when fighting." He hiccoughed.

What am I saying? They do not need to know anything about Kipp.

Yet he added, "Maybe you can teach him to change into something other than a canine, or a pig. I know he can do it, but he does not believe so. After seeing you in action ...." He looked at Kipp, "How old is too old to become *Shayot*?"

Jamal shook his head. "Hauss is too old. He's a man."

Irwin snickered, "Just barely."

"Puberty tends to be the cut-off. But we took in one adolescent. His voice had changed, but he ... he was still very young in the mind. I guess it depends on the circumstances."

Kipp paid close attention to their conversation, his eyes fixed on Irwin. They stared at each other, and Irwin directed his comment toward Kipp. "Hear that, Hauss, you could become a *Shayot* if you act young enough. And I can stay on for proper training of my Erthin skills." Kipp's brown eyes never left Irwin's, but his face softened—trying to fight back a smile.

Jamal egged them on, "Sounds quite appealing, doesn't it?"

"So does touring Urthis uninhibited," Irwin said. "But that probably will not be the case."

"I feel sorry for Hauss."

"Why?"

"His future is unknown, whereas yours seems certain."

"How so?"

"I think *They* look at you as some tasty morsel *They* get to share. However, Hauss, *They* just want him gone."

15

SECRET SIDE MISSIONS

Night had settled in, but you could hardly tell. Deep in the jungle, it began to rain. Large droplets fell through the canopy, and soon the roadway was muddy; splashes of slimy water flew up onto them on the wagon seats. Irwin was sentry now on the first wagon, while Kipp drove theirs right behind. Jamal sat next to Kipp, and Bejorn napped in that wagon, snoring loudly. Jorge drove the wagon where Irwin held the sentry position, and Teigahn also slept. His nap was inaudible. No one could change positions until the next stop after sunrise—Bejorn's orders.

It was their fourth day of the rough ride through the oppressive jungle, and Irwin had heard assurances they would sleep in Nuaki Village this very night. It was almost sunrise when the wagons rolled to a halt along a boggy marsh hugged by the roadway. Trees shaded the edges of the large open area, and a perimeter roadway circled the up-kept bog. The morning sun shone on them and glistened across the murky water. Everyone dismounted to stretch their legs and ease their stiff backs and butts.

Jamal, Kipp, Jorge, and Irwin were told to find fresh produce that would be growing in and around the marsh. So, they began to pluck mature stocks of water chestnuts and watercress; scoop up cranberries, wild rice, taro and other native species propagating around the bog. Each man had been given a basket and sent to gather all he could. Meanwhile, Lieutenant Bejorn and Corporal Teigahn strolled along the perimeter roadway. Irwin saw them turn down a freshly cut corridor.

Kipp and Jorge went in one direction, and Irwin followed Jamal who knew what to pick. Keeping an eye and an ear toward Teigahn and Bejorn, Jamal whispered, "I hear them talking about the carriage Hauss spoke of. They say it hasn't arrived in Nuaki Village."

"Really?"

"It could be late. Those first three days heading south are the worst with all the aggressive animals. But straight on from here, it's easy." Jamal paused, adding, "It's possible the carriage had problems, but we would have seen it along the way."

The Lieutenant and Corporal had disappeared into the cut corridor into the jungle, away from the bog. "Where are they going?"

"That's the old road; usually it's overgrown."

"The old road?"

"A narrow path from here to old Nuaki."

Irwin made a sound deep in his throat.

"About sixty years ago, Nuaki Village was upstream from where it's now," Jamal explained. "They say the men outgrew the post. It's a rubbish of a place—partially dismantled, burned in spots. I think something happened, and that's why they abandoned it. It looks totally broken and not a place for the *Shayot* to live.

"What's funny is they used the same floor plan. I don't think the new place is any bigger than the old."

Jamal pulled up a handful of watercress plants; Irwin did the same. The Clan-Duin pretended to be looking for more but kept his attention on the Lieutenant and the Corporal and the path where they had wandered. He loudly sniffed several times, apparently picking up a scent.

"What is it?"

"Something's not right," Jamal whispered.

"Let me take a guess. The carriage deviated from the route to Nuaki Village, down that old road, and they are wondering why."

Jamal glanced over at Irwin.

He said, "Why else would we stop? Does Nuaki Village really need watercress and cranberries? They want to know why the carriage left the road."

"You sound like you know why."

"That carriage was never bound for Nuaki Village. Somewhere, someone believed it was, but ...." He watched the two officers pace up and down the jungle path beyond the bog—they were looking at the ground, the trees. "It is a decoy sent by Dephen Ishik, although your superiors believe it was sent by their fellow PCP from the north. The carriage was sent for Hauss to follow. Though some thought it was for me.

"I was told it was loaded with rations before being sent on to Nuaki Village. But why would they load it with provisions? You said it yourself; Nuaki Village is self-sustaining. If you needed anything, it would be clothing or metal."

They both watched the officers walk further into the jungle again. "And your wagon has everything Nuaki may need: empty casks and jugs, and whatever is in those boxes."

"Where do you think the carriage went?"

"That carriage is on its own mission. The men driving it are working for Dephen Ishik. They might say they are PCP, but that is a lie. They have been under Dephen's control for many moons. This is all a ploy. Hauss might have fallen for it, your superiors too, but I have not. Hauss believes his girlfriend is in that carriage, but she is not. She left our path before that carriage arrived in Arenu Village."

"You sound full of yourself, Samuel."

"I know Dephen Ishik wants us out of the way. He wants me locked up tight behind Nuaki Village walls. As for Kipp, Dephen wants him gone."

Jamal lowered his voice. "Sounds like a Gypsy story."

Irwin sensed Jamal was not himself but being manipulated by a Telepath. "Gypsy stories are not this complicated, Corporal Teigahn." He let the Telepath know he was on to his shenanigans. "This is reality. Dephen Ishik is smarter than all of you. You have all been conned."

He noticed a change in Jamal's demeanor that gave away the Telepath in control. Irwin had seen the effects many times over and placed his hand on Jamal's forearm; the Clan-Duin blinked, and his eyes dropped to the grasp.

Jamal's voice shook, even though his body was steady. "What just happened?"

Be practical, do not startle.

"You need to practice being quiet with your mind when around me."

"They took my mind?" Jamal's voice rose; his body tensed. "They know not to do that!"

"Do not call attention to us," Irwin whispered, keeping a tight hold, keeping calm. "There is no need to get heated, Jamal."

"They know better than to fuk with me!" Jamal frothed and spat, "Teigahn knows better! I'm gonna fukin' kill him." He tried to pull away from the grasp.

Irwin braced himself, struggling against the headstrong Clan-Duin. "There is no need, Jamal."

"They call me heathen when I .... I've been told they'd tie my mind into knots if I didn't .... I could kill him so easily. I could be a fukin' moth and kill him and he wouldn't even know it."

"Take a couple deep breaths, Jamal, please. I will maintain contact with you, keeping them from accessing your mind."

His words broke Jamal's rage, "You can do that?"

"I can do a lot of things they will never know about."

Jamal was studying him.

"If you really wanted Teigahn dead, I could do it for you right now with a flick of my finger."

"Please do!"

"It is not in my nature to kill. Nor do I enjoy fighting."

"Teigahn fukin' deserves it!"

"There are worse offenders out there who do not deserve the death I can bring."

Jamal began to calm down. "You're like the Bearer of Admonishes, aren't you?"

Irwin remembered Kipp saying that, or something like that, when they first met. "Although I have heard of him, I am not him. Nor would I want to be." He wanted to release his hold on Jamal. "Will you be alright if I let go?"

Jamal's nostrils flared. "Yeah. I won't go after him. Not yet."

"Not while Bejorn is there." Irwin knew that if Jamal acted on impulse, he would be incinerated by Bejorn the moment he tried to murder Teigahn.

"What was I gonna do while they had me?"

"They were just using you—your eyes and ears—to listen in on our conversation."

"Fukin' assholes."

"That is the best label for those types."

Jamal patted Irwin's shoulder. "You know, you're alright Samuel. First impressions aren't everything. I won't make someone's smell the reason I don't like them."

"Thank you, I think. It would be hard for me not to hate something or someone that reminds me of Death."

Jamal eyed his superiors menacingly. "We should pretend like we're still working."

The two moved further along the edge of the bog, past the old road.

Only the donkeys had been allowed time to eat; the horses remained hitched to their wagons and were napping. When Bejorn and Teigahn returned, they perked up. The donkeys were given commands, and the baskets of fresh food were secured along the side of the lead wagon.

Bejorn stayed with Irwin's wagon, and Teigahn took his seat, rather proudly, on the leading vehicle. "Jamal. Kipp. WithBejorn. Samuel. Jorge. WithMe," Teigahn ordered, and the men scurried.

Once the donkeys were loaded into the wagon, Jamal began his nap next to them. Bejorn sat with Kipp on Irwin's wagon. Jorge took his position, facing the rear. Irwin sat at the edge of the bench, ready to jump into the jungle's arms if Teigahn tried to touch him, his mind again.

After a while of rolling on silently, Teigahn said, "You are correct." He spoke slowly, thoughtful of each word said.

"Correct?" Irwin said, rather apathetically, "About what?"

"The carriage. Dephen Ishik."

Of course I am.

"We be close to Nuaki," Teigahn said, "Dephen Ishik visited long ago."

Irwin sat straighter in the seat but said nothing.

"I have met him," Teigahn said.

"You have? What was your impression?"

"Controlling, arrogant, above others."

"When did he come through Nuaki last?"

"Long before I was alive. I met Dephen in Arenu many years ago. He spoke about his travels. A proud world traveler he was. Recalled wild stories about old Nuaki Village."

Irwin looked at Teigahn, took a breath to speak, but swallowed his disappointment.

"You have permission to view the book of travelers. Admiral Argustos has chronicles—much information on pages, including your grandfathers."

That explains how Admiral Ubic had those pictures and information on my great grandfather and his brother.

"I saw the descriptions of those Sampson brothers on the pages, and the images; they were very detailed. Are there records like that on Dephen Ishik?"

"Yes. And in the same log."

Irwin then realized, "You were the one who looked up the Sampson brothers and brought those parchments to Admiral Ubic."

Raising an eyebrow, Teigahn nodded and smiled. "Perceptive."

Yes, very. "I can be, sometimes." He waited, listening to the wheels on the road. "Did you actually believe that the carriage was sent by the PCP of Ahradah?"

"Yes, and no." Again, there was a long, contemplative pause before Corporal Teigahn spoke. "Scoundrel Dephen Ishik is. Comes from Ishik Empire. He might say he never harms volatiles, YetIKnowHeUsesThemForPersonalGain." Taking in a deep breath, Teigahn regained his cool and added, "Hypocrite, he is."

"When Dephen last came through, was the southern roadway to Daos well-kept?"

"Maybe. Much changes because of Ishik regime."

"Why do you say that?"

"Alliance."

"Alliance? Is there an alliance between the Ishik Empire and Nuaki Village?"

Teigahn said nothing, but Irwin noticed his head shake slightly.

"Do the PCP cater to the Ishik Empire, or is it the other way around?"

Teigahn kept quiet.

What are you hinting at, Telepath?

He tried not to stare but could not help but look at the Lieutenant, attempting to read him. After a bit, his eyes drifted back to the jungle that had changed over the past few days. He saw more flowering plants, and the aroma overtook his senses.

The wagon rattled on, and they were deep in the jungle again. The humidity left a sort of mist in the air that hung heavy and damp and hot enough to irritate Irwin's throat. He wanted warm weather; he got it.

Teigahn said, "Admiral Argustos requests you when we arrive."

Irwin rolled his eyes. "Of course he does."

Just great.

"Are there any more stops between here and there?"

"None necessary."

Of course. They are keeping Kipp and me apart. They do not want us to talk. I wonder what they have in store for me.

He tried to calm his resentment toward the Telepaths.

Do not get ahead of yourself. Be peaceful, and they will be too.

Heaving a deep sigh that turned into a yawn, Irwin stretched his legs and arms.

I am tired. But I need to be prepared for whatever happens. As long as Kipp is safe. There will be no casualties.

He almost fell asleep but couldn't help keeping an eye and an ear alert.

They were coming to a place where the trees had been thinned, allowing sunlight to filter through the canopy. Slivers of light played on their faces. The rain let up and the flying mud had abated, though their clothing was wet and muddy. It would be dusk before they arrived in Nuaki Village; the landscape was now very well maintained. No longer was the gnarly undergrowth of the jungle out of control, threatening them with bugs and snakes. Random foot-trails from animals and possibly humans could be spotted.

After a while, Jamal switched places with Bejorn, giving the Elementalist time to rest. Teigahn handed off the reins to Irwin and took a brief nap as well. Jorge stayed on the bed, not wanting to be close to anyone.

16

ADMIRAL ARGUSTOS

Teigahn was awake by the time the jungle parted into orchards.

Rows and rows of apple trees afforded an entryway to the grove. Apple trees turned to pear, plum, date, and mandarin; the aroma of citrus filled their noses—lime and lemon. Irwin spotted fig, avocado, banana, and almond trees by the river, hidden from view until the last half kilometer.

As they drove on, the evening shadows grew longer, taking hold of the descending darkness. Lanterns and torches glowed along Nuaki Village's perimeter wall, a bridge, and the land access point. It was dark, but there was light toward the end of the copse at the river.

Up ahead, thunderous hooves raced parallel to the river—toward the bridge. The sounds of the galloping spooked Irwin's horses. Jamal snapped at them, and Irwin looked back to see both geldings jumping in-place then pacing sideways off the road. They were steered back and pulled steady by Jamal's muscular arms and curses. They whinnied toward the running herd (even the donkeys bellowed) at the young black horses following their dams toward Nuaki Village. Some of the younger steeds skidded around the corner onto the bridge—rumps flying, kicking out, and bucking. Their hooves beat across the stone footing toward the immense fortress. A herd of goats and sheered sheep followed the equines. A dozen pigs and Clan-Duin shepherds were last over the bridge.

The lead-wagon's horses whinnied, pulling faster than before—wanting to race home with their comrades for supper. Teigahn shouted incoherent words at the agitated beasts, pulling violently on the reins to keep them quiet. Irwin grasped his seat, hoping not to be thrown from the wagon.

A flock of crows screeched at all the commotion as they flew over the treetops and roofs toward Nuaki Village. Two jaguars lay at the threshold of the stone bridge beneath an archway. He was unable to tell if they were real or statues. They did not move as the eager animals raced between them, and their eyes remained forward and steady as the wagons approached.

But the statuesque jaguars were not statues, after all. Their eyes glistened and followed the lead wagon. Irwin jumped from his seat when they stood up as the wagons passed. The horses pulling the lead wagon did not flinch when the dark cats moved. He looked back at his own horses. They rushed past the bridge's entrance—tails tight against their buttocks—if only to be pulled back by Jamal.

Once through the archway and on the bridge, a tall fortress loomed above a growth of trees along the river's edge. It did not feel or look hospitable.

Calling this a village is a cruel joke for weary travelers.

A tall black spire pierced the sky. The river curved around the tower and around the omnipotent fortress. The footprint of this village was like that of Arenu Village, with one exception—it did not span the river. The waters coursed around its stony façade. The fortress walls looked impenetrable.

Large wooden doors stood open at the entrance, and the horses clamored through a tunnel into a courtyard. The jaguars crawled through the tunnel and mutated into fierce-looking men who closed the thick doors behind the two-wagon caravan, picked up their hanging sarongs and dressed before walking away.

Stopped briefly, Irwin's wagon was parked alongside the tower, meanwhile the one on which he rode backed up to an enormous set of double doors that in turn opened to a large storage room just beyond where men emerged and surrounded the wagon. Irwin dismounted, and Teigahn kept close.

Teigahn shouted at Irwin, "Follow, now!"

He did not have any time to see or talk to Kipp. Jorge began un-tacking the horses from his wagon, while Bejorn kept Jamal and Kipp unpacking Nuaki Village's wagon. No one seemed to notice Teigahn escorting Irwin away from the courtyard.

This is it. Be kind. Show mercy.

But will they?

I must show mercy. I will not be like my father.

Irwin did not want to leave Kipp behind, and he glanced back at his seemingly aloof friend. Teigahn shifted his position, trying to touch Irwin. He had to watch those pasty white hands.

They are going to try to touch me. Think of previous experiences. Remember when I was chained? Remember being beaten by the chain. Remember when I was thrown off the cliff? Or the time I was tied up for days, left to starve—left for dead. Think those thoughts; that way, if they come into my mind, they are in my territory.

In no time, Irwin and Teigahn were surrounded. Irwin had felt the men waiting around the corner. They were all Erthin in some capacity. Half a dozen gruesome,

Talented men surrounded him. None of them held blades. They didn't need to. Irwin was ushered up several flights of stairs.

Teigahn led the procession down a stark corridor and into a meeting room. A wall of mirrored windows across the courtyard appeared as ghost twins to the building in which he now walked. He noticed how this would be a good vantage point for any Telepath to have of those below.

A bald man with deep wrinkles sat facing an apprentice, a younger platinum-blonde Telepath who was busy scribbling in a ledger. They had been talking but hushed when the procession entered the room.

Irwin guessed this was Admiral Argustos.

He is old—possibly Dephen old!

The aged Telepath turned to scrutinize him. The Metalist felt golden teeth in the back of Argustos's mouth—but the man remained tight-lipped and steady. Irwin kept his mind still.

Three Telepaths, he guessed to be middle-aged, were seated on a couch in the center of the room. They each had receding (or mostly balding) hairlines and were otherwise non-descript. Two empty wooden chairs—ornately carved and cushioned—had been positioned at a formidable wooden table. Two full-blooded Erthins and two Clan-Duins hid in the corners. They had all been awaiting his arrival.

He felt everyone's metal. He was outnumbered, and he measured the situation. *I could kill them all right now. Be steady, keep calm.*
Breathe.

"Have a seat." The youngest Telepath on the couch motioned to a stuffed chair.

He looked around one more time, his senses alive and keen. The place smelled of old men who had not washed in many days—their garments dirtied and soiled. The couch and the big chairs were stuffed with musty horsehair. Bookcases bowed from the weight of dust-covered books. Portraits of past admirals hung evenly on the wood-paneled walls. Nautical treasures—a compass, a brass telescope, a partially rusted spear, a bludgeoning bat for fish—had been hung between and around the paintings. A stuffed swordfish was mounted over the door. At the far end of the room, Irwin recognized a framed map of Urthis.

He felt jewelry on several of the men; Admiral Argustos had adorned himself with several silver and gold rings and earrings—some spiraled through his ears. He wore a tattoo of an eagle gripping grapes in one talon and a snake in the other—the snake glittered with golden flecks burned into the Admiral's forearm.

Other ornate tattoos had been drawn along his right arm. Irwin guessed there were others underneath his partially clean clothing.

Admiral Argustos spoke with a voice loud enough to be heard down the hallway. He had a spiteful drawl. "I arrived in Nuaki Village 'bout sixty years ago—not a land lover. I've spent much time on the open ocean, meetin' her wrath, witnessin' her splendor. I've met many people, civilized and not. I've dealt with countless atrocities. Kept men alive. Or brought death—all because I could." He cleared his throat, coughed.

"I've had to adapt my ways over time. The men here are horrible, who, like me, have seen and done many thin's, all treacherous. We've all dealt out many a card, played many a game, and continue to win if only by our cunnin'. The men below are valuable in tellin' me what type of urchin I be dealin' with when a new mate arrives. This allows me to gauge how things'll go while ye-be settlin' in." He sneered, displaying a gold tooth.

Irwin remained standing, taking note of all the faces. Teigahn and the other soldiers stayed close. The Erthins near the windows were air-yielding. He could feel one of them muting sounds and voices from outside; nothing could penetrate. One Erthin was a young Elementalist, possibly there for intimidation purposes. They grimaced as he studied them. The two soldiers behind his shoulders kept their eyes to themselves.

"I'd been in Mavar's position ..." Admiral Argustos pointed at the younger Telepath taking notes. "... 'bout four moons when two brothers walked into our village. They were headin' north, fleeing Daos Territory. They were twins and were about five years older than you. They were mangy, dehydrated, and hungry. We offered them use of our amenities, as we are hospitable people."

Irwin stared at Admiral Argustos, harrumphed to himself at the word 'hospitable'.

"Yet soon thereafter, we found those men were not suitable guests. The soldiers here could smell somethin' wrong with those brothers." Again, Argustos paused—his blue eyes wanting to read Irwin's thoughts. "Believin' they were worst of the worst of the worst. And they were."

Irwin tried to appear stoic, but inside, he was an emotional windstorm.

This must be some kind of telepathic trick. He wants me to do something, say something. Be calm.

Calm? He's up to something. I can see it in those cold blue eyes. I hope they do not hurt Kipp. Or kill him. I cannot keep him safe anymore.

Maybe I should leave him a message in the wagon. Just in case.

Admiral Argustos's voice rose as he ranted. "They cheated in card games. Lied about themselves: who they really were, about their actual powers. Those bastards killed over three dozen men, took metal reserves, stole horses, and set this place ablaze. We've been searchin' for them and their relatives ever since."

I should kill them all. It would be easy. Breathe. Be calm, do not kill. The Admiral just wants to talk.

He was afraid to breathe.

Yeah right! He wants to do more to me than talk. I know that look. Just like Jebadia and Albert all over again—plotting, calculating.

Admiral Argustos's eyes twinkled. "You look like Edger Sampson, but you behave like Edwin. Unlike Admiral Ubic, I believe you know your ancestors." Argustos paused, maybe hoping Irwin would reveal himself and his family. "Your father, Albert, for example, he has shown his face many times in Kobiton. And the rumors about what he did in Chinochi .... We know he's violent. What I want to know is which man was his father? Edwin or Edger?"

Chinochi? I do not want to know.

Irwin maintained eye contact.

I believe the Admiral is trying to provoke.

Mavar interrupted, "Sir, your accounting is inaccurate. There is no record of three dozen men being killed, just Admiral Staeon and his assistant."

"Not everythin' that happened was written down," Argustos said, lips barely open.

The apprentice harrumphed. "Sir, I don't think he resembles either picture we have."

"He does! I recognize those eyes."

Mavar reached over and pulled a book from the top of a pile—opened it to a marked page. "It was written 'Their faces are oblong, gaunt from lack of food and hydration, eyes set close together, beady-silvery, hair silvery-gray, body type lean, medium muscle build.' Samuel Irwin's face is more effeminate, rounder, possibly resembling his mother, and his hair looks more sandy-brown than silver. Although, he has the lean muscular body type."

Silence fell over the room.

Admiral Argustos coughed several times and then caught his breath. "You've demonstrated the same arrogant behaviors as your elders, Samuel Irwin Miner. We know you can't be trusted with your powers. Even if you've the air that you do not know how to use them, we know you do; you're just good at being deceptive, much like your ancestors."

The men hovering around him backed away.

Cut them all up. Hurt them before they hurt me! Keep calm, breathe. There is no reason to be like father, to decimate. Remember, we just want safe passage.

He licked his lips. "I know I have given you Telepaths the impression that I am shifty. I do not trust others easily. Now I clearly did not know about my powers in Onj Raha. If you have been watching me and my family, you would know that I am naïve to this world. I come from the mountains and am not a fighter. In Onj Raha, I was out of my element. I-I was provoked by situations and people."

A Telepath on the couch scoffed, "That's your excuse?"

"I have always been a peaceful person, Admiral Argustos, Sir. I have never meant to harm anyone. That was the way of my father and grandfather, but not me." He bowed his head, indulging the Admiral the same way he would have his father. "I am new to Urthis, so to speak, naïve about how things work."

Argustos growled, "Don't placate me, boy! You've already demonstrated Talent and intelligence. You've shown my men how coy and keen you can be on the trail."

"I did not hurt any of your men."

"You provoked."

He regarded the ancient Telepath. "You live in a fortress full of men who provoke."

"You'll be under scrupulous supervision in the brig. Preemptively, of course."

"What for, exactly?"

"You're not trustworthy."

"And everyone else in this village is?" Anger furrowed his brow, and he spat, "This is exactly what Dephen Ishik wants!"

"You're right, my boy!" Everyone chuckled. "While Dephen is changin' the regime, you and the Clan-Duin will be disposed of."

Caught off guard by Argustos's admission, Teigahn had the millisecond he needed to bludgeon Irwin unconscious.

17

<u>NUAKI VILLAGE</u>

A light mist fell before daybreak, but Kipp slept until a clamoring of horse hooves jolted him up from the hard bed. Shepherds passed by, chasing a constant stream of animals flooding out of the dark stables. Several spunky yearlings brought up the backend of the barrage and frolicked with lambs and pigs as they headed out for a day in the pastures.

Kipp watched and worried about where Irwin had gone. He looked around the wagon. No Irwin. His heart beat hard against his chest; he sat up, feeling prickles up and down his back. He reached into his pocket and tapped the special coins together, but nothing happened. "Where are you, Irwin?" He scanned the fortress. No Irwin. He climbed out of the wagon. He went to Jorge's open door in the stables, but the Empath was not in his chamber. He spun around. Jorge was in the middle of the stable, pitchfork in hand, staring at him. "What are you doing, going into my room?"

Kipp walked toward Jorge. "Where's Samuel?"

Jorge shrugged, tossed aside the pitchfork, and grabbed Kipp's arm. "Let's go ask." He pushed Kipp toward the stairs. "And don't be angry if you don't get the answers you want."

"Why wouldn't I get answers?"

"Telepaths."

Admiral Argustos's office door was open. The understudy, Mavar, sat at a small desk shuffling through a mound of papers. He looked up when he heard Kipp snort and Jorge clear his throat.

"How might I help you?"

"Where's the Admiral?" Kipp's voice was thin and shaky.

"And you are?" The Telepath studied Kipp and smiled smugly. "Oh, that's right, you're Samuel's friend. Hauss Kipp is it? Or is it Kipp Hauler?"

Unnerved by Mavar, Kipp barked, "Where's Samuel?"

"Resting, I suppose. He and the Admiral talked all night. My hand cramped up while writing their lengthy commentary. I must finish these notes before I forget what all they talked about."

"Where would Samuel rest?"

"We have extra sleeping quarters in the tower." Mavar pointed toward the enormous tower.

"Why wasn't I offered a bed?"

"You're not really allowed to be here. The only reason you haven't been kicked out is because Samuel requested you stay." He glared at Kipp. "Maybe you should go make yourself useful, offer to help in the kitchens or something." He gestured for the two of them to leave.

Kipp stomped. "I need to see Samuel right now."

Mavar lifted his eyes again and said, "You don't need to see Samuel now."

"I don't need to see Samuel now," Kipp responded, hypnotized.

"You're hungry and want to go eat."

"I'm hungry and want to go eat."

Stifling a yawn, Mavar ordered, "Jorge, take him away."

"Yes, Sir," Jorge groveled and then reached for Kipp's hand. "Come on, let's go get something to eat." He pulled Kipp through the hallway and back down the stairs.

Once they landed on the ground floor, Jorge left Kipp to fend for himself, sent him on to the dining area. Kipp stopped, put his hand in his pocket and fingered the special coins Irwin had given him. 'Never lose these.' He heard those words as he stood alone and lost in the courtyard. He smelled breakfast and his belly growled, but his eyes were drawn back up to the windows. He saw a shadowy figure looking down at him from the fourth-floor windows. Without another thought, he hustled toward the dining area.

Kipp piled his plate with bread, fruits, and thin slices of meat. He then took a seat at a mostly empty table. He stuffed his mouth full of food, barely breathing between bites. By the time he was full, Jamal appeared and sat down next to him.

"Good to see you made it through the night."

"Why wouldn't I?"

Shoveling food into his mouth, Jamal asked, "You gonna come and train with the *Shayot* today?"

"I'm not sure. I need to find out what Samuel will be doing." He felt as though he was wandering inside a dark tunnel.

"Why do you care what he's doing? By now, he's in cahoots with the Telepaths."

"Why do you say that?"

Jamal shrugged, still busy shoveling and chewing his morning meal. Kipp stood and headed back toward the wagon. Once there, he tried to remember what he needed to be doing. Every time a spark of reason came, his focus was drawn in another direction.

He went to the Hole to do his business but left as there were men waiting in line. Back at the wagon, he sat hoping for a turn in the Hole soon. He did not want to wait in line. Then he moved around in the wagon, reviewing the annoyances of the morning. The blanket fell from the metal bed. He was about to replace it when something inscribed in the metal caught his eye.

Go to bog. Find the carriage. Find Yace.

He flung the blanket across the bed and sat down on the chiseled words. He put his hand under the cloth to feel those words—making sure he was not just seeing things. "You left me a message," he said, thinking of Irwin. But without another breath, he tried to blank his mind. He knew not to think about anything.

Telepaths will hear it!

He held the coins in his hand, clanked them together again, hoping Irwin would respond—hoping the coins would rattle or levitate off his hand.

Nothing.

"This is no good," he muttered, and a familiar shiver rippled down his spine. "I know they have him. Fuk, now what do I do? Go to the bog, find the carriage; find Yace." He shed his clothes and stuffed them and the coins inside the metal lockbox.

The courtyard was full of life. Locals were starting their daily routines. Kipp dove from the wagon, hands forward, mutating into his canine form. He raced through the open doorway, across the bridge, through the orchard and down the roadway, retracing their journey into Nuaki Village the night before—back to the bog.

The further from Nuaki he raced, the more he remembered of the day before. Out here—speeding away from the dark and dreary fortress—his mind cleared. He remembered smelling Yace at the bog. He reflected on the day before, on their arrival.

It was mid-morning by the time Kipp reached the marshy area. Thirsty and out of breath, he drank his fill before following his nose around the giant bog. Her scent had been left between trees on the side of the bog where he and Jorge had foraged for food. She had relieved herself away from the trail the carriage had taken. Wheel marks and broken overhead branches revealed where the enormous coach had pushed its way through the jungle, possibly with Erthin help. There were broken branches all along the overgrown roadway where yesterday he and Jorge had strained to see what the Telepaths might be investigating.

It was obvious that Erthin powers had been used to manipulate trees, branches, shrubs, and rocks, pushing them back and recreating the old road for the carriage to pass through. There were wheel marks on the ground where it had stopped and waited for the roadway to be cleared. Downed trees and hefty rocks had been rolled off to the side.

Kipp followed the recreated roadway, returning to the river. He raced along the jungle-lined corridor. The muscles in his canine legs flexed and tightened like that of a panther on the hunt. For a time, the mangled road took on a manicured look. He was nearing the old Nuaki Village fortress. Between the trees, he made out a steeple and tattered roofs. As he got closer, he could see holes in the brick façade. The building looked and felt haunted. Shadows flickered with sunlight; windows in dark rooms came to life.

He stood panting in an old, worn-down fruit grove. He heard a group of *Shayot* boys approaching from the river, and he jumped into a patch of overgrown brambles where he watched the boys pass. They raced along the old road, shouting to each other and heading the way Kipp had just come.

He remained still and out of sight. He waited for the horde to pass and then continued to follow the roadway.

Suddenly a pack of Erthins raced up a side path from the orchard, and Kipp had to duck from view again. He crouched low as a dozen young Erthin *Shayot* paced along, keeping in stride with each other as they passed.

The closer to the river and the old fortress he ventured, the more anxiety flooded his veins. What if he were to be caught? Would they banish him on the spot? Or would they just kill him? He stopped in the middle of the old road. "The carriage wouldn't have come this close to the fortress. The *Shayot* live there, and I don't think they would let them pass. Then where would the carriage go?" He surveyed the land, trying to calculate, as Irwin would have done.

Wheel tracks turned from the road. There was bent grass, barely noticeable, but Kipp could see and read the signs. The carriage had crept through the orchard and continued due west. So did Kipp.

"How's that no one saw it, or heard it? Maybe they came through at midnight." Kipp analyzed the wheel marks as he pattered between them. They were not easy to spot. "I bet that Earth Erthin fixed the grass so that no one would notice." His nose followed where the carriage had gone, and he held close to the haphazard trail.

West of the old fortress by nearly a kilometer, the river twisted out of view from anyone down river. It was there, a low point and widest part of the river, where the carriage passed through the rushing water. Kipp changed out of his canine form to his two-legged self and used his height to see up and down the river bend. "No one could've seen them here. How'd they know where to drive? Dephen must've been here before."

A push of air accompanied by a sonic boom flushed out all the animals close-by, pushed tree branches around, flooded the sky and ground with leaves. Kipp had to catch himself to keep from falling over, but he kept his eyes on the direction of the blast. Rattled to his core, he watched hundreds of birds take to the sky.

"Dang me. I hope that wasn't Irwin."

The birds flew around like starlings coming to rest at sundown. Colorful birds, large and small. They floated between the trees, up and down the river's avenue, unsure if they should come to rest.

Another explosion took him by surprise and threw him into the water. Trees bent and birds scattered, flying for their lives.

"Fuk, I bet that *was* Irwin." He looked toward the east, barely able to see the old Nuaki Village fortress now. "Well, if I was a bird, I could find out what's happening." The thought floated around in his head. "There's no harm in trying."

Seeing all those birds flying with vigor provided Kipp with an opportunity to free his mind and seize the shape he wanted to be. He jumped into the air and allowed his body to follow through his silent command, *Be bird*. His arms became wings, feathers grew over his body, and his legs lifted protectively.

Kipp had mutated into a white crane. "Holy Hakra! I can fly!"

18

HOW TO KILL IRWIN

Irwin slowly slipped back into consciousness.

"We've tried everything." He heard Bejorn talking to Admiral Argustos. Argustos was angry. "I don't think you've tried everything."

"After he was nearly bludgeoned to death—and that didn't work—we tried simpler tactics. Can we suck the spirit out of him? Can we mentally command his body to stop working? Can we command his mind to believe his body's dead?"

"That happened under Mavar's stint!" Andel snapped.

"Can we hang him? Can we crush him? Can we cut off his head with a sword? The answer to all of that is no." The defeat in Bejorn's voice was evident.

"You couldn't cut off his head?"

"Sir, his body absorbed the metal." Bejorn had lost his edge, the one he had pressed and pressed last night, or however many days ago that was. Irwin was not sure.

"Captain Andel, you're supposed to hold on to him," Admiral Argustos chided, "keep his mind still, make his body believe it's dead."

"That happened on Mavar's watch, not mine!" Andel hissed. "And I have been holding on—though I don't like it."

No one was watching Irwin now; he was aware they all believed he was unconscious.

"Even Dawson had problems with his mind, Sir," Bejorn interjected.

"You're killing a man! You might not like the work, but you are supposed to get it done." Argustos was snarling now. "His mind isn't allowed to have a voice anymore. He must be permanently silenced."

Andel repeated Bejorn's words, "Dawson had a hard time too, Sir! This man's hard to break."

"Mavar didn't complain," the Admiral reproached Andel.

Bejorn cut in, "Sir. If I may—"

Argustos cut him off. "What other tactics have you tried?"

Andel sounded impatient. "All of them! He's tried all of it, Sir."

Irwin kept his eyes closed, but he could still see through his thick eyelashes and out the periphery of his eyelids. He had been strung up in the center of a circular torture room, each appendage held tight with ropes secured to the stone walls. He was sure they were in the top of the tower—inside a massive training room. There were all sorts of fighting accessories, gizmos, and gadgets for torture, unmovable obstacles, and high scaffolding he had witnessed and endured. The walls and floor were reinforced—no sound could escape—and there were no windows and only one way in or out that he could see.

Earlier in his life, Irwin had borne everything imaginable to cruel and sinister minds. Inadvertently, his grandfather and father had prepared his mind and body for the gratuitous torture techniques of these men of Nuaki.

Bejorn said, "There's one tactic I've not tried. But you and I've talked about it."

"You're not allowed to do anything that brash until you've exhausted all options." Argustos's voice rattled; he was on the edge of a coughing fit and cleared his throat. "Now tell me what all you've tried."

Bejorn said, "The men and I have tried everything imaginable. Many Clan-Duins died trying to rip him to shreds. It seems his flesh is poison to them."

"You let them rip him apart?" The Admiral gasped. "Was he still awake?"

"No. Everything we did, we did with intention. Dawson held on, tricking his mind, making it believe he was dead. Meanwhile, this little shit is poisoning men with his flesh and blood. No wonder the Clan-Duins call him Death."

"Did you bury him?"

"We threw his body off the scaffolding, tried hanging him. Then brought down the stones on him. He was crushed, mangled, and we left him to die. But once we pulled back the boulders—though he looked flattened—he was still alive. Everyone thought he was dead. No one heard a heartbeat until he began breathing again."

"How'd he heal from all that!?"

"I haven't the faintest clue, Sir. I have allowed every Erthin who wanted to try their rendition of incinerating, breath rescinding, drowning—"

"Did you fill his lungs with sand?"

"We've lost all of our powerhouse Erthins: Clide, Fritz, Grendel, Rhyly. They're all dead."

Andel added, "It's almost like what he did in Arenu, Sir. But scarier to witness."

"Yes, it is." Bejorn agreed. "They can't even try to …. They're just …. He just assimilates them. And every time that happens—every time he absorbs one—he wakes up. It invigorates him and his regenerative power. We have to make sure there is a Telepath holding him the entire time."

Argustos asked, "You can't turn it off?"

"No, Sir, it's on at an innate level," said Andel.

"Are you certain you're tricking his mind correctly?"

"I know how to manipulate the mind, sir," Andel grumbled at his superior. "Maybe someone else can take my place for a while?"

"Dawson and Mavar already did six hours each. You're only three in."

Andel's lips quivered, and he let out a muffled weeping sound.

Argustos turned his attention to Bejorn. "Have you tried to take his life using a healer?"

"Yes," said Bejorn.

"And …?"

"Do you see Nandhu here?"

"No."

"Exactly my point! Every Erthin power performed backfires. I think it's time for me to try my—"

"What did I say about that, Bejorn?"

"Sir!"

"What about the alchemists? Did they try their acids and poisons?"

"Acids did nothing but burn holes through his regenerative flesh and into the floor. He was unaffected by the acids." Bejorn scoffed, admitting, "They also poisoned him. They did that after dumping a vat of acid on him. We all assumed he was weakened by then. I was assured it was the most lethal dose of poison too, but …."

"But what?" Argustos was growing impatient.

"He's still alive!"

"Did you try to kill him while poisoned?"

"Yes."

Andel shouted, "That's how Nandhu died!" He folded his arms and glared at Irwin.

"Do you know how many men we've lost *trying things* while he was mostly dead?" said Bejorn.

Argustos looked over at Irwin. "He should be dead all right."

"Well, he's not," Bejorn said through clenched teeth. "There must be something more we can do to him than what his ancestors have done. When I first met him, touched his hand, I thought he might be an Elementalist. He's got all the powers in equal parts. Maybe that's how he's able to affect the men. But it's like his powers work at an infinitesimal level—"

Argustos interrupted. "It's possible his mother was Erthin. Though he doesn't look it."

"I can't explain what is going on here." Bejorn's voice shook with fear. "I think this is ... well, it's beyond Erthin."

They moved closer to Irwin, assessing him. Argustos said, "Coterie." And they all exhaled simultaneously.

Bejorn then inhaled loudly, "And if he is?"

"If Lady Gretchen were still alive, she could drink his blood and tell us his origin story." The Admiral added. "No matter what, he needs to be destroyed."

"If I try my spell on him now, before he wakes, I'm sure it'll kill him."

"It'll kill you too," the Admiral's voice was stern and at the same time, wary. "Out of the question." He must have seen Irwin take a breath. "Looks like he's coming back."

"I hope not. After Nandhu poisoned and burned him with acid, Samuel should be closer to death. I wish I hadn't ... I wish I had stopped Nandhu. I saw it all happen. Everything slowed right before Nandhu was taken by Death. If anything, Nandhu's power pulled Samuel back from Death's grasp. I shouldn't have allowed Nandhu to try anything."

"You think?" Argustos was now sarcastic.

"We should have waited," Bejorn whispered. He was staring at Irwin. "The poison should've killed him, I'm sure of it."

"Have you tried anything since then?"

"I ran out of formidable men, Sir. That's why I called for you. I don't wanna harm more of the men below trying to kill this vile creature. We've lost many outstanding soldiers to him already," said Bejorn. "Frankly, Sir, I don't know what else to do. We've tried everything!"

"You've not tried everything. Not every contraption in this room has his blood on it."

"We cannot use any metal on him. He absorbs it."

The Admiral strode over and grabbed Irwin's foot. "He appears to be conscious. Maybe not fully awake, but ...." He recoiled and took a step toward the door. "You need to destroy him, and with no more casualties."

Irwin was fully awake—unmoving and his mind clear of thoughts—but still listening to the conversation.

Bejorn spoke, "If you'll let me have my way, Sir, I know I can—"

"Out of the question, Bejorn! We might as well use all the Erthins together and try—"

"We did that sir," Bejorn grumbled.

"You did? How many men did you use?"

"Five. And we combined their powers, forcing what we believed was complete destruction on this man."

"What happened to the men?"

Bejorn raised his voice, clearly angered that Argustos was not getting the point. "They're dead, Sir! All of them! They were all sucked into his body—just like Barnst was."

"If Gretchen was still alive …" Argustos muttered, "… we could ship him off to her and let her have some fun."

"Isn't General Gepson taking over for her?"

"Yes. But it'll take Gepson a while to learn how Gretchen did things; she had her own style—her own way of working with Clan-Duins." Argustos sighed and looked again at Irwin, "If only the Lady had killed you, and not the other way around."

"We could still send him to Gepson." Said Bejorn.

"This man will need a telepathic guard every minute of every day to keep his mind quiet." Said Andel with a trembling voice. "He's strong."

Bejorn said, "Who would we send to guard him?"

Andel piped up, "Not me!"

Argustos wanted to know, "What's so horrible about holding his mind?"

"Whatever you twist his mind into believing, he makes it worse and then sucks you into his nightmare."

"You're supposed to be the one creating nightmares, not him."

"His head's screwed on wrong, Sir. He somehow can take the vision I give him and twist it. And since I'm holding on, he makes me somehow a part of it. I can't control what he does."

"You can't control him?!"

"It seems most of his life was a living hell. But adding to what's already happened to him …. It's like he wants things to get worse."

"You should use positive moments from his life and twist them, not bad ones. I thought you were taught better."

"I tried that!" Andel squawked. "He doesn't have any good memories."

Argustos raised his voice, clearly impatient. "Use a recent memory."

"You don't understand, Sir, he has no happy memories. Not even his most recent memories have anything positive that I can twist into a negative. All his life he's been shit on. It's depressing." Andel took a step back from Irwin. "Maybe you should be the one who holds his mind, Sir. You're stronger than any other Telepath here. You know what to do. Maybe you can twist his mind into believing—"

"Try drowning him in a tub, or a bucket, this time."

"Sir?!"

Admiral Argustos stepped close. "I understand, Bejorn, that you haven't tried every technique."

"We've already tried drowning this asshole!" Bejorn met Argustos's eyes straight on. "Nothing works! But, of course, the spell I have, Sir. The needs of the many outweigh the needs of one. Please, let me do this, Sir. I promise he will not survive."

"You're the last Elementalist in Nuaki. We cannot sacrifice you. If Nandhu, Clide, and Rhyly are dead, and we know of no others coming here anytime soon." The Admiral coughed, nearly choking. "You need to think this through, Lieutenant. Try a more old-fashioned approach." Argustos turned on his boot heel, exited the room and descended a hidden staircase, leaving the top floor of the tower in Lieutenant Bejorn's care.

"Old fashioned?" Bejorn scoffed. "I'll show him old-fashioned! Tell Samuel's brain it's dead while I pour a bucket of water across his face. Grab his hair; pull his head back and cover his face with a cloth. You'll have to really hold him down while I water-board him." He stalked off, probably to get a bucket.

"I don't care what the Admiral thinks, I think you should do that spell you keep talking about," Andel said when the Lieutenant returned.

"I have to give my life to do it."

"But the needs of the many—"

"Trust me, Andel, you and I, we're reading from the same book. But Argustos wants me to continue to do things *the old fashion way*. The problem with that logic is that we've tried it all."

"You know what you're doing, Lieutenant. You don't need the Admiral to advise you on what needs to be done. You've made many hard decisions already concerning this bag of excrement. You've seen many good men die. Trust your judgement," Andel said with a hint of telepathy Irwin could hear in the man's tone and word usage.

A long time passed while they stood next to Irwin, meanwhile staring at one another. Irwin watched the two men through tight eyelashes, still pretending to be asleep. Bejorn muttered, "I might be able to use another person's soul in exchange for my own."

"How do you know you have to use a soul to make your spell happen?"

"It's required!"

19

THE NEEDS OF THE MANY

Lieutenant Bejorn placed his hand on Captain Andel's shoulder and appropriated his life energy. Andel fell forward, his body slamming into the floor; he was dead. The Elementalist had used Andel's life force and created a bubble of power potent enough to execute Irwin once and for all. Equal parts of earth, wind, water, fire, and the spirit of death—he churned the bubble of power around in his hands.

From purple to blue, the energy ball glowed and grew, slowly at first; it transformed to green, and the energy kept churning, now changing to bright yellow. The orb swelled significantly while Bejorn beheld it in his hands. Yellow turned to orange, then red. The energy bubbled—radiating powerful heat. Red mottled into purple, completing the cycle, and it started all over again. Colors of spirit energy rolled from one into another, oscillating fluidly, and the ball of energy grew larger and larger while it hung in the air between the Lieutenant's hands.

Bejorn stepped close to Irwin.

Irwin's head hung from a rope that clenched it in an upward position. Slowly his eyes opened, and he saw the electrical charge Bejorn was summoning in his hands. He closed his eyes, shielding them from the energy. He pulsated his magnetic energy outwards.

The air between the two men vibrated as their powers met. A blinding spark of white energy burst, and Lieutenant Bejorn was instantly absorbed by Irwin. The nuclear ball of energy Bejorn had created was also integrated into Irwin's flesh. Usually, he could flush out Erthin powers, but this was a unique spell that was meant to contain and refrain before overloading the host.

BOOM!

Believing he could absorb the Elementalist's spell and dissipate the energy it had created was Irwin's only mistake. White light tore through his body, spewing it in every direction. Fat, muscles, ligaments, sinew, tissue, and skin were no more, only bones and innards—already coated by metal—remained. He screamed out as his whole body was nearly incinerated from within. And just as rapidly, it began to regenerate.

As the deafening burst of energy emanated away from Irwin, it blew out the tower's upper exterior walls and popped the cone roof clean off, sending it flying into the river. Below him, the flooring burst into pieces and the ropes that bound him were incinerated. Everything within a fifty-foot radius had been instantaneously decimated.

Once the restraints vanished and the ball of energy ceased, Irwin's body succumbed to gravity, tumbling three floors below, crashing through ceilings and floors, falling with chunks of stone wall, broken flooring supports, bricks, and flaming pieces of wood and roof tiles. Not sure how high it had been to the top of the tower; he was unsure what to expect next. He crash-landed into a sparring room, debris raining all around and on top of his mangled body.

Only a few of the men who seconds earlier had been sparring managed to jump out of the way of the massive cave-in. Once those men realized what had happened, they tried pulling stones, blazing pieces of wood, and dusty debris now smothering their fallen brethren.

Irwin, too, was partially buried. The weight of stones and flooring was heavy on his bones, especially his rib cage and spine. He heard the muffled cries of men dying—being crushed—below his wedged position. He tried to move, but was pinched and broken. Nevertheless, with the metal in him, his body could maximize its metaphysical healing abilities. And although he had to regenerate those parts and pieces necessary to live, it was all nearly instantaneous. The pain was excruciating as his body regrew ligaments, tissue, muscle, fat, and flesh. The regenerating always hurt more than the injuries.

He cried out in agony, and those outside the wreckage heard him. He was under heavy piles of rubble, and it was stifling, yet refreshing.

I am alive.

He felt large stones being eased off his fleshy legs. He managed to muster enough strength to help hoist the loosened stone from his back.

Two Erthin/Clan-Duins—who had been fighting one another moments before—leaped into action and were helping the injured. They found Irwin among the wreckage, but neither offered a hand up. He looked to be a partial skeleton whose body was re-growing its muscles and flesh before their eyes.

The soldiers jumped back at the sight of him. He saw their faces and then the sunlight shining down on them. He was dazed by it all, as was everyone else.

But then he realized it would all happen again.

His skin had grown back just in time to start changing color. From his usual ashen flesh to purple, then to blue, Irwin's skin-color shifted.

I need to get out of here.

He shouted. "Where are the stairs!?"

"Did you do this?" an assertive Erthin/Clan-Duin asked, ready to brawl.

This was the spell cast by Bejorn. He wanted to hydrate himself, but he had to take care of himself and those around him. "I need to get away. None of you are safe!"

The startled men of Nuaki Village were ready to spar with him. Three partial Erthins charged up their powers, ready to decimate the Metalist. But the moment they started firing their powers on him, he absorbed those Erthins and all their eruptive energies.

BOOM!

The floor Irwin had fallen into was blown out, and whatever rubble remained was obliterated into fine dust particles. Bodies and bricks intermingled in the air, swirling around and away from the destruction. From two-hundred feet to one-hundred and twenty, the tower of Nuaki Village came down, floor by floor, and all because of Bejorn's radiant spell. Everybody, alive and dead, on the upper floors had been incinerated, except Irwin.

Once the bubble of energy blew out, he fell down another floor into yet another sparring room—thankfully barren of students. He woke atop the rubble and felt his body regenerating again. Now he understood what was happening.

There was a pattern to the churning power Bejorn had given him; slowly it built toward a climax before what could only be described as the kind of explosion that could wipe out the entire planet. This would happen again and again unless he found a way to stop it. He scrambled to get up, to orient himself. He spotted an open door leading to a darkened stairwell and ran toward it, his mission to exit the tower.

Where is Kipp!? He better be safe.

He felt for the coins.

Why do I feel him in the box? I thought I left him a message about Yace. Was that even real?

He tried to swallow his fears, but his throat was too dry.

I cannot be sure about anything.

As he ran, Irwin was able to coat the wagon frame and everything in it.

No one is safe. Where do I go? What should I do? Do not panic!

Flying down the stairs, he nearly fell into the backside of Admiral Argustos who was also fleeing down the stairwell. The old man had stopped for a coughing fit. Argustos looked up at Irwin.

His flesh was changing color again, almost too red now, and he had only a second to say, "I am not sorry," before his skin pulsated white energy, blowing a giant hole in the tower's side.

He plummeted down another story and landed inside a dark room. He could see the ceiling and heard stones tumbling and the tower rumbling and groaning, readying to collapse. Irwin managed to stand upright—his body repairing—and took off running, ignoring the pain while he ran on bones and tendons. It took no time for muscle and flesh to grow back, completing his body's regeneration.

He sped down another set of stairs, knocking people over as he went. He needed to get away from everyone, if only to keep them all safe.

Shit. Shit.

He did not know how to take care of this continuing problem.

What do I do? Where do I go? No one is safe. I do not want to kill them all!

He shivered down to his soul. He could barely draw oxygen down his parched throat.

He guessed that only three floors separated him from the base of the tower. But he did not reach the main doorway before blowing up again. This time, he coated his skin with metal to keep it from being blown off as it had before. The pain from his body being ripped apart was beyond anything he had ever endured; he did not want to bear it again. He understood that being buried by all the heavy rubble was just as bad.

Irwin used his Earth Erthin powers to push rubble off himself and continued his race to the ground floor. This time, he did not falter, but tumbled and fell along with the rubble as it fell.

He bumped along, trying to surf the river of rumbling debris.

Ugh, ouch, ugh! Bejorn deserved what he got.

How long between explosions? I need to count. I cannot focus. Breathe. Keep calm. What about Kipp? He is sealed in the wagon. He should be safe.

At the end of the churning pile of rubble, Irwin took off.

Where do I go? How can I protect everyone else? The forge! Seal myself in. They have iron and copper too! I must absorb all the copper. Ground this shit out of me. But I do not have time to get there before exploding again. Shit!

He used his wagon as a beacon to find the exit. He was racing against time. The second he threw open the exterior door, he realized he was not yet out of the massive tower. There was a passage between the courtyard and the tower; he hid there. Men shouted to put out fires and to find out what was going on.

I do not want to kill any of these people.

He peered out from the alcove, past his wagon, toward the forge across the courtyard.

The barnyard across the way appeared barren. The southern facing wooden door was locked, but the doorway to the north was open wide. No one was fleeing; they were too busy diffusing the situation.

No matter what Irwin did, he would not make it anywhere outside the alcove before exploding again. The power bubbled, ready to explode. He watched his metal hands turning purple.

He looked down the long corridor, descending into the excrement Hole and smelled the foulness. He looked out the alcove's opening again and saw several men running toward him. His body lit up the dark recess—he was glowing bright yellow.

He summoned metal from his wagon to surround him, creating a thick, yet small, sphere to protect all who approached. The emanating colors of his skin brightened the interior walls of his protective metal sphere, and finally, the percolating energy violently discharged. The building above him rumbled—a warning of its eminent collapse.

As soon as he felt safe, he threw the metal back onto his wagon. The liquid metal flew around Clan-Duin soldiers who were advancing, startling them. Shouting and grunting, the men sounded hesitant to approach the alcove. He could feel them coming and he decided to step out into the open, catching the soldiers off-guard.

Hands up, fear rattling his voice, Irwin said, "None of you are safe. Go! Run! Get away from here—from me."

The burliest Clan-Duin of the bunch dove toward Irwin, fangs out, ready to chomp. He did not want to fight, but threw up his silvery fists. Hungry for blood and vengeance, three of them attacked at once. There was no way for them to pierce his hardened flesh, and Irwin doled out punches and kicks.

Even though his skin changed colors, no one backed down. He counted while beating the vicious attackers.

Twenty-nine. Thirty.

"I will not regret this," he told the angry Clan-Duins as the deep-seated power boiled out once more.

Those who stood defiantly before Irwin were incinerated.

He left a circular divot in the ground, and another hole in the tower—this time at the base. The building rattled, threatening to fall on him. Not wanting his best friend and their personal possessions buried, he shoved the metal-coated wagon through the closed southern doors. They burst open, wood chunks flying. The gleaming wagon slid across the long stone bridge.

Now that the southern doorway was open, the men of Nuaki had another option for fleeing the destruction.

Irwin raced for the forge.

Thirteen. Fourteen. Fifteen.

He counted and his feet flew across the cobbled courtyard, straight for the open foundry.

Turning purple now, he entered the stone room that held all Nuaki Village's workable metals. Once inside, he lifted his hands, and the entire room was at once coated with iron.

This should give me time to think.

He needed to calm his mind and assess this situation with both eyes open.

Thirty-two.

BOOM!

The iron-laced room contained the explosion, yet rocked Nuaki's exterior walls and foundations. Once the energy had let loose, Irwin summoned all the copper in the room to coat his body, hoping to ground this rampant power.

I need to think grounding thoughts. Grounding thoughts; meadows, butterflies, flowers.

How do I get out of this? Should I go into the jungle? Be on land, on grounding soil. Where trees can fall on me after I explode?! No. I need to stay away from everything—keep all life safe.

He felt the urge to cry, to sob, but he could not falter for even one second.

What if this is how my life is from here to the end? What if this does not stop?

BOOM!

One. Two. Three.

He counted until thirty-two and erupted again.

He sat and counted again. The next few blow-outs he only counted to thirty-two, but by the third time he was able to reach thirty-three. Soon he heard a voice shouting at him from beyond the barricade.

It is Kipp!

Shit.

Keep your cool. You cannot help him if you cannot help yourself. Let this explosion happen, then go talk.

20

<u>Finding Sanity</u>

"Irwin?!" Kipp was hollering, his back turned to the forge when Irwin opened the door.

"I am glad to see you!" Irwin beamed with relief. He tapped his toe, counting down the time until the next explosion.

"What the fuk Irwin!" Kipp spun around. "They say you killed all the Erthins and the Telepaths. There's only something like sixty men left, they say, and that's out of two-hundred and somethin'. What the fuk? I thought you were gonna use your words—diplomacy, you called it."

"Calm down, Kipp."

"The tower is demolished. That whole side of the fortress—look at it!" Kipp turned toward the crumbling wall and its smoldering remains.

Irwin took his friend the by shoulders. "I have to ... I have to go."

"WHAT!?" Kipp screamed, and the door to the forge closed in his face.

Irwin flung himself into his metal cell, allowing his body to change color, explode, and rattle and thunder what was left of the fortress's exterior walls. He heard Kipp ranting outside the forge. He opened the door and stepped into the afternoon sunlight.

"They tried to kill me, Kipp. This is ...." He looked at his hands, pulling back the metallic façade to see his pale flesh. "I cannot control it, Kipp." He held back the urge to sob. "I do not know what is happening to me. I do not know what to do."

Kipp's eyes glistened golden. "Hey, it's okay, Irwin. We'll figure this out."

"I explode on the count of thirty-eight. The energy is dissipating, but slowly. And the magnitude of the energy of these explosions will bring this whole place down." Their eyes locked. "I am holed up in here hoping that everyone who can get out is out. I do not want to be on land, but I am not sure I want to be here either."

"How'd this happen?"

"Bejorn. Do not worry, he got what he deserved." His hands started to turn color again. "I will be back."

This time Kipp saw the flesh changing colors.

"What the fuk is that? Why is that happening?"

"It is a spell," and he recoiled back into the dark forge—now his lair.

The building rattled, shaking loose mortar and scraps of wood as he exploded.

Kipp pointed upward when Irwin stepped out of the room again. "We might wanna leave this place. Looks like you're gonna bury yourself within the next few ..." He jumped back, away from falling bricks. "... next few explosions."

I am defeated.

His shoulders sagged. His head shook with deep regret. "I do not know what else to do, Kipp. I feel safest in here, and if they are all out there, then they are safe—safe from me."

"Bejorn cast this spell?"

"He created a ball of nuclear energy, which I assimilated along with his body and soul. I thought I could ground it out, but ...."

"Jorge said he saw men on fire running around. He got all the animals out after the second explosion. And I felt it two kilometers upstream. He said it sounded like the end of the world." Kipp rubbed his neck. "Looks like it to me."

"You said only sixty or so men got out?"

"Yeah." Kipp watched him as his flesh changed color. "At least you know when it's gonna happen."

Inside the dark chamber, he let the energy blow. When he was back outside, Kipp spoke with barely a breath.

"The men are in the orchard. They're a morbid bunch. They were betting on how fast this place would crumble when I found them. Some were placing bets on you and Bejorn—who would win, until several of the raptors ..." he pointed up toward the spiraling birds, "... said they saw no one fighting outside—only the explosions and disintegration of the buildings."

"Do they have our horses?"

"Yeah, Jorge has them. He used them to pull a wagonload of animals out of the stables."

"I am a monster."

"Yeah, you are! This is why my nose told me not to be around you when we first met."

"I am Death."

"You're something, that's for sure."

His body was heating up again, his skin shifting colors. "Stay here. I will be back." Irwin sealed himself in.

Send Kipp on. He needs to find the carriage; he needs to see the truth. I cannot convince him otherwise.

When he opened the door, Kipp spoke first. "I got your message."

"You did?" Irwin rubbed his head, yawned. "So that did happen."

My head is messed up from those Telepaths.

"I was unsure that really happened." He stifled a yawn. "So many things have transpired since last night. So, you got my message, and ...."

"I smelled her at the bog the other day when we were there."

"You smelled her?!"

"I smelled her twice—well, once. But when I went back this morning, I smelled the same spot to be sure my mind wasn't playing tricks on me."

"Wait, you are saying that ...."

"Yeah! She's with the carriage, Irwin. I knew she wouldn't take a boat. Well, maybe from Lady Gretchen's place to Arenu Village, but she got back on that carriage in Arenu Village."

"How sure are you, Kipp?" His body was warming again, but he did not want to leave the conversation. Nevertheless, he stepped inside, closed the door, exploded, and then returned to Kipp.

"I smelled her," Kipp said. "I know her smell. No one can fake that!"

"Did you follow it?"

"I did! I followed the carriage's trail. They used Erthin powers to make that tunnel we all saw back at the bog. They drove toward an old fortress but changed course through an overgrown orchard, which was tough to find."

"Where did it go?"

"Crossed the river."

That might explain why it deviated from Nuaki Village.

"So, did you find the carriage, Kipp?"

"No. Someone decided to explode and cause a ruckus." They laughed—a moment of lightheartedness.

"So, you came to watch me decimate Nuaki Village?" Irwin did not need to keep counting—tapping his toe—he could feel his body warming and the energy percolating. He stepped back into his lair.

"Well, since I didn't get to see how you destroyed the Hall in Onj Raha ...." Kipp watched the door seal in front of him again.

Irwin smiled when he stepped back out from his lair, his worries melting away if for only a twinkle. "You actually think she is with the carriage?"

"Yeah, I'm positive she is. I'd bet my life on it!"

He looked around, happy to see Kipp again, eager to find Yace. "Well, I am in no shape to follow the carriage. You will have to, but do not get too close. Not without me."

"I don't want you to have all the fun."

"You think this is fun?"

They stared at each other, flat-faced. Kipp smiled, "Oh. You were right!"

"Huh?" Irwin said, "What about?"

"I can fly!"

Irwin nearly flew from the floor himself. "About time you tried! I told you, you could." He receded into the dark forge.

"That's how I got here so fast after following the carriage. It crossed the river, just beyond the old Nuaki Village fortress. That place looks haunted!"

For the brief time he was inside the forge, surrounded by the resonating iron metal, Irwin saw a correlation he had not thought of. "I think my great grandfathers were the ones who destroyed that old fortress. How ironic that I would do the same thing to this one," he had returned to Kipp from the safe hold.

"What? Wait. How do you know that?"

"The whole Nuaki community moved from there to here about sixty years ago, about the same time my great grandfathers arrived. They were a little older than I am now when they came through—back then. From what I was told, they were ornery men and were said to have killed at least thirty, maybe more."

"That fortress looked broken, for sure. And I saw some of those *Shayot* kids. They look mean, beings I wouldn't wanna cross. And Flinn's getting that type of training right now from Leola and Alio. She's gonna be a deadly assassin; I know it."

Irwin stared off.

The tortured life we Metalists lead.

He felt his temperature rise and stepped back into the forge.

"I wonder if that's how Dephen's men knew of the old road." Kipp muttered to Irwin's back as he sealed himself again.

I am glad to see Kipp can use his brain for investigative purposes.

He exploded. As he once again returned to the light, he said, "Oh! You were correct, Kipp!"

"Who? What?! Me?"

"Dephen visited Nuaki Village. Teigahn told me."

"Wow! Me, right about something? How long ago was that?"

"Long before Teigahn was born. Possibly around the time my great grandfathers were here."

"Dang me. You think they knew about each other?"

Irwin shrugged.

"Why's the wagon out on the bridge?"

"To keep the tower from collapsing on it."

"It collapsed alright! The river is strewn with all kinds of stuff." Kipp rubbed the back of his neck. "You gonna be alright in here?"

"I do not know what else to do."

"Well, then, I'm gonna get the horses and the girls."

"Good idea. Get going before you cannot."

Irwin was left to explode.

"You should get out too, Irwin." Kipp yelled. "You'll bury yourself in there. This entire wall looks ready to collapse, and those two sections will probably follow; they're all attached."

Irwin put his hand on Kipp's shoulder. "Tell the men I am sorry for destroying their home."

"Somehow, I don't think they'll believe me."

"This was not my fault, Kipp. The Telepaths were going to do what they wanted to me. It did not matter if I went willingly or not. They want me destroyed. I am realizing that nothing can destroy me except time, or a cave-in."

But they tried that, and I did not die.

"Well, this is about to cave-in." Kipp pointed at loose bricks. "I'm not hanging around to watch it all fall on you, immortal or not. Get out while you can, Irwin, please."

Irwin shook his head, feeling the weight of Nuaki, and all the others he did not mean to kill. His flesh was changing colors. "Go Kipp." He stepped back into the dark room now encased in iron and closed the door.

This time, his explosion rattled roof tiles loose; several rows streamed down off the tall peaks, shattering on impact. Kipp jumped out of the way and took to the air in his crane form. Irwin opened the door and watched Kipp's slow lift to flight.

Be safe, Kipp.

Kipp sailed across the rooftop. The village groaned, and Irwin returned to the hot cell.

21

<u>DOOMED</u>

Irwin remained inside the metal enclosure, where he felt safe. He knew the weight of the fortress was literally on him—as heavy as his conscience. Nuaki Village was nothing more than crumbling rubble. A few sections of exterior stone wall stood weak and battered, but there was nothing inside the mounds of smoldering wreckage. It would take a long time to sift through the remains if the few who remained wanted to rebuild.

He pondered Bejorn's Elemental spell. Although the power still radiated and burst, he felt it dissipating.

Maybe I am not doomed.

Just as he had done when he was buried alive at Lady Gretchen's, Irwin sent up a metal rod through the wreckage. It pushed past countless feet of heavy debris before finding the surface and the probe broke free. He pumped more metal into it, expanding the tube enough to allow fresh air and the waning light into his dark cell.

It was late afternoon, almost evening. He could tell by the angle of the sun's rays. Using all the metal in the forge, he climbed out into the wasteland he had created. Nuaki Village was nothing more than piles of stone. The smell of lingering death seeped into his nose and heart.

He watched crows circling above against a surprisingly blue sky. They had been circling the wreckage all day, watching, waiting for him to emerge. They were all Clan-Duins acting as eyes for the Telepaths who had escaped the destruction. From the north, Irwin could feel the presence of knives, some moving and some idle along the riverbank; they would be strapped to the remaining men of Nuaki Village. He chose to ignore the natives for now—more curious about the destruction he had wrought.

He saw a body move around a mound of rubble. He felt a knife affixed to a leg, felt it climbing over piles of debris, heading straight for him. He followed the movements and shadows, and then saw that it was Jorge.

Jorge's empathic appearance was that of Yace stepping over a heap of roofing, looking for signs of life.

He called out to Jorge, "Do not come any closer." He was changing colors again. "I cannot control the blast. And I do not know the radius of the burst."

Jorge watched with wide eyes as Irwin's metallic body glowed and shifted colors—purple, then blue—until the cycle ended in bright white light. Jorge shielded his eyes from the blinding light. He was far enough to not be flattened by the decimating power.

He called to Irwin, "What's going on, Samuel?"

"Nothing anyone can help me with," Irwin sighed. "Just so you know, I did not want this. I do not want bloodshed and destruction on my hands, and I never did. I am a peaceful person, Jorge. I did not mean for any of this to happen. You must let them know that."

"How'd this happen?"

"The Telepaths know."

"You killed many men today."

"Yes, I know." Irwin's shoulders hung like weights tied around his neck.

"Is this fallout from Lieutenant Bejorn's prohibited spell?"

"Yes. This was his spell. But you would not have that knowledge, Jorge. You might know who all is dead, but you would not care who created whatever spell that brought down Nuaki Village. Who am I really talking to?"

Forty. Forty-one.

"It's me, Jorge."

"No. You are a Telepath using Jorge. Who are you?"

Jorge's facade morphed from Yace to Albert with a menacing look. He did not reply as he watched Irwin's metallic façade change colors.

Irwin took a few steps back to blow up and then advanced swiftly toward Jorge. He grabbed Jorge's forearm, shedding the enigmatic appearance and Telepath's hold.

Jorge blinked and pulled away from Irwin's grasp. "Why are you holding me?"

"You were being used by a Telepath. I freed you from their mental grasp."

"Oh." Jorge softened his attitude and his posture. "Well then, thank you."

"You are welcome. Did you know you had been mentally taken?"

"It happens all the time with those telepathic bastards. They all hate me."

"Well, it is obvious that they like you for something. They sent you to talk to me."

"It's unnerving." Jorge upturned the side of his lip in disgust.

"Do you know what they want?"

"I know they want you to leave, but they're worried that you're just catching your breath before killing the rest of us."

"I do not want to kill! I have never wanted to. It is they whom harbor all this hatred and disgust toward me, not the other way."

"Sounds about right. You gonna do something about it?"

"No." He turned his attention toward his wagon, driving away in a southward direction.

"I think you should," Jorge egged, "I think you should kill the rest of those telepathic mates and all their cronies and be done with Nuaki Village."

Irwin stepped back twenty paces and pushed out the boiling energy. "Why do you want me to do that, Jorge? Are they so deserving of death? It is quite permanent, you know."

"Nuaki Village," Jorge was dramatic, opening his arms wide. "The worst of the worst live here, and you wanna save them?"

"You are not the worst of the worst, are you?"

"There're far worse offenders than me here; you're right, but none of them deserve to live."

He stared at Jorge who he now saw in his own image. "You have never seemed threatening, to me at least. But you say I should kill everyone?"

"You could spare me."

Irwin chuckled, "Why would I spare you if I am going to kill everyone else? I might as well kill you all. I do not think that anyone would miss the worst of the worst." Irwin let go another deep sigh, "But then that makes me worse than any of you, and that is not me. I do not want to be considered the worst of the worst, nor do I believe I am. I do not want to kill anymore. Understand?" He felt the energy growing warm from within, and his skin changed colors again.

When the first explosions happened, the energy radiated a hundred feet, but now the blast was only about twenty feet all around. First came a blast of flames, then hurricane wind, then water as intense as the bottom of a towering waterfall, and finally the earth elements; the powers of these explosions sought to ignite, suffocate, drown, and obliterate all remaining carbon atoms within its sphere. Anyone standing too close to Irwin would die instantly.

Jorge shielded his eyes, but looked back at Irwin as soon as the bright light receded. "Why does that keep happening?"

Irwin walked over and touched Jorge's arm. "It is Bejorn's own spell. A spell that Admiral Argustos argued should not be used."

"I've always hated Bejorn."

"Well, he is dead now, so you do not have to worry about him anymore."

"Good riddance. How'd he die?"

"He is in here." Irwin patted his chest. "I absorbed him and this powerful spell he created to kill me."

"Bejorn couldn't kill you? Impressive."

"No. But he tried." Irwin's eyebrows lifted, "Oh, he did try!" They both chuckled.

"He always boasted that he could kill anyone anytime." Jorge added, "Oh, and it looks like you killed all the Erthins."

"That is what Kipp said." Irwin understood now what had happened. The energy that first emanated took all Erthin lives within several kilometers, obliterating them. He believed he could feel those souls added to the ones he had already assimilated.

"I witnessed Emett and Loc burn up at the forge." Jorge held a horrified look. His eyes said it all. "I think you killed all the Erthins everywhere, Samuel."

Irwin stepped back for another explosion. "No!" He was haunted by the idea that he killed more than the men close-by. "No, I did not kill all the Erthins."

"You sure? There are none alive that lived here. Even the *Shayot* Erthins were killed."

"The *Shayot*?" His heart sank.

I do not want to kill innocent children!

"I heard the Telepaths say your power is unlike anything they've ever witnessed. They really want you dead."

"You actually heard them say that?"

"I've heard a lot of things about you today." Jorge confessed, shrugging with an impish grin.

"I know I extinguished over a hundred Erthin lives today." He saw Jorge mouth the number. "There were countless others who also died—who did not need to."

"Oh, they deserved what was coming. Trust me on this," Jorge said.

Irwin closed his eyes and stepped back, feeling the energy grow again. Most of the Erthin men killed had been in close proximity—within or around Nuaki Village—while others killed, further away, were most likely Shayot and their teachers. He put his hands over his face, hiding his tears from Jorge. "I killed many of your people today. I am truly sorry."

"These are not my people," Jorge sourly replied. "My people—if they're still alive—live somewhere else on Urthis." Jorge shielded his eyes when Irwin changed colors.

After exploding, Irwin said, "You do not think your people are still alive?"

"No. I'm the last Empath."

"That's a bold statement. I know I am not the last of my kind, even if those Telepaths want me to be."

"That's what I've told myself for years. They've also told me I can never leave."

"Why?"

Jorge scoffed and stepped out of range of Irwin's Metalistic grounding powers. His empathic being shone like Irwin's. "I can't go anywhere. I'm not a welcome sight. I scare people who don't know me."

"When I first met you, you wore a robe and kept to yourself. I did not know what an Empath was."

"I wore the robe to stay warm that morning. In Arenu Village, most people are accepting of me."

"Most? Very few were hospitable to me."

"You look Mortal. You even act like one."

"Looks can be deceiving, my friend."

"And you were challenged there too!"

"Yes, I was."

"And they lost. Man, they lost!" Jorge snickered. "I wouldn't wanna be on your bad side."

Irwin closed his eyes. His body was ready to blow. He counted his steps back, and when he stopped, he called to Jorge. "I do not want to be seen as an angry or bad person, Jorge. Do you understand that?"

Irwin detonated with all the force either of them could imagine.

"I do, but *They* don't."

"Who is in command? Do you know?"

"Command?" Jorge snorted. "Teigahn's in command—the dumbass."

"Corporal Teigahn?!" He muttered, "He is a minion not a commander."

Jorge snorted and snickered.

Irwin's head and heart both hurt.

I wish I had never left the mountains. Warmer weather was not worth all this bloodshed.

He did not want to think about all whom he had killed. "Kipp said there are about sixty people still alive."

"There's about seventy people. But not all of them are at the river. There're shepherds tending to the herds east of the Nuaki, although I heard several of those Erthin/Clan-Duin mixes …" Jorge's laugh had a sinister edge. "… burst into flames while all the chaos was happening. Even though they were close enough to the river to extinguish the fire, they died anyway."

"Horrible. I am horrible." He slunk away.

I am not fit to be alive. Yet they could not kill me, even with the wrath reminiscent of Jebadia. And there is nothing I can do to remedy any of this.

He exploded.

I cannot let this get me down. But I killed again! I said I would not, and I meant it. None of those men deserved to die.

"It's not that horrible." Jorge said.

"No one deserved to die today." Irwin was weighed by his remorse. "Except, maybe Bejorn."

Yes. That man definitely deserved to die.

Irwin added, "He said it took a soul to make his spell. So, he killed the Telepath who was supposed to be controlling me. Corporal Andel, I think his name was."

"Andel? Huh. I don't remember seeing him today."

"Well, he is dead, but by the hand of the Lieutenant, not me—I saw it."

"Dang, that's malicious."

I need to get away from these people. I need to save them from me.

"'The needs of the many outweigh the needs of the one.' Bejorn said that right before …."

That is how I feel right now. My needs do not count. I must think of everyone else.

Jorge laughed at hearing those words come from Irwin. "Bejorn loves to say that. Of course, he's usually victorious."

Irwin wanted to sink to the floor. He was physically and mentally exhausted.

"You hungry?" Jorge asked.

Sustenance. Yes.

"I have not eaten in what seems like days." He was famished and dehydrated. "Yes, please, that would be nice. And some water too, thank you. Thank you, Jorge." He wondered aloud, "Why do you want to help me? I thought you feared me." His body warmed. It was time to move away, to protect Jorge.

"As I see it, I'm safer with you than any of those Telepaths."

After he exploded one more time, Irwin said, "Possibly. You seem to know I will not treat you like a pawn. And they know I will talk to you. So, you are not afraid of me anymore?"

"As I said, you're the lesser of the evils."

"Are you sure of that?"

"I'm not sure of anything right now." Jorge turned to leave but veered back toward Irwin. "Fruit and water?"

"Yes, thank you." He was humbled that someone would be nice to him after all he had done.

He moved around the island of rubble piles, assessing all his options; all the while exploding less and less.

I am an abomination. I am not safe anymore, and I should not be with Kipp. My flesh and blood could kill him. But I made promises. Now they are promises I cannot keep.

I cannot save Yace.

I should never have left the mountains. What was my reason for leaving father?

Irwin snorted at his momentary stupidity.

How could I forget he left me? Left me for dead!

Had I not left the mountains, I would never have learned about myself, my abilities. I would not know what I now know.

But I have killed so many people.

So has father.

This just shows I am no better than him.

If I had not left, I never would have met Kipp. I would not know what love is.

Love? What do I know about love? I know Kipp loves Yace! He will never love me … barely tolerates me.

I must remember that this is all about Yace. She needs me. But how can I help her when I am like this?

Fuk. We are in deep trouble. What are we going to do? How are we going to get to her before …?

Yace is a sacrificial lamb, just like Kipp and me. This is how Dephen wants it. He wants me captured, killed. And he wants Kipp lured to his death too. He is so clever he convinced the PCP that my coming here was all their doing.

What did Admiral Argustos say right before I was bludgeoned? 'While Dephen is changin' the regime, you and the Clan-Duin will be disposed of.'

That cannot be true. Then they would be in cahoots. Maybe he said what he said to catch me off guard long enough for Corporal Teigahn to act. Damn, I hate Telepaths.

He watched the river flow to the east.

He took a seat, watched the trees along the south bank sway with a twilight wind that had come in from the west. "I hope Kipp still wants to be my friend after all this."

I need to get to him before he finds the carriage. If Yace is not there, he will be so angry.

Now that Irwin was out in the fresh air and not physically contained, the explosions' radius was becoming smaller, and the bursts of energy took longer to come. By the time Jorge returned, Irwin could count to fifty-seven before discharging.

When he saw Jorge, instead of taking the water or the fruit being offered, he grabbed Jorge's arm, making sure Jorge's mind was his.

Jorge chuckled. "I wasn't sure they were gonna let me come back to you. We argued, and an agreement was made."

"What was the agreement?"

"That I can bring you this food and water as long as you leave immediately."

"Right now?"

"Yeah. They say you can go on to Daos, but you're not allowed to go north."

"Really? Teigahn said that? May I talk to him?"

"Why do you want to talk to that asshole?" Jorge recoiled from Irwin's grasp.

"I know you do not want to allow him access, Jorge, but I would like to talk to Corporal Teigahn. He might be the only one who will understand what I have to say."

Jorge folded his arms across his chest. "I am not sure I want any part in ...." Without warning, he froze and could not speak.

When he recovered, his voice and his demeanor were changed. "You wish to speak to me? Why?"

Irwin curled his lip at the hasty takeover of Jorge. "I am done with all you Telepaths believing that you can manipulate without discord. And you cannot keep me from going or doing as I wish. I am done with manipulation of me and my friends. I vow to keep them safe from your mental grasp."

"You cannot keep them all safe."

"I can and I will."

"What about your friend Kipp Hauler?"

Irwin could feel his metal wagon rolling farther away. "He is safe." Yet he knew Kipp would not be able to fend for himself if a Telepath was near, but all the Erthins close by were dead so ....

"How sure are you?" said Teigahn.

"Teigahn, I want you and your telepathic friends to understand that mindsets cannot be permanently altered. Believing that you have all the power, all the ability to control others, will be your downfall. I am here to let the people know that they are just as powerful as any other being, including Telepaths. We are all equal. We all have the right to live unimpeded. You and your manipulative friends have been warned. The more you try to control others, the more they will gain control of themselves. Be prepared!" He reached up and grasped Jorge's arm with force, pulling the Empath back to himself.

Jorge said, "Wow, you look angry!"

"I let them know what I think. By the way, you should have no reason to fear Telepaths. We are just as strong as them, if not better!"

"Yeah? How so?"

"Because we do not use telepathy to spy on others—to get our own way."

"Ha. That's a lie. They're better than us because they use their powers, their telepathy, to get their way." Jorge spat on the ground. "They enjoy taking advantage of others. You can't stop them. No one can."

"As long as I am around, I can keep you safe from them, Jorge."

"That's foolish thinking. You can't keep anyone but yourself safe. Even then ...." He pointed at Irwin's skin, transmuting colors again.

Irwin stepped away. "You are right. I cannot keep you safe. But I want to." He exploded. "None of us deserve to be telepathic pawns."

But we all seemingly are.

Jorge held the flask and meal safe and offered it to Irwin when he returned.

"Thank you." He appreciated Jorge's kindness, even though he was hesitant to fully trust the Empath. He drank what he could, ate a whole banana and half an apple, and then handed the food and drink back to Jorge when he moved back to discharge again.

It was almost dark. The smell of charred flesh still lingered in the air. Smoke smoldered up from under piles of rubble. The cloudy sky shone hues of orange, then purple. Dusk fell over what was left of Nuaki Village. Firelight radiated from the north side of the river. Irwin turned toward the south and calculated his next move.

Jorge asked, "What are you gonna do now?"

"I think I am ready to head south." He studied the horizon with tired eyes.

"You know you need to move your feet to head south."

Irwin's skin glowed once again. Anyone looking his way could see the progression of colors emanating from his body. "I must wait. I do not want to blow up the bridge."

Jorge took a few steps back, allowing Irwin his space to explode.

After this blast, Irwin started running. He did not want to destroy anything else, including the southern bridge. At breakneck speed, he nearly made it to the other side, but his skin began to glow.

Irwin threw himself over the side of the bridge and into the water. Ripples radiated around him and then water shot up and rained down along with dead fish. Thirty feet from land's edge, he swam to the bank and lay on the ground and blasted forth another time. He fell back into the water. Shaking himself off, he clambered up the bank and began walking away from Nuaki Village.

22

<u>DUPED</u>

Kipp saw the rest of Nuaki Village collapse and believed Irwin to be dead. He recalled Irwin saying, *'I can only die from old age, or a cave-in'*.

He wiped tears from his face. "There's no way he could've survived that!"

He had to go on, find Yace, but it was Irwin who was supposed to save her. "How am I gonna do this now? There's no way to rescue Yace. When I come to her, I'll be under her control. I'm damned without Irwin."

But he would not forsake his mission. He was just not sure what to do next. Forcing the horses onward was all he could do for now. He didn't want to stay anywhere near Nuaki Village. He had to figure out how to save Yace without Irwin. But for now, that task felt insurmountable.

"She has to be up here somewhere."

He believed the carriage had rerouted to stay hidden. But Dephen's goal would remain the same: get to Daos. The carriage would have to return to the road going there, so Kipp led the horses onward, and he hoped to be there to meet him, to rescue Yace somehow.

Darkness enveloped Kipp, and he lit the lantern. It swayed rhythmically, casting haunting shadows. Jungle animals were preparing for the night, and they bellowed and cawed and growled and hissed. The wagon rolled on and the night quieted. After a while, the horses slowed their pace.

He had been lulled into a waking stupor when the smell of charred flesh and campfire hanging low in the humid nighttime air wafted into his nose. He pulled the horses to a halt and applied the brakes on the wagon. It creaked as it came to a stop on the roadway. He jumped down and gave apples to the animals to eat while he was gone. Leaving the wagon parked in the middle of the road, Kipp carefully approached a somewhat hidden camp.

"Why do I smell dead bodies?" Kipp wondered, inspecting the campsite through the foliage. It was difficult to get a good look without being seen.

Whoever it was, their campfire was burning brightly, lighting the trees above. Dark horses were tethered to nearby trees. And there it was, the colorful carriage in the middle of what would be the old road—partially masked by dense foliage.

The camp was eerily quiet, except for the croaking of frogs, the chirping of nocturnal birds and creatures. He did not hear any human murmurs, nor did he smell any other living beings besides jungle life—only the pungent scent of burned human flesh.

He approached the apparent barren camp with caution. Those tethered horses nickered at him and looked toward the carriage, hinting to something or someone inside. Kipp dropped to his knees, snuck around several trees—his eyes, ears, and nose all on high alert.

Anxious to step inside the camp, many odors wafted his way. He peered through the foliage. One of the horses pawed, begging for Kipp's attention—that horse had a story to tell.

The horses had witnessed something, but some were more spooked by the gruesome affair than others. They must have all heard the explosion and felt the wind from the blast, but with it came another rippling effect that had instantly incinerated all the full Erthins in the camp. Men burst into fire and incinerated into nothingness. Their ashes blew away like lit sparks from a campfire. One partial Erthin/Clan-Duin, however, had caught fire and raced around the camp trying to put himself out before crumpling into a heap of charred body and bones. It had been the flailing and screaming that had probably scared the horses most of all.

Kipp took a step back, mortified by what he had just seen through the horse's mind's eye. "What a horrible way to die."

A campfire was still burning, and a small, skinned animal was cooking over the fire. The men Kipp had just seen burning up had died during daylight hours. By now, the fire would have gone out and the food would be charred. "There's still one soldier alive." Kipp scoured the camp, smelling everything, including Yace's essence. Her scent drifted from the carriage.

He crept around the camp, hiding in the brush, sneaking up to the carriage door. He slowly opened it, panting. He sprang inside where he was met by a musty feline Clan-Duin odor that laced throughout, even the bedding and the curtains. Repulsed, Kipp rifled through baggage and personal effects on the bed, searching for any sign of his beloved.

"She must be here. Where else would she be?"

Kipp and Irwin had been following Yace for many moons, or so Kipp believed. He had smelled her scent back at the bogs, so he was certain they were gaining ground, still on her trail. The carriage held signs of her. Her scent lingered.

Then he spotted one of Yace's pouches hidden under a blanket. Inside were two perfectly rounded metal rocks—encased and smoothed by Irwin—along with several throwing knives that Irwin had rebalanced. He also found her small handmade leather doll Dana had given her after she became a Gypsy many years ago. These were her treasures that had been left behind. "She's on the run. I need to catch up."

Kipp stuffed Yace's treasures under his shirt and left the carriage door open after leaping to the ground. He stepped around the coach; the smell of Yace's excrement was profuse. There were two metal containers attached to the back of the carriage. He lifted the lids and looked inside—one held her scat, and the other her urine. Dephen's soldiers had been leaving her scent markers all along the way for Kipp to follow. Dephen and his men knew Kipp would use his nose and his heart to follow Yace.

He had been conned.

He shouted at the top of his lungs, "FUK!"

He had never felt so blind, so stupid, so humiliated. He should have known Yace was not close. They had bonded sexually. They had a connection with each other. They could sense how the other was feeling, or if the other was hurt or killed. Dephen had severed that bond without Kipp knowing.

He stood in the middle of the camp, seething; he wanted answers—dumping empty sacks and boxes over, trampling on and tossing blankets into the brush. Nothing would soothe his rage. He emptied the pack bags onto the ground and kicked around the contents. By the time he was finished, he crouched panting in the heart of it. The abandoned camp had been thoroughly ransacked.

Those soldiers and whomever had been there for more than one night. "They've probably been spying on us!" His nostrils flared. "Dang me. A fukin' decoy. Irwin was right. Fuk!

"I didn't want Irwin to be fuking right! FUK!" He yanked drying clothes down off the limb of a tree and kicked over the roasting food, scattering embers, smoldering coals, and bits of meat. He tore everything out of the carriage. He came across a stash of money—a few dozen gold pieces in a wooden box. There were also plentiful rations, as many as Irwin had bought for them. There was even a keg of alcohol.

"And I thought Yace was excessive! She obviously gets that from her father."

He tossed all the soldier's belongings out onto the ground; stealing what he deemed of use. While he was stuffing the valuable stash in ration boxes and bags, he heard the donkeys' bellow. They were often much keener to the movements in the jungle than the warhorses, and quick to warn against trouble.

He jumped from the carriage and crept toward the donkeys, a box of food in hand. He came face to face with a hefty canine Clan-Duin. "You must be the last of Dephen's soldiers. I was wondering when you'd show up."

Hackles up and growling deeply, the canine hurdled at Kipp. But already on high alert, Kipp used the box of food to block the first blow. He advanced with force, tossing the box at the Clan-Duin. The second time they tussled, he grabbed onto the soldier. They moved in tandem with the velocity of that impact; Kipp fell forward and threw his adversary away from his body. The canine slid on his side, but jumped back onto his feet in one motion. This gave Kipp enough time to ready himself for another attack. He was ready to let out all his wrath.

He wanted this canine soldier to transform into his two-legged form so he could be questioned as they sparred. The aggressive Clan-Duin jumped for Kipp, lunging at his throat, but that maneuver was counteracted, and the dog was tossed into the brush.

As his opponent jumped up on his four feet, Kipp demanded, "Where's Dephen?"

The canine lunged again, and Kipp whipped his leg high into the air, kicking the vicious dog's face. Hitting the ground hard, the Clan-Duin canine stumbled and struggled to regain his footing. "Tell me where they went!"

Laughing, the dog flung himself toward Kipp and spun around as he made contact. Immediately, Kipp's arms were pulled behind his back in a lock-hold position. The canine landed on Kipp's back, mutating as he went, and straddled him.

The naked Clan-Duin soldier leaned down and whispered, "Your precious Yace is dead."

Although his body was pinched, Kipp knew that if he mutated into a small enough creature, he could squeeze out between his opponent's legs, somersault, and mutate back into his two-legged form before this stranger knew what had happened. He leaped back onto his feet, rubbing his right shoulder.

The soldier smiled and jumped into the air, mutating into a bird with a wide wingspan, and attempted to fly away into the night. Just as fast, Kipp transformed into his new crane body and both birds went for each other, each for the other's neck. They both sought blood, vengeance, and death.

Blows were dealt. Blood poured. Bones cracked. It was a battle of wits and metamorphosis. The screeching of each bird pierced the night jungle. Any nearby creature was either running away or trying to get out of the battle. The horses shuffled around the trees where they'd been hitched, snorting and whinnying. The donkeys brayed for all the world to hear.

A loud popping of bone announced defeat.

Landing on the ground with a loud thud, Kipp was at once his two-legged self. He howled in pain. His right shoulder had been dislocated. It burned and throbbed. Behind the howling came the adrenaline; Kipp was not done with this fight. His right arm hung limp, but he lurched forward with his only capable hand, reaching for the Clan-Duin opponent who had followed him to the ground. The soldier jumped to the side, drawing Kipp's eyes to Yace's pouch; it was only a few feet away.

"Did you think you were a match for me? I'm a trained *Shayot*!" The soldier sneered as they both looked at the pouch, both aware of its significance.

It took Kipp but an instant to untangle the satchel's drawstrings and pull out the two throwing knives. If he had not been injured, the first throw would have hit its mark, but it flew right past the soldier's face.

"You throw like a child," the soldier roared. No time to blink. The second knife pierced his eye—a precise hit. The naked soldier fell over, dead.

Alone again, Kipp screamed out in agony. He looked at his shoulder—tears of pain welling in his eyes—as it hung limp at his side. His fingers hurt to touch, and his arm hurt to move—most undoubtedly broken.

"DANG IT!" He shouted, and pain shot through his body.

Horses nickered.

Using the side of his head as a brace, he stood, leaned against a tree, and rose to an upright position. His left arm cradled his right. He managed to take a few steps across the camp and kicked the soldier to make sure he was dead. "Dang me! I didn't get any fuking answers!"

He was bleeding with rage. Not only had he been duped, but now he was banged up and without hope of ever seeing Yace again. Blood dribbled from his broken nose. His eye and cheekbone throbbed. He felt the broken ribs on both sides of his chest, noticed a dislocated left thumb, and was certain his shoulder had been dislocated when they had fought while in flight as their bird selves. He stumbled toward the carriage, hoping Yace's leather bag of herbal remedies was in the pile he had dumped onto the ground. There it was, on top of the pile filled with herbs meant to help him rest and sleep, along with roots and powders for pain and swelling and a vial of poppy milk for the worst of it.

He licked his finger and stuck it into the turmeric pouch, and suckled the powder. He found a root of valerian and bit off a sizeable chunk. He drank it down with poppy milk. Gagging, he tried to keep all the nasty tastes from coming right up again. "Yuck! Ugh. I hope this gets rid of the pain."

He stumbled to the half-drunk cask of ale. "I might as well lay down and die—but with ale in me." He lay down below the spout and poured the alcohol into his mouth. After a long drink, he waited on the ground—hoping either the pain would end, or he would pass out or die.

23

<u>JORGE TO THE RESCUE</u>

Irwin advanced through the blackened jungle. Before each explosion, he could see his surroundings as if in daylight. But the darkness would soon return, leaving a pothole in the earth each time.

I wish this all could have been avoided. I wish Kipp would believe me when I say what I know to be true. I wish I had never left my mountains.

He tried to recall one of the tunes Bernard the Bard had sung as they had trudged through the snow down the mountainside oh so long ago. The words were not easy to remember, but the tune came to him like an old folksong.

From behind him, Jorge asked, "What are you humming?"

He had known Jorge was following—feeling his magnetic energy—many paces ago. All the same, Irwin jumped and turned. "Why are you here, Jorge?"

Jorge shrugged, but Irwin sensed there was some personal agenda at hand.

"Seriously, Jorge, go back. I cannot have you around me."

"I'm safe if I'm this far back."

"I am a ball of destruction."

Jorge chuckled. "Have you seen the bumps you've made on the road lately? The divots you're making are not like what you wrought in Nuaki. Besides, I'm not afraid of you."

You should be.

"Why are you following me?"

"Because I don't wanna be a pawn anymore."

After yet another detonation, Irwin walked over to make contact with Jorge's forearm. "They just let you go?"

Telepaths are shifty. I am not sure I can trust him.

"They don't control me," said Jorge. "They haven't been able to for quite some time. I just do as I am told and don't balk. That is not being controlled, that is being complacent. There is a difference."

"That is horseshit, Jorge, and you know it. They had control of you earlier today. They can take control whenever they want. Why are you here?"

"I want to go to Daos City. I want to find my people."

"And you think because I am going that way you are invited?"

Eyes locked. It was dark, but as Irwin's skin began to rotate colors and heat, he could see Jorge's face and his expressions in the light. "It's okay. If you don't want me to come, I'll take the old road back."

"Old road?"

"It's up here a little ways." He pointed down the darkened roadway.

"Does the old road go to the old Nuaki Village? Is it the road that starts at the bog?"

"Yeah," said Jorge. "It's possible I could stay with the *Shayot*. Although, I'm sure everyone else will take up residence there until Nuaki can be rebuilt." He paused. "It's possible I'd be welcome in Arenu Village, but ...."

"Do not follow me," Irwin said. His silvery skin glowed yellow and then orange. "Go to Arenu Village ..." He exploded. "... take passage on a boat bound for Daos. You would get there faster than we will."

"Why don't you take a boat?"

"I am not so sure about the ocean. I saw several storms from the shoreline on the way to Arenu Village—violent waves and churning water." He shook his head. "I would not do well in those conditions. Stuck out on the ocean, nowhere close to land—a vicious storm with swells taller than trees and hard winds strikes your sails and tosses you overboard. And suddenly you are holding onto a small hunk of hull with no hope for recovery." Irwin shuddered.

"Well, when you put it that way ...." Jorge fell silent.

Irwin could hear him jogging to keep up.

"A few years ago, when visiting Arenu, one of those types of storms hit," Jorge began a tale of the sea—his own story. "Waves blew up and over, cresting the eastern wall. The wharf flooded. So many boats were crushed. But the sounds of the waves crashing against the fortress .... Everything echoed. It was so loud. If there hadn't been Erthins, the whole place would've been decimated. They kept everyone safe—protected the fortress. I was with Ron the whole time. We felt the walls rumbling every time one of those enormous waves hit. It was something!"

"Do you always stay with them when you visit Arenu Village?"

"Yeah. I prefer to stay with Ron and Arrol. Not too many people like me in Arenu either. I could work for my keep at Gritty Titty, but that's not what I enjoy. I much prefer the stables—to be around the animals, cleaning up their shit—not getting it from others. But I probably wouldn't be allowed to work in the saloon, anyway. You know how intolerant pirates can be. That's why I stay hidden with the Eunuchs upstairs at Gritty Titty, and I work in the stables in Nuaki. I prefer to stay in the shadows. Darkness suits me. No one sees me, except the animals I care for. I couldn't do that in Arenu. That place is too open."

"They appeared more accepting of you than me. At least you look Talented."

They followed the roadway in silence for some time until Jorge offered him some water.

"Yes, please!" Irwin felt as though he had been parched for days.

Jorge passed the flask and went on. "I've never felt like I belonged in either place." He capped the water flask and said, "Oh, and you were right."

"About what?"

Second time today.

"I know how to defend myself. I'm a trained *Shayot*, you know. But like you, Samuel, I don't wanna fight."

"So, you want to find your family?"

"Yeah. I've been told that in Daos City there is a large section that allows people of Talent to live. Daos Prime, I think they call it. Though I'm not sure my people would be there, it'd probably be a good place to start."

Irwin exploded twice before he asked, "Do you know where you were born?"

"Out on the ocean. All I know is that my mother was a pirate, or something like that. She must've been raped, or maybe was a whore. That's how I came to be. Like I said before, there's no others who look like me."

Silence enveloped them again, and they ambled on through the night.

It was nearly morning when they spotted a light in the distance—the lantern on Irwin's wagon. They smelled burned flesh, and the odor of defecation hung heavy in the humid air.

"Ugh, Hakra," Jorge muttered and pinched his nose.

Irwin stopped, holding Jorge to his side, and whispered, "Let me go first."

They could barely see into the dimly lit camp from the backside of his wagon, and there were, to his surprise and joy, his Jennies eating foliage along the road's edge. Jenn Jenn came to him for a scratch; he nuzzled her and crept around the wagon's side. He edged past Roper and Bodi, touching them as he went. Then his body began, yet again, to make ready for the detonation.

I am silly for thinking I could remain hidden.

He stood, his skin shone colors, and then he blew. If anyone was in that camp, they surely saw and heard him.

He called in a whisper, "Kipp?"

The horses nickered at him as he moved toward the trees where they were tied. He patted their haunches, and there, between their rumps, he spotted two naked Clan-Duins. Both were beaten up. One was obviously dead, the other ....

"Kipp! Oh shit, Kipp. Kipp. What happened?"

"I thought his name was Hauss?" Jorge stepped through a block of foliage. "Woah. What happened here?"

"Kipp," Irwin bent over his unconscious friend, listening for a breath, feeling his bruised chest for a heartbeat. His hands shook. "Oh, Kipp."

"At least he's not that guy."

"He is alive. I hear his heart. Kipp, can you hear me?"

"He looks dead."

"Kipp," Irwin whispered, "Please stay with me." He touched Kipp's forehead and chest, inducing spirit energy into the banged-up body. He called on all the spirits he knew and all the healing he was capable of.

"Irwin. You gotta go do your thing." Jorge pointed to Irwin's arms—he was about ready to explode.

Irwin raced away from the animals and his friends in time for another blast and then ran back to Kipp's side.

Jorge stepped over to the cask lying on the ground and rattled it. "Feels about half full. You think he's just drunk?"

Irwin ignored Jorge, pleading with Kipp, "How hurt are you?" Again, he placed his hands on Kipp's chest.

"What are you trying to do, Irwin?" Jorge leaned over Irwin and Kipp.

Irwin said nothing, eyes closed. He was assessing the damage to Kipp's body. Heat radiated from Kipp's shoulder—a measurement of the damage. "His nose, ribs, cheek, and eye socket are broken. There is tearing of muscles, but the worst is his shoulder." Irwin cocked his head sideways, trying to feel all Kipp's afflictions. He summoned Kipp to wake.

"Ugh." Kipp was groaning now.

"Kipp!"

"Irwin?" Kipp's breath reeked of alcohol. "Are we dead?"

"No, we are not dead."

Kipp struggled to open his eyes. "Yace. Yace! You saved her. I knew you would." "That is not Yace, Kipp. That is Jorge."

"Yace. Yace."

"Oh, for fuk sake, I'm not Yace," Jorge growled.

Kipp continued making drunken sounds. "I love you. Come back, my beloved." He tried to reach with his injured arm, "Oh, fuk. Oh, fuk." He passed out again.

"Kipp? Kipp! Kipp, what is wrong with you?"

Jorge had been walking around the camp. "I found this bag of herbs and stuff. It looks recently gone through." He passed the satchel to Irwin who was cycling through colors again.

He shoved the bag back at Jorge and ran from camp.

While Irwin was again discharging and exploding, Jorge sifted through the leather bag—opening pouches, smelling roots, and tasting herbs. "This smells like turmeric root. This is chamomile. Here is mint and black elm bark. This is witch hazel. I think this is valerian root, and salt, and, um, the vial is poppy milk."

Irwin examined roots that had been recently chewed.

"If he ate the valerian and mixed it with the ale and poppy milk, his heart could stop." Jorge studied Kipp, his hand on Irwin's shoulder.

"What?"

"It's happened with men in training who were hurt before a healer could get to them. *Shayot* are supposed to be able to handle the effects of milk of poppy, mushrooms, Tabaci, and other barbiturates. But that mixture can kill."

"Barbiturates?"

"Mind and body altering drugs."

"Shit. Kipp?!" He looked down at his beloved friend. "If I had to guess, I would say he ate the herbs for pain and swelling before he drank the ale, hoping to pass out. I am sure he knows what to do if he gets hurt, but probably did not know to not mix the herbs."

Kipp, do not die. Please.

"That's really stupid."

"Kipp's logic is, sometimes ...." He made a *Shayot* hand signal that meant dumb.

"Well, he probably won't die, but you'll wanna watch him, keep a close eye."

Irwin kept his hands on Kipp's chest, tried again to summon Kipp to consciousness. Jorge watched. "What are ya doing?"

Flooding Kipp with wakeful energy, Irwin thought aloud, "Maybe I should just let him rest."

"Ya think?"

"He is hurt. I should heal what I can and not tell him later."

"Why wouldn't you tell him?"

"Kipp does not think I am capable of healing him." Irwin wiped his brow. "He wants me to have formal training. But as with everything else in my life, I have learned as I go. And with over two dozen healers absorbed in my body, I can summon their power."

"How about summoning their knowledge?"

"I wish I could. If any of them could be alive and here to teach me, that would be—"

"If you have their power in you, then—in theory—you've got their knowledge, right?" Jorge grinned. "How hard could it be to actually heal your friend?"

"I do not want to hurt him." He knew how to heal bones; he knew what it felt and sounded like when they were mending. But muscles, tissue, organs, and ligaments—how they mended was foreign to Irwin. His own body innately did those repairs.

Kipp coughed and blood spurted from his mouth.

Jorge said, "You know what that means, right?"

"No!"

"He's probably drowning in his blood." Jorge seemed amused by the situation, and by Irwin.

Immediately, Irwin rolled Kipp onto his side.

"Ouch! Oh fuk, oh fuk." Kipp groaned, his eyes were swollen and one eye barely open at all.

Irwin pulled Kipp back toward him while his friend gurgled. He rolled Kipp toward his folded knees.

Kipp coughed several times and then fell back to sleep. Irwin cried, "No, Kipp. No! What do I do, Jorge?"

"Well, he's probably punctured a lung."

Irwin leaned close and listened to Kipp's breathing. His lungs were sputtering. "What would you do, Jorge?"

"Well, if you have the healing abilities of so many healers, I'd try healing his lungs."

Hands on Kipp, Irwin tried to pull the sitting blood from the lungs.

It is like water, pulling water ... but his body needs water, so you are just clearing the lungs, clearing the airway, letting air in, pushing the blood out.

Jorge reminded Irwin of his coming explosion.

He wanted only to keep his focus upon Kipp, yet the darn nuclear energy continued to percolate, interrupting him every time.

During one incident, Kipp awoke while Irwin was touching his eye socket and nose bones—fusing them back together. He reached for Irwin's arm. His brown eyes wide. "What are you doing, Irwin?"

"I am trying to heal you."

"No, don't please!"

"But I am almost done. Your nose, your eye–"

"Don't heal me."

"Alright, I will not heal you." He pulled his hands off Kipp who fell back into sleep.

"What the fuk was that?" Jorge called from a stone seat he had found near the smoldering fire pit.

"I think I should be done for now."

"But are you?"

"No."

24

MOVING THE WORLD

Jorge was able to put Kipp's dislocated shoulder and his left thumb back in place. He cleaned wounds, made poultices, wrapped bandages, and maintained a calm for both Kipp and Irwin.

Irwin kept on exploding for another two days and nights. He was exhausted. He was also angry at himself for not being of more help—having to ask Jorge to do the brunt of the work, including cooking. But Jorge didn't seem to mind being ordered around.

On the third morning, Irwin decided it was time to continue toward Daos Territory. He knew they were heading for a harsher landscape. The humidity remained as thick as his heartache about their situation.

While Kipp was healing, Irwin had turned inward. He had time to sit, feel, think, and to come to a deeper understanding of his situation—his newfound powers. On a profound level, he had come to an awareness—an innate knowledge—of organic matter, the elements, and how to masterfully manipulate these to his advantage. Not only did he see how fire was made with carbon dioxide, water vapor, oxygen, and nitrogen, now he could control each on a basic level. He could excite all carbon-based forms, lifting organic matter with a whirlwind of power. Now the task of moving their vehicle down an overgrown roadway was possible instead of insurmountable.

I believe I know how the road was created through that boulder field back in the Kruluver Mountains.

Every day was filled with new wonders, excitement, and self-discovery as Irwin led the two men, the donkeys, the horses, and the wagon down the gnarly old road toward Daos Territory.

One of the gifts from his newly charged power was the ability to heat anything with his bare hands or feet. He realized he could boil water just by holding a container between his arms or legs. There was no need for fire, and at this point, it was too humid to enjoy one. Their daily ration of rice was cooked by Irwin in minutes—a new trick, a new Talent, to perform at every meal.

As much as I feel cursed, I must thank Lieutenant Bejorn. He opened my awareness to all my Erthin gifts. And I must thank Admiral Argustos and Lady Gretchen for letting me know that maybe I am more Talented than my father would ever have given me credit for. Both said I was Coterie. And if I am, does that mean I'm related to Yace?

I always knew there was something different about me. Albert and Jebadia made me wrong for that difference; they tried to kill me for it. But out here, no one can make me wrong for being myself. Nor can they stop me from exploring all I can do.

He felt happy for the first time in a very long time—maybe ever.

Without his ability to manipulate the earth, they would have had to abandon the wagon and travel on foot. It would have taken much longer through the overgrowth and undergrowth on the road from Nuaki Village to Vidigen—the first township in Daos Territory they would come to. Time was of the essence. But instead of being on Yace's heals and closing in, Irwin was not sure she was savable any longer.

I must hope, for Kipp's sake, that we can still rescue her. Thankfully, Kipp is so out of it, he does not know what is happening.

Kipp had to be sedated for the drive in the bumpy wagon. Though Irwin tried to make the ground flat as possible, there were still rough spots. He hoped they had enough poppy milk to make it to Daos; Jorge assured him they would be able to purchase more once there.

As he walked ahead of the wagon clearing the landscape, he heard Kipp bellow, "It hurts! Too bumpy! You're going too fast! Stop. Stop. Stop! Owwwwch!"

"Irwin doesn't wanna slow down," Jorge grumbled from the driver's bench.

"Yace? How'd you ...."

"For the fuking ump-teenth time, I'm not Yace!"

Kipp was dazed, "Dinill?"

"I am not Dinill either, or Flinn, or your mother, or anyone else you fukin' know. Shut the fuk up!"

Kipp barked, "Fukin' Telepaths, leave me alone."

"Why can't you just heal him, Irwin," said Jorge. "Let's be done with all this bemoaning horseshit."

Ahead of the horses by ten strides, Irwin glanced back. He heard the conversation but did not want to get into it. "Kipp asked me not to, and I will respect that."

Kipp cried, "Irwin?!"

Time for another dose of poppy-milk.

I do not want Kipp to know what all we have done to heal him already.

Kipp reached for Jorge. "Have you been healing me, Irwin?"

Jorge turned. "Yes, I have! And against your will. What'll you do about it?"

Irwin was ahead of the horses, moving trees, brush, large stones, and decaying matter from the overgrown roadway. He did not want to stop, but he heard them arguing. Jorge looked, to him, like Jebadia. "Jorge, please do not antagonize Kipp. He needs to heal."

Kipp's voice cracked. "Please don't heal me, Irwin. I'm hurting bad."

"You're a dumb Clan-Duin," Jorge spat.

Irwin put up his hand, palm toward the horses, and they all stopped. Even the jungle held still right then.

He strode toward the wagon. "I am beginning to realize that you dislike Clan-Duins, Jorge. But please stop badgering him. It is not helpful. He needs to heal."

"And only partially healing him is helpful to no one."

"I'm not dumb, you're dumb." Kipp stuck out his tongue at Jorge. "And you're disrespectful. Don't use your powers on me!"

Jorge moved his hands, pretending to strangle Kipp. Irwin grabbed his arm, and Jorge's reflective appearance shed. Kipp saw him for who he really was.

The sight of the real Jorge startled Kipp, and he brought both hands up to cover his eyes. He screamed out in pain, "Ouch! Oh shit! Oh, shit. I forgot."

It would take time for Kipp's torn muscles to heal.

Eye level with Kipp, Irwin put his hand on his friend. "Be still, Kipp. All this pushing and pulling around will only make the pain worse."

Kipp's eyes were closed, "Dang me."

Softly, Irwin assured him, "You know I will never hurt you. I wish you would let me heal your injuries."

"No! Don't touch me, don't touch me. Please." Kipp's eyes popped open at Irwin's touch.

Jorge asked, "What's your aversion to being healed by Irwin?"

"He's not trained!" Kipp said. "He doesn't know what to do. I want a trained healer. A trained healer." He closed his eyes.

"I know how to heal myself," said Irwin.

Kipp whispered, "That means nothing to me. Nothing."

Jorge said, "Yet he's been healing you while you sleep."

Kipp's eyes flew open. "You'll mess me up, Irwin! Maybe that's why I hurt so much. Please don't; you're hurting me. Please. Please don't touch me." He closed his eyes again. Irwin could hear his rhythmic breathing and the loud rasp in his lungs.

He sounds like me when I was a child being beaten. I cannot do this.

He took two steps back, feeling guilty for what he might have already done. Jorge's appearance changed—this time he appeared to be Albert—Albert filled with rage. "I am sorry for trying to help, Kipp. I will not touch you again unless asked."

Jorge rolled his eyes. "Oh, for fuk sake! You give in too quick."

"What is your issue, Jorge?" Irwin snapped at the Empath. "I get that you do not like people and that you enjoy provoking. Why is it so hard for you to just be nice every once in a while?"

"No one's ever been nice to me, except you," Jorge confessed. "For whatever reason."

"Yeah, why are you nice?" Kipp muttered.

Irwin glared at him.

Jorge spoke with a sense of hesitation, licking his lips, "Everyone, and I mean everyone, including Lieutenant Bejorn, Corporal Teigahn, Jamal, Admiral Argustos, all of them. They all hate me. Yeah, sure they tolerate me, but not really. No one wants to see me; I remind them of someone they once knew. I was banished to the stable yards at four for a reason—not a good place to grow up—constantly inhaling the odor of shit.

"You're lucky your upbringing was isolated, Irwin," Jorge said, not knowing the extent of Irwin's past life. "I was beaten, sodomized, taken advantage of all the time. No one ever bothered to think of me. All they thought of was who I reminded them of. Do you know how fukin' twisted in the head that is?"

Kipp stared at Irwin. "Who is he talking about?"

"Our life stories followed similar paths. Jorge, the thing is, what happened to us in the past is behind us now. It defined us then, not now. What we do, how we act and speak now, defines us now. You do not have to continue to hate. We do not." Irwin pointed to himself and Kipp.

Kipp murmured, "Well ...."

Jorge snorted. "You think it's wrong for me to have hatred?"

"Yes," said Irwin. "You do not need to have it, not here, not with us. Just because you dislike Kipp does not mean you cannot get to know him."

"He's Clan-Duin. They're all the same."

"What ...?" Kipp tried to yell out.

"That is a narrow-minded thing to say." Irwin glared at Jorge who now shifted into Jebadia. "Maybe you should close your eyes and hear what he says before judging him. What about Arrol or Ron? They are Clan-Duin."

"They're different."

"Because they are eunuchs?"

"No!"

"Because they enjoy sleeping with the same sex?"

"No."

"Then, in what way are they different?"

"Because," was the only excuse Jorge gave.

Kipp snickered.

Irwin's silvery eyes flushed golden. He did not want to intimidate; he knew to remain calm, but the metal within swirled. "If you are going to have a problem with all Clan-Duins, but give exception to ones who have been castrated, or enjoy same-sex partners, then you are being unfair to all Clan-Duins."

"You think it's fair for them to be castrated?"

"That is not what we are arguing, Jorge. Either Clan-Duins are all the same or they are individuals like you and me?"

Kipp, mostly sober now, watched Irwin intently throughout the argument. He smiled and nodded.

After a while, Jorge said, "I can *try* to be nicer to Kipp."

"Good." Irwin turned his attention to Kipp. "And Kipp will try to remember that is Jorge in the driver's seat and not a family member, or a Telepath warping your mind."

Kipp looked away.

Irwin's golden eyes examined Jorge again, and finally he said, "It would be nice of you, Jorge, to remember that *you* decided to join us on our way to Daos City." He turned on his heel to take the lead position.

"Without me, you two would've died. Maybe you should thank me!" Jorge shouted.

Irwin heard him.

That is an exaggerated lie. We would not have died. True, it would have been harder to do everything, but....

He called back, "I have thanked you every time."

He was exhausted—all the running, the torture he had endured at the hands of the Telepaths, exploding, more killings—and now the escape to an unknown destination with an injured and incensed Kipp.

I thought I got away from all this. I hate badgering. I do not want hostility, and why is it that Jorge reminds me so much of Jebadia? Oh, I know, because he looks like him right now. Maybe I should have told him no, that he could not come with us, to take another way on his own. I guess this is where I learn how to set boundaries.

He stepped ahead of the animals and felt them on his heels once more.

The days slipped past like a mountain ice flow in winter. Irwin labored to split the jungle, to remake the overgrown channel so the wagon and livestock could move through the dense undercover. Kipp was mending and was now well enough to help with driving—giving Jorge a reprieve now and then.

While it warmed Irwin to see his friend feeling and doing better, that meant the old Kipp was back and would assert himself. Jorge was new to their group, and Kipp was less than accepting of that. They squabbled about everything—how to hold the reins, how to tell what time of day it was, the difference between bird calls and a monkey call, how to breathe, and on and on. It all reminded him of Albert and Jebadia's arguments oh so long ago.

This is worse than Yace and Kipp. At least Kipp conceded to Yace. Kipp will never concede to Jorge, and Jorge will not back down.

Jorge estimated travel time from Nuaki Village to Vidigen was eighteen days—back when the road was a road and not an impenetrable jungle. It took them twenty-six days once Kipp was rehabilitated enough to go that distance. At some point, the dark and dreary jungle turned from thick foliage to vast nothingness. The trees and underbrush were now a flat swath of bamboo forest. The gnarly jungle had disappeared.

Now we really must be cautious.

Irwin took a seat next to Jorge. He had stopped exploding. He couldn't remember exactly when, but this realization lifted his spirits. But now he had to be within an arm's length of Jorge to conceal his Empathic power. Kipp hunkered down on the bed. Having changed into his four-legged hound body, he stared off through the bamboo lining the road.

Large spider webs occluded the view and had to be cleared while Irwin kept the creepy crawlers off the wagon and watched agricultural workers through the seemingly endless bamboo silhouettes.

The thick bamboo forest went on and on until water trickled across the road and the horses paused for a drink. Up ahead, rectangular swaths of ground crops littered the landscape. Despite the pleasant aroma of flowering peas, there still lingered the unpleasant scent of human defecation. Life in Daos was a step back in time from the rest of Urthis. It occurred to Irwin as they passed by agricultural lands that people here were not as experienced in planting and harvesting food as those to the north.

He saw women working bountiful fields; he saw gray-haired men turning muddied grounds with yoked oxen. Children as young as three years worked alongside their mothers, older siblings, aunts, or grandmothers. Thatched baskets hanging from their sides were heaped with harvested crops.

A few looked up to see the wagon and the enormous black horses passing. Irwin and Jorge sat together on the wagon bench, both staring forward.

Irwin said, "I do not see boys older than eight or nine in the fields. Why is that?"

"You won't," said Jorge.

"Why not?"

"Once a boy reaches his tenth year, he's sent off to work in the iron mines. Don't be alarmed if all you see are old men."

The city-village of Vidigen was indeed barbaric compared to any other place Irwin had seen on this seemingly endless journey. Two-year-old children and babies were strapped to older adults. Irwin noticed an old woman watching over a dozen children who were playing with sticks and rocks. Some were just toddling around. They appeared lost.

Anemic looking goats wandered loose, grazing on tufts of grass here and there. Chickens ran wild. Children and elderly women were naked and sat in shadows between houses, perhaps to stay cool from the oppressive heat. There were no trees, large grassy areas, or flowers to be seen.

They came across a pack of older men gathered, sitting or standing, all wearing baggy pants and vests, hats; all smoking amidst spirals of white smoke rising into the afternoon sunlight. The pipe being passed between them could have been opium or Tabaci. The old men watched them with interest.

Irwin said, "Do you know if they speak our language?"

Jorge shook his head as they were approached by four middle-aged men. The most rotund spoke with a harsh, unusual tone. They twanged, popped, clicked, and used their hands expressively.

Jorge spoke Daosian and interpreted. "I asked them where we can purchase produce."

"What all did he say before you spoke?"

"People who come from the north aren't allowed in Daos."

Two men jabbered, moving their hands in a violent gesture indicating the wagon must go back, must leave.

Jorge elbowed Irwin. "Show them your money."

"Why?"

Without further conversation, Irwin made four golden coins appear. Jorge grabbed them and tossed them to the Daosian natives.

"They won't let us pass."

"Let me give them a blade."

"No. They might take that as a hostile gesture. But the coins can be traded with visiting ships."

Looking at the harbor, Irwin could not see an entrance to the ocean. There were about a dozen middle-aged women, four buildings down, huddled underneath in the shade, working on looms, weaving colorful silken fabrics. "Tell them I come for their fine cloth," Irwin pointed at the weavers. "And I will pay a fair price for every ream," he said. "We will also take several hundred pounds of rice, some dried fish, produce, and a cask of any hard spirit they might make." Having studied these people as they rode into Daos, he caught on quickly that, even along the wharf, women did most of the work.

A dinghy rowed up and breeched the beach as their wagon arrived. Two ladies who had been hiding from the sun under a hut ran to retrieve the fisherman's baskets—filled with fresh-caught, yellow-skinned fish. They ran back and began the filleting process. The fisherman strode up the sandy beach and joined the congregation of men in their afternoon smoke out.

Irwin reached behind his seat, grabbed an empty pouch, and filled it with silver coins. He turned around and jangled the heavy sack so that everyone could hear the wealth he was bringing. He tossed a few more coins out for the men to catch and inspect. Words were exchanged among the natives. Soon the men were chortling wildly and greeted Irwin and Jorge as if they were old family members. They descended into the throng of men who had surrounded the wagon.

They were tossed around between the inebriated men who were laughing and groping for more money. Luckily, Jorge managed to stay close to Irwin, his empathic powers hidden for now. They were pushed along by the men of Vidigen and into an herbalist's shop. Pipes were pushed into their mouths and vapors inhaled—no choice in the matter.

Jorge seemed to be more accepting of what was happening than Irwin. The locals also seemed more willing to talk to Jorge, probably because of his looks and understanding of their language. He noticed the Empath smoked whatever came his way. Irwin—on the other hand—was cordial, but after only two tokes on a pipe, he took a seat, hoping his mind and his eyes would stop spinning.

25

THE UGLY SIDE OF DAOS

Two large baskets with heaps of colorful silken fabric were placed at Irwin's feet. Another man brought a bamboo sack of turnips. These and other offerings were piled before him, all hoping to get some of Irwin's money.

An old man covered with scars on his arms and face—wispy white hair lifting in the breeze—brought out his two beautiful whores. They were naked teenage girls with alluring and nearly perfect bodies—free of scars, piercings, or tattoos. Their faces were painted, highlighting their eyes and lips—colorful feathers decorating long and shiny black hair. While they were clearly fed better than the women and children Irwin had seen along the way, their brown-black eyes were as desolate as the wind-swept desert on the far side of Arenu Village. He felt each young woman's despair as they looked to the ground in response to his greeting—as tender a smile as he could muster under the circumstances.

A drunken man stepped in front of the two women—promoting and hoping to sell several pouches of fermented goat's milk at a high price. Another man, covered with pockmarks, brought numerous flasks of his homemade rice wine. Both men argued in favor of their beverages. The man with the girls clapped his hands, summoning the women to dance. No music, but they sang as their bodies hypnotically swayed in unison.

Dried goat's meat and cheese, fresh fish wrapped in seaweed, and thin rice cakes were passed out by two boys who Irwin guess couldn't be older than five years. They made sure he tasted these wares. Irwin and Jorge were showered with everything they asked for and more. Every Vidigen man was hoping to take home money. One man shared a bowl of boiled crab legs, another presented bamboo root sticks with a deep bow. Jorge encouraged Irwin to spend as much as he wanted on these people who were hungry for money and attention.

Soon, seven young girls, no older than twelve, were paraded before the strangers. Timidly, they stood naked and under the scrutiny of all Vidigen's older men. Two girls wept.

Jorge nudged Irwin who was sampling the fermented goats' milk. "Um, how should we handle this?"

Irwin swallowed the bitter drink, his lips twisting from the sour taste. "Do they want us to buy them?" Jorge nodded. Knowing he could purchase all the girls, he replied, "We cannot."

"We will dishonor many agreements with these people if we don't take at least one."

The smoking and soured drink kicked Irwin's anxiety into high gear.

What do I do? Buy them all. Take them away from here. But where? Daos City? Maybe they could find a life, a future there.

Irwin heard Albert's grizzly voice say, 'They are females. All they are good for is reproduction.'

He closed his eyes to hide tears.

I do not want this!

His eyes still closed, he asked, "How much?"

"For which one?"

His voice dropped. "All of them." Slowly his eyes opened, noticing one of the innocent girls standing in front of him. Her lips trembled and her left eye twitched—she watched him and shook.

She is frightened. I do not want this burden.

Jorge said, "Did you just say all of them?"

Kipp whined from the wagon bed. The wagon had been sitting out in the tropical sun and there was no water or food readily available. The horses and donkeys had been neglected. Irwin jumped up and turned to attend to the problem.

Jorge kept to Irwin's side. "Wait! You're gonna buy all of them?"

Irwin moaned, "This is not what I want, Jorge. Food, spirits, clothing fabric, but not women. Maybe that is what you and Kipp want, but not me."

"I don't want any of them!" Jorge said. "But I don't want to upset these people, either."

"What are you worried about?"

Jorge whispered, "There's a Telepath among them."

Irwin looked at all the men huddled under the shade. None of them had blue eyes or blonde hair, but still sensed that Telepaths could be amongst these locals. All these men with dark brown hair and nearly black eyes were watching them intently. "How do you know?"

"You probably can't feel it, but I can. Kipp probably does too," Jorge said, motioning to their four-legged friend. "If we don't accommodate these people, we probably won't live through the night."

"That sounds a bit far-fetched, Jorge," said Irwin. "You know I will not allow anyone to hurt you or Kipp."

They stopped at the wagon. Jorge said, "They're watching us." He looked over his shoulder at the quiet gathering.

Although several men were busy eating and drinking, the conversations had died. Many of them were eagerly studying Irwin and Jorge.

"I know." He pulsated his magnetic power, feeling for metal, noticing a copper bell hanging above a doorway five buildings down the wharf. He put a hand on Jorge's shoulder, asking again, "Do you really sense a Telepath?"

"Yes, and now that you've touched me, I feel clearer in the head."

I am not sure I believe Jorge. I do not see any Telepaths. A blonde would be easy to see among these dark-haired men—of course, I know better than to look for the obvious.

Irwin eyed the congregation, looking for anyone with blue eyes. "I need you to ask them where we can put our animals out of the sun for the day. Maybe somewhere with grass, although I do not see any green spaces."

Irwin released Jorge's arm but remained close.

While decisions still hung in the air, Irwin found a bowl and gave Kipp some water, then petted him, quietly asking, "Do you sense a Telepath?"

Kipp shook his head and eyed Jorge who appeared impatient—tapping his foot, waiting for Irwin to make up his mind.

Sensing Jorge's irritation, Irwin grabbed another empty satchel and filled it full of coins. "We are buying what we must." Irwin reiterated his earlier sentiment. "And we will not stay here longer than today. And we are not here to save anyone but Yace."

"We're gonna continue on tonight?"

"Maybe. I do not know for sure." He reached up and touched the crown of his head and closed his eyes. "My head is a bit fuzzy from all the smoke."

"A little more alcohol and that'll go away," Jorge chuckled, patting Irwin's shoulder.

The situation was becoming uncontrollable. He rolled his eyes at Jorge; stared at Kipp as a reminder to 'guard the wagon.'

Kipp whined again, looking at Jorge who was clearly still antsy; he was studying the throng of men. Irwin put his hand on Kipp's head again, then turned away and walked with Jorge back to the shaded area.

The villagers argued as to where the horses and donkeys could rest. Once a decision had been made, the wagon was driven to a long drying house—smelling of fish—and parked parallel beside it. Kipp now had shade, but was unable to see Irwin and Jorge. But he had a good view of their animals.

Irwin and Jorge were given the option of allowing their animals free-roaming access or keeping them corralled below one of the huts.

I do not trust these people. I fear they might eat one of my donkeys.

A decision to corral them that night was made, and they returned to the smoke shop where food, libations, and young girls were passed around. The local men greedily chortled as they groped and squeezed the young girls, obviously scared for their lives. There was nothing Irwin or Jorge could do, short of killing every greedy man to save the girls from the old lechers. Jorge joined in the juvenile games. He knew to follow along, though he might not have wanted to. Irwin sat with arms folded and a sour glare.

"You need to loosen up, Irwin," Jorge whispered.

"I am loose." Irwin continued to drink and eat the food offered but would not take part in the drugs or debauchery.

Jorge stood next to Irwin. "Maybe we buy some rice wine. I like that better than that sour milk shit."

"I am not sure I like any of it," Irwin grumbled. "But if you want, we can get rice wine."

Throughout the afternoon, many of Vidigen's men tried to make deals with Irwin while Jorge interpreted. He pressed the issue again. "I think we should take one of the girls."

"And do what with her?" said Irwin, chin down and his scowl deepening. "Neither of us is going to make her our wife. And Kipp would have to stay a dog the whole time if we brought one along."

I cannot stand this. Any of it.

He looked toward the calm waters in the bay.

Just get what we need, Jorge, please. I want to be done with this place. Breathe. Keep calm. We will be gone from here soon enough.

I never want to return to this place.

"If I saved one of them, I could not just let her be free. I know what happens to innocent young people out there in the real world; just as you do, Jorge." He saw again how terrified the girls were. "They are too young to be in any place other than home with their families. I do not want that responsibility."

"You could always sell her," Jorge suggested.

"What?" Irwin protested, "No! I do not want to be a part of the slave-trade. And I am not going to kill her, either. No, she is better off here with her people."

"You're cold-hearted sometimes, Irwin."

"What?"

"We'd be saving her," said Jorge. "She'd never have to worry about us hurting, raping, or beating her. These men … they enjoy the young a wee bit too much, don't you think?" He reminded Irwin, "We both know what that's like."

"I am not buying any of them." He wanted to cry.

I want to save them all, but I cannot. Not here, not like this. Too much is at stake right now.

He did not want to deny someone the opportunity for freedom, but now was not the time. "We are not in a place where we can be so carefree, Jorge. We have a mission to uphold," he said through gritted teeth. "Just get us what we really need, please."

"And if they ask about—"

"If they ask why we are not buying any of those girls, tell them we will be back through and will then have enough money to buy all seven. Tell them we have friends who love young Daosian women."

He listened to Jorge make the demands and explanations to the natives.

As the sun settled to the west, baskets of freshly picked produce were brought from the fields to the wharf and lined up to display. Eager men stood proudly next to their merchandise, hoping to be paid.

Slightly drunk now, Irwin and Jorge bought half of what was being offered and packed it away in the wagon. Neither were very fond of the alcohol, but they bought one flask of rice wine and a bladder of fermented goat's milk. Even after Irwin packed away the alcohol, the merchants continued to share their liquors freely. Jorge asked to buy Tabaci, opium seeds, and refilled their vial with poppy milk. The natives threw in a bamboo pipe for free. In all, Irwin spent two pounds of silver and received many hundreds of pounds of food and supplies in exchange.

It was a good night, but Irwin would not soon get over the reminder that human trafficking was prevalent in Daos Territory.

It was dark when the locals drunkenly stumbled home. Jorge and Irwin were inebriated and unable to hitch their horses and drive, so they pulled out a wool blanket and laid it out on the sandy ground. They would sleep under the moon and stars and any local staying up to spy.

Jorge faced Irwin, and Kipp kept his vigilant post on the wagon, though he looked down from his perch at them from time to time.

Irwin placed his hand on Jorge, making sure no Telepath was present in his mind. He looked deep into Jorge's light brown eyes. "I am sorry for arguing with you about buying those girls. It tears me up knowing what will happen to them. It was never like that in Datzar.

"And, yes, I know I can do something about it, but not now. I cannot bring anyone into our dilemma ..." He looked toward Kipp, and then turned his attention back to Jorge. "... including you. It compromises Kipp's and my mission. You are innocent, Jorge."

"Innocent. Ha!" Jorge smirked.

"I do not want to see you get hurt by me, or by anything that may lie ahead. Kipp and I already know what could be in store, but you do not. Honestly, I do not want you to know. It just makes you a liability. Trust me—you do not want to be a part of what I can no longer avoid."

"Why are you acting like this is all on you, Irwin?" Jorge said, his voice flat. "You know you have friends." He pointed at Kipp.

Shaking his head, Irwin said, "Kipp is here for support. He knows he cannot help me; neither can you. We know that whatever is before us is for me to take care of, not Kipp. We know what Dephen is trying to do. We are too far away to stop him now."

How are we going to save Yace? She could be dead already. This is an uphill climb with no end in sight.

His heart hurt. "No matter what I do, I see this going 'five ways to Daos'."

Jorge chuckled, "That's a common saying in Arenu, and Nuaki too. It's a way to say that no one gets out alive."

"That is how I feel right now."

"Then, why do it? I mean, you've said that he-she's gonna assassinate the standing Emperor. And, from what I understand, the Ishik family are all Coterie. Supposedly, Coterie are all powerful, more so than you. Your friend doesn't stand a chance. So, what's the point in trying to save her?"

Kipp whimpered. Irwin said, "Yace is Coterie too. Her father, Dephen, is from Ishik descent. He might be a bastard, but he is smart. And with him in possession of her, Dephen could easily assassinate the standing Emperor of Daos."

"If he's a bastard, then she's one too. That means their powers are watered down. Your friend can't be all that strong. And even if she were, that wouldn't make her immune to pure Coterie powers. They're all powerful. They know all, see all—just like any other corrupt Telepath. Teigahn's a bastard Coterie too. Strong with his telekinesis and telepathy. Some of the things he could do ...." Jorge paused, but it was clear to Irwin that he did not share what he knew. "But he couldn't stop you. That should show you that Coterie aren't infallible. But your friend, she's as good as dead. You should give up before you get killed too."

Irwin said nothing.

"Everyone dies, Irwin, including you."

"My grandfather and father tried to kill me several times, as did Bejorn. Even I have tried to kill myself a few times. Nothing can kill me, Jorge. At this point, only time can—"

I do not want to talk about myself.

"—But if we can get to Daos City before she does ...."

Jorge spoke over him. "If she took voyage on a boat at Arenu—from what I understand—it takes something like fourteen days to get to Daos City from there. Well, on any Erthin-yielding ship, it takes fourteen days. Those mortal sailors, it probably takes a moon's time, maybe more, to get there. At any rate, most likely she is there by now."

Kipp growled.

"Most likely she's already tried to kill the Emperor. But since he's Coterie, he probably already knew she was coming. No doubt she's dead."

"Dephen is smarter than that. He knows how to manipulate a situation. I believe he would infiltrate, lie low, and strike when he can."

"He couldn't infiltrate a family of Coterie."

"Dephen could. He is Ishik. He might be a bastard, but .... He is powerful. He can do anything he wants. I would put nothing past him. Besides, he used to live in the palace. He probably knows all about the place—how to infiltrate without being detected."

"You actually think he's that good?"

"Yes. Not only did Dephen manipulate an entire village in his distant past, he also recently convinced PCP in Ahradah, and several of the masterminds in Arenu and Nuaki Villages, that I was being brought to them by their own kind—when in reality we have been following Dephen's trail all along. I would not put it past him to take full advantage of the Ishik Regime."

"How do you know he manipulated an entire village?"

"Nonbry, one of Kipp's fellow Gypsy, told us the story."

"How'd he know?"

"He was there when it happened."

"Is Nonbry a Telepath?"

"Yes."

"And you're believing him?"

"Yes. I believe Nonbry, even if he is a Telepath," Irwin said. "Some elders are here to help us, not hurt us."

"Says you."

"I would not have believed Nonbry had I not witnessed everything I have so far. Look Jorge, you might not understand our mission, but I need you to realize that we have been taken advantage of and that traps may be set for us."

"Are you trying to scare me?" Jorge said, "Cause it's not working."

"We watched our friend, Yace, touch a dead body. It came back to life and then the specter within it took over her body and her life. You should be scared of what we are following."

"Sounds like Erthin magic, not Coterie."

"It is okay that you do not understand. Probably best."

"What you're saying sounds dubious," Jorge said. "I mean, if you really just wanna tour the world, go for it; you don't have to make excuses to me, Irwin."

"This is not an excuse." Irwin's eyes adjusted beyond Jorge to the hut where their animals rested. "We cannot delay more than we already have. I do not want to rest tonight for long. Just long enough for my head to become unclouded. I want to be moving before daybreak."

There was a long pause. Jorge put his hand on Irwin's chest. "To be an effective savior, you need a good night's sleep."

Irwin's mind would not stop swirling, even if his body already had.

I cannot save anyone, not even Yace. Not those innocent girls. I cannot think about the ones in Arenu village. This is all too much to bear.

He closed his eyes. "Right now, I cannot sleep."

With a flirtatious look in his eye, Jorge said, "I can help you sleep."

"Oh? How are you going to do that?"

Jorge leaned forth and planted a kiss on Irwin's lips.

Startled by Jorge's forwardness, Irwin glanced up at Kipp. "That will not help me sleep."

"You're so uptight, Irwin." Jorge gestured toward Kipp, "I know he agrees with me. I've noticed that you have a hard time enjoying the very moment we live in. Why are you always looking forward? Why can't you just be comfortable here and now?"

Irwin had no answer.

"Why *do* you always think of the future?"

"I must think of all the outcomes that could befall us."

"Nothing will befall us tonight," Jorge chuckled. "Besides, if something happened, I know you'd kick ass." He stared at Irwin. "You're worried."

"I am not worried."

"Yes, you are." Jorge poked Irwin's chest.

Sighing deeply, Irwin said, "Okay, I am. I have a lot of worries—most of them are about Yace and what is happening to her right now."

"Worrying about your friend is like paying for a debt you've yet to incur, Irwin. You're good with money. Besides, you can't help her now. She's not here to be helped, and you're nowhere near her to help. What you need to do is stop worrying so much about everything. Just relax."

Irwin sighed again.

"Just be comfortable with yourself."

He lay there, then he said, "The reason I cannot be comfortable is that I was never allowed to in my entire life."

Jorge laughed, "Wasn't it you who said, 'Our past is behind us?'"

Irwin rolled his eyes.

"I allow you to be comfortable. I think Kipp would too."

The dog whined.

"See, he knows you need quiet time, downtime, time to relax and not be thinking or doing."

Heaving a deep sigh, Irwin responded. "I have quiet time."

"When?"

"When I am walking, moving jungle pieces around."

"That's work, not quiet time. I think you're confusing the two. When you work, you must think about what you're doing. That doesn't allow for quiet—in the mind—time. Doesn't sound like much fun to me."

Irwin did not know how to respond to Jorge.

My past is behind me. My past is behind me.

"Do you ever just lay back and do nothing, think nothing, watch the clouds go by, let the day take you wherever it takes you?"

"No. I was never allowed. What about you—were you able to relax in Nuaki Village?"

"Yeah, we had downtime during the day. But going to Arenu Village is a good example of a break." He continued to study Irwin. "Do you ever just sit around watching the world pass you by?"

"I would, but not in the sense you are suggesting." Irwin recalled the dark mines, staring at the coal walls and wishing to see brilliant landscapes when he was a child.

"You never took time for yourself?"

"No." Irwin thought about his hasty response and added, "Well, I had a place. It was outside of the mine, up the slope. I would go there to stash my metal or to get away from Jebadia's wrath. But it was exposed to the elements, and not the best place to relax." He remembered the view of snow-covered mountain tops from that perch.

"You need to learn to relax, Irwin."

"I know how to relax." They heard Kipp laughing; it sounded like he was coughing.

"No, you don't. Let me show you how." He pushed Irwin back onto the covered ground and then leaned alongside the Metalist, staring and smiling lustfully. His hand was soft on Irwin's chest. Jorge caressed Irwin's torso and arm. His hand drifted. He petted and smelled while leaning forward to kiss Irwin's chest and neck.

Lying there stiffly, unable to figure out what to do, Irwin said, "I am not sure you should do this."

"Doing what? Showing you affection?"

"It is just ...."

Jorge pulled back, holding a flirtatious smile. "Accept that I love you."

"I do not think I am drunk enough to ...."

"You need to be drunk to enjoy love?"

"No. It is just that ...."

"You don't accept me."

"No, it is not that." He glanced up at Kipp, their eyes locked.

Jorge whispered, "You want Kipp."

Crushed that Jorge knew his secret, Irwin closed his eyes and sought out Jorge's lips. They kissed passionately. Jorge's hands were warm as they caressed Irwin's body. They pressed against each other. Irwin did not pull away from the warmth or the closeness. Finally, Irwin let go of the worry and stress and allowed himself to succumb to his desires.

26

<u>Understanding Feelings</u>

Jorge kept his arm across Irwin's abdomen all night long. At daybreak, Jorge rolled away and walked around the wagon to do his morning business. Irwin lay still, contemplating his life.

I cannot believe I did that. I just had relations with Jorge. It was amazing. But I was pretending. The whole time I was pretending he was Kipp. I am so ashamed. I should not have allowed myself to indulge like that. It was wrong of me. All of it.

But Kipp has gone and enjoyed many a lady, and without any emotional hangups. He has never seemed to care about Yace's feelings when he does it. How can he be that way? Maybe it is their relationship. Maybe they are alright with the feelings of infidelity.

How can I experience what I want and without feeling bad about hurting others?

I cannot. That is not me. I am so confused. I want Jorge, and I want Kipp. Maybe I want them to be the same person.

All I know is that I should not be fantasizing about one man while I lay with another. That is not fair to either of them. What about me? What about what I want?

I want what I had last night. Jorge made me feel loved. I have wanted that for a long time. I am glad Jorge was sensitive. And kind. He was amazing.

I cannot wait for tonight.

Irwin rolled over and noticed Kipp staring at him from the wagon bed. He smiled, "Morning."

I know he saw it, saw us. I feel such shame. I cannot look at him.

Jorge was back, and off they went to get the horses and donkeys and gear up for departure from Vidigen. The first sun's rays lit across the sparse land and the locals who had come out to the fields—women and children—filed down the wide thoroughfare toward the fields and their day of work. Irwin had no doubt that from sunup to sundown, these were the people who worked hardest for little to no reward.

He kept glancing at Jorge.

I wonder what he is thinking. I wonder if we will do it again tonight. My belly keeps bouncing, worse than the wagon. Will he want to? Did he do it just to make me feel better, or does he really care?

Jorge is hard to read.

I wonder if he wants to talk about it. I know Kipp would, but Jorge is not Kipp. And Kipp would go on and on about parts and such. I want to talk about feelings and such.

I feel so confused right now. This is so new. I just want to know what to place importance on. I want to know what Jorge thinks. He said he loved me. I said it too, but it was probably the alcohol talking. I want to know what he is feeling, but I am afraid to ask.

When they were finally rolling forward, people stepped aside to let the wagon pass; they stared expressionless at the enormous black horses pulling the load and the tiny donkeys peering over the back of the wagon bed. The vehicle wagon sped faster as they approached a bridge—a crude draw bridge hoisted by a bundle of rocks hung over the scaffolding. For now, it was down, allowing workers to pass. The waterway beneath the bridge flowed out to a shallow bay. They drew to a stop and waited for a crowd of laborers to pass.

On the southern side of the harbor, a gutted body had been tied and nailed onto a cross. What was left of the skin draped from the bones, picked clean and barely held together. While the clothing was torn and now just shreds of fabric, it still resembled PCP garb that soldiers from Datzar would wear. It had been there for many days; there were bugs and birds fighting over what was left—even the bloodied clothing. The scavenged body had been left as a warning for those with Talents to stay off Daos's shores.

Kipp whined as they passed by the deceased. Irwin glanced over his shoulder. "Do not worry, Kipp. I will keep you safe."

"You can't keep him safe," Jorge scoffed.

The truth in those words silenced Irwin for the rest of the morning. He tried to forget the decrepit conditions in which the people of Vidigen lived—what they faced every day of their lives.

As they traveled beyond the city limits, there were still workers walking along the roadside or already laboring in the fields. Nothing changed as they rolled past one sparse field after another. Irwin kept his eyes to himself, biting his fingernails, hoping the scenery would change, but it never did.

After a while, Irwin leaned into Jorge, placed a hand on his thigh and whispered, "Thank you for last night, Jorge. You were right."

The Empath glanced at the hand, then stared ahead, ambivalent. "We can't be obvious like that again. Not out in public."

"What do you mean?"

The wagon rattled along a little further and he said, "People like us are frowned upon here in Daos Territory."

"People like us, meaning ...?"

"Those of us who are attracted to the same sex."

"I thought you liked women too."

"Being a gender fluid hermaphrodite means I can be attracted to both," Jorge tried to explain. "Although I appreciate women, I understand men better." He patted Irwin's leg and smiled. "I feel we have more in common."

"You mean you can choose whom you like?"

"No, attraction is attraction. I am not attracted to Kipp, whereas you are."

Irwin fidgeted and looked over his shoulder.

"What are you so worried about? He knows you lust after him."

Kipp could hear their conversation; he was riding right behind the driver's seat. Irwin could feel those brown eyes on his back. He whispered, "Can we not talk about this?"

"Why don't you acknowledge your feelings, Irwin? If you don't, they'll eat you up! I know Kipp would agree."

"I acknowledge my feelings. I just do not like to talk about them."

"Why not? Your feelings matter, Irwin. You matter."

Irwin snarled. "What about your feelings, Jorge? What did you feel last night? You said that you loved me, but today you have been cold to me."

"Cold? I love you, Irwin! And last night, all I felt was love for you. Did you feel it?"

He was still unsure about what he felt. "Yes."

"Hm. You feel anything else?"

Irwin flushed.

"Ah, you felt shame. Why?" Jorge waited for Irwin to respond, but he couldn't. "Did you actually want me or were you dreaming of Kipp the whole time? You know you can't lie to me, Irwin. Your feelings are too revealing. That's why you need to acknowledge them."

His heart raced. Irwin felt trapped by this moment, afraid to speak, to confess his truths.

"You need to acknowledge your feelings, Irwin. For him. For me. You can't just stuff them down and ignore them."

Irwin tried to ignore the jab.

"Face it, the sooner you acknowledge how you feel, the better it will be for all of us. I know Kipp would agree with me."

He glanced over his shoulder at his Clan-Duin friend. The wagon rolled on.

After a while, Irwin replied, "Last night made me feel accepted. And wanted. And loved." He squeezed Jorge's thigh. "Maybe you are right about me needing to own up to my feelings. As a child, I was beaten for showing any feeling, any emotion. I always thought that no one cared. But it is obvious you do."

Jorge slapped Irwin's shoulder and cackled. "I've always cared for you. I know Kipp cares too. The sooner you fess up to your feelings, the better you'll feel."

Irwin grimaced, held his tongue.

This is where I should tell him exactly how I feel. But I am still trying to figure that out. I said I loved him, but is that really true?

I am afraid to know my feelings, to say them aloud. I do not want to hurt Jorge's or Kipp's feelings. But they both show their feelings—are not afraid to admit them.

The contents of the wagon rattled as they bumped along down the unkempt roadway.

Irwin sideways glanced at the Empath.

How do I feel about Jorge?

I like him. He is different, pokey, but…. I enjoyed our time together. He made me feel special and wanted … meanwhile I was thinking of Kipp.

Ugh. I must get over my love for Kipp. He has Yace. He does not want me.

All I want is someone who will be by my side. Dedicated. Helpful. Hopeful. And Jorge …. He can be that, though coarsely …. And he is someone who loves and accepts me.

But what if our relationship does not work? What if he finds someone else along our way? He said he loved me, but how he looks at me when he says it is not very convincing. I know he is coming along to look for his people in Daos City. What happens if he finds them? Will he still want to remain by my side? Will I want him to be there with us as we rescue Yace? Ugh. Suddenly I need to calculate for more things to go wrong if he is there. I do not want harm to come to Jorge. Nor Kipp.

Thinking about his Clan-Duin friend made his heart skip.

I need to breathe!

I do not think this is me acknowledging my feelings. I am only thinking of my anxieties and insecurities. I hate feeling this way. Lost.

It was easier to believe that people did not care for me. But if Jorge cares, then maybe I should too.

An echo of Jorge's voice rattled his mind. '*Kipp cares too*'.

He shook off his internal conversation and focused on the road ahead.

Silence enveloped them while the wagon bounced down the road; whiffs of white clouds flew past overhead. Irwin thought one took on the shape of a mountain goat. He had not seen one of his beloved goat friends in a long, long time. The wagon hit a rut and jarred him, reminding him why he left the mountains. He wanted something different, a life to call his own—not something his father created and demanded. He did miss the monotony, the quiet—Jorge had made him realize that.

I am disappointed that we have not shared intimacy since that first night. Maybe he is afraid that we will be caught. Though why would anyone care what we are doing? We are not doing it with anyone but each other.

Maybe he is waiting for me to initiate. Ugh. I hope it is not that. I have such a hard time reading Jorge. He is so gruff. When would be a good time to initiate? He is always tired after driving all day, and complains more than Kipp does. So hard to read.

Maybe Jorge needs to be drunk to feel uninhibited. I know it helps me feel freer. I might be more willing to initiate if I am drunk.

Maybe he is waiting for me to figure out my feelings for him. I do have them. Moreso now than before. Could it be love? Or is this lust? I wish I could tell the difference. Thankfully, I have not thought about Kipp in that way since that day. And how Jorge was with me. It was a way Kipp would never be—wish he was.

Maybe I am not over Kipp.

Look at Jorge. I can see something happening between us.

But ... Kipp.

Ugh. I am hopeless.

I wish I could figure out what my heart wants.

It wants Kipp to be like Jorge.

That will never happen.

Jorge took the reins most days. He enjoyed being the driver, taking this job seriously; meanwhile, Irwin worked on multiple projects—mostly sewing. He stitched a hole in his boots; he used one of Kipp's PCP shirts as an outline for a pattern to make more. The reams of material he had bought were large and long enough to make several brightly colored shirts. He decided he would make his partners at least two shirts each, one long-sleeved and the other sleeveless. Kipp, for now, would remain a quiet dog who lay on his bed.

They passed small mud-home villages huddled along the sides of the road as they drove through land's end. Row boats made of logs had been dragged onto the beaches. Clothing hung on lines strung between palm trees and flapped in the sea breeze. Irwin spotted old men with girls. He could hardly bear what he knew to be true. He saw babies on the laps of elderly women; the mothers were likely out in the fields.

They drove on and on past endless rows of dilapidated mud houses where families lived in squalor. The road was muddy and more and more rutted the farther into Daos Territory they traveled. Irwin was sickened by the horrific conditions in which the people of Daos lived. He could not wait until they were done with their mission. He wanted to save them all, but there was no way to change an entire society—not without a complete regime change.

I cannot think that what Dephen is planning is a good thing. Overthrowing the Emperor and taking control of Daos Territory. Nonbry said that would be a horrible outcome. Could Dephen actually do that? Anything is possible. He has shown me he is powerful, but he is also power hungry. Or maybe that is all part of his plan. Maybe he intends to make changes for the better! Or maybe this is all about revenge. A suicide mission. He does not care about anything; he just wants his brother dead.

He huffed aloud for no one in particular to hear.

He is old and stuck in a youthful body. He is liable to do anything at this point.

But if that is his plan, can Dephen reverse centuries of neglect and negative mindsets?

Irwin wondered what the landscape would look like if the people were treated better, given help and allowed to live in a free society.

What an ambitious thought. He is Coterie; he could be the All-powerful ruler of the land. Then how am I to counteract him? Maybe what Dephen is trying to do is for the best of Daos and its people. But Nonbry said …. Yet a change is needed. These people …. I understand why the PCP would support Dephen's plan.

What am I saying? I cannot forget about Yace? He is using her and for his own personal gain! If he cared about her, then he would have cared about us. No, we cannot stop.

But imagine, for a moment, Dephen conquering a male dominated empire in a female's body. From what I have seen, especially Daosians, women are not honored—they are disrespected. Maybe that is the ultimate twist!

He laughed at his thoughts and toked on the Tabaci pipe Jorge passed him. He had not enjoyed the taste of either of the alcohol beverages, but relaxed from a few puffs of the smoke.

He ignited a flame at the end of his finger to light the bamboo pipe. His newfound powers continued to amaze him. He did not feel that he was all that powerful until he reflected on his past.

I am not as powerful as Yace. As a Coterie, with full knowledge of her powers, she would be unstoppable. And with Dephen manipulating her, all the people will submit!

Irwin blew the smoke from the pipe and watched it lift into the air.

Telepaths like to talk. What if the Ishik's know Dephen is coming? What if they know Dephen's plot? What if they are following along, waiting for the moment to take him down? The master manipulator manipulated by his own game. Yace is innocent but would be found guilty because he has control over her.

He took another draw on the pipe and, while coughing, passed it back to Jorge.

We must save Yace at all cost. We cannot give up on her, even if ... even if I cannot think about more negative stuff. We have come so far, we cannot stop.

But what if ... what if Dephen's will is to better the people of Daos? What if Dephen wants to set these people free? Why would we stop him?

Ugh. This smoke is clouding my judgement.

Think about it. We offered to help long ago, and it was dismissed. Dephen has his own plan that never included us. He does not want us around Yace, and he is going to do what he is going to do. He knows I can save Yace from him. Dephen's desires are his own; we cannot just let things happen. We must find her before it is too late.

When the sun dropped below the horizon, the wagon slowed. They only stopped long enough to allow the horses and donkeys time to rest. Irwin and Jorge would take turns sleeping and driving. There were no conversations about feelings, about heartstrings, about a future together. Irwin felt burdened by his conscious, and the want to please everyone. And at the same time, he had to keep his focus on the immediate goal; Yace's rescue.

Nearing the next large village five days south, they spotted another cross holding a crumbling skeleton stretched across the top.

Irwin calculated that they had enough food to get them to Daos City. On they went.

27

SPACESHIPS

They camped outside villages—away from prying eyes. Often, they would lie in fields, or outside a bog—of which there were many. Kipp could be himself at night now that he was stronger and able to move without restrictions. Although many days had passed since leaving Vidigen, the sweltering heat and humidity was relentless.

One cloudless evening, they stopped to give the horses a break and some water at one of the canals along the road. The sky bled from orange to dark purple, from which the first few stars broke through. It would be a moonless night; they had seen the moon set to the west just before the sun dropped from sight.

Irwin stuck a finger in his ear, rattled it around, and looked up at the sky. "Do either of you hear that?"

"Hear what?"

"Now I feel something."

"What is it?"

"It is hard to describe."

"Why's that?"

"It is metal, but different."

"Different how?"

"We might be nearing another large village or ...." A bolt of lightning streaking up from the ground shot across the night sky. He pointed, "What was that?!"

Jorge dropped the orange. "What was what?"

Irwin pointed up and looked at Kipp. "Did you see that?"

Kipp had been off relieving himself. "I saw it! I've seen them before, they are, um, what did Yace call them ...?"

"Light streaking up?" Jorge said, "I've heard stories from sailors. I think they're called spaceships."

"Spaceships? That was not a ship! It was metal. I saw it; I felt it!" Irwin's silvery eyes bulged.

"Yeah, spaceships." Kipp's eyes bulged too. "Oh, fuk, this isn't good!"

"Spaceships? That was metal, Kipp, and metal cannot fly."

"This isn't good," Kipp continued to mutter.

"Maybe we're closer to Daos City than we thought," said Jorge, looking skyward.

"I didn't know Daos had spaceships," said Kipp. "I know Akarah has them. Yace and I saw them there for the first time several years ago. I think she said the Al'Lieur Isles have a spaceship port too."

"Daos, Akarah, Ieree, and GnSaan are supposed to be the only cities on Urthis with spaceship ports," said Jorge, his chest bulging with the pride of knowing this.

Irwin gasped. "How do you two know this?"

"Living with the Gypsy," said Kipp.

"I've heard stories, seen things." Jorge said.

Irwin tried to grasp this new language, new ideas. "You both know that there are spaceships made of metal and have never told me?"

"I didn't think it mattered," Kipp said, rubbing his neck, "until now."

Jorge butted in, "In Nuaki, we're taught about all the many beings who live and visit Urthis. I've seen some interesting-looking people come ashore in Arenu." He smacked his lips. "You probably don't know this, but most people living on Urthis are non-native."

"While traveling with the Gypsy, I saw many things," Kipp said in a reverent tone Irwin had never heard from him before. "There're some weird creatures out there. I've seen men with long foreheads and V-shaped nodes starting at their nose and stretching up to their hairline. There are blue-skinned people, green-skinned people, and red-shelled people. People with tentacles for hands, one-eyed people. You think it up, it's out there."

"Non-native, blue-skinned people? What the …!?" Irwin's jaw hung open, too stunned to close his mouth.

"Your people probably aren't native to Urthis," said Jorge.

Kipp agreed. "Yeah, Irwin's family definitely came from somewhere else."

Jorge sneered at Kipp, "I know Empaths are non-native."

"Us Clan-Duins, we're from Urthis," said Kipp, smiling proudly.

Jorge jeered. "Telepaths definitely are not."

"Neither are Erthins," Kipp snorted.

"They wish they were," Jorge laughed.

Irwin finally regained his ability to speak. "What about Mortals?"

Jorge and Kipp agreed, "Oh, yeah, they're definitely native."

"How do you know?"

Jorge shrugged as if he'd been asked to solve a complex problem.

Kipp said, "Where else would Mortals come from?"

"Well," Irwin said, "If you are suggesting there are other worlds that are inhabited only by Telepaths, or Erthins, or Empaths, who would refute the idea that Mortals do not come from somewhere else too?"

Kipp said, "They are people who just happened to be born without Talent."

Jorge turned to Irwin. "Do you feel the metal now?"

"No. And I never really felt it, it was like ...." He pointed to the horizon. "I could hear it and that was how I felt it. It was like a high-pitched ringing. I could tell what was happening to the metal. Felt it heating as it ascended."

While looking intently at Kipp, Jorge asked Irwin, "Can you feel the metal in Daos City from here?"

Closing his eyes, Irwin allowed himself to magnetically feel—pulsating like a bat's sonar. He felt something. They were close to a larger village, about two kilometers away. "We are close to something, but it is not Daos. Cities have a different tone than a town or village."

"If you think Onj Raha or Ahradah was metal filled ...." Kipp's voice tightened. "Dang it, Irwin, you're gonna lose your shit in Daos City."

"I can keep my cool, Kipp."

Kipp stared back. "When Yace and me were in Akarah, a monstrous city, by the way, there was an inner city inside the main city. You had to show your power to get in—that was fun. But once inside, that's where the spaceship ports were ... there were these wide-open spaces with hundreds of people stepping off metal ships." His eyes widened, and his voice rattled with fear. "Irwin, if Daos City is anything like Akarah, no one will be safe."

Rolling his eyes at the implication, Irwin said, "I have much more control over myself now than back in Onj Raha."

"Every one of those ships is metal!"

"You remember how I was in Ahradah?"

"I do."

"Nothing happened."

"Nothing?" Their eyes locked.

"We were escorted out of the city, nothing more," said Irwin as though he had just out-bid someone at an auction.

"You call that nothing? You sprung a trap we knew was there, stole tons of metal, killed Erthins, took their fiery shots into your ... and then we were followed by a legion of PCP for days beyond Ahradah!"

"Kipp! I only killed three Earth Erthins, and it was only because they harnessed their power and would have used it against us. I know I am a magnet for metal. And their blood was calling for me to .... But I have control!"

Kipp tittered.

"And the reason we were escorted was because I decided to save someone who was wrongly imprisoned."

"No," Kipp insisted, "The reason you were escorted was because of what you did in Onj Raha. What happened in Ahradah, *that* was extra."

Jorge joined in, "Don't forget about Nuaki Village."

Irwin did not appreciate this attack, and he pointed at Jorge. "That was all Lieutenant Bejorn. Had he not tried his Elementalist spell, Nuaki Village would still be standing. Most likely you would still be there, Jorge." He took a heated breath. "But because of Nuaki Village and Bejorn, I understand my Erthin powers so much more. Now I have control over all of it—all of me. How much more reassuring do you need?"

"I know you, Irwin." Kipp waved his finger at the Metalist. "You've been away from metal for a long time. Last time you came into a village that had it ... remember?"

Irwin growled, "It was the sneers and jeers and pushy attitudes that—"

"And the forge. I saw how you got when the forge was being worked."

"It was not the forge."

"It didn't help," Kipp went on, "All that and more will be in Daos City; I guarantee it."

Jorge downed a gulp of water and said, "Do you think your friend's been caught yet? You know once they do, they'll know all about you, if they don't already."

"You wish they knew," Irwin growled. "If they do not know about Dephen and Yace, they will not know about me."

"You positive?" Jorge said, not backing down. "What if they've already captured your friend and they know about you? What'll you do then?"

Take a deep breath. Stay focused.

"We have our mission. I cannot worry about people believing they know me when they have not met me. Telepaths do not scare me."

Jorge softened. "You sound scared."

"I am not scared."

"You should be." Jorge echoed the same sentiment that Yace had once upon a time. "Telepaths are everywhere. Who's saying that they're not all talking about you? Waiting for you."

He is good at making me question my decisions, just like father.

"For as isolated as Daos appears to be, I find it hard to believe that the Telepaths here would communicate with those outside of their territory."

Kipp said, "Telepaths can hear anything."

Irwin glared at him.

"Yace told me. She says they can hear all lines of communication, much like what Nonbry told us in Arenu Village. It's possible they've heard all about you."

"Yes, I know that they supposedly hear all." He said, recalling Admiral Ubic boasting about what the Telepaths knew about him and his family. He heaved a deep sigh. "I assumed that being in Daos, surrounded by tall mountains and angry jungles, so removed from the rest of the world—would make it harder."

Jorge said, "Assuming anything about a Telepath is a bad idea."

Irwin closed his eyes, remembering the Telepaths in the rooms in Arenu and Nuaki Villages.

Corporal Teigahn kept silent in that dark room; he was there as a witness, a broadcaster just like those two Telepaths on the couch in Admiral Argusto's office. They all watched and listened to the conversation unfold and were probably broadcasting to all Urthis's Telepaths, 'Come see us kill Samuel Irwin Miner.'

He blew a powerful breath.

Telepaths might think they know me, but they do not; they only know what I have shown them. But they know about me and my family.

He shuddered.

"What's wrong?" asked Jorge.

After a long time, Irwin said. "So what!"

"Huh?" Kipp had started to nod off and jerked awake. "What?"

Jorge asked, "What do you mean, so what?"

Irwin shrugged like a petulant child. "They do not know me; they only know of me. If they want to fear me, let them. I know I am not the person they portray me as." He looked at Kipp. "We have our mission; get Yace and get out of Daos. We should not worry about the details between here and there."

They do not need to worry. I will figure out the details.

"You know you're not immune to telepathic manipulation," said Kipp. "Remember Lady Gretchen?"

"She could not kill me. None of them can, and they have tried."

"She was bad," said Kipp. "Who's saying there're not worse people out there? In Daos City even?"

"Worse than those I have already killed?"

Jorge was dusting off the orange. "Kipp's right, you're not immune to telepathy—none of us are. In fact, you'd be worse under their influence. I hope no one gets ahold of you, Irwin. If they do, we're all fuked!"

Irwin glared at Jorge.

Kipp muttered, "I hope there's a Talented district in Daos."

"They've apparently a Space Port," Jorge said. "Of course they'll have a Talented District. Probably one of the largest!"

Kipp grumbled, "Hopefully it's nowhere near the spaceships."

"Most likely it will be," said Jorge, smirking.

They both looked at Irwin, who was openly flustered. He walked away from camp—taking up his Jennies' lead ropes.

I want to be alone.

Kipp and Jorge called out in unison, "Don't go far!"

28

<u>DAOS CITY</u>

I rwin refrained from conversing with his friends for a full day. He was angered that Kipp did not believe that he could control himself and his powers; he was furious at Jorge for provoking him like Albert and Jebadia would have.

They noticed his withdrawal. There was nothing they could say or do that would put Irwin at ease, so they allowed him time to be broody.

All I want is to prove I can contain myself. They have nothing to worry about.

This would not happen before their arrival in the city of Daos.

Early in the morning, they passed through the village Irwin had felt the night before. There were acres and acres of pastures on the south side of this village—filled with animals and mostly barren of grass. Cows, pigs, and goats stood idle, unwittingly awaiting their inevitable future—being served up as supper. They bickered loudly for space, for food. And the smells were foul indeed, especially when they passed the chicken pens.

For a full day, the landscape looked like this. After a while, there were more houses and other buildings lining the roadway. Two and three-story structures took on a new look with thick thatched roofs. The road turned into hard packed dirt, beaten down by time. People darted out of the way of the wagon. There were no green spaces, no rolling hills, pastures, or parks.

This concrete-like landscape swelled from slightly crowded to overwhelmingly crowded in just a few hours' drive. As they made their way past the thatched roof houses, Irwin heard and recognized screams and cries of abused children. The stench of human waste was as strong as it had been in the other villages or towns along the way—another sign that the Ishik Empire didn't care about their people, even those living in Daos City.

As twilight fell to darkness, the end of their arduous journey was upon them. Perhaps they were close to finding Yace after all this time, all these kilometers. The capital city of Daos was massive—growing from the heart of the city by at least fifty kilometers. It was possible now that they had breached city limits halfway through the day and continued rolling toward distant towers that reached for the sky. Once the sun had set, the looming buildings were lit like a blacksmith's hearth, light glowing from hundreds of windows.

Corner post lamps gleamed at crossways where streets and avenues intersected. They kept on going, passing through a changing city landscape until, after a while, the part of the city through which they traveled fell to a hushed quiet. They had not seen any more spaceships zipping up to the heavens, even though Irwin felt them, and he was curious as to why.

Jorge urged the horses on until they passed through a section reeking of waste and garbage. Despite the stench, it was late and so they slept restlessly in the wagon, the horses still hitched for fear they might be stolen; the donkeys were tied to the backside. Kipp curled up where the donkeys had ridden inside the wagon. Irwin took the metal bed and Jorge lay on the driver's seat. They switched positions when Irwin woke so Jorge could rest better. By then, it was almost dawn; Irwin picked up the reins, and the horses perked up, ready to continue after a quick snack of oats and apples.

Irwin's gaze lingered on the towering buildings off in the distance. He could see beyond the elongated structures where enormous bullhorns—mirroring stone spires—pierced the sky above the colossal structures. They emitted a low hum that Irwin felt in his toes. The giant horns symbolized a protective barrier that no one could see. A barrier that only Irwin could feel. He didn't like it, but still they rolled forward at a steady pace.

Odd as it seemed, they still had a distance to travel before arriving. He daydreamed, wondered what the veritable city of Daos would be like, and fantasized about finding Yace. He kept driving southward.

Jorge woke much later and took a seat next to Irwin. After a while, he handed off the reins.

Jorge fondled the dirty leather reins and asked, "We're still on the same road we've been driving, right?"

"Yes. It has made a few slight turns. But is still the same road."

"Slight turns?"

"Up a small rise, and once a jag at a meeting of two major roads." Why did he have to explain? "It is the same road, just wider."

"You know, they probably won't let us into the main part of the city with the wagon."

"Why not?"

"Horse shit."

"There is human shit everywhere and they are going to balk about horse shit?" Jorge shrugged.

The wagon rattled on, only stopping once for a train of human-pulled carts to pass. They still had not seen any trees or parks; no place for children to play except in the streets—and there were a lot of children.

"When do you think we will arrive in the main part of Daos?" Irwin asked.

"You see those buildings way over there? That's the actual city—this here is an outlying district."

"How can you tell?"

"That looks like a city. This doesn't."

"How would you know? You grew up in a stone village."

Jorge glowered. "I've heard stories."

"We have been driving through this district since this time yesterday," Irwin said. "How large can this place be?"

"Bigger than anything you've ever imagined," Jorge said.

Irwin looked back at Kipp huddled on the bed, watching this strange world pass. He wanted to ask Kipp about Akarah, but his canine friend did not notice his stare. He looked back again at the towers that seemed to never get any closer.

The further into the city they journeyed, the tighter the buildings became—now five and six-stories tall and still outlining the horizon. The farther they traveled, the hotter and muggier it became. Irwin began to think of the city as its own type of jungle. By late afternoon, the air was so stifling he could hardly breathe. They all gulped water as if marooned in a desert and stopped several times to water the horses.

There were more women than men in the streets—men were under awnings or standing in their shops, selling their wares. And the only animals they ever saw were ones for sale at the butcher's shops—boxes of chickens, crates with pigs—all doomed for slaughter. People moved from the wagon's path; no one smiled, but many glared.

"I hope we find the inner city soon," muttered Jorge. "Beginning to feel unwelcome here."

Five blocks later, they were halted by half a dozen heavily armed Daosian soldiers dressed in red uniforms. "Think they're here for you?" Jorge elbowed Irwin.

Two soldiers approached, while the others stood blocking the wagon. Only one spoke, his Daosian tongue hot, his dark brown eyes jumping from Irwin to Jorge.

Jorge said, "They'll let us pass, but only if we pay."

"Of course," Irwin said while rolling his eyes toward the cloudless sky.

Their transition into the active city where metal rang all around had been subtle. It wasn't until these soldiers standing before them with impressive drawn-out swords that the ringing became noticeably intense. He could feel that everyone else who passed had coins, metal trinkets, jewelry, teeth, or anything that amounted to these weighted swords.

Stay focused. Must not summon any metal other than my own.

He made twelve silvers, two for each man standing in their way. The armed men stepped aside, allowing the wagon to travel across a long bridge into a panorama of substantial buildings. Now the road was cobbled. Had they entered the central part of the city?

"We're not allowed to travel beyond the inner-city gates with the animals; they're prohibited," Jorge told Irwin.

"Inner city gates? Where are those?"

"Up ahead, somewhere."

They were still on the same road they had been traveling since their exodus from the Jungle of Datzar. They were heading straight into the city, the road never winding or turning very far off their southerly course. Now they were surrounded by rust-colored buildings, mostly one or two stories taller than the last part of Daos. After a bit, they saw two greenish swaths of land up on either side of the encircled City Center beneath the crown of the towering stone horns. There were trees, but not much grass, that aided in occluding the southern views. Beyond the trees and towering horns, a wall rose from both the southeast and southwest, encapsulating the urban landscape. On the far west side, a beautiful grassy hill protruded above the wall. Wildflowers and occasionally a lush tree, four-times the size of the others, were one of only a few peaceful sights among the maze of stone and mortar.

They moved on through a forest of gangly buildings—on down that main road and then east onto a long avenue in search of the stable yard to which they had been directed.

I am feeling lost. Stay composed. Ignore the ringing.

Jorge pulled the reins, and the wagon came to a halt amid the stench of death.

Plugging their noses, Irwin and Jorge stepped down from the wagon, keeping close to one another. Kipp remained in the wagon-bed, partially hidden in his canine form. They went into the covered stables and were greeted by two young boys who were mucking stalls. They did not stop, but did point at the man in charge.

The stable manager was lazy-looking, well-fed and rough-hewn. He wore an open woven garment showing off his yellow-skinned Daosian body. Jorge spoke, and the man chortled. "Where from?"

Jorge muttered, "Oh good!"

"North," said Irwin. "We come to sell our wares in the inner city. I am a cutlery specialist. We need a place to keep our animals for a few days. How much will that cost?"

"North you say. Huh." The stable manager looked toward the doorway at the huge warhorses pawing at the cobbles. "Those eat much."

"Yes. But the small ones eat one-third as much."

"Seven silver per horse and five silver for each small one per day. You pay upfront, now." He thrust out his hand.

"I have silver," Irwin said, rummaging in a pant pocket and producing the silver pieces.

"How many days do you stay?"

"You think two will be enough?" Irwin looked at Jorge. He did not know how long it would take to locate and retrieve Yace. "How about this? I pay for two now and if necessary, I will come back in two days to pay for more."

He handed off several stacks of silver pieces to the stable manager—who double-checked the count and pointed at the wagon. "What of dog?"

Irwin looked over his shoulder at the empty wagon. "What dog?"

"I saw one dog!"

"No," Jorge chuckled, "we don't have a dog."

Kipp must have overheard the conversation, mutated into a much smaller form, and was hiding.

"Pay to park wagon."

Pay to park?

Trying to remain calm, Irwin felt metal moving every which direction—singing to him.

He is trying to take advantage of me!

Through grit teeth Irwin asked, "How much?"

"Four per night."

Jorge balked. "For an empty wagon?"

"It does not eat, or shit, and you want four per night?" said Irwin. "We might as well leave it on the road."

The portly man waved his finger, "Stop in road not allowed."

Jorge haggled, "Two."

"Four." The stable manager's nostrils flared.

Jorge snarled, "Three."

"Four," the stableman stepped closer.

Irwin fished out five coins. "This is all I have left, sir," he said, looking at Jorge while handing over the silver pieces. "When I get paid, I will return the favor."

Oh, how I hate being hustled!

The rough stable manager shouted in Daosian at the young stable hands. They jumped and headed to the wagon, guiding the horses into the barnyard. It was obvious they had maneuvered wagons in and out of the stable yard many times. One took the donkeys and ushered them into a stall; the other used the still-attached horses to finesse the wagon between a flatbed dray and a two-person cart.

Once the wagon was parked, the boys unhitched the horses; Jorge and Irwin retrieved their belongings.

Jorge leaned into Irwin. "We won't ask about an inn. I bet he'll charge for that information too."

"I want to be farther into town before finding a place to sleep," said Irwin.

In a rat form, Kipp jumped into Irwin's saddle bags as he tossed Kipp's personal bag across one shoulder. Irwin was careful to hoist his own across the other shoulder—he had fifty-pounds of silver rocks at the bottom of his baggage. He handed Jorge two bags; everything else would be left behind—mostly empty ration boxes. Camping gear, horse tack, and everything else of value was hidden in the large and heavy metal lockbox. He did not want to worry, nor did he want to carry everything they owned.

Before they left the barnyard, Irwin paused. He saw baskets of long grass and wooden buckets filled with water being given to their animals. The young stable attendants seemed eager to please the new boarders. He smiled, gave a pat to Jenn Jenn and turned to leave.

Jorge took the lead. Irwin kept a step behind. They walked back the way they had come, back to the main road.

"I'm hoping we'll interact with more bi-lingual people." Jorge said, sounding a bit impatient.

"Me too," Irwin smiled. "I would like to understand what is being said."

"I don't think there is a Talented District out here beyond the wall. We need to find a way into the inner city." Dark brown Daosian eyes were upon them.

"How far do you think we will have to go to find it?"

"You saw how vast Daos was from a distance." Jorge said. "This place is many kilometers wide and just as many long. I don't think anyone could actually travel this entire city, end to end, in a day's time."

"We have been in this city for almost two days and have not reached the city center? I do not want to sound impatient, but how much farther must we travel? I do not want to be too far from the animals."

"I don't know. Don't you have a map?"

"Only of the territory; not the city."

"Maybe we'll have to find one."

He couldn't stop worrying about the animals; he did not trust that stable manager. "You think our animals and the wagon will still be there when we return?"

"If they aren't, you can unleash your wrath," Jorge chuckled.

"Maybe you should use your powers of persuasion," Irwin hinted with a raised eyebrow.

"No, I think we should let loose Kipp. Let him tear up that fat fuk. How about that?"

Kipp squeaked. "I do not think Kipp wants to be a part of the conversation." Irwin could see the rat huddled on top of his clothing, trying to peer out the edge of the bag without falling onto the street.

29

<u>Daos Prime</u>

Side by side, they walked with the masses. Irwin had never imagined this many people living all in one place. He was overcome with claustrophobia a few times. People were heading home, and eventually the crowd thinned out. Occasionally, the constant vibrations from all the metal that surrounded, and from the invisible spaceships sailing away, gave him vertigo. They paused a few times to catch their breath and gaze with wide wonder.

They hiked up a slight incline to an enormous portal in the wall and straight into the heart of Daos City. They now stood at the feet of the towering buildings they had seen from afar two days before. Between twenty and twenty-five stories tall, the buildings and the monstrous horned towers cast long shadows across the center of the city. A sort of false darkness fell.

Was this the inner city they thought they were looking for? Everything was modern compared to the roughened cityscape they had just traveled through. The streets had lanes for those who walked and those who were driven around. All the buildings were painted and well-maintained. There were receptacles for trash along the streets, and there was no excrement pooled in the roadway. A few horse-drawn carriages, glamourous in size and substance, carried what appeared to be wealthy noblemen and women—perhaps on their way for an evening out. The horses even had poop-catchers between their back legs. But there were no spaceships. No colorful aliens.

The unfamiliar low hum Irwin had been feeling the last two days was still a constant, but never grew louder, never rocked him like the metal would. He was positive it emanated from the large bull horns that they continued to walk towards. Were those magnetic horns there to hide a space port beyond Daos City's farthest towering wall?

They wanted to find a Talented District before daylight warped into darkness. They looked for signs to point them in that direction, but there were none. A water fountain shot sprays from the mouths of peculiar-looking sea creatures: a statue of giant cats leaping through and around old banyan trees in the center of an enormous park. They looked for people of color, for people with Talents—none could be found. The few they had seen were following their wealthy Daosian employers.

Daos City appeared to adhere to the same principles the PCP did in other places—non-natives walked behind benefactors. Although it might have seemed that they had transitioned into a city that promoted forward-thinking, this was the usual patriarchal society—women and people of Talent were not seen as equal to Mortal man here.

On and on down the never-ending roadway, they tried to find a place to belong, to find Yace. Finally, the thoroughfare narrowed as they approached a tall perimeter wall. Were they nearing the edge of the City of Daos?

Irwin paused to take a drink and looked back at the way they had come. "I feel like we missed something." He took a long drink. "Do you know where we are going, Jorge?"

"The stories I've heard say the main road in is the main road in. I've seen the maps. I just don't know why there aren't any signs, no Erthins. No Aliens. No nothin'!" Jorge took the flask from Irwin's hand and chugged most of it.

Exhausted, Irwin fell into a state of despair. "You are saying there is more to Daos?" He pointed up the hill they were about to climb. "What about the other side of that wall?"

"Possibly. Yeah!" Jorge sounded confident. "People back there called this place Daos City Center, not inner city. The inner city is where people like you and me go."

"Center and inner mean the same thing." Irwin was hungry and tired. He wiped sweat from his brow.

"City center means the center of the city. Inner city can be offside or just beyond the center. Maybe you should feel for those spaceships. We should have seen them by now!"

"I feel metal everywhere," Irwin said, not wanting to hear the metallic sounds. He tried to clear them.

Jorge said, "I was told there are aliens here. You know, people who aren't from Urthis. I honestly don't think we're there yet. We gotta keep walking."

"My feet say we should turn back, go another direction."

"The road in is the road in," Jorge insisted. "Pull out your map; let's look at it."

"No, I have seen it too. I believe you. I know this is still the main road, the road in." Irwin waved his hand, signaling Jorge to lead again.

They followed an older couple along the incline into a residential district. The couple turned off the avenue two streets before it came to an end at the forbidding stone wall. Here, on the last street that followed the wall, the western giant stone horn hid the descending sun. The stone wall was four stories tall and as dark as the spires. They had reached the end of the road.

They drank more water.

"Fuk," Jorge muttered, passing Irwin the flask. "Now, where do we go?"

He pointed at two soldiers hidden in the shadows. "We should ask them."

The afternoon light was rapidly fading. The soldiers were hidden in recessed alcoves along the dark stone wall, watching them, and stepped out of the darkness—dressed in the same red uniforms they had already encountered.

The first guard spoke Daosian, and the second one asked, "You look lost; may we help you?"

Irwin glanced at Jorge, who said, "Yes. We seek sanctuary."

Both soldiers looked Irwin and Jorge up and down. "Sanctuary?"

The other soldier said, "Sanctuary is given only to travelers from afar."

"You must prove you are worthy of sanctuary," said the other.

"We're not from around here," Jorge said and took an enormous step away from Irwin.

Immediately, both soldiers muttered, "Empath." They sounded both bewildered and excited to see Jorge.

Second one nodded, smiling, "You may pass."

"Yes, you may pass," agreed the first.

Irwin asked, "May I pass?"

"You walk with an Empath, but you help him look Mortal."

Flushing his skin with silver, Irwin asked again, "May I pass?"

Stepping back, both soldiers nodded. Irwin had silenced them with his metallic trick. One grabbed a hidden tapestry—a doorway to the other side. "Welcome to Daos Prime," he said. "Had you arrived beyond sundown, we wouldn't have allowed passage."

With a lift in his step, Jorge stepped toward the portal and asked, "Where can we find an inn?"

The first soldier said, "The best inns are along the water."

"No, the best are on the cliff," argued the other.

"You will not have any problems finding an inn," said the first. "They are everywhere. May luck be with you."

Irwin smiled, "Thank you." He followed Jorge through the hidden doorway into Daos Prime.

The sky held a golden hue, and the residential district they found themselves in was terraced, allowing all the individual whitewashed homes a view of the giant harbor beyond. The houses on this side of the tall wall were colorful, ornate, and even had charm. There was much more greenery here than in the other parts of the city: bushes of flowers, ivy climbing terraces, blossoming trees; patterned curtains fluttering from open windows, and colorful clothing flapping on laundry lines strung between houses. Daos Prime was more modern than the rest of the capital city of Daos Territory. It was as if they had transcended to another place and time. Here they were able to see the spaceships lifting off from their port—turning invisible as each ascended into the sky.

And that low hum he had been feeling the last two days was indeed a magnetic barrier that kept the native Daosians from seeing the technological wonder that Daos Prime was.

Irwin took up his saddlebag, slowly knelt, and opened the bag. "They said we are welcome here," he said, and Kipp jumped from the luggage.

Transformed into his two-legged self, he said, "About time! I thought I'd suffocate in there."

Jorge said, "I think those soldiers were Telepaths."

"They looked Daosian to me," Irwin said. "How do you know they are telepathic?"

"I just know," said Jorge.

"He doesn't know anything," Kipp grumbled. "They smelled Daosian to me." He pulled on a pair of cut-off shorts. Jorge did not wait for them and walked on ahead by five steps. Kipp called to him, "Aren't you gonna put a hood over your head, or something? You know, in case you offend people."

"They said I'm welcome here," Jorge scoffed. "If people approach me, believing I am someone I am not, Irwin can shed my spell."

"You feel that safe here?"

"This is the inner city. All Beings are welcome, and I do mean all! I shouldn't have to worry about anything. There is no eye for an eye here, and you can't be called out just because you don't look right."

Irwin asked, "How do you know?"

"Daos Prime is unlike any other place on all Urthis," Jorge said. "That's why it is both feared and revered."

Irwin and Kipp glanced at each other, neither fully believing in Jorge's knowledge of the city. But they picked up their bags and began to follow.

Kipp tossed his heavy sack over the other shoulder. "Dang me, Irwin, how much silver is in here?"

"Twenty pounds."

"You have me carrying twenty pounds?"

"You could carry my bags," Irwin offered with a smile. He was packing over fifty pounds of silver, gold, and personal luggage.

Kipp felt the weight and backed down. "That's all yours."

Irwin chuckled, wiped his sweaty face, and slung the bags over his back.

It was cooler here than on the other side of the stone wall. The breeze off the wide wharf was constant. The road slowly widened as it descended out of the dense residential area. They passed an extensive park with more water fountains and beautiful flowering shrubs. Throngs of people walked along; a few were driven by horseless carriages called rickshaws. They were made of wood, although they did pass one made of metal—it was larger, seated six people, and the driver was on a bicycle—another fresh sight. Other rickshaws were pulled by lean runners, clearly well versed in the road systems of Daos Prime.

"I've heard of those," Jorge said. "Sometimes they're called horseless carts."

"They have those in Akarah," Kipp said.

"That would be one way to get around quick," Irwin muttered. "I feel like we have been walking all day."

Jorge said, "More than half of it, at least."

On this side of the wall, they could see the palace. It overlooked Daos Prime and sat back from the wall, partially hidden by trees and rolling hills.

As they descended into Daos Prime, the palace disappeared behind buildings and into the growing twilight. You could see one of the palace's white slate rooftops or spindly towers glimmering in the starlight. Irwin made a mental note of the palace's location as the road ahead turned away.

The layout of this part of Daos was much like the city center. Masses of residential housing flowed downhill from the tall stone wall toward the wide bay below. Seagulls were soaring and squawking, looking for perches in one of the many parks where large trees hid rows of houses. Far below, the streets that wound through the bay shimmered; you could see wharfs and docking systems for boats, still busy as night fell. They finally spotted the spaceship parkway along the bay.

They soon learned that the inlet passage between Daos City and Daos Prime was the only way to get around in a timely manner. It was also the only way the two cities were truly connected. Everything else was kept separate by the giant wall behind them. They also learned that most of the natives did not know about Daos Prime, and many of those who lived in Daos Prime did not know about the other side of the wall.

They passed small and large crowds; most were not of Daosian lineage. Some appeared Mortal, while others were obviously Talented or aliens from other worlds. No one looked out of place here in Daos Prime. Everyone they encountered was welcoming and inviting. It was an odd sight compared to the rest of Daos Territory.

How could they all be oblivious to the atrocities happening on the other side of that wall?

The road turned and ran parallel to a cliff; restaurants and glamourous inns hovered along the cliff's edge overlooking the city below—an amazing view of the harbor and the turning nighttime sky. The roadway followed the cliff for several hundred feet before descending into the main part of the city. They saw the interstellar docking stations equally spaced along the perimeter of the harbor. Right after sunset, several spaceships lifted into the sky—like backwards shooting stars—leaving tracers one could follow until they were out of sight.

The road zigged and zagged down the cliff's edge, diving deep into the towering cityscape of Daos Prime. On they walked until they encountered a range of different types of beings. From dwarf to giant and all shades of skin colors and markings, the people of Daos Prime were out enjoying the evening.

Those wearing only fur walked alongside fully clothed people. Women with purple hair and pink skin put on an acrobatic show at one intersection—an open area—and onlookers crowded to see. A few blocks later, they passed a throng of men with tentacles for hair, fishy-smelling clothes, laughing and haranguing one another as they entered a busy eatery.

Everything and everyone were buzzing, including Irwin's head. He took it all in, trying not to be overwhelmed by everything he saw, heard, and felt. There was a lot of metal here in Daos Prime, and the songs in his head were deafening. He had to practice his breathing techniques and ignore his desire to manipulate it all; the metal trumpeted in his ears.

Jorge walked several strides ahead of Irwin and Kipp. They tried to keep up, but Irwin was so impressed by everything and everyone, Kipp had to pull him along. He too stopped to gawk at beings who looked like lobsters but were not; they were entering a small bar.

Kipp stepped in closer to Irwin. "How you holdin' up?"

"Fine." He was tired from all the walking and carrying the heavy baggage. "Though, I am ready to stop for a while."

Kipp said, "Jorge seems to know where to go."

"I do not believe he does."

30

<u>WINE. WHISKEY. ALE.</u>

"I'm hungry," Kipped flung his heavy bag to the other shoulder.

"Well, I'm tired. Maybe we find an inn." Jorge's eyes were already half shut.

"We passed by an inn two blocks ago. Didn't you see it?" Kipp snapped back.

Irwin's stomach growled, and he was in no mood to listen to these two argue. "I agree with Kipp's hunger. Food first." This reminded him of the earliest time he could remember visiting Kobiton with his father. Everything was new and exciting—bright colors, sounds of everyday living, and people happily going about their business. It had been dazzling to his young eyes.

"No, I saw no inn." Jorge turned his head, scanning the landscape in every direction. Irwin could see that the Empath was also overwhelmed by the sights.

He placed a hand on Jorge's shoulder. "Are you alright, Jorge?"

"I never knew a place this big existed. I mean, I was told that Daos was a city that took a day to walk through, but I thought a day meant a sunlit day, not two days and nights. This place is spectacular." His excitement rose with his voice. "Arrol and Ron would be so amazed by all of this. It's everything they said it would be and more, that's for sure!"

Kipp said, "I smell food this way."

Jorge squeezed Irwin's arm. "How are you feeling, Irwin?"

"I am fine." If they were walking, he was not as overwhelmed by the volumes of metal surrounding him. But when he paused, Irwin could feel it, heard it singing lustfully, calling to him from every direction.

"Food's this way." Kipp strode into an eatery half a block away, not looking back for an okay sign from Irwin.

Without a sign of objection, Irwin and Jorge followed him into a bustling establishment where all the workers were green-skinned and purple-haired. They wore black clothing and white aprons—did not approach them when they entered. Several looked their way as they entered Pammi's Platters. Irwin and Jorge were out of place—probably looked too Mortal in the alien-run enterprise. Jorge kept close to Irwin, muting his empathic powers. Kipp was the only one who fit in with his dark features.

"This is a little awkward," Jorge whispered to Irwin.

Kipp said, "Dang me, there're no open tables down here." He peered up at the upper floors, open to below, and spotted a few barren tables. In the center of the ground floor where they stood looking around, there was a stage that included idle instruments.

Irwin struggled to remain calm. There was metal constantly moving around and through him. He closed his eyes and felt Kipp moving back and forth at his side; Jorge moving in closer on the other—they were all anxious, almost ready to leave.

A server approached. "Three for a table?"

Irwin said, "Yes, please."

She motioned for them to follow. "This way."

She led them to a spiral staircase leading to the second floor—as loud and busy as the first. Windows were open and a subtle breeze flowed through the open, but crowded, room.

He inhaled the aroma of cooking fish and some kind of vegetable he couldn't place.

They were led to a corner booth amid the soft roar of people talking, eating, and scraping their chairs back and forth. "Your server will be with you shortly." She handed them hand-printed menu cards and walked away.

They settled into the U-shaped booth, adjusting bags and baggage. Irwin sat between Jorge and Kipp; Jorge studied the menu, and Kipp looked the place over. They could see up to a third floor, as busy as the first two. Pammi's Platters was packed with patrons.

"I wonder what type of entertainment they have here." Kipp said. His attention returned to the booth and on his menu—food always Kipp's priority.

Irwin looked out the window, watching those below strolling around. There did not seem to be any obvious codes-of-conduct here in Daos Prime—no menacing-looking men in dark blue uniforms. He saw only cheerful people, and that melted some of the angst in his soul.

"You think they have wine?" Jorge was also considering the menu.

Irwin muttered, "I hope they have whiskey."

"They should," said Kipp. "What's on the menu, anyway?"

Jorge snapped, "Can't you read?"

"I can, but not that handwriting." He pushed his menu toward the center of the table.

"They have salmon bisque, crawdads and clams, a spicy seaweed sandwich that is mostly vegetables, no meat," Irwin softened. "You probably do not want that. There is also chicken and noodles and lamb bites with dumplings."

"Oh, those last two put together sound tasty!" Kipp licked his lips, his eyes sparkly with enthusiasm for the first time in a long time.

"Order whatever you want," Irwin said. "This meal is well-deserved." He slapped Kipp's shoulder. "We made it."

Whatever that means.

Now all we must do is find Yace.

He knew that feat was nearly impossible.

"About fukin' time, right?!" Kipp cracked.

"I can order anything?"

"Of course, Jorge, anything you want," Irwin said.

"How are we gonna find Yace?" asked Kipp.

A green-skinned, male waiter wearing a thigh long black tunic, matching shorts, and a long white apron wrapped tightly around his mid-section, holding a small ledger, stepped up to their table. "Good evening, patrons. What are you drinking tonight?"

"Wine."

"Whiskey."

"Ale."

The server smiled, nodding as he wrote their order in the small notebook. "Anything else? Have you decided what you want to eat?"

Jorge replied first. "I'll take the salmon bisque."

Irwin asked carefully, "Where is your lamb from?"

Kipp elbowed Irwin and answered, "Chicken and noodles."

"I will take the crawdads and clams, please and thank you," said Irwin.

"Will that be all?"

Kipp pointed at a server passing off a loaf of bread to other patrons, "and one of those."

"Anything else?"

"Make my whiskey a double," Irwin added. "Thank you."

"Alright." The server checked his list. "One glass of wine. A double whisky and an ale. The salmon. Crawdads and clams for you. And chicken with noodles. Excellent. Your drinks will be up quickly." He then left.

After a bit of stunned silence, Jorge said, "A male waiter? Who would've thought of that?"

"That is what I was thinking," said Irwin, "a pleasant sight to see. All we have ever seen are women working these jobs—all the while trying to keep men's hands off them. It is disgusting, really."

"You probably won't see that here unless we're at a brothel," Jorge said. "After this, we should go find an inn."

"I think we should begin searching for Yace," Kipp said. "Irwin only paid for two days at the stables. It'll take us time to find her in this place!"

Jorge snapped, "He can go back and pay for more days."

"The quicker we find her, the quicker—"

Jorge cut him off. "Did you think it'd be that easy?"

"It was before," Kipp said. "I smelled her then."

"Daos is vast," said Jorge. "We've been walking all day and haven't seen one person with blonde hair."

"We'll find her."

"No, you won't," said Jorge bitterly. "She's probably dead by now."

Pushing the table toward Jorge, Kipp snarled, "You don't know that."

Irwin snapped, "Will you two stop arguing? Yace is not dead. And, yes, we will find an inn. We will look for her and we will find her." His eyes were on Kipp.

"Tonight?" Kipp had not let go of his panic, his fear that Yace was lost to him.

The metallic songs grew louder and louder. Irwin closed his eyes, trying to calm his anxieties; tried to measure his breath. Meanwhile, small and large spaceships continued to fly into and away from Daos. The non-stop hum of all the metal people carried and wore, both close and up and down the streets, was deafening to Irwin. He ground his teeth, trying to fight his urges. But when he opened his eyes, both friends looked aghast at the sight of him.

Kipp jumped. "Irwin! Keep control. There's silver swirling in your eyes."

Jorge added, "Should we leave?"

Irwin blinked several times, washing away the swirling metal. "I will be alright. I was fine while we walked. But now that we are sitting, being still, I feel everything. The metal is loud—almost unbearable."

"Fuk! We shouldn't be here." Kipp grabbed at his bags. "We need to go."

"I am alright." Irwin measured his breath, focusing on each inhale and exhale. "I will be alright."

He could see that Kipp and Jorge were not convinced.

"I knew this was a bad idea." Kipp fiddled with the handle of his bag.

"I agree. We should go." Jorge reached for his pack.

"You two are overreacting. I will be alright." Irwin assured them while telling himself to hold still.

Keep it together. I need something to do. A drink. Some food. Please, hurry, server!

"No, for once Jorge's right, we need to leave. I'm familiar with that look."

As Kipp scooted to the edge of the booth, their server reappeared. "Here you go." He placed their drinks down along with three glasses of water. "Your order comes to fifty-five credits, or Rupees."

"Credits or Rupees?" Irwin said. "I have Hakran silver pieces. What is the monetarily equivalent?"

"Fifty-five Hakran pieces."

"It is the same?"

"One Rupee is one Hakran piece. If they weigh the same, they're the same; the pictures don't matter here."

"That is good to know." Irwin shoved his hand into his empty pocket and proceeded to make the coins. "Thank you," he shilled the shiny silvers, stacking them on the table.

"Thank you, gentlemen. Your food will be ready shortly." The server smiled, took the coins, shoved them into his pocket, and moved on to the next booth.

Irwin picked up his drink and chugged it down. As their server walked past their table, he signaled for him to come back.

"Is there something else?"

"Um, yes," said Irwin. "I would like another double shot. But I was hoping to buy a bottle if I can, please."

"An entire bottle? We only sell shots."

"Yes. This is a good whisky. We just arrived in Daos Prime. And I do not know where to get a bottle at this hour. I feel I need an entire bottle to suit my cravings for tonight." He felt his friends watching him.

"I can ask about selling you a bottle, sir. Not sure if it'll happen."

"Thank you for trying."

"I'll take another ale," Kipp said, chugging down the remainder of what was in the mug in front of him. He passed the heavy glass to the server, and they all watched him walk away through the crowded room.

Once he was gone, Jorge asked, "Are you sure you need an entire bottle, Irwin?"

"Yes."

I am hoping it will help dull my senses.

Though they sat in silence, Jorge and Kipp kept their eyes on him—he stared forward, ignoring them, though he was aware they were watching, aware of their concern.

"You gonna be alright, Irwin?" Kipp pressed.

Irwin opened his mouth, but at first no words came out. The two waited. "The first place we need to search for Yace is the palace."

Keep focused, talk about plans.

"Kipp, I leave this for you to do. With your ability to shapeshift, you can infiltrate those palace walls easily. Jorge and I will walk around the harbor. We will ask in every establishment we pass, see what may have happened of note recently in the palace; maybe someone knows something. It is possible we can find a Telepath, maybe talk to Nonbry. He might know something. He has Dana at his side." Those two were back in the Gypsy camp, maybe on the road, but either way, they were long ago and far away.

"Oh good! You've been thinking about Yace."

"Of course I have, Kipp. And now that we are here, it is going to be a challenge to find her."

"I hope she hasn't tried anything stupid."

Jorge sneered, "Most likely she has. Most likely she's already dead."

Kipp jerked the table toward Jorge.

"Please, you two, your bickering is not helpful." He rubbed his forehead and leaned back in the seat.

Jorge persisted, "What about an inn?"

"We will find one and rent a room for the day."

Jorge and Kipp echoed each other. "For the day?"

"We must consider that there are fewer people out during the night than in daylight. So now is a better time to find a scent and get a location on her. I do not think it will be as easy during daylight when all the people are out. Besides, we are used to very little sleep. We need to seize our time here and not get caught up by our personal needs."

Kipp sniffed. "You need a bath, Irwin."

"We all need one, but not now. Maybe tomorrow, when the city is busy, we will take a reprieve. That is what has cost us so much time in the past." He studied Kipp. "We cannot give in to our needs, not yet. Dephen certainly has not."

"Are you fooling me," Kipp snapped, "Dephen gave into his needs everywhere along the way. If we find them before something bad happens to Yace—"

"We have been lucky, Kipp, but our luck may have run dry. Daos is a big place. We must use our wits, be quick on our feet, and use our cunning to find her."

"I'll find Yace," Kipp was adamant, "and you'll save her."

"I hope so."

Jorge spread his arms across the table and hung his head. "I don't get to rest until tomorrow?"

"If you do not want to help, we can find an inn and you can take the night off, Jorge." Irwin said, "Yace is not your problem. And it is probably best you are not seen with us, anyway."

Jorge said, "What if something happens to you, Irwin?"

"You are worried about something happening to me?"

Kipp and Jorge answered in unison, "Yeah!"

A small wooden cutting board with fresh baked rye bread, served with a saucer of butter and stabbed in the center with a knife, was placed on their table. Then a mug of ale and the bottle of whiskey were set down. Their arrival of their server silenced their conversation. "That will be fifty silvers for the bottle of whiskey, and three for the ale refill."

Jorge gasped, "Fifty! That's robbery."

Irwin said, "It is unopened, Jorge." He made the silvers in his pocket and pulled them out. "Fifty silvers is worth it to me." He pushed the payment across the table. "Thank you."

"Since you're all new to the area," said their server, "I should let you know that the best place to buy spirits is down along the southern docks. Spirit sellers are down there usually around midday. That bottle would only cost you twenty unless you barter for more. The more you buy, the cheaper it gets—sometimes."

"But you're gonna charge us fifty?" Jorge sneered.

"Jorge." Irwin blasted him with an angered look; then smiled at the server. "Thank you for that information."

"Hey, I'm just charging what I was told." The server said.

"Robbery," mumbled Jorge.

The server smiled. "I'll bring your food momentarily." Irwin thanked him again.

He said, "The man is nice. Let up on him."

Jorge elbowed, goading. "I think he likes you, Irwin."

"How can you tell?"

"Oh, I just know these things," Jorge said, "How he looked at you, after looking at all the rest of us. How his smile grew a little wider when he spoke to you. And when you thanked him, he liked that, too."

Kipp looked stunned. "You think our server likes Irwin?" He reached for the bread, cut off a piece, and chomped on a bite.

"What's not to like about Irwin?" Jorge said, smiling.

Stuffing his mouth, Kipp rolled his eyes.

Irwin reached for his bottle of whiskey, opened it, and poured his glass half full.

Jorge squirmed. "I still can't believe I am here in Daos Prime! Ron would be so jealous right now if he knew." He took a contemplative sip of wine. "Maybe I'll walk around with you tonight, Irwin. We can look for Empaths too. Those guards knew what I was, so there must be more here like me."

Kipp said, "I'm amazed I haven't seen any other Clan-Duins yet. Do you sense any Erthins, Irwin?"

Jorge was fantasized. "Maybe there is a commune, a safe place for my people. Yeah, I should go with you, Irwin. We can see the sights together." Jorge leaned into Irwin with lustful eyes.

He ignored Jorge, emptied his cup, and said to Kipp, "There are no Erthins in here, but there are three next-door." He pointed at the far wall.

"What?" Jorge looked startled. "You-you can actually feel Erthins?"

"Yes." Irwin grinned, pouring himself yet another glass of whiskey. "Two of them are Wind Erthins, the other is a mixture of water and fire."

"Are they full Erthins?"

"One of the Wind Erthins is more powerful than the other. But I cannot tell if they are full-blooded or part."

"You should have seen him in Arenu Village, Jorge," Kipp sniggered. "He counted over two hundred."

"There were two-hundred fifty-three in Arenu village," Irwin confessed. "There were others, but they were too far away to count individually."

Jorge said, "Arenu Village has something like four hundred Erthins. Most are crossbreeds. The rest, telepathic crosses."

Silence fell over their table once more. They sipped their drinks and watched others in the room.

After a while, the server appeared. "Here're your meals. Will there be anything else?" He asked—eyes on Irwin again.

"Thank you." Irwin levitated a coin to the server. "A token of gratitude for the swift service. We will let you know if there is anything else."

Jorge added in haste, "I'll take another glass of wine."

"Ale, please," Kipp said. They both pushed their empty cups toward the table's edge.

"Yes." The man nodded, taking the coin and the two glasses away. "I'll be right back."

"This place is pleasant." Irwin pulled his meal toward him. "This is where we should meet up before finding a room tomorrow."

"I just wanna sleep in a comfortable bed tonight." Jorge expressed his exhaustion.

Irwin said, "Alright, we will find an inn, drop off our heavy bags, then go find Yace." He picked up a shell-cracker and tiny fork and broke his meal into edible bites.

31
Conquering Emotional Attachments

The food was good, seats were comfortable, and those who filled the room were entertaining to watch. Irwin asked the server about where they might find a nice room and he was told that the barkeeper's sister owned a large inn one block away. They were set.

The people who ran the inn were hospitable, offering them built-in latrines, running water, bathing rooms, and clothes-cleaning service; of course, that all came as extras. Once they found out the base price for one room was forty silvers per night, they opted to take the amenities, which cost another five silvers and to share one room.

Their room was on the fourth floor. The innkeeper told them they could use the lift or take the staircase up to their room. Kipp was unsure of this lift, yet followed Irwin and Jorge as they entered the box. After the door closed, they were then swooped to the fourth floor faster than it would have taken Kipp to hike up the stairs. They were all unsteady as they departed the electric lift.

Their bedroom was enormous—a giant bed was centered between two windows that opened to the night sky. They settled into their room and readied themselves for their night out.

A tall oak dresser hid a wall-mounted urinal and a washing basin with a faucet. Two wicker seats with plush-looking pillows were nestled against a matching table; there was a bin for dirty clothing next to the door. The room had everything a weary traveler might need; if they put out their dirty laundry, a maid would pick it up—clean, fold, and return it by early morning.

Impressed by it all, including the key to the room, they were motivated to go back out and scour the streets for Yace and for any Empaths that might be about. After they washed up and put on clean-ish clothing, Irwin and Jorge were ready to walk the streets. Kipp took to the sky in his bird form.

Riding the lift down, Irwin said, "I can feel the mechanics of this thing."

Jorge clutched the side rail. "Do I need to worry about this contraption?"

Feeling the motor turning, valves pumping and gears moving in unison, the Metalist shook off the impulse to manipulate the lift to move even faster. He was transfixed by what he felt. Jorge said his name again. "Do I need to worry about you doin' somethin' stupid?"

"No."

They both laughed and took up hands.

Irwin still could not shake the intimacy he had shared with Jorge. He had never been that close, that trusting with another.

Although I hope Jorge finds his people, I also hope he wants to stay with me. Once Kipp and Yace are reunited, I will be sad that I do not have someone to lean upon. Although I am not sure I have deep love for Jorge, I know I have something with him that we can nurture, grow together. I need that in my life!

Although his emotions were still confusing, he was working on understanding them and sharing them with others.

"I am glad you are here with me." Irwin squeezed Jorge's hand.

The spacious lobby was fitted with plush couches and other cushioned seating, end-tables, and immaculately painted walls. A display of fruit for the guests to enjoy had been placed in bowls on a table near the greeting area. They walked across ornate carpets, and the front desk woman smiled and called out, "Have a good evening, patrons."

They were out in the night air that had cooled considerably by a breeze off the harbor, though it still felt sticky—humid. If not for all the tall buildings, more wind could have whisked away the stifling and sticky air.

"Let's go this way," said Jorge, taking the lead.

There were many unique looking people, most appearing Mortal-like, walking the streets and enjoying the evening. Jorge and Irwin felt watchful eyes as they walked along a path past a section of storefronts.

They walked along the expansive harbor where they passed several taverns and brothels. Irwin noticed that there was less obvious contention between the men and the women in these places—more respectful interactions. Nevertheless, all sexes strut about preening themselves as sexual objects; they had put themselves out there for everyone to ogle.

Passing another brothel, it looked just like any saloon Irwin had ever been in, except alcohol was prohibited. There were signs next to the doorway stating that drunk and disorderly customers would be removed. Gargantuan creatures in bright orange clothing stood aside the open doorway. It seemed quiet from the street view. There was no bar for people to step up and order drinks, only cushioned couches, chairs, and gaming tables inside the brothel's large front room. Only a few people were there talking to the colorful and erotic creatures within—Irwin guessed most had already been taken upstairs. Creatures of color and different skin with skimpy clothing, painted faces, and wild hairdos paced along a balcony, calling down to all who passed by. After taking it all in, Irwin and Jorge walked past the brothel and slipped into a quiet tavern.

They ordered drinks.

Jorge engaged a middle-aged Erthin bartender. "We just arrived in Daos today and are wonderin' if there's an Empathic community here."

The bartender shrugged. "Where you two from?" He was studying them while waiting to be paid for the drinks. He had a bushy goatee and wild, curly hair pulled back in a knot at the back of his head.

Irwin passed him ten coins for two glasses of wine. He said, "A small village on the west coast called Goshee—near Gustin. My friend here is an Empath. We were told there is a commune here for his people."

The barkeep sounded bewildered. "In Daos Prime?"

"Yeah," Jorge replied, "Of course, that was several years ago when we were told this, but we're hoping it still exists."

"I don't know of an Empathic community. You know, if you were to go to the Hall of Civilities, they'd know if such a place exists."

Irwin was curious, "Hall of Civilities?"

"Yeah, but they're not open now. I'd try first thing in the morning when it's not busy."

"Where is the Hall located?"

"Downtown. Next to station seven, up from West Wharf. You can't miss it—gigantic building. Large doors. Anyone lookin' for a residential pass has to go through those doors."

Jorge pressed, "What about the Palace? Do you know if Empaths live there?"

"The Palace? You mean the Palace of Ishik?"

Jorge nodded.

"That place is a steel cage. No one goes in there unless invited; and from what I know, no one's ever invited."

"So, nothing ever happens in the palace," Irwin said, glanced at Jorge.

"We residents aren't privy to that information," replied the barkeep. "Besides, the Emperor is only here for the people of Daos."

Irwin asked, "Daos meaning the whole territory?"

"Yes, of course! Daos Prime is not ruled by the Ishik Empire, or Hakra, or anyone else. This is a galactic city under the rule of universal leaders who believe in the common good for all kinds. Daos Prime is a city for tourists really—visitors and workers come here every day from all over the known universe. This city's been here for over millennia and will always be here. We are a powerful city and cannot be owned, or ruled, by anyone."

Jorge said under his breath, but loud enough to be heard, "Ishik's are Coterie. They could control it all if they wanted."

The barkeep sneered. "The people of Daos Prime can't be bullied by anyone, including supposed children of gods—Ishik, or anyone else. They didn't help keep Urthis safe when the sky rained red. Millions of people died back then. That Empire did nothing but preserve their own perverse race. If you ask me, the Ishik owes us! We kept their people safe."

"Would the people of Daos Prime know if something happened to the Ishik Empire?" asked Irwin. "Like a battle within the compound, or an assassin taking out the standing Emperor?"

Raising an eyebrow, the barkeep said, "As I said before, Daos Prime residents are not privy to that information."

"So, if someone came in and killed the Emperor, Daos Prime would be none the wiser?"

The barkeep's smile veered sinister. "We might not know what happened but would be secretly happy if something did! Some of us, like myself, who live and work in Daos Prime, know what happens on the other side of that wall. We know how the food is brought to our table. We know how the people of Daos Territory suffer. The Ishik's don't care about them. Never have; never will." He paused, glanced at the bar; he leaned in close and whispered, "If given the opportunity, we would help those on the north side but those who aren't native to Urthis aren't allowed to interfere with the present habitat of the planet."

"You're Erthin!" Jorge said, "You're native-ish."

Irwin asked, "How come you cannot help?"

"I wasn't born here. And those of us who live here are restricted from going there. We can trade with the merchants, but ...." He looked out the window to the north. "We're not allowed to help the Daosian people in any way. We don't look local, and to be seen offering help, well, that's against Daos Prime rules."

Irwin said, "You look more local to Urthis than some of the people we have seen today."

"There're rules here?" Jorge looked at the barkeep, taking him in as though there was no one else in the world when they spoke, as he did with everyone.

Irwin watched this new friend, Jorge—considered that might be the foundation of being an empath; to take them in and only them when encountered.

"There are many types here in Daos Prime. Some of us might appear more local than others." The barkeep studied Irwin and Jorge. "But we're not barbaric like them. Daos Prime is for happy people, and that's how we want it. Everyone is equal here and our rules are better than the Ishik Empire's rules—we don't tolerate Telepaths manipulating the population. They are discouraged from living in Daos Prime, and only a few do."

Jorge gasped, "You're saying there're no Telepaths here?"

"There are some. We call them Psychic Attendants. A few advertise their services. You'll find one along the southern side of the harbor, but most live on the northern side of the wall. They tend to live solitary lives—keep to themselves."

Irwin muttered, "Psychic Attendants."

"That's a fancy name for Telepath," Jorge was amused.

The barkeep lowered his voice. "Most people don't like Telepaths."

"I understand," said Irwin.

"Just like everywhere else on Urthis, they're not to be trusted. But especially the ones here in Daos. It's possible that one of those Psychic Attendants would know of an Empathic community."

Jorge and Irwin both took a drink from their mugs, processing what they had just learned. "We were in another tavern earlier," Irwin said, "for supper, and noticed that they only employed green-skinned people."

"There are several places that only hire Ivians. Some places selectively hire those types—loyal to those types. As you can see, I don't care who you are or what you look like, so long as you don't cheat or lie; those types can live on a boat stuck in the doldrums."

They all laughed; Jorge and Irwin guzzled more of the tasty spirits. After a brief silence, Irwin asked, "Have you hired on any female servers recently?"

"All my workers have been with me for years and are quite loyal to my saloon, except Sally. She came on after this last winter's storms." He glanced at a voluptuous woman who had extra of everything, including giggles. She winked at the barkeep and waved at Irwin and Jorge.

"Any chance that was over two moons ago?" Irwin asked.

"About half a year ago. We've bad monsoon seasons. The weather drives many visitors and workers back home. Most of my people love their job, but not the weather."

Jorge said, "You're Erthin. Shouldn't you be able to control it?"

Rather emboldened, Irwin thought.

The barkeep laughed, "I'm not a weather manipulator! Just a humble proprietor who loves drink, food, and people."

After a bit of chatting and laughing together, Irwin and Jorge moved on to another saloon—quieter places where they could keep to themselves. At each saloon, they ordered a drink, sometimes two. They ate a late meal at the Wealthy Witch where they once again quizzed their server. Like the rest of them, no one recalled seeing any Empaths anywhere in Daos, nor did they know much about the palace and its inhabitants. No new servers had been hired. Finding Yace would take more than two days.

By the time they stumbled back to the Inn, it was late, and they were drunk. Irwin used his own metal as a beacon, bringing them back without getting more lost than Jorge predicted. Riding the lift, Jorge held on to Irwin—belligerent and beleaguered. He almost passed out in his arms. Back in their room, they collapsed onto the bed, leaving no space for Kipp.

Irwin woke late that next morning—he felt Kipp sleeping next to him.

Am I dreaming?

Irwin moved closer to Kipp, smelling his musty scent, and eventually waking him.

Rubbing his eyes, Kipp turned over. "You two smell like a tavern."

"Where is Jorge?" Irwin was still groggy and hung over.

"He's passed out against the wall next to the urinal."

There was Jorge, partially sitting, but mostly propped up against the wall. "What is he doing over there?"

"He puked at some point." Kipp muttered.

"I did not think we drank that much," Irwin said and laid back. "Of course, we had a drink at every bar we stopped at." He watched Kipp roll off the bed and head toward the urinal. "How was your night, Kipp?"

"I'm sore."

"Sore? What did you do?"

"I flew, and flew, and flew. Dang me, Irwin, Daos is enormous."

"I thought you went to the palace."

"I did, after flying around the city. I thought I'd see the entire view, you know, check everything out. But man, Daos goes on and on." He came back to bed and lay down.

Irwin got up to relieve himself.

"I take it you did not smell Yace?"

"Holy Hakra, Irwin! I don't know how we're gonna find her."

"Well, she is in one of two places—either somewhere in Daos Prime or walking the palace halls." Irwin nudged Jorge with a foot as he stepped away from the urinal. "Hey Jorge, time to wake up," he whispered.

"He's passed out," said Kipp.

"Must not drink so much," Irwin said and returned to the warm bed.

"He tried to keep up with you, didn't he?! That's like me trying to keep up with Yace. Maybe tonight you two should do less drinking and more talking."

"We went to seven taverns. No, eight." He tried to remember where all they had been. "Yes, eight, but we learned very little. But we did find out that none of those places has hired on any new females in the last few moons. And there is no Empathic community here, but a few of the locals said they had seen Empaths before. At one stop, Jorge was flaunting his powers—clearly asking for attention."

"Jorge's a weird one."

Irwin wondered why Kipp seemed to dislike Jorge so much.

Shaking off his confusion, Irwin propped himself up on his elbow to keep an eye on Jorge. "I noticed that some people we talked to had very negative views of the Ishik Empire. Apparently, a good portion of them know how their food is brought to them, where it comes from. They know quite well how the natives are treated," Irwin said, remembering their conversations last night. "A few even expressed that the idea of the Ishik Empire being destroyed was a good one. But at the same time, they were not sure if there was a better option. The feelings about the Hakran Empire were neutral at best. But no one seemed to like the idea of Telepaths being in control of either Empire, so ...."

"Ha! Wouldn't it be funny if you were right," said Kipp, "... the PCP and Dephen plotting together to take down the Ishik Empire?"

"Funny?" He changed the subject. "Today, I thought we could all look around together."

"Together?" Kipp pointed toward Jorge. "You think he'll be ready to go any-time soon?"

They looked at Jorge sleeping against the wall, drool smeared on his cheek and the wall. Irwin asked, "How was the palace?"

"It's a fortress of a place—as big as any village I've been in!"

"Really?" Irwin noted Kipp's concern.

Just how Yace would act if she were apprehensive.

Kipp said, "Yeah, three times the size of Arenu Village."

"Really? Arenu Village was pretty big."

"The whole compound is contained. There are quarters and segments, but all of it appears interconnected. And that hillside we saw. There are wolves and wildcats and horses running free all across there."

"And ...?"

"There're all Clan-Duins, Irwin!"

"Clan-Duins can be horses too?"

"No—well, maybe," Kipp paused, "But there are Clan-Duins and Erthins everywhere. It's kind of like they're waiting for something. I hope it's not us."

Irwin studied Kipp.

Kipp was worried. "I flew and flew."

"Yes, you said that."

"I surveyed only a few of the rooms and the gardens—it's massive, Irwin. I'll have to go undercover tonight, check out the inside of the palace."

"Undercover? Alone?"

"As a mouse, or a rat—some small form that allows me to get around without being noticed. I need to get inside and smell for Yace. I think she's there, hiding out, waiting for the right time to assassinate the Emperor."

"Maybe; while you are there, you can look for Empaths too. For Jorge's sake." Jorge was waking up. "He was sad that there was no Empathic community."

Yawning, Jorge asked, "What ... what are you two talking about?"

"Last night."

"Fuk, I don't wanna do that again." Jorge put a hand on his head. "Ugh. Water?"

Irwin retrieved a half empty flask. With a wave of his hand, he filled it and passed it to Jorge. Guzzling half the water, Jorge cleared his throat and asked, "What're we doing?"

"Are you in any shape to walk and talk some more, Jorge?"

"Shit, no." Jorge took another large drink. "I wanna sleep on the bed. You two go; I'm gonna stay here and recover."

Worried he had gotten his friend too drunk, Irwin asked, "Will you be alright?"

"I don't know." Jorge took another drink. "My head hurts; my eyes hurt. I wanna sleep on something more comfortable than this wall."

Kipp offered his spot on the bed. "Take it."

"What're you two gonna do?"

"I am going to continue to wake up," Irwin said. "Kipp seems to have more energy than us."

Pulling a sleeveless tunic out of his bag, Kipp tittered, "I didn't get drunk!"

Slowly climbing onto the bed, Jorge said, "We found you a brothel." He pointed in the opposite direction of the brothel.

"Oh," Irwin held his hand out to Kipp, "If we want to talk to Nonbry, we need to find a Psychic Attendant. That is what they call Telepaths here. I do not recall seeing any blue-eyed, light-blonde-haired people anywhere yesterday. Did you, Jorge?"

"I don't wanna talk to Nonbry," said Kipp. "He'll not be pleased."

Jorge lay down and closed his eyes. The flask still in his hand, it rested against his belly. "Not that I recall," he said, smiling. "Hm. I'm alright with that."

Kipp said, "Who wouldn't be!"

"What are you going to do, Kipp?"

"I'm gonna get breakfast. Can I have some money, please?"

Irwin made a dozen coins fly out of his hand onto the bed. "There you go." He then drew out a small knife. "Just in case."

The look Kipp gave Irwin said, 'I don't need it.'

Irwin insisted, "Keep it on you, anyway."

"I've got those coins you gave me. I'll put them in my boot; that way I don't spend them." He fished through his bags for the coins and dropped one into each boot. "There, you happy?"

"Thank you, Kipp."

"I think it's stupid; nothing will happen to me. It's you I worry about, Irwin." He opened the door and was gone.

Irwin wondered if his love for Kipp was merely one young boy's longing for love from another. These thoughts plagued him—got in the way of their mission to find Yace.

Jorge grumbled, "Man, he's pissy."

"He is just upset that he has not found Yace yet."

"We just got here. Did he think it'd be that easy?"

"Probably."

"Dumb Clan-Duin," Jorge muttered under his breath as Irwin moved off the bed.

He went to the saddlebags and pulled out an almost empty satchel of dried fruits. He turned around and there was Kipp, lying naked on the bed. He knew it was Jorge, but still his heart leaped.

If only I could pretend and feel alright about it. But Jorge does not smell like Kipp, or act like him. It is not fair to Jorge. Life is not fair. But I do have warm feelings for Jorge.

He lay next to Jorge—Kipp vanished. Irwin munched on dried strawberries, sort of ignoring Jorge.

Jorge muttered, "Ummm, berries. You alright, Irwin?"

I do not care if you are not Kipp. I want intimacy, I want love. I want to give in to my urges. I do not want to hold back anymore. I want what you and I shared a moon ago.

Irwin then leaned into Jorge. Their lips met; a bite of strawberry was shared. The satchel of dried strawberries was soon buried under their bodies and smashed into the blanket. He felt it smeared across his backside, but this time Irwin let his inhibitions go, surrendered to his desires.

32

<u>METAL MADNESS</u>

I rwin and Jorge awoke entwined in each other's arms—warm and sweaty. They used the washbasin to clean up and cool down. They dressed and looked for and found the restaurant where they had eaten the night before, Pammi's Platters. For the midday meal, the eateries' menu had been changed to easy-to-prepare meals of soups and sandwiches. They shared some vegetable soup and a goat cheese sandwich. A day of carousing around the city, and meandering along the bay toward the Hall of Civilities had begun. On the streets there were many going about their business, working, playing, and wandering around.

Irwin's feet hurt, so they found a shoe store that was two stories tall and filled with countless types, shapes, and sizes of boots and shoes. Some were made of leather, others cloth or wood; some were tall, short, big healed or flat; anything one might want for comfort or style, or both. Irwin bought himself and Jorge each a pair of well-fitting, comfortable shoes.

He was drawn in by the sights and sounds wherever they went. Jorge tried to regulate his impulses—especially when Irwin was drawn to the spaceship docking stations.

"I see a blonde," Jorge said, pointing to a medium-sized person about sixty feet away, back turned to them. She disappeared.

"We must follow her." He could not let her go, and they began chasing after the woman who disappeared into the crowded streets.

Irwin and Jorge pushed through crowds, searching for the blonde-headed person they hoped to find. Irwin grabbed Jorge when he spotted the ends of blonde hair fluttering as they raced around the corner of a building. Now they were in hot pursuit until Irwin reached for the blonde person's shoulder. When he turned around, Irwin realized he was face to face with a man.

Both were startled. This man had beautiful blonde locks—for a man—and comparable in length to Yace's hair. He looked telepathic, but clearly, he was not a family member of Yace's. His face was long and gaunt, and his nose was arched—probably broken a few times—with bushy eyebrows and a long fore-head.

"I am so sorry. I thought you were someone else," said Irwin. He turned away, embarrassed.

Jorge chuckled.

They continued on down the avenue in their new footwear, looking up as they passed twelve and fifteen-story buildings. "How are we going to find Yace in a place like this, Jorge?"

"You probably won't."

"Look, your negative sentiment is not helpful."

"You're hoping for a miracle, Irwin. She's gone. When will you accept that fact?"

"Yace is not gone."

"Then tell me where this illusive, strong-willed Coterie woman is."

Wiping sweat from his face, Irwin said, "She is here somewhere."

"You're lying to yourself, Irwin," Jorge said. "Your female friend is gone. You already know this. You're smarter than Kipp; you know what's happened to her. She's—most likely—dead. Meanwhile Kipp will go on, loyally, trying to find someone who left him in the first place. So what if she's mentally taken over? That probably happens all the time! Telepaths are conniving; you know this. We both know this! And Kipp, he'll never let go of her. He is Clan-Duin and too stupid to realize—"

"Stop, Jorge! Stop badgering, please!" Irwin barked. "Kipp is smart in his own way, just as you are smart in your own way."

"That's one way to put it."

"We are going to find Yace," said Irwin, "and we cannot be deterred."

"You seem so sure of that, Irwin, but she's gone. She's gone! You're smarter than this. Don't follow that Clan-Duin's nose. Maybe this is where the two of you part ways. You stay here with me and let him go; let him find her." He ran his fingers up and down Irwin's arm.

Irwin pulled away. "I am the one who is supposed to find Yace."

"And how are you gonna do that?"

"Jorge, we just got here. Do not lay into me about what needs to happen, or what will never happen." He heaved a deep, forlorn sigh. "I must go back to the stables tomorrow and pay for the animals." His eyes drew up between two buildings to the slope they had descended the night before. "It will take me all day to get there."

"Maybe you should leave tonight."

"I cannot leave tonight; we have work to do." He watched an orb fall from the sky and land a short distance away.

"Then how're you going to .... Hey, where're you going, Irwin?"

He stepped away from Jorge and ran toward the docking spaceship.

They were lost to each other. He had not seen Jorge struggle to move around a group of aliens. But he heard people gasping, calling out to their loved ones, and then angered to see someone they did not wish to see. But Irwin's eyes were fixed on the dozen or so idle metallic ships. "Aluminum, Chromium, Titanium, Tungsten, Copper, Zirconium ...."

"Hey, what's your problem, Irwin?" Jorge shouted, out of breath.

He watched creatures exiting and entering the spaceships. From behind them, half a dozen lobster-looking beings—possibly the ones they had seen last night—pushed past them toward their ship. It was obvious that those six creatures were in a hurry; he watched them hustle toward the landing pad.

"You left me back there." Jorge looked distressed.

"Sorry," he said, still hypnotized by the ships and not caring so much that he left Jorge behind. He was clearly conflicted. This morning had been amazing, but Jorge was not Kipp.

I must stop comparing them. Must remember Kipp's desires. And it is not me.

Rectangular, oval, round, flat, misshapen—each spaceship was unique, as were the array of beings coming and going. It was a busy afternoon at Daos Prime's Interstellar Port. Ships were landing and taking off—turning invisible before shooting upward into the brilliant blue sky—reflecting sunlight as they defied gravity with ease.

Irwin could feel Jorge at his side, jumping from one foot to the other. He ignored him. He was unmoved and watched another ship land; watched green-skinned, purple-haired creatures emerge from this strange sky wag-on—Ivians.

That is right, Ivians. Where are they from?

They looked like servers at Pammi's Platters and Illian's Inn. They stepped around Irwin and Jorge and climbed a flight of stairs. He had seen a marketplace up there earlier.

Kipp called from the top of the stairs, "Irwin?!" He ran down the steps holding the handrail, jumping the stairs two at a time.

Irwin was happy to see Kipp—his best friend. He could not imagine a world without this sometimes-annoying guy in it. "What are you doing here, Kipp?" He could hardly contain his delight.

"I should ask the same of you," he said, stepping in front of Jorge to get closer to Irwin.

"Where have you been?"

"Where haven't I been, Holy Hakra! I went to the north docks, then the western docks." Kipp swung his arm around, pointing here and there around the bay. "Then the southern docks. There are four piers around this wharf, and all the buildings are massive; it's like they're made for giants. Then I went that way." He pointed again. "Daos Prime is massive! There're so many people everywhere. What've you two been up to?" He was breathless with excitement.

"Just looking around."

"Irwin bought me shoes and a pouch," said Jorge, showing off his new attire. "We thought we saw Yace."

"You did?!"

"It turned out to be a hideous man with pretty hair," Jorge finished.

"Did he look like Yace?" Kipp stared at Irwin.

"Not really," said Irwin. But his attention was elsewhere.

Kipp grabbed his arm. "You alright, Irwin?"

"Yes. I am looking, that is all."

"Daydreaming's more like it," said Jorge.

An ocean breeze whipped at their hair and tumbled debris around the streets. A swirl of dust picked up a small child's skirt. A flock of seabirds rode the wind surf along the lanes.

"We should leave this area," Kipp pulled Irwin by his shirtsleeve. "Come on; let's go get a bite of food down by the docks."

"Why?" Jorge was inquisitive, or was it suspicion?

"Pretty workers," Kipp gleamed.

"We're going to the Hall of Civilities," Jorge told him. "We're gonna see about my family—where they live."

"We can go there any time, Jorge," Irwin was exhausted by Jorge. And now he felt refreshed by Kipp's presence. "Who knows, we might see an Empath today just walking around." He took up with Kipp, keeping pace.

They all three meandered away from the spaceship docking port. Irwin hustled toward a jewelry seller. The man was shouting and showing off his gleaming jewelry; gold rings and necklaces were pinned inside his petticoat and shone brilliantly in the afternoon sunlight. But then Irwin noticed the merchant's fancy jewelry was not made of gold.

It is all just well-polished bronze. And for the price, he is ripping off people.

He leaned in close and muttered his sentiments to Jorge and Kipp; they both chuckled.

"There're merchants all over Urthis who do that," Kipp told Irwin; Jorge agreed. "They sell wares, saying it's one thing, but you could guess it's fake. Just like those pots Yace stole. You could tell right away they were improperly made, but she never knew."

Irwin glared at the animated trader. "I am half tempted to steal some of the silver he has stashed in his pocket. Teach him a lesson."

"It won't teach him anything," Kipp said, "But go for it, if you must, I won't stop you."

Deep-sea fishermen were moored at the docks. They ate from the same food stand where Kipp had stopped earlier. The pretty shuckers remembered him and gave him two free oysters for bringing more patrons to their stand. Jorge made a face and spat them onto the ground. Irwin made a face but still swallowed the strange textured things.

It was late afternoon and Kipp said he was ready to go back to the Inn for a nap. He urged Irwin and Jorge to come with him. They needed energy to search for Yace again when night came. Irwin led them to the Inn without one wrong turn. Jorge marveled at such keen awareness of the city's layout, but Kipp knew Irwin was using his powers, letting his own silver guide him back.

The comfort of their room was welcoming to all three weary men. Kipp lay down on the bed, but Irwin and Jorge decided to bathe first. They went to one of the communal bathing rooms on the same floor, and at least for now, it was empty.

Jorge chose a private room with a tub.

They enjoyed their first proper bath since Arenu Village. First, they took time trimming facial hair and ragged locks. Then they bathed, scrubbing each other's back, flirting, and frolicking. They were enjoying each other; something Irwin felt he needed more of and wanted more of now.

Kipp napped, taking up the entire bed, but jolted awake when the two men flung open the door.

"Good, you smell better," Kipp muttered, rolling over and out of the way of Jorge, who had plunked himself onto the bed.

"You should smell yourself," Jorge grimaced.

"You are going to bathe, right Kipp?" Irwin shimmied into one of his hand-made sleeveless shirts. He liked this one in particular because of its maroon color.

Kipp looked tired. He blinked several times, rose on his elbow, and looked toward the window. There wasn't much daylight left. "Better do it now, I guess."

"Better hurry. The tubs were filling up when we left," Jorge taunted, and then turned to Irwin. "Are we going back to that one tavern?"

"Pammi's Platters?" Irwin knew what Jorge was thinking. "Yes, we can do that, though I want to go back to the Wealthy Witch too. They had those seasoned potato stringy things. Tasty!"

"Wait for me?" Kipp grabbed the bag of bathing supplies.

"Of course, Kipp," Irwin noticed Jorge shrug. It was obvious he did not care, maybe even wanted to leave Kipp behind.

"Just meet us there?" said Jorge. "We'll have an ale already for ya."

Kipp looked crushed in a way Irwin had not seen before. "Fine. See you then."

Irwin knew Kipp wanted him to wait—he was willing to—but Jorge had his own desires. "There are personal showers—if you do not want to bathe. You could be done quick if you go now."

"Alright. I'll be back soon." Kipp scooped up his clean clothing.

Once Kipp left the room, Jorge grinned. "Good job gettin' rid of him. Let's go."

"No. We are going to wait."

"Your lust for Kipp has gotten in the way. You know that, right?"

"I know he does not love me. I am alright with that."

"That's not what I am saying, Irwin. Your feelings for him shadow your true desires. What you really need to do is leave him. That way, you can finally acknowledge your feelings for me."

After a deep exhale, Irwin admitted, "I like you, Jorge. But I am not in love with you. Not like I am with Kipp."

"See there, you acknowledged yourself. Your true desires. And we know they'll change over time." Jorge ran a finger up and down Irwin's arm. "Like can grow into love. And it's time you accepted the fact that Kipp will never love you. Not like I do."

"How you show your love is harsh, damaging sometimes."

"At least I'm expressing my feelings. That's something you still need to work on!"

This conversation again.

Shaking his head, Irwin sat next to Jorge and kept his eyes on the door. "I know to not allow my feelings for Kipp to get in the way of what needs to happen. Our goal is to rescue Yace. Nothing else."

I have been withholding my feelings for him since Arenu Village.

"You're still having a hard time with that. I can see it. You either need to confess your feelings and accept the rejection, or just move on!"

He refrained from breathing, afraid Jorge's words would continue to smack him.

"What about after you find your friend, Yace? Will you tell him then?"

"No."

"Why not?"

"My feelings for him do not matter. Besides, he does not need to know." Irwin's voice cracked. "I am good at holding back my feelings, my emotions. I know not to let them dominate my ... my everything. I know to keep focused, to follow through, no matter what."

"But why? You're ignoring yourself and what you truly want."

"Emotions get in the way. They do not matter. Not here. Not now."

"That's horseshit Irwin! You need to feel. And if Kipp won't give you want, what you need, then you should move on. Move on to me."

"I do not want to have this conversation again, Jorge."

"If you don't acknowledge your feelings, Irwin, they'll eat you and everyone around you alive."

He is trying to provoke me.

"You do not know what you are talking about."

"Then tell me. Tell me why you are quiet when you should be fierce? Tell me why it's so hard for you to be you!"

"You do not want to see me when I am fierce."

"I don't think you've ever been fierce. Like mad in love and willing to do anything about it, fierce."

"Oh, I have." He lied.

"You have? Is it comparable to how you were at Nuaki Village?"

"It is similar." Irwin knew he was afraid to acknowledge many things about himself and his feelings for other people. He wanted to ignore it all.

His silvery eyes never left the door. He felt four people move away from the lift that had just stopped near their room—heading to the rooms beyond. Every person carried at least one knife, coins, jewelry, and other small metallic things that sang as they walked past. He used the metallic parade as a diversion.

"I don't believe you. You know what, Irwin, you need to be more in touch with yourself or you'll reduce yourself to a recluse."

He listened to the metal sing.

"Hey Irwin, are you even paying attention to me?"

"Yes."

They sat quietly and then Jorge asked, anger rising in his voice, "What do you want from yourself, Irwin?"

"I want to rescue Yace and see Kipp reunited with—"

"Wrong. You want Kipp all to yourself, but you'll never get that. Can't you see that you two are not meant to be? And this whole finding Yace shit, it'll never happen. It's like finding a needle in a haystack. And all I have to say is good luck with that!"

"We will find Yace."

"You'll find Yace, and then what?"

"One thing at a time, Jorge."

"Imagine Kipp being reunited with Yace. And then what?" Jorge would not let up. "What happens with Irwin then? What about you?"

Irwin spit the question back at Jorge, snapping, "What about me?"

"Exactly!"

"Why do you provoke, Jorge?"

"Because you need it. Because you let me." Jorge's eyes twinkled. "Because I was never allowed to push people around, but it always happened to me." His smile showed off his crooked teeth—he looked wicked. "You need it. I see it! You need to acknowledge fundamental parts of yourself, Irwin."

"You think I need to be pushed?"

I am ready to hurt you, Jorge. Please do not provoke me.

Jorge read Irwin's body language. "Aw. Look at that. You wanna kill me! That's cute," he winked.

"I do not appreciate it, Jorge. And I do not appreciate you implying my feelings matter to you, nor do I appreciate being provoked."

"Your feelings *do* matter to me. They might matter to Kipp. But they should matter to you too!"

He quietly said, "They do."

"Me provoking is just a way for you to feel those emotions." His voice was clouded now.

Irwin tried to keep his resolve. "You know, Jorge, at some point I might forget to keep calm. Think about what all you have seen me do before you push me to do the same. Remember, death is permanent."

You might be right. I might not know what love is. I might love you too, even though you provoke me like this. Is it possible I love Jorge? I have wanted it for so long. But I really do not know what love is, what it feels like.

"Oh, you won't kill me." Jorge appeared tickled by the conversation.

You are right. I will not. But my feelings are jumbled. It is hard to know what to do. And I do not want to be provoked!

The room fell quiet again. Irwin allowed the metallic songs, now echoing everywhere, to distract his attention from Jorge. It seemed to him that Jorge wanted him to explode. In a place like Daos Prime, he knew he would not be able to handle himself if he let go.

Between the choruses and acknowledging my emotions…. I could destroy so many things, so many beings.

After a long time, Jorge jumped to his feet. "Well, I'm gonna get us a table at Pammi's Platters. Guess I'll be seeing you and the Clan-Duin later." He patted Irwin's back and went to open the door, then turned around. "Can I have a few coins for drinks?"

Without a pause, Irwin passed over a dozen silvers and watched Jorge leave the room. He lay back on the bed, his thoughts swirling.

What the shit am I going to do? How will I rescue Yace with Jorge being Jorge?

Well, if Jorge finds his people, I feel fine in leaving him with them.

Do I?

Yes, he is abrasive, but I have something with him, even if I cannot define it just yet. What if he finds his people and they live here, and he wants to remain? I will have to let him go. There is no way I can stay here in Daos. This place will set me off.

But what if there is not a commune of Empaths? Will Jorge want to stay with us, with me? I mean, Daos Prime has everything. Everything but me. I cannot stay here. I will remain with Kipp and Yace.

But what if Jorge is right? What if we never find Yace? I know Kipp will continue until the end of time looking for her. And then what? Will I continue to follow him?

His shoulders and stomach sank.

What am I going to do?

I feel like Jorge is trying to corrupt my mind, my thoughts. No, he is just tempting me with something I desire. I want to be happy with someone—someone who accepts me for me.

But that cannot happen. Not now. Kipp and I have a mission.

And when it ends ... what about my happiness? I have never had it, or allowed it, but today ... today I feel like I have it with Jorge, even if he provokes. He lets me have contact; he accepts me with all my flaws, most of them.

He laid back on the bed, eyes plastered on the wooden ceiling.

This is all fleeting. Once Jorge finds his people, he will forget about me.

Maybe I do not want Jorge to find his people. He makes me happier than being alone with my thoughts. But he is abrasive. Maybe he can learn to be less coarse. Ha! I cannot expect that. He took all the negative things that happened to him in his life and allowed them to fester. We are much the same. Maybe that is what I am attracted to. Jorge makes me feel safe. He does want me to be happy. I want that too. But I want it with Kipp.

Jorge is right. My love for Kipp has compromised our mission. I must move beyond him. Let Jorge be my happiness.

I am sure this is how Kipp feels about Yace. She barely tolerates him, and he adores her—would do anything in his power for her. It seems we both want something we cannot have. At least we have that in common. Oh, if I could have with him what I've had with Jorge.

I just wish ... I wish I could meet someone like me, like Jorge, but someone who is not jaded by their past.

Jorge is the only one I have met like me so far! I think people like me, those who need and desire what I do, are a rarity. What about Arrol, Ron?

They are proof that I am not alone.

33

<u>Daydreaming</u>

The door flung open. Kipp stepped into the room, partially clothed. He smiled at Irwin. "Jorge didn't wanna wait, did he?"

"No."

"What a shit, Irwin! Jorge's an asshole. I hope he finds his people soon."

"I understand why you two dislike each other. But I wish you were able to get along."

"I get along with him as long as he doesn't call me stupid, or make fun of me, or provoke, or all the other annoying things he's done ... all of it!" He pulled a sleeveless shirt over his head. "What I don't get is why you like him so much. I mean, he's pushy with you, he goads you, he does things to you I wouldn't do. Why do you allow it?"

"He reminds me of my father and grandfather."

"You miss being harassed and beaten?"

"No. I do not miss that. I wish Jorge was nicer with his words, especially toward you."

"I just don't get it, Irwin." Kipp sat next to him, tying his old worn boots. "What does he do for you that makes you like him?"

Irwin's eyes dropped to his hands.

I can pretend he is you.

"I do not know."

Kipp did not press the issue, but his eyes glimmered gold. Jealousy? "You ready to eat?"

Trying to pull himself out of his depressed mood, Irwin lifted his eyes and forced a smile. "Yes."

Out of the room, down the lift that had become routine to them, they strolled out onto the cobbled street. Pammi's Platters was easy to find on the next block.

Jorge was sitting in a booth on the first floor. He waved. A glass of wine, a mug of ale, and a cup of whiskey were arranged on the tabletop just as Irwin and Kipp settled in.

"Thank you, Jorge," Irwin spoke softly, still trying to regain his good mood.

Grabbing his mug of ale, Kipp held it up, urging the other two to do the same. "A Prost!" He clinked his mug against Irwin's whiskey cup. "To finding Yace!"

"To finding Yace." Irwin needed the pick-me-up. He needed to not think about his feelings, or Jorge; he needed to focus on the plan.

They ordered food and more drinks. No one needed more alcohol by the time they left Pammi's Platters. Kipp returned to the Inn to drop off his clothes before taking to the sky. Irwin and Jorge meandered through the streets of Daos Prime. Again, Irwin was drawn to the spaceship landing area.

They walked around twelve-foot-tall creatures and followed a menage of men into a gigantic chamber where creatures fought until someone tapped out in metal lined cages. Everyone seemed to be betting, voices echoing throughout the grand hall. Most of the fighters were Mortal, at least in nature.

Irwin and Jorge were shoved toward the front row of the main cage, where a gory fight was taking place a few feet away. Men with powers fought for blood and money behind thick glass walls inside a large octagonal room. Blood splatter from previous fights had not been cleaned from the floor or windows. They watched for two rounds: men placed bets and greedily scooped up their winnings. Outside the octagon, men amped up from watching fights were engulfed in a brutal fight of their own, but were swiftly kicked out by gruesome, lizard-like bouncers.

They were getting another taste of Daos Prime's lifestyle. Jorge was enthralled by the sights, as was Irwin—but probably in a different way, for different reasons. Jorge wanted to stay to watch the next fight, but Irwin pulled him outside. When twilight fell, several spaceships took off into the twinkling sky. Irwin stopped to watch, but Jorge reached over and took his arm, pulling him away.

"Why'd we leave the fight? Was it so you could watch the spaceships again? Can't you ignore the metal, Irwin?"

Trying to give Jorge all his attention, he replied, "I hate fighting."

Jorge snorted, "All right, where to now?"

There was a fire dance show a half block away, and Irwin was drawn to the spectacle. Three teenage Erthin girls were juggling flaming orbs, shooting fire out their mouths, and making sparks fly from their arms and legs while they performed gymnastic maneuvers. There was a crowd gathering.

"You're walking around like a lost child, Irwin."

He ignored the jab, kept his eyes on the fire dancers. One made a flaming hoop and her two partners backflipped through it.

"Oh, look at that, honey!" A ten-foot-tall woman called back to her even taller husband who was dragging along their two five-foot tall children. They stepped past Irwin and Jorge to get a better view of the dancers. "Let's get a shot of this," she giggled, pulling out a sleek metal device from a large purse.

Irwin's eyes went from the dancers to the device. Once he saw the image of the fire dancers holding still on the front of it, he gasped, "Excuse me, Ma'am, what is that thing you have in your hand?"

"Oh, this? It's a camera. You must be a non-native." She snapped a picture of Irwin, who was standing apart from Jorge. "Isn't it cute, honey? They've never seen a camera before?" She took several more pictures of those in the crowd watching the fire dancers.

"Come on," Jorge grabbed Irwin's arm, pulling him from the mob.

He heard her snap a few more pictures.

"People around here are annoying," Jorge said, navigating them toward the northeast side of the bay.

"Where are we going now?"

"Away from that freaky lady."

"Maybe we could look for Yace down by the docks."

"You think she'd be there of all the places?"

"Possibly. Kipp said he saw every type of creature, including Telepaths, down there."

"You're not looking for one of those Psychic Attendants, are you? You know, they won't be out walking around where everyone else is. They'd be in the shady part of town."

"No, I just want to watch everyone." This time Irwin led—Jorge half a stride behind.

They passed sweet-smelling dessert bars and boisterous taverns. Many varieties of music wafted past as they meandered—soft sounds of harps, rhythmic drum circles, piano sonatas, and a melody of stringed instruments. These choruses were as sweet and drawing as the metal Irwin felt; Daos Prime was indeed its own type of orchestra.

They found a boardwalk that hugged the lengthy bay that stretched on for many kilometers, following the curve of the land around a small peninsula. After a while, Irwin found a bench and motioned for Jorge to sit with him. There in the moonlight, they watched reflections ripple across the waves. The breezy air smelled of the sea. They gazed at birds diving into the water for an evening meal.

Buildings on the other side of the bay were lit with neon signs and outlines of blue, purple, orange, and pink. The neon colors mixed with the starlight on the waters below. People of every race walked past. Some were jogging, others pushed baby carriages, roller-skated, or strolled peacefully with friends. Irwin and Jorge saw a lot that night, including a boat full of Mortal passengers.

Two Erthin men who had been working as shipmates emerged from the low-lying dock and strode tiredly up a long gangplank. They grunted as they pulled ropes across the access point, closing their boat business for the day. They said farewell and departed in separate directions.

Irwin stood and approached one of the Erthin sailors. Jorge followed. "Hi," said Irwin, "I was wondering where you sailed in from?"

"Central Daos, why?"

"Central Daos? Is that on this side of the wall or the other?"

"Central Daos is on the north side, but we taxi to Fisherman's Wharf, Boat Bay, Canal Jetty, and a few docks along north and south Daos Prime six times a day. We take workers back and forth. There's another boat that hits all the eastern ports for non-natives like us. They make a stop here too, but their final harbor is that one." He pointed across the bay. "They work with the crabbers and fishers."

"How much is the fare to the north side?"

"What are you doing, Irwin?"

"I have to pay for the horses tomorrow. The gate up at the top of the hill is closed until morning, and if I walk, it will take all day to get there. And another to return. Maybe it is possible I take a boat instead." Irwin asked the Erthin sailor, "How early do you cast off?"

"Just before first light. My buddy, Joe, will be takin' that shift. We switch shifts. He works early morning; I do the afternoon-evening runs. Today, my buddy Carl rode along, helped blow air." He chuckled, watching Carl amble away. "It's a simple route, but more fun with friends. So, where'd you leave your horses?"

"About five blocks in from the wide canal that has roads on either side."

"Oh, that *is* a walk from here!" The Erthin sailor laughed. "Your best bet would be to get off at Canal Jetty and follow the road inland."

"Sounds like a plan. Thank you."

"Oh! And it's two tokens for a one-way trip."

"Token, is that the same as a Rupee?"

"Nah. For a Rupee, you get four tokens. You want some tokens now?" He rummaged in his pocket, pulling out several small bronze pieces—a quarter the size and weight of a silver piece each.

"You leave before first light and make six rounds?"

"Yeah, it takes just over two hours to make one round trip," the Erthin explained patiently. "If I wasn't Erthin, it would take much longer." He held out a heaping handful. He was ready to exchange four for a silver piece.

Irwin took what he needed and paid for it with his one silver piece. "Up and back should be all I need."

"What if you have to go again?" Jorge was watching him closely.

"You are right, Jorge, can I get eight?" He passed over one more silver, took four more tokens. The exchange was made, and the Erthin left.

Jorge chuckled. "That was convenient."

"What is funny is I was just thinking about how I was going to get back to the stables in a timely manner, and then along comes that sailor."

"Dumb luck," said Jorge, keeping to Irwin's side. "So, have you given much thought to my proposal?"

"Your proposal?"

"To leave Kipp and his problems and stay with me." He placed his hand on Irwin's waist, trying to pull him closer.

"Stay with you, here?"

"Well, if I don't find my people, then there is no sense in staying here. We could go anywhere we want. I mean, the entire universe is at our disposal." Jorge said, pointing to an ascending spaceship.

It was a tempting proposition, except for the fact that being inside a metal space-voyaging-vessel might not be in his best interest.

"I know I said I might want to visit my home world, but I did not really mean it."

They took many silent strides before Jorge spoke again. "We could stay here."

"That is not an option for me. As soon as I can, I am getting out of here."

"Why?"

"There is a lot of metal here."

"I hadn't noticed," said Jorge sarcastically. "It's that bad?"

Pulling out his hidden flask, Irwin took a sip of whiskey. "Alcohol helps. It makes me not want to summon all of it around me, but the songs are deafening at times."

"Songs?"

"Do not worry about it. I have myself under control."

Mostly ... unless provoked. Ugh! I am so much like father.

Irwin ran his hand through his hair, something he did a lot lately when thinking about Albert.

I understand so much more about him. Maybe the mountains are the only place for me. Keep calm; remember the plan; get Yace and get out—try not to kill everyone.

"You sure? Maybe we should go back to the room and rest."

I cannot take time off. I must find Yace. But how? In a place so large and so diverse. Kipp is not taking time off. He is searching the palace right now. I hope he finds her.

"No, let us go back to—"

Jorge wagged his finger. "We're not going back to the fukin' spaceships, Irwin!"

"The Wealthy Witch." Irwin was getting more and more irritated by Jorge's assumptions. "I want to try one of those salami sandwiches and have more potato strings."

34

<u>Kipp's Conscious</u>

Kipp returned before dawn. Irwin had left to catch the boat. He woke Jorge, who shouted, "Fuk off. He left to go pay for the horses," and rolled over and went back to sleep.

Finding a spot on the floor, away from Jorge, Kipp curled up in his canine form. They both slept all morning. Jorge woke before the sun was at high mast and slipped out of the room.

As soon as the Empath was gone, Kipp jumped onto the bed and rested comfortably in his two-legged form. He dreamed the dreams of a peaceful man, but when Jorge came back, Kipp jumped up and left Jorge in search of breakfast.

His first find was a bakery. Believing regular bread and hard-rolls would be sold there, he discovered that they only served frosting-covered cakes, cupcakes, and cookies. He bought one sweet treat and walked down to the fisherman's docks in search of something not so sweet. The Clan-Duin preferred nature's sweets—honey, apples, oranges, peaches, or strawberries.

He ate fried crawdads on a stick for his next meal and seaweed-wrapped fish fillet for the third meal. He tried ice cream, to his delight, then tasted something called iced coffee that was not as wonderful as the ice cream. The last of the silver Irwin had given him was spent. His stomach satisfied, he returned to the Inn, passing someone who looked like Irwin going out the door.

"Irwin?!" Kipp called out several times before realizing, "Jorge!"

Jorge stopped, turned and waited for Kipp. He had looked like Yace, then Irwin, and now the closer Kipp stepped toward him, Jorge turned into Nonbry, then Hauss—they all appeared to be disgruntled. Kipp forced himself to think of and engage with Jorge—he knew the conversation would be coarse.

"What?"

"Where're you going?"

"Patti's Platters."

"Man, you sure like that place."

"They've good food."

"You know that food is probably made by a special kind of cook. They use their powers to make food taste better than it is."

"Oh, I know," said Jorge. "We had one of those in Nuaki; his name was Bob."

"Bob, what a snippy name. Isn't that something women do?" Jorge said nothing, turned to leave, but Kipp kept up. "You think we'll see Irwin soon?"

"He left before first light. Who knows?" They walked in silence, and then Jorge muttered, "I wish I knew how he does that. He just knows when to get up."

"It's that weird Erthin shit he's got going. Man, that's a long walk. I hope he makes it back before tomorrow."

"He took a boat."

"A boat?"

"Yeah, there're boats that taxi people between ports and on both sides of the wall!"

"Yeah, I know about the taxis. I took one yesterday and paid for it with kind words. She was such a pretty Erthin." He added, "Well, good for him, better than walking, that's for sure."

"Yeah, Irwin didn't wanna walk all day."

"I wouldn't either," Kipp said. "Daos is much bigger than Akarah. I remember in Akarah, we could walk across the entire city in a day. But this place ...."

They went to Patti's Platters, mostly empty of patrons during the mid-afternoon. It appeared that most restaurants either closed or cut back workers at this time. Kipp wanted to sit at a booth, but Jorge went to the bar.

Pulling out a silver rock from a hidden satchel, Jorge asked, "Where can I cash this?" The barkeep looked Jorge over. He was obviously put off by his appearance and how it changed, wavering in his sight. Blinking a few times, the barkeep focused on the rock.

Kipp whispered, "What are you doing?"

"I have no silver, do you?"

"I just spent my last few coins."

Barkeep looked at the two young men. "You know what it weighs?"

Jorge shrugged. "Don't you have a scale?"

Kipp reached for the rock, picked it up and tossed it around. "This is three pounds."

"Three, you sure?"

"Yeah."

Jorge said, "I took the smallest rock I could find."

"Three pounds?" The barkeep assessed. "That's one-hundred and eighty Rupees."

The waitress stepped up to the counter. "Three pounds is over two-hundred Rupees."

"Only if it's pure silver. Is this pure silver?" The barkeep bounced the rock in his hand.

"Of course it's all silver," said Kipp.

The waitress stared at Jorge, obviously confused by his appearance. "Tavian?"

"I'm not Tavian," grumbled Jorge, keeping his attention on the man behind the bar.

"He's that fellow the other servers were talking about yesterday," the barkeep said. "For pure silver, I could get two-hundred Rupees, for three pounds!"

The waitress looked baffled. Her eyes rested on Jorge for only a moment and shifted toward Kipp. "I'd take it to the bank down the street for better value than you'll get here."

Jorge asked, "Where's the bank?"

"Five blocks down, take a right, then three more. It's not too far," the waitress replied, clearly mesmerized by him.

"I'll give you cash now, one-hundred eighty Rupees," said the barkeep.

Jorge did not seem bothered by the exchange. "Sure, I'll take it."

Kipp leaned into Jorge and whispered, "Irwin could probably make three-hundred coins out of that rock."

Jorge smirked. "He's not here to do so, and I'm hungry."

"There's a pouch of coins in his baggage."

"Really, I didn't find it."

"I don't think you looked very hard," said Kipp.

The barkeep turned away and knelt to open a safe below the counter. Pulling out a sack of Rupee coins stamped with a raptor grasping grape vines; he stacked coins in rows ten-high.

"Thank you for the trade." Jorge took the coins and shoveled them into his pouch. He passed a handful to Kipp. "Here ya go, Clan-Duin. I'll take a glass of red wine, barkeep." He placed a half dozen coins down.

"Drinking this early?" Kipp chided.

"It's midday." Jorge pointed at the man pouring wine. "Besides, he was nice enough to trade coins for a rock, so I might as well spend some of this money here."

Kipp huffed, "That was Irwin's rock to spend."

"He would've given it to me. This way, I don't have to wait for him. Why do you care, Clan-Duin?"

"Did you ask him if you could take his stuff?"

"He lets me do what I want; I don't have to ask permission—unlike you."

Kipp held a low growl, wanting to say something, but suddenly heard Irwin's voice chiding him for wanting to argue with Jorge. Instead, he took the twenty Rupees and settled down at the other end of the bar. He wanted to be far away from Jorge, but his stomach held him hostage.

"A mug of ale and a bowl of clam chowder," Kipp said.

He heard Jorge snicker at his decision to order a drink. Kipp hated everything about Jorge; he wanted to leave the bar as soon as he finished eating. The ale was placed between Kipp's hands, and not long after, the clam chowder was delivered. Jorge's meal took longer to be served.

Few people came or left the bar while Jorge and Kipp ate their meals separately. As he wiped his mouth and pushed his empty bowl and mug aside, a shrouded person stepped between the two of them. He thought nothing of it until that person moved away from the bar toward the restroom. Kipp noticed Jorge's eyes following the shrouded person who stepped around Kipp. His pastel orange robes billowed as he strode away from the bar and down the short hallway.

Jorge took a large bite of his meal, drank down the glass of wine, and did not make eye contact with Kipp. He also moved toward the restrooms. Jorge gave the impression of deception—glancing over his shoulder, avoiding eye contact with Kipp, and disappeared around the corner.

Waiting, Kipp counted. He reached seventy and realized Jorge was not coming back. The Empath had left the building. Standing up and pretending to go to the bathroom, Kipp saw a backdoor open to the alleyway. Jorge and another person's urine were combined in the bathroom. Some had been splashed on his feet, and the scent was carried and dropped along the way, leaving a trail.

"Why be so sneaky?" He followed the scents, inhaling the odor of the other person. "Smells like another Empath." He went to the end of the alley, following the smells down three blocks and up four.

Jorge was now shrouded in the same pastel colored robe as his escort. They zigzagged through the streets and rushed into a colorful but small bazaar.

Kipp saw Jorge and the shrouded person joined by two others who wore the same color clothing. He watched them march along together, but they separated on the other side of the bazaar. It was hard to tell which pair to follow. Kipp knew what they were trying to do. They wanted him off Jorge's trail. Both pairs went in opposite directions and Kipp rushed to an alleyway to morph into a bird. He flew his clothing up to their hotel room, tossed the threads through the window, and took to the sky in search of the shrouded ones.

Once he spotted the soft pastel pair of hoods, Kipp followed from overhead. They knew how to cover their trails, but from where he was, nothing could get past him. Occasionally, one of them would glance over their shoulder to see if he was still following. None of them bothered to look at the sky. When Kipp found the second pair of cloaked travelers, he shadowed them too, but sporadically sought out the other pair. That was when he noticed both pairs were climbing toward the same object.

"What are you up to? Where are you going?" Kipp pursued the Empathic congregation as they hiked the streets heading west. He watched them leave the city center, moving toward higher ground. He hung to the scent of them all.

His Clan-Duin instincts were always keen. He stuck to their trails. The two sets joined one another upslope in a dense residential district. The group slunk down a street before pushing Jorge into a three-story residence. It was there that they locked the door behind themselves with a loud snap that echoed with finality.

"Dang me!" Kipp landed on the stoop, smelling the wooden door. He caught whiffs of more people inside, in addition to the ones he had already been tailing. "I need to find Irwin."

Irwin missed the return boat at Canal Jetty by only a few minutes. It took him extra time to find the stable yard that morning. Every street in Daos City looked the same—rust-colored stone and mortar. He waited along a northern wharf, miffed about this day. He would not arrive back at the southern wharf until early evening.

This was supposed to be a quick trip.

North of the Canal Jetty there was an open market partially covered and inviting. He ate steamed fish on freshly baked rolls and watched the sights. Native Daosians were hard at work selling and showing off their wares and designs. It seemed that the Daosians who lived in the city were far more creative with their time than their rural neighbors; their clothing, pottery, woodworking, and leather designs reflected their freedom.

After a while, Irwin found a bench near the bay and from there watched boats and anglers up close; some were ferrying locals to other ports. He watched the sun move across the horizon; the afternoon wore on. The breeze was warm and filled with sounds of hungry gulls. Just in time, he saw the taxi-boat's colorful sail in the distance swiftly gliding toward Canal Jetty.

He stood and started walking, wanting to be in line and on that boat. His stride was swift and determined, but as Irwin walked along with the boat in his sight, he was hit in the head by a blackbird.

A violent collision, the bird flew into him again, circling his head and chirping angrily. It soon seemed like the bird was insisting Irwin follow it. He watched the boat coming; the one that would return him to Daos Prime, but now realized this was Kipp trying to get his attention. The bird shot between two buildings, down a very narrow alley, and landed. Then he mutated into his two-legged form.

Kipp gasped for breath, "Jorge was kidnapped ..."

"What?"

"... by an Empath. There were others too!"

"Where was this?"

"Pammi's Platters."

"Kipp!" He raked his fingers through his long hair. "The boat back is coming. I have to go."

"It won't be fast enough. He needs your help now!"

"It is faster than running through the city." Irwin glanced over his shoulder, trying to see the dock. "Look, Kipp, if you want me to help, I need to get on that boat."

"They knew I was following. Went into a market thinking they could lose me. They joined up with others wearing the same robes."

"Did you follow them?"

"Of course. And they all ended up at a house far upslope from the bay."

"How many are there?"

"At first there were just the four. But once I smelled the house, I realized there were more. Maybe a dozen."

"A dozen?"

"Yeah! There were a lot of smells at the door they took him through."

Irwin groaned, pacing backwards. "I need to get on the boat. I missed the last one. I would have been back already had I not. I must go." Irwin jogged backwards; the taxi-boat was probably docked—but only long enough to allow people off and on.

"Dang it!" Kipp bellowed, leaped into the sky, and flew after Irwin.

Seeing the boat readying for departure, Irwin shouted and waved. He would not miss another boat; not again! They had cast off one of the two ropes; a gangly man at the dock held onto the last rope while Irwin raced down the planks. He jumped and landed on the deck at the last second. His momentum helped push the boat away from the dock.

"Thank you," he panted, grateful for whatever delay the shipmate might have rendered.

"Tokens," the Erthin from last night asked Irwin. "Ah, it's the boardwalk fellow. Hey! You made it."

"This time, yes." Irwin passed him a token. "Let me know if you need any help getting back to the southern ports."

The Erthin captain took the small token, and filling his sail full of air, he sent the boat speeding forth. "Help, why?"

"I am Erthin."

The obvious, red-haired, olive skinned, wind yielding Erthin chortled. "You're no Erthin."

Irwin pulled the wind from the sails. The boat slowed.

"Wow! I don't sense your abilities."

Irwin coolly replied, "I have been taught not to display my powers unless I must."

"Wow, you're that well-trained?"

He nodded. Kipp landed on his shoulder. Irwin turned his head and smiled at the small black bird. "Hi, friend."

"An Erthin, an' somethin' else!" He gasped, "I've never seen a bird just land on someone before unless they have food in hand. Is that yer pet?"

He said nothing, but smiled at the compliments. He glanced at Kipp, who stayed with Irwin the entire ride back—the taxi made several stops.

They passed an eccentric part of town attached to the north side of Daos City where bright red painted houses layered the hillside. From there, the boat flew along and passed a mouth to the open ocean where the wind blew harder and Kipp dug his claws into Irwin's shoulder. "Ow!" On either side of the inlet passage, tall bluffs provided protection from the elements for the city-folk, keeping hidden the wonder of Daos Prime from those who lived in the main part of Daos City.

The speedy boat sailed past what appeared to be a barren island full of trees and flowering plants. The moment they passed the long stone wall's invisible line through the waters, the view changed to whitewashed houses. The residents up on the hillside had a perfect view of harbors, docks, and glimmering sunsets. No one departed from the boat at the next stop, and no one waited for the taxi.

Further past the island, their boat-taxi parked at a dock off a serene beach. There were people relaxing, strolling along the edge of the harbor. Half a dozen stepped off the boat, but no one came aboard. Children were playing in the sand along the shoreline.

The next stop smelled of fishy odors. Only one person stepped off, but four boarded and took seats next to one another. The sails filled once more, and the boat lurched forth. They glided down to the southern tip of Daos Prime, passing an ocean access where the breeze picked up again. A gull dived at Kipp who made no indication of playfulness.

At the next dock, the local scene was landscaped with radiant blooming gardens, so bright they could see them far away from the shore. Only one other boat was moored there. It was a peaceful place—no one was around except two dockhands helping taxi-boats park.

Casting off, they sailed around a similar boat heading south. They glided into the main harbor of Daos Prime, stopping at every pier. Irwin watched the spaceships—still mesmerized at the sight. Kipp flew off his shoulder when their boat pulled up to the city center dock, and Irwin stood by the railing, ready to depart.

35

<u>For Jorge</u>

He jumped off as the boat settled alongside the dock and nimbly followed Kipp's flight up the gangplank past a spaceship landing pad. He climbed up many steps, hurrying to follow Kipp's haphazard flight pattern—he noticed the Hall of Civilities a block away. Drawn from the hubbub of the city center, Irwin ran through an extensive park, racing to keep up as Kipp darted in and out and over the trees. Finally, they were in a seemingly endless residential area.

Kipp flitted back and forth, urging Irwin to go faster.

By the time they reached the large townhouse, the evening sky had already turned dark shades of pink and purple. Indigo shadowed the eastern seaboard. The western mountains had long since swallowed the sun. Lights from the buildings across the bay twinkled like stars in the night sky. Irwin thought that maybe some of the lights were spaceships.

Was this the Mortal side of town? Most of these people on the avenue appeared untalented. They were northwest of the central port in Daos Prime, east of the palace by several blocks.

Kipp landed at the front door where Jorge had been hustled through. He looked up as Irwin's feet came to rest. In a flash, Kipp mutated into his two-legged form, naked yet unabashed.

"He's in there." Kipp said, out of breath.

Irwin huffed too. "How positive are you?"

"Completely." Kipp inhaled. The scent of his urine marker left from earlier could be smelled by both.

Irwin assessed his options. "You will want to be in your Clan-Duin form."

Kipp could see metal swirling around in Irwin's eyes. "Should I even be here?"

"Yes, I need your nose."

"You're gonna be alright, right?" Irwin heard him muttering, "Please don't kill too many people."

"Are you going to change or not?" Their eyes locked for only a moment, and Kipp slipped out of his two-legged form, mutating into a rat.

Irwin knocked on the door. He heard children playing inside, giggling, and running around the house. There were murmurs of adult voices, and a middle-aged Daosian man opened the door. He was dressed in the same drab clothing those on the north side wore—appearing out of place in Daos Prime.

"Good evening, Sir," Irwin said. "I am looking for a friend of mine. He's about as tall as me. I heard he visited this house a while ago. I am hoping to speak with him if he is still here."

The man spoke Daosian, using aggressive hand gestures. He seemed insistent that Irwin leave.

"Jorge. I am looking for Jorge," Irwin hollered. "Jorge, are you in there?"

The Daosian man continued to spit and flail.

Irwin glanced down at Kipp, worried that this wasn't the correct house. But the rat nodded and stepped closer to the doorway, sensing his hesitation. Finally, Irwin grabbed the Daosian's hand and immediately the telepathic spell placed on the man's mind melted away. He became meek under Irwin's grasp, stepping aside, cowering, allowing the Metalist to enter.

Something sinister is at play here.

He stepped further into the house—around the quivering Daosian man. The children held still, all eyes on Irwin as he stepped past the front room doorway. He continued into the house. Kipp led him down the entry hall, past a stairwell that led upwards. The rat did not pause.

Into the kitchen, Irwin opened an in-out swinging door, startling a woman holding a young baby against her bosom. She was stirring a pot. She screamed, as did her child. Were they an alarm, or just scared?

Kipp squeaked at Irwin from around a corner next to a tall-but-narrow door. Irwin put his foot between Kipp and the door to keep his friend safe. "Let me go first."

The shrill cries were hard to ignore, but Irwin did. He opened the door and peered down a stairwell. A flame shot toward his face and Irwin stepped into the oncoming fireball, his hand extinguishing the flame. He wanted whoever was down there to see that they could not stop him. He descended the stairs, loud footfalls announcing his arrival. Once on the stone cellar floor, he was assaulted by a barrage of Erthin fire coming from two combatants.

"You think you can hurt me?" He stepped forward, unflappable as he now was in these situations. He spun his index finger around in circles, flicking the flames back onto the instigators. The Erthins deflected the rebounded flames, and using the same force, attempted to boomerang the fireballs back at Irwin.

Irwin pulled the fiery balls into his hands and snuffed them out. "Where is Jorge?!"

No one answered, but now the Erthins assaulted him with all they had. Unamused, Irwin snapped his fingers and assimilated the fire blowing Erthins. He hoped the other two Erthins in the room would pause for thought and resign from fighting. Unfortunately, they only saw Irwin's actions as a hostile attack and tried to suck the air from his lungs and attempted to drown him.

He gasped; pushed the water out of his skin. It dripped off his arms and down his clothing, pooling onto the floor.

I have no time for this!

He churned up his own elemental spell between his hands, radiating red energy and heat. It slowly grew. "Either you tell me where Jorge is, or I will kill you!"

These warriors were not there to negotiate, nor did they cease with their tricks. Wind whipped, tossing boxes at Irwin. The water maker attempted to take all the water from Irwin's body.

Tossing an Elementalist spell on the two soldiers, they sputtered and gasped and burned to ash.

Kipp stepped out of his mutation, eyes wide, and jaw slack. "I didn't know you could .... You just ... instantly they ...."

"Yes, get on with it, Kipp."

He shook his head. "Jorge is here. Or was. I smell him, but it leads ...." Kipp sniffed and stepped across the cellar toward a stone wall. "... through this wall."

"Through it?" Irwin stepped up and placed his hands on the wall. Beyond the ancient stone and mortar, he felt an opening—a hidden passage. His hands fumbled across the pieces of brick, summoning a metal lever on the other side, opening the secret door. A trigger stone to the left of the doorway sank into the wall as the passage opened.

Kipp kept to Irwin's side, smelling the roughened surface on the other side. "Yeah, Jorge went this way alright. He placed his hand right here. I smell fear and stress pheromones, and ...."

Irwin pushed Kipp back into the basement. "I do not know what is going on here. Hold back until I find Jorge."

"You really think that's a good idea? You might need my help."

"If we are battling Erthins or Telepaths, I do not want you compromised."

"Me, compromised? You're the one who's been compromised!"

"What are you talking about?"

"Jorge compromised you, Irwin, and our mission. If you weren't so fukin' smitten for him, we would've found Yace by now."

"What is that supposed to mean?"

"You know what it means." Kipp tossed a hand around the air. "You know what …. Maybe-maybe Jorge left under his own free will."

"Do not do this, Kipp. If Jorge needs our help, we will help him."

"It's probably just a ploy to take you away from me—from our mission."

Irwin's silvery eyes narrowed. "Then why would Erthins stand guard in the cellar of a house you saw him go into? Why would you have brought me here in the first place?"

They stood in the quiet; the woman and child above had stopped screaming. Finally, Kipp replied, "Telepaths."

"You might be right about the Telepaths. Another reason you should stay behind."

"But you'll need me. My sense of smell."

"Wherever this leads, Kipp, those people who took Jorge are going to answer to me. You do not want to be around for that." He turned, stepping into another corridor.

Kipp appeared to heed Irwin's warning.

Irwin followed the corridor that led to a fork in a longer passage. Right or left, it was his choice. There were no sounds. The tunnel was far enough below ground that only the ringing of metal in locations above and beyond was present in Irwin's ear. A flame hovered over his head as he marched along the passage. There was no sign of anyone else.

After jogging for at least a kilometer, he began racing through the tunnel. It felt like it could go on forever. But soon, the passageway forked into another lengthy corridor. He hated how quiet it was. Not an echo of footfalls, nor a hard breath except his own. Irwin stopped again to assess his options.

"Where do you think this goes?" said Kipp, catching his breath.

Irwin jumped. "What the shit!"

"Do you sense any Erthins?"

"No." He headed to the right, walking away from Kipp who kept one stride behind.

"I forgot to tell you. I didn't smell Yace anywhere in the palace last night, but I didn't get into all the rooms either."

"Jorge and I, we went down the boardwalk, between docks, but did not see her."

Kipp fretted. "What are we gonna do, Irwin?"

"For now, rescue Jorge."

Kipp groaned. "But-but maybe he found his people—left under his own accord."

"You flew all the way into Daos City to find me and tell me Jorge was kidnapped by an Empath, surrounded by shrouded goons, and now you are saying he went peacefully," Irwin snapped. "Which is it, Kipp? Did Jorge find his people, or was he kidnapped?"

"Both."

Irwin raked his fingernails across his skull. "I know you dislike Jorge, but we cannot allow him to be killed, or worse. He is just as naïve about this place as we are."

"He was devious about leaving Pammi's Platters."

"Devious, how so?"

"How quickly he ate and didn't make eye contact with me once when going to the bathroom."

"And your instinct told you to follow. You knew something might be wrong. Why else would you have come to find me?"

"Because I know you've feelings for him," Kipp replied.

Is Kipp jealous?

"I know you do not understand why I like Jorge, Kipp. He is abrasive, I get it, but I understand why he is like that. You do not and that is fine.

"Look, I appreciate you seeking me out after seeing all that. You knew I would be worried about him had you not followed. And thank you for leading me this far, but you do not need to stick around and pretend you want to be here. You should be out there," he pointed to the roof of the tunnel, "up there, flying around the palace."

Irwin stepped forward.

"You think you'll be able to find Jorge down here?"

"Did he go this way, or that?"

"He went this way."

"Do not worry about me, Kipp. You go. Find Yace. I will find Jorge and bring him back to the Inn."

"What if he chooses to stay with his people?"

"I will not deny Jorge the happiness he seeks. I just want to know that he is alright." Irwin walked away, but Kipp wasn't ready to part just yet.

"What if they took him to their secret lair, then allowed him to leave? What if he's back at the Inn now?"

"Why would people go to great lengths to steal someone away, if only to let them go so soon?"

The Clan-Duin rolled his eyes. "You know I hate riddles."

"Just go, Kipp. I will find Jorge whether he is ahead or back at the Inn."

Kipp mutated into his canine form and raced back in the direction they had come.

Irwin took off in a jog, following the passageway as it twisted and turned underground. His sense of direction had been obscured. The corridor led up and down and then intersected with yet another corridor—this one crooked, and it ran back and forth, up and down, heading in the opposite direction he had just come; or did it?

I am so lost.

After three left turns—scared he would be stuck in the depths of Daos Prime—he stopped and felt for his metal back at the Inn. There was metal everywhere overhead, but not his. He pulsated out further, and realized his metal was far, far away.

Where in Daos Prime am I?

He could not stop—he had to go forward. He did not want to backtrack, not now. But he was hungry and thirsty and ill prepared.

One hundred feet ahead, the corridor took a sharp right turn, and ten steps ascended to a dark wooden door. Irwin hunkered down, listening through the door. He felt a pair of Erthins walk past. He flexed his Elementalist powers and located and counted one hundred and thirty other Erthins nearby. He felt even more blades.

Now where am I?

He placed his hand on the door lever. Slowly, quietly, he pushed the door open and looked out. He found himself somewhat hidden by a large gazebo, mostly covered with clematis vines and surrounding hedges of flowering shrubs. It was pitch-black in the gazebo. He slunk through its shadows. He sat down and pressed his back against a stone wall—the backside of the gazebo. Once his eyes adjusted, he noticed a hanging seat held in place by chains secured to overhead beams. He crept behind the seat, watching, listening, and feeling for movement.

Still on his knees, he summoned the courage to explore further. Inching closer to the clematis, he peered out a wide-arch-doorway. He darted across a flower garden toward an elegant house and hid beneath a bushy tree—the tallest plant in that section of garden. There were fragrant flowers and white rock walkways meandering through the extravagant garden. He spotted another house with tall windows, all open and with flowing curtains pawing the edges of covered balconies.

He heard the crunching of stones and two sets of feet walking the white path. He held his breath. A pair of Erthin soldiers clad in red strode past, side-by-side. They were similarly dressed to the soldiers at the entrance to Daos Prime and at the bridge they crossed before boarding the animals.

I am glad they are not Clan-Duins.

He moved around the tree away from the soldiers' eyes. He looked up at several of the towering windows and felt a vaulted room singing with an awesome amount of metal.

Is this the palace?

There were also substantial amounts of gold in both these buildings.

I must be at the palace. Wonder if Kipp is up there.

36

BLOOD AND ASHES

As though he had heard Irwin, Kipp descended from the sky. Landing right there, he mutated from his bird form back to his two-legged self. "Jorge is in the palace—around that corner, up on the second floor."

Irwin jumped. "Why do you keep scaring me?" He had to catch his breath and stared at Kipp. "You found Jorge?!"

"I smelled him, yeah. There's other Empaths with him too."

"Empaths! You saw them?"

"I smelled them. All of them, including him."

He patted Kipp's shoulder. "That nose of yours!"

Kipp smiled. "What do you want me to do now?"

"Go back and look for Yace. Do not be near me. I do not know what will happen when I rescue Jorge."

"You're positive you don't want help?"

"Not at the expense of your life. If Yace is not here, she must be out there. Do what you do best, Kipp, go smell for her."

"What are you gonna do?"

"Rescue Jorge."

"But what if ... what if he wants to be here?"

They stared at each other. "You think he wants to be with his people even though they live under the rule of the Ishik Empire?"

Kipp shrugged, picked at a low-hanging flower. "It's possible."

"I will ask Jorge what he wants. Which room was it?"

"Around that corner, three, no four porches down, second floor."

"Thank you, Kipp."

"Good luck."

He watched Kipp fly toward the balcony and room where Jorge was being held. He followed on foot and rounded the corner and came face to face with two Clan-Duin canines. They lunged; mouths open wide, teeth snapping. But

Irwin tore at them. They did not have time to make a sound; they were sliced into pieces.

Irwin saw and felt more soldiers coming his way and stole around the corner, waiting.

I do not want to kill any others. I just want to see Jorge without alerting the entire palace.

Two Erthins sped toward him; again, he assimilated them, but more were on their way.

He slipped into a large, slightly overgrown, and very prickly rose bush. Closing his eyes, he felt for all the Erthins in the palace compound.

One hundred thirty. A dozen are Elementalist. Interesting. For Coterie to condemn people with power, they sure have a lot of Talented serving them.

Another pack of soldiers, half-Erthin and half-Clan-Duin, sped to where their brethren had fallen. He felt their approach.

Should I assimilate all those I feel? No, I am not here to do anything other than save Jorge. Get Jorge and get out. But what if….

He slipped around the back of the rosebush into another prickle bush. "Ouch." A thorn drew up his shirt and pierced his spine.

A pack of Clan-Duin dogs heard him before their Erthin counterparts saw him cowering in the bushes. He had no time to figure out how to escape without hurting them all. Instead, he pushed his hands up, stood, and said, "I surrender."

"Samuel Irwin Miner," a voice boomed from two Erthin soldiers. It was obvious they were being manipulated by a Telepath.

"How do you know me?"

"We've been waiting for you."

The Clan-Duin canines growled at him, ready to attack. More soldiers amassed. He felt most of them coming, except for the Clan-Duins in animal form.

"Who is we?"

The soldiers all laughed.

"I demand to speak with Emperor Ishik."

He could have done any number of things right then, but he chose not to.

I cannot allow myself to be bullied.

"Take me to your Emperor. Now!"

Thirty-four Erthins and as many Clan-Duins, surrounded him like bees on flowers. They escorted him into a large ballroom, stopped and waited for their master to arrive. The room was enormous, two-stories tall; the ceiling was patinaed aluminum embellished with animal and ivy scenes. The marble floor showed no apparent cracks that would have indicated slabs. The sheer curtains he had seen from outside were drawn open along several tall windows, allowing a warm early morning breeze to float across the hall. It would be another hot-humid day.

Every set of eyes was on him, assessing him. No one came closer than an arm's length. "When is your Emperor coming?"

Half of the room answered, "We are here."

"We have always been here," remarked the other half.

"Ha! Nice trick. Maybe you can show your face, Dephen." The men laughed. "Somer?"

One soldier stepped close to his face. "We've been waiting for you. Samuel Irwin Miner. Watching from afar, wondering when you'd arrive."

A ripple of fear cracked Irwin's tight back.

"How many have you killed, my little Sleeper Assassin?"

Sleeper Assassin? Where have I heard that before?

He tried to keep his voice from crackling when he said, "I do not know what you are talking about."

All the soldiers echoed an amused chortle. "Don't lie. We know what you've done. All the destruction and chaos ... what a lovely surprise to the Hakran Empire, don't you think? All the Telepaths in the world didn't see that coming. Too wrapped up in their own undertakings and geopolitical stunts. For them, it's all about status, not necessarily power. It should be about power. And those who've conquered it shall reign supreme."

Irwin blinked, sweat dripping into his eyes. It was stifling.

They all moved in unison. "But now you're no longer necessary. Know that we appreciate you. All you've done for us. My little Sleeper Assassin."

Was it Admiral Argustos or Admiral Ubic who called me a Sleeper Assassin?

"I am not a Sleeper Assassin."

A smirk grew on the representative's face. "Nuaki Village. Ahradah. And to a lesser extent, Onj Raha. That was more you than us, but we knew what could happen."

"None of that was you. That was all me. And I am not a Sleeper Assassin. No one has corrupted my mind. No one has forced my decisions. Everything I have done, I did with my own intention. No one else influenced me."

"Are you sure? You've met many Telepaths along the way. In a way, they've all had a hand in influencing your decisions."

I cannot let him provoke me, corrupt me. I need to get to my friends.

Again, a sinister laugh bellowed from the surrounding congregation.

"I am not falling for your telepathic trick."

"This is no telepathic trick. It's the truth. Think about it!"

The ringing of metal and those words made his mind swirl. But those words were much like his father's. Cold. Calculative. Truth or not, Irwin was ready to retaliate. And then Nonbry's voice floated around Irwin's mind, 'Repercussions from an assassination would be catastrophic. We can't allow that to happen.' Rage was trying to close off his throat and dry his mouth.

"Did you kill Somer?"

"We don't kill."

More wicked laughter.

Irwin shouted. "Give me Jorge."

"We're not the Sleeper Assassin. You are. We are here to meet the needs of the many. People like Jorge. He finally has what he wants. We can give you what you want too. We know you've dreamed of finding someone who will love and accept you. We can give that to you. Right now. Your beloved Jorge has dreamed of finding his people. And now he is with them. He wants to be here. His family is here.

"We know he wishes for you to be his bedfellow, but your record for being easy to handle is smudged with irregularities; especially when you're around people of Talent. And that chameleon skin you wear is not invisible to those of us with moral vision. We know who you are, what you are. We know of your ancestors and their origins. We know what you can become. And we also know what will become of you if you do not stay here with us. Your only option, save death, is devotion to us."

He stuck his chin out. "I demand to see Jorge. Now!"

Although it was just one man speaking to Irwin, the rest of those soldiers continued to watch their interaction from every angle. None of them moved, but still they blinked in unison.

"Demanding isn't allowed. Deliver your eternal devotion to us and you'll be able to live here with Jorge, happily ever after."

Whether this is Dephen or Somer, they know too much about me. Stay vigilant. Do not fall prey to his words.

He clenched his jaw. "Why would I do that?"

"Your other friend has."

"Friend?"

"You know who we're talking about."

Irwin whispered, "Yace?"

"Yes. She's happier now. And a wonderful addition to the family."

His heart pounded. "You have Yace?"

"Yes, we have her. She is soft and fun to play with. But of course, your friend Kipp already knows this."

Breathless, he said, "I want to see her."

"You cannot."

"What of Jorge?"

"No. Not until you deliver your devotion to us."

He shifted his posture and everyone surrounding him moved with him.

Keep calm.

His voice deepened, "I want to see Jorge and Yace, now!"

"No. Not yet." The green Erthin eyes tried to stare through him. "First, you must deliver yourself to us. Let free all your causes. Once you deliver yourself to us, you can do whatever you wish. Until then ...."

"I cannot do that," Irwin replied, shaking his head. "I will not!"

"I'm sorry to hear that. Now, this moment will be forever etched in your mind. The moment you made the worst decision. You could have saved them all by giving up yourself. But you didn't. Selfish bastard. And now all of you will suffer the eternal consequences. On your deathbed, remember this."

The Erthin standing close charged his powers, readying to incinerate Irwin. His brethren followed suit. Their powers began to combine.

Irwin shuffled backwards half a step, and said, "I would not do that if I were you."

Those energetically charged hands reached for and grabbed Irwin. "You are foolish to believe that I will regret this," he said, looking deep into the green eyes. In that moment, the Telepath, this person of Ishik descent, could not see through those Erthin eyes, nor could he hear directly. Contact had been made. Spells were broken. Now he had to use all the other eyes and ears in the room.

Irwin was ready to shed his calm, ready to release his power. Songs were ready to be orchestrated, pulled together into a great symphony. There was enough metal in this ballroom to kill everyone standing around him, and Irwin allowed his imagination to flower. The aluminum above molded easily into an enormous grid and was brought down on the unsuspecting soldiers, killing them instantly.

No one had a chance against the Metalist. He tossed down the severed hands still holding his forearms and stepped across the heaping pile of cut up bodies; blood flooded the floor, spilling toward the double doors where Irwin made his way further into the vast palace.

Sixty-eight soldiers had been instantly and brutally murdered.

Irwin did not care. He felt he needed to prove to himself that he was still in control. That this Telepath wasn't puppeteering him. In fact, he tried to push that total nonsense out of his mind. He didn't need anything else to cloud his judgement, or this task.

The Telepath in charge, whether Dephen or Somer or someone else entirely—Irwin wasn't quite sure—sent more soldiers after him. He felt them moving toward him, counted boot steps echoing along the palace corridors. He ran down the wide hallway, hoping to find Jorge and Yace—at least one of them was upstairs. A dozen Clan-Duin soldiers descended an enormous formal staircase, ready to rip him to pieces. Unfortunately for them, they never got the chance.

A sense of calm flowed over Irwin, and now he did not care what happened to any soldier who stepped before him. He had only one thought on his mind; find Jorge and Yace, and escape.

After slaughtering another dozen men with a flick of his wrist, Irwin raced up the stairs. He spotted four Erthins on the second floor guarding a set of double doors. Whatever, whomever they were guarding, must have been important. Twirling his hands, they, too, were melded into his flesh. He rushed to the doors, threw them open. Now even he could smell the Empaths' essences. "Jorge!"

"In here Irwin!" called Kipp.

He raced past a grand living room, down a short hall into a colossal bedroom. Kipp stood at the foot of the bed. Yace sat on the bed with two Empaths who looked like her. They were all frightened, but said nothing. The moment Irwin was bedside, their Empathic spells were shed and the real Yace appeared. The two Empaths on either side were exposed as their true light orange skinned gender fluid selves. They looked nothing like Jorge except for the light-colored eyes and curly hair.

"Touch her!" Kipp demanded.

Yace grabbed the arm of the Empath to her left, seemingly fearful of her friends.

Irwin leaned forward and touched Yace's foot. She screamed, jerked her feet away and pushed her body into the Empath on her right. They held each other in fright.

"Yace." Irwin's eyes pleaded for her to recognize him.

"Yace." Kipp moved toward his long-lost beloved, looked longingly into her vacant blue eyes. "Irwin?"

"Yace." He leaned onto the bed. "Do you remember us?"

One of the Empaths began laughing, that same sinister chuckle as the soldiers. "Surrender now."

"Or something worse will happen to you," said the other in a deep voice.

"Give us your soul," said the first.

Irwin reached up and touched their feet, releasing Yace and those at her sides from the telepathic spell. "Kipp, we have to get her out of here."

"Did she just ask for your soul?"

"It is a telepathic trick. Where is Jorge?"

"In the other room." Kipp pointed.

Irwin felt several Erthins heading their way. "We are not safe here. Do not let anyone touch you." He rose and left the room for the adjoining entry chamber. With a wave of his hand, he sealed that door in a coat of metal; no one would be able to enter or exit.

Kipp followed Irwin into the room where Jorge slept. Stopping at the foot of that bed, Jorge was entwined in three sets of arms, all holding him tight—a radiant smile on his sleeping face.

Irwin's soft contact woke Jorge. His eyes shot open, surprised to see the Metalist.

"Irwin! What are you doing here?"

"I am here to rescue you."

"Why? I found my family," Jorge said euphorically.

"Are you sure you want to be here? We know how the Ishik Empire treats its people."

"Give us your eternal devotion or doom will follow you," Jorge's voice changed, powerful and angry. He laughed with the rest of the Empaths who were now awake.

Irwin touched every person in the room. They all teetered between consciousness and telepathic influences. He heard the rest of the concubines coming down the hall. They were all chuckling 'Doomed' with a devious echo.

He placed his hand on Kipp's shoulder and whispered, "I must end this." All the concubines, Empathic or not, entered the room, including Yace—all controlled by the grand-master Coterie.

"Dephen. Somer. Whoever you are! I am coming for you," Irwin said, lunging forward, touching all of those who charged at him. He struggled to break the telepathic spells. The devious chuckling never ceased.

It does not matter if I touch them and shed the spell a thousand times. They gave themselves to the Ishik empire. Whoever this is, they have full control over them.

"Kipp, get out of here," he shouted as the Empaths and concubines came into their own minds. "I know what I need to do."

Those with Jorge were back under the Telepath's control; they jumped from the bed, tackling Irwin. No doubt this Telepath had not yet realized the extent of Irwin's power and his ability to shed telepathic spells. Although he was buried under bodies that kept shifting in and out of consciousness, he allowed Kipp that moment to escape.

Irwin never imagined he would fight women. He pushed back and threw down many of them while escaping the crowded bedroom. He managed to lock most of them in, but two pressed past and raced after him into the adjoining room filled with plush couches and chairs.

He used his Erthin powers to push those two around the room and opened the doors to escape their clutches. From the concubines' arms into a dozen soldiers waiting outside, he jumped.

It did not matter which direction Irwin ran, he would have to fight.

He heaved a deep, foreboding sigh.

Fine. I will kill them all. Leave no one alive.

Allowing his rage to explode, Irwin assimilated half of the Erthins who were trying to burn him alive. He sliced the Clan-Duins who were diving for his flesh into pieces. No one would survive the violence he summoned. Using the absorbed metal, he created ten orbs, oscillating them around his body. Anyone bidding to fight him was cut into pieces. Walls and ceilings and woven tapestries were splattered with blood; red pools dotted the marble flooring and carpets.

He stalked everyone inside the palace; listening, feeling, and waiting for someone else to make a move. He was far gone, his emotions and thoughts removed from his mind. For now, he had found inner peace—the feeling was glorious.

At this point, it did not matter who he killed; every man, woman, and child inside the palace walls were all decimated, as were any soldiers trying to put up a fight. While bringing down the Ishik house, Irwin reflected on what the Telepath who spoke through the Erthin had said. How he would forever remember this moment, the reasons for letting go of his energy, summoning the anger and wrath his father and grandfather grew within him—and themselves. In this time of reflection, Irwin wondered if indeed he had been manipulated by Dephen. The aged Telepath had access to Kipp, but Irwin always tried to use his best judgement and against his friend's feral opinions. He wondered how that could have happened. How could he have molded Irwin into an assassin without telepathic words or touch? Or were those words meant to cloud his judgement in this moment? Rile him up?

Was Dephen, or whomever, trying to trick Irwin more than they already had?

None of that seemed to matter. The wickedness of the Telepath's words lingered, spurring further decimation of the Ishik Regime. And the deception that now shrouded Irwin hastened his anger against those who were after him and his friends. As the blood continued to fly, bodies were left in his wake.

He continued to draw energy from everything he had witnessed not only today but while traveling through Daos Territory. Their journey had been emotionally heavy at times and with many burdens. All the faces he had seen along his voyage since arriving in Vidigen: the young girls offered up for sale; the wailing malnourished children; the boys being forced onto trade ships—it all came to a boil right then.

37
<u>Escaping Chaos</u>

After seeing all the blood and bodies he had lain to waste, Irwin sunk into his own mental storm. It was midday, and he was tired and hungry.

He approached the concubine doors. They had been set aflame. Only charred, the fire had not penetrated the metal barrier he had created on the inside. He removed his metal lock and pushed open the doors, startling everyone in the room. They were clothed in hooded robes, including Kipp. They stared in horror at Irwin.

Kipp was the only one happy to see him. "You're alive!"

"Of course I am alive."

"Yace needs you." Kipp started to say but was cut-off.

"Irwin, I would like you to meet Diasa, the eldest of us!" Jorge leaned on their shoulders. "Tihil, Mati, Ili, and Sitir." Their dark brown eyes stared at him.

"Many thanks to you for bringing Jorge to us," said the one named Mati. When they spoke, their voice held multiple tones which probably aided their ability to cloak and mimic. Even with their enigmatic appearances disabled, their pure form was of an almost iridescent tone. Their orangish-yellow skin tone and hair matched. Small tight curls clung close to their scalp, and they too were lanky, just like Jorge. Yet they seemed more comfortable with their bodies than Jorge had in the past.

"I am happy for you all."

"Many thanks to you, Master Irwin," said Diasa.

Sitting at Jorge's side, Diasa resembled him until Irwin knelt. He affected all the Empaths close by, within at least an eight-foot radius. Everyone who sat around gasped for air when they saw what Irwin's magnetic power revealed.

Five of the concubines were Empaths. The remaining seven were mixed-breed Erthins, Clan-Duins, and Telepaths. They had never seen the Empaths as the Empaths saw one another; only Empaths saw each other for who they really were and not the shapeshifting creatures they appeared to be for everyone else.

From behind Irwin, one of the most beautiful redheaded Erthin's he had ever seen, asked, "Do you affect everyone like this?"

"No, only Empaths."

Not believing him, she pulled her curly red hair back from her ears. Her green eyes had flecks of amber, and her face was freckled. She was tall and thin. Her hand felt ice cold as it touched Irwin's warm flesh. "Huh. No. I felt nothing."

One of the more exotic concubines laughed at her. "Why must you always inspect, Holly?"

"You are amazing," Holly said to Irwin, and he blushed.

Several of them laughed at Holly. She blushed too, looking away from Irwin and around the room at her peers. It was good for Irwin to see that they were not put off by him or his power.

Jorge was the first to ask, "What happened out there?"

"Do you want to know the truth?"

Kipp said, "You killed them all, didn't you?"

"You are all safe now. But if anyone is still alive, they know I will hunt them down and kill them." The silver swirled across his irises—he could feel it, now familiar.

Several pleaded, "Please don't kill us."

Reaching to comfort Diasa, Irwin tenderly placed his hand on their forearm. "I will not hurt anyone in this room. I am just letting any Telepath who escaped my wrath know that I will find them and kill them."

"Irwin, are you alright?" Jorge looked startled.

"Can you touch Yace again?" Kipp's voice cracked. "She's not acting right." He sat by her side, staring into her vacant blue eyes.

Irwin went around, touching all the concubines, and then sat with Kipp and Yace. He held her hands, but she did not respond. Kipp whispered, "She doesn't remember me," his voice trembling.

He knelt and took Yace's icy hands. She stared forward, blinking erratically.

Kipp said what Irwin was thinking, "What the fuk, Irwin? Why isn't she coming back to us?"

Parched and starving, Irwin licked his dry lips. He looked at Kipp. "We need to get out of here."

"Irwin?!"

"We need to get out of here," he stood and said again, "We need to go." He watched the dozen concubines stand, ready to follow. One of them threw a silken hooded robe over his shoulders, like the ones they wore.

Jorge stepped along Irwin's side. "Stay behind me." He pushed Jorge back from the doorway, then peered out and took the first steps toward the staircase. Jorge and his family followed; Kipp and Yace were at the back of the line.

The hallway was littered with blood and pieces of bodies. They descended the stairs to the ballroom. He tried to ignore the horrific sight, but the women could not. They shrieked and cried, yet stayed close to Irwin.

The carnage was indeed repulsive to witness, but this was the only way Irwin knew to go—straight through the ballroom. He ignored the mass of cubed body parts heaped near the wide-open doors. He summoned an open window to become a doorway. They went out into the gardens single file, except Kipp and Yace. Kipp was struggling to keep Yace focused.

Irwin brought them to the gazebo. He asked Jorge to take the lead and stood at the doorway, watching each female escape into the darkness and the long tunnel from where he had come. One of the Erthins lit the way. Meanwhile, Irwin waited for Kipp and Yace to step up. Once they were all through the portal, he sealed them inside; no one would be able to enter or exit from this direction unless they were an Earth Erthin.

"She's not herself, Irwin," Kipp said once more as they ran away from the palace.

Irwin stepped alongside her and placed Yace's free arm up across his shoulder to help Kipp escort her.

She leaned in and banged her head against Irwin's ear. He stopped her.

"Yace, what are you doing? What is going on?" He did not want to be angry with her, but shook her, "Yace, look at me."

She did, but then her eyes drifted up to the stone ceiling.

"What the shit happened to her, Irwin? Your powers should work, right? You can ground out Dephen, right?"

"I do not know what is going on, Kipp. I know my touch should work. But it is not!"

"Dang me, Irwin!" Kipp bemoaned, and they resumed jogging. "What are we gonna do? I think they took her memories. She doesn't know who I am!"

"You are getting ahead of yourself, Kipp. We do not know that for sure."

"Dang me, those fukin' Telepaths messed with her mind. She'll never be the same."

"Kipp, calm down, please."

"Dang me!"

"I know this is hard for you. It is hard for me too! I know my powers work. They have been working all morning."

"Yace'll never be Yace again."

"You are not helping, Kipp."

"Fuk you, Irwin, what've you done?"

"I have rescued Yace and Jorge and all these people," he tried to keep his patience with Kipp while holding onto Yace. "I murdered the whole Ishik Empire. Women. Children. Ugly old men. I killed all their staff too. Liberated an entire country from selfish dictators. What more do you want me to do?"

All the women and Jorge stopped and shouted from up ahead, "Hey Irwin, which way?"

Not needing any more stress, Irwin grumbled under his breath, "I thought they would know the way."

"They should," said Kipp, "right?"

"They might have been under telepathic control." He closed his eyes, ringed in circles from lack of sleep.

Kipp saw Irwin's duress and patted his back. "I'll lead them. If you got here coming this way, I will be able to track your scent back to that house."

"Thank you, Kipp."

What would I do without you?

Kipp scurried around the Empaths and women, all now with their hoods off and sweating from the escape. They had traveled only a small portion of the way—only Irwin knew how much farther they had to go before being topside again.

Kipp finally brought the party of sixteen back to the basement of the townhouse. Night had fallen again; it was about the same time of night they had passed through the house the first time. No one was home. There were no sounds or smells of anyone.

They all tiptoed into the front room. Many took seats, resting their tired feet. Irwin peered out the window. He saw people walking by, swinging baskets of food, and probably heading home. He did not want to leave just yet. They needed to wait until it was completely dark.

"What are we doing?" Jorge asked.

"Waiting."

"For what? I thought we needed to leave."

"The owners of the house are not here, and we need to make a plan before going out into the world."

Kipp stood at the edge of the congregation, holding Yace. "Should we worry about being followed?"

Irwin took in all the innocent faces. "I think we should all go back to the Inn."

Jorge insisted. "Sixteen people won't fit into our tiny room."

"I can rent a few more rooms. I have more than enough silver to help you all find your way—wherever you want to go." This felt reminiscent of his time at Lady Gretchen's. "You are all strong beings who deserve to live as you wish. I am glad I have helped you out of that pit, but only you can set yourselves free."

Diasa asked, "Is there any way we can repay you?"

Irwin forced a smile, "My payment is Yace. She is why we came here. She is why you all became free today. Well, she and Jorge are the reasons. Besides, I could not allow you to slip away." His eyes locked with Jorge's.

Jorge took Irwin's hand and kissed the back of it. He gave him a seductive look and then pulled him into a loving embrace. "Thank you, Irwin. Thank you for everything, including the warmth in my heart."

Irwin blushed, glanced at Kipp, and pulled away from Jorge's hold. "It is agreed, then. We will return to Illian's Inn. Keep to the shadows; do not acknowledge anyone."

"Those in Daos Prime will not look twice at us," Diasa told Irwin. "We are accepted here."

"That is good to know," Irwin said, noticing the distraught Kipp. He stepped to his side and whispered, "You and Yace are ready to go?"

"I guess so."

Irwin pulled up Kipp's and Yace's hoods, then his own, and headed for the door.

Following his lead, hoods came up and dozens of feet plodded down the cobbled road. A slight breeze thrust away some of the hot stagnant air lingering in the city of Daos. Two by two they went, Irwin and Jorge leading. No one on the streets seemed to notice.

38

<u>Picking up the Pieces</u>

Once they arrived at the Inn, they had to wait for the front desk attendant to return. Kipp took Yace up to their room. Jorge stayed with Irwin, leaning into him with the happiest of grins.

The young Erthin-mix receptionist got off the elevator and jumped, startled to see the large group. "Oh! I'm so sorry. It's been quiet all night." She made her way around the group and said, "Oh, it's you, Mister Samuel."

"Yes, I would like to rent out a full floor for my friends."

"A whole floor—all ten rooms? We have a penthouse on the eighth floor. It would fit everyone here—seven bedrooms, giant beds, a private kitchen, and balconies all the way around. A private pool and tub, showers and—"

"Yes, that sounds perfect. How much?"

"Is this just for tonight?"

"Ten nights, minimum."

"Ten nights?"

He looked back at the cluster of hoods gathered behind him. "If they wish to stay longer, they will be able to pay at that time."

"Ten nights comes out to one thousand credits, or Rupees."

"That's a lot of money, Irwin," Jorge said.

Diasa gasped, "Goodness, you don't have to do this."

He did not care; metal was metal. Irwin could make up enough coins to pay for all those nights. "That comes to be about ten pounds, correct?"

Counting on his fingers, Jorge said, "Wait, only ten pounds?"

Irwin summoned the coins from his pocket, stacking them in rows of ten. "Yes, why?"

"I sold your three-pound rock for one-hundred eighty Rupees."

"What?" Irwin was slightly offended that Jorge had taken it, but more miffed that he had been ripped off in price. "I have a satchel of coins in my bag up in the room. I thought you knew about it."

"Kipp might, but I didn't."

"Umm, these are not Rupees," the desk attendant told Irwin. "I know you are from the north, but how many coins do you have from there?"

"Of course, you would want Rupees, not coins with Hakra on them," he said, tired from this day.

"Not that it matters," she said nervously.

"But it does. It is okay. I am not offended."

"Around here they are nothing more than salvage metal, really. I mean, I know silver is silver, but no one around here uses Hakran coins. We prefer Rupees or credits. I could trade them at a bank, but I'd have to wait until tomorrow."

"Can I see a Rupee, please?"

She studied Irwin as he continued to place rows of coins down on the wooden counter. Making coins was automatic for him and he watched her slip a key into a lockbox below the counter, open it, and pass him a Rupee to inspect. He quit pulling Hakran coins out of his pocket, studied the Daosian Rupee.

A grape vine held by falcon talons was stamped on one side, a $1 symbol stamped on the other. Irwin concentrated on the image, etching it into his mind.

He felt it in his hand and gave it back. He placed his hands over the silvery stacks. Summoning the image was a challenge. He had to make the change to every coin under his hands.

He had already made just over two hundred coins with Hakra on them, but, as it turned out, it was easy to change the stacks into the Daosian Rupee. He had to calm the songs. All the metal in that large atrium room, including the metal lock box near her feet, vibrated. His eyes remained closed until he felt Jorge's hand on his shoulder.

The Empath could tell that Irwin needed some comfort. The entire room vibrated, startling everyone. "Keep calm, Irwin," Jorge whispered.

Breathing deeply several times, Irwin opened his eyes and pulled his hands back. All the coins had changed faces. Metal sang louder, wanting him to wield it like he had inside the palace. He had to keep calm and find his focus. He shoved his left hand into his pocket.

Just make coins. Breathe.

He began pulling Rupees out of his pocket, ten at a time. It was hard—at first—to change the emblem, but the more Irwin thought about it, the easier it became to mass produce the Rupee. The currency flew out of his hand and into his pocket. He stacked them on the counter.

"How is it you carry that much money?"

Jorge watched the front desk attendant lean across the countertop. Trying to keep her eyes above the counter and not on Irwin's fast hands, Jorge rubbed the back of his neck and chuckled. "He always carries lots of cash."

She picked up a coin and looked it over, tossed it in her hand before placing it back. "Feels and looks real."

The Empaths moved around nervously. Irwin kept summoning coins from nowhere. He was now pulling metal from the floor. The vault holding hundreds of pounds of metal was located below Irwin's feet. He continued to count and replicate.

After placing the last hundred coins down on the counter, he put his hands calmly behind the money. "As you can see ...."

"All Rupees! How'd you ...? You're not Mortal, are you?" The woman smiled at him. He felt accepted for once.

Placing a finger to his lips in hopes she would be quiet, "I am just trying to help my friends have a better life."

Nodding her head, the young woman placed all the coins into the lock box below the counter. "We have only ten keys to the penthouse suite." She turned and retrieved all ten keys, placing them on the counter. "If any of you leave, make sure you have a key." Her face was soft, as was her demeanor.

Stepping around the front desk counter, the receptionist waved the group toward the lift. "See, there's a slot you place the key into. It will take you directly up to the penthouse. The lift will only hold ten, so you will have to take turns—the only downside of taking the lift. There are stairs," she pointed, "for emergencies, or if you'd rather take them and not bother with the lift."

Stepping away, she smiled at Irwin. "I hope you enjoy your stay at Illian's Inn." She asked, "Would you want reimbursement for your room, Mister Samuel?"

"No. I will keep that room. I just want my friends to have quiet comforts while they are here."

"I understand. We will make sure all their needs are met." She headed back toward the front desk.

The lift was crowded when it hoisted the Erthin mixes and Empaths to the penthouse. Irwin rode along to make sure Jorge and his family were tucked in and happy with their situation. Then he headed for his own room.

He took the stairs, allowing the echoes of his footfalls to calm his internal dialogue.

I must remember that none of this metal is my metal. I shall not take it as mine. But it wants me to ....

Sweat dribbled down his back.

Stop calling me. I am not interested in your sirens.

Oh, how I miss my mountaintop.

Back in their room, Kipp was sitting on the bed with Yace who was leaning into his shoulder. He was crying; she stared forward—still catatonic.

Irwin closed the door. "What can I do?"

"Fix her."

"I have made as much contact as I can, unless it requires full skin on skin," he said, and Kipp glared.

"Fuk that shit! We need to get out of here." Kipp looked around the room, at their bags still stacked as they had left them. Folded piles of cleaned clothes were heaped in the laundry basket.

"Kipp, you are being irrational. We need sleep."

"You'll be hunted down, Irwin. You assassinated the Emperor. Killed his soldiers."

"By whom? They are all gone, Kipp, every one of them. If the PCP really wanted a regime change, it has come."

"What if there are holdouts, like those soldiers at the river crossing?"

"I killed the Emperor and all his men. All the Ishiks are dead, except Yace. And if there are soldiers left behind, they probably do not know what has happened. I think we are safe for now."

"You've gone crazy, Irwin. That metal messes your mind up!"

"I wish I could say I regret it, but I do not. Everything they have done, everything we have witnessed along the way here—those people deserve better. Shit, I hate saying it, but I believe Hakra and PCP are better for the people of Daos than the Ishik Empire."

"You're fukin' crazy!"

"Have you forgotten all the brutality we saw during our trip here? I think the people of Daos have suffered enough!"

"That kind of shit happens all the time, everywhere. I'm not even considered a person in most places unless I pledge loyalty to the PCP. Even then, I'm classified as a dog no matter what type of Clan-Duin I am. Besides, didn't Nonbry say something about not killing everyone?!"

Irwin grumbled, "You are not helping, Kipp."

"Fuk you! I've always tried to help you!"

Exhausted, Irwin went to his knees. "I only want the best for you. The best for Yace and you," he paused and then his words came softly, "I did this for you." And then the tears fell. He put his head on Kipp's knees.

"That's a horseshit of an excuse, Irwin." Kipp too began sobbing.

Both men cried for different reasons. Yace remained mute.

"What the shit Irwin? Yace isn't Yace. We need her to be Yace again."

"Psychic Attendant?"

"No."

"Then we take her back to Nonbry."

"How?! We don't even know where he is."

"Once again, I say Psychic Attendant."

"No."

"We will not get anywhere, Kipp, if we do not talk to Nonbry."

"No. You're gonna fix her. Nonbry said you would."

"Do I look like a Telepath?"

"No, but you're supposed to fix her. You're supposed to bring her back—to banish Dephen."

Irwin turned to Yace, taking her hands in his. He held them tight, trying to catch her gaze. She peered at him, looked at him as if she had never met him. Her pale blue eyes fell to his hands, perhaps trying to understand his tight grasp.

"See, there, she's looking at you."

"I am holding her tightly. She does not flinch or cry. She only wonders why."

"Can you hear her thoughts?"

"No, I read it in her eyes." Irwin stared at Yace; his brow wrinkled. "I still think we need to find a Psychic Attendant. Talk to Nonbry—ask him what we can do."

"Maybe we can use Yace to call for Nonbry."

"If she is unable to acknowledge us, how will she be able to contact Nonbry?"

They both stared at Yace, then at one another. "Dang me! What are we gonna do? I don't want anyone touching her mind that isn't you or Nonbry."

"I am not telepathic and Nonbry is not here."

"Then we take her to him."

"We do not know where he is! And that brings us back to the root question and the reoccurring answer."

Kipp shouted, "Don't say it!"

"We need to see a Psychic Attendant!"

"No. No. NO!"

"You are being irrational, Kipp." Irwin kept his focus on Yace—so blank. "A clean page," he muttered aloud.

"A clean page? What do you mean?"

"They said Telepaths are not welcome on this side of Daos, right?" He let go of Yace's hands, stood up and glared at Kipp.

"Yeah, something like that."

"Which probably means they live on the other side of the wall."

"I don't wanna talk to—"

"Kipp, we have no other option."

"If you would do what you are supposed to, she'd be back already!"

"I have been!" Irwin tried to stay calm. "You are being irrational."

"I'm being irrational?!"

He stared at Kipp.

I hate to do this….

"Kipp, go to sleep." He placed his hand on Kipp's shoulder, and the Clan-Duin succumbed to Irwin's Erthin powers and fell backwards. He adjusted Kipp so he could rest peacefully. The miner then stepped over to Yace and saw a questioning look in her eyes.

"Do not worry about him. He is tired. I just want to focus on bringing you back."

She said nothing. Her muteness made her appear meeker than usual. His hand brushed stray strands of hair from her face.

"Yace. What did they do to you?"

Just as soft as he had been, she reached up to brush his face in the same manner. Closing his eyes, Irwin leaned into her.

Why is my power not working? What is going on?

"Just when I thought my journey with you two is up, another twist."

Why did this have to happen? How can I fix you if my touch cannot help?

"Kipp is going to be so angry when he realizes we are going to see a Psychic Attendant. Oh, Yace." He held back a sob. "I do not know what else to do."

He backed away, feeling the weight of the world. He needed to meditate, to ground out all the bad thoughts and the lustful metallic call from all around the city. He liquefied the remaining fifty pounds of silver he carried in his baggage, encapsulated the walls, ceiling, and floor. He needed to sit, be quiet, and listen to the harmony of his metal.

Yace stepped forward and felt the wall as the metal washed across it like water flowing back onto a beach. She was obviously impressed by the sight, running her hand back and forth on the reflective surface.

"You are a blank piece of paper, Yace. They stripped you mentally. You have nothing to work from. I can only hope we find a Telepath that can help you."

She did not acknowledge him.

He reached over and held her, scooping her up in his arms and placing her down next to Kipp who was snoring. He summoned her to sleep, pulling a thin blanket across the two of them.

He stood over his friends, watching them sleep. "We will fix this together," he muttered and found a spot on the floor.

39

<u>ONE LAST KISS</u>

He left the Inn early that morning and went shopping—the next leg of their adventure would require supplies. As he was leaving, he looked at Kipp and Yace curled up together, hoping they would still be that way when he returned.

On the way back, he carried bags and bags of perishable food on his back. Drenched in sweat, he left some oats down in the lobby behind the front desk. Upstairs, he reached for the doorknob and Jorge swung the door open from the inside.

"There you are! Where've you been, Irwin?"

At the same time, Irwin spoke to Kipp, "Do you think you can change into a donkey?"

"What?"

"I bought us enough food for the next ten days. I figure once we are far from the city limits, you can hunt. Jorge and I can steal if necessary."

"Woah, I'm not going anywhere," Jorge waved Irwin off.

I knew it.

A pang of sadness wrang his chest. "You are going to remain in Daos Prime?"

"Yes. You should too." Irwin had never seen the Empath smile that wide! "You're the first person who ever gave me hope. I didn't know leaving Nuaki Village was even possible, but you were so determined to find your friend. You let me join in your crusade." Jorge kissed Irwin. "Thank you, Irwin. Thank you for giving me a chance at a new life." Again, he kissed Irwin.

Kipp groaned.

Pulling away, Irwin was embarrassed by the outpouring of emotions. "Thank you, Jorge, for helping us when we needed it."

Jorge drew Irwin in for a hug, whispering, "He will never love you like I do; stay here with me."

I want a new life too. With you. But I cannot stay here, Jorge. The ringing is frightening. If you were to come with me, that would be perfect. But I know why you want to stay.

Why was it so hard for him to say what he felt?

Not wanting to acknowledge any of these emotions, as the previous night had been full of them, Irwin closed his eyes and found his focus. He opened his silver-swirling eyes and looked at Kipp again. "The reason I ask if you can change into a donkey is I bought about a hundred pounds of food, mostly for the animals, and these bags are for us."

"Now I'm your pack animal?"

"I can handle most of it until we get to the north side of the wall. But yes, I need your help. Oh, and we are going to leave today."

Jorge gasped, "Already? You'd be safer here in Daos Prime. This is a sanctuary city. The moment you go anywhere else ...."

"I cannot stay here any longer."

"It's the metal, isn't it?"

The songs are deafening!

"I am not supposed to live in a city, Jorge. Especially one this big. Besides, Yace needs help from people who are nowhere close to here."

Kipp sounded meek for a change. "You talked to Nonbry?"

"No. Any Psychic Attendant is going to be on that side of the wall, not here. And I will not go there until tonight."

"Aren't you supposed to pay for the horses today?"

"Yes."

"They're probably at the butcher's by now." Jorge argued.

"Ekaro knows I will be back later today." Irwin said, "I told him I would be. I did not want to rush back."

"It's midday already," said Jorge. "You won't make it there in time."

"He knows I will be late." He watched Jorge roll his eyes and then turned his attention to Kipp. "We will leave today on the last taxi-boat. You will be in this form until we reach the northern dock; at that point, I would appreciate it if you were a donkey. It appears that it will be us three. I will carry our personal baggage, so you are not crippled by all the weight."

Kipp held Yace. "Maybe you should try grounding her out today."

The solemn look Irwin gave Kipp said it all. "I cannot help her. I have tried."

"Try some more!"

"I do not need this, Kipp! We must speak to Nonbry. We will find a Psychic Attendant."

"Before or after I haul all that food around?"

"Don't be sore at me for not being able to help, Kipp."

"Have you even tried?"

"Trust me, Kipp, I believed what Nonbry told me; I believed I would be able to help. He said I would be the only one able to remove Dephen. But this is beyond removing an old spirit. I believe she is still in her body, but her mind has been wiped clean. You are correct, Kipp. Yace has no memory of us. She is like a new sheet of paper."

"Wait a moment. You said that last night!" Kipp looked down at his hands. "You said that. We were arguing, but then ... did you hit me?"

"No," Irwin's voice dropped, "You fell asleep."

"I don't think so."

"Trust me, you did."

Jorge's eyes drooped more than usual. "Can't you just pay for a few more days and come back?"

"No."

"Did you use your powers on me again, Irwin?" Kipp was pressing his suspicions.

"You fell asleep holding onto Yace. You were both very tired last night—do you not remember?"

"I wanna go out with you one last time." Jorge was trying to draw Irwin's focus back to him. He ran a playful finger up and down Irwin's forearm. "I wanna thank you for everything you've done for me—for changing my life for the better."

"I'm sure we were arguing and then we weren't," Kipp said. "I think you put me to sleep. Did you do it to Yace too?"

"I watched you two fall asleep."

"You're lying to him."

He glared at Jorge, then smiled and grabbed his hand. "Yes, I would love to go out with you one last time." He turned to Kipp. "I will be back soon." He threw two-dozen Rupees at Kipp, "Get yourselves some food, maybe her some clothing."

"You're leaving her with me?!"

"You have been missing her for many moons. Spend time with her. Maybe that is what she needs."

"She can barely function!"

"But she can function." He pointed at Yace who was trying to use the urinal. She straddled it, began urinating, groaning—she had obviously been holding it for a while.

Irwin felt confident leaving Yace with Kipp. She wasn't completely catatonic, just unable to function without guidance. Jorge pulled at Irwin, and they left the room.

Once they were in the lift, he asked, "Was I too rough with Kipp?"

"Oh, for fuk-sake! You're so willing to do anything for him. You've gotta stop it, Irwin. He's gonna ruin you."

"I know I was stern with him. But Kipp is in no position—" *mentally* "—to solve any problems."

He has given himself over to the problem, wallowing in it.

"He believes only I can fix this situation, which I cannot. I have tried. And he will not take my advice about finding a Telepath so we can talk this over with Nonbry."

"It could be worse."

"Worse? How? Yace is mute and seemingly without her mind. And there is nothing I can do. I have tried everything. I do not know what else to do."

"Well, you can't beat a dead horse."

"Actually, you can," he said, "but it is dead so it will not feel it."

Jorge took Irwin out, just as Irwin had for him and indulged them both—using the silver he had taken from Irwin's bag.

They enjoyed an afternoon of food, drinks, dances, and a long walk, talking about what their future held. It was a nice departure from the normal routine. He took it all in, including the spaceships—one last time.

I do not want this to end. But it will.

I cannot count on anything to last, or anyone.

At least I have this. These last few moments with Jorge.

When they returned to the Inn, Irwin pulled Jorge in for an embrace. "Thank you for allowing me to be me, and to experience happiness." They kissed.

Jorge pulled back. "You should keep on being happy."

Glancing over his shoulder at the door to the room, Irwin said, "It is hard."

"When you love someone who won't love you, yeah, it is." They embraced again. This time, it was long and lustful. "Take care of yourself, Irwin. I hope you find someone who loves you as much as I do."

"If you love me, then you should come with me, with us."

Jorge shook his head. "Albeit a tempting proposition, I finally have my family, my people. I always felt like they were out there. And they were. Awaiting my return. I really feel that Daos Prime is the only place we can live and feel truly free. I wish you would stay."

"If the circumstances were different ... If I were not allergic to all this metal, I would."

Jorge placed his hand on Irwin's face. His light-brown eyes unwavering with their love. "I understand. Know that I will always love you, Irwin. I'm gonna miss you."

The Metalist stared at the Empath for a long time, trying to interpret his jumbled feelings for the other man. "I love you too. Thank you, Jorge, for everything."

Slowly, each man turned away from the other. Jorge headed to the lift, and Irwin opened the bedroom door. It was barren. His heart stopped, but then he remembered: *They are probably out eating, enjoying time together.*

Or he lost her.

"I need to remember to be nice to Kipp; he is having a hard time."

He has had a hard time since Yace left us. He can be so insecure; it rubs my nerves raw. I thought he was a man. At least I get a little quiet time before they return.

He lay on the bed, eyes transfixed on the ceiling.

40

<u>FINDING HOPE</u>

Kipp was shaking him. "We got lost. Irwin, we're gonna miss the boat!"

It was almost dark. "Shit!" He jumped up and stuffed his folded clothes into bags. Kipp was doing the same while Yace watched them rush around the room.

He picked up the bulk of the heavy baggage. "Grab those bags, Kipp. I will take everything else. Oh, I need to give these bags to Jorge's family. Maybe you can take those."

"You have to see him now?"

"I will be right back." He summoned the door open. "If you get all this out to the lift, I will help load it on and pack it from there."

"Fine, I'll do it all." Kipp griped.

Irwin ran, summoning the lift to the fourth floor. He pushed the lift doors closed, and his stomach turned as it rose to the eighth-floor suite.

There were bowls of fruit on the kitchen table. The room smelled of oranges and peaches, and there were short citrus trees in planters at the corners of the room. He heard murmurs coming from outside. The doors were open wide to the evening sky, and the concubines were enjoying a hot soak in the cooling twilight.

Several shouted when seeing him. "Irwin!"

"I bestow to all of you these two reams of silken fabric and my last forty pounds of silver. If you are thoughtful about it, that amount can buy you many things.

"I am leaving you my wagon as well. Jorge, do you remember where it is? The stables are called Rosko's Yard; Ekaro is the man who you should ask for. It is next to Lolo's Meats, where it smells of death. You can cash it in for more silver or take it and do with it as you wish." He called to his friend who was exiting the pool, nude. "It is worth at least fifty pounds. I would not take anything less, but you should ask for sixty. I have modified much of it; Jorge knows what I have done."

"It's impressive, just as you are." They embraced. "I thought you had left." Jorge kissed Irwin.

He felt himself blush. "We are late to leave."

"Better get going then!"

Several of the ladies came over to assess the amount of silver being given. Two tried to heft the bags, and Irwin said, "Have Jorge help you with that. He knows how heavy they are."

"Yeah, I sure do!" Jorge planted one more kiss on Irwin. "Be safe, my friend."

"As safe as I can be." Irwin winked, turned, and left the penthouse.

I hope they will be out of harm's way. I cannot protect them. They know Daos Prime; they know how to live, but only as concubines—perhaps they have other resources.

Irwin dropped the lift four floors and opened the doors. Kipp had dragged everything down the hall, leaving Yace for last. He was pulling her along. They lugged everything into the lift. Irwin closed the doors and pushed the lift to the ground floor.

"How in Hakra did you carry all that food?"

"I used the metal."

"You're gonna do that again, right?"

"I just gave it all away."

"You what? Why'd you do that?"

"We do not need it."

Kipp stared at Irwin.

The elevator door opened and now they had to heft all the bags of food and belongings out into the darkening day. Irwin called to the front desk hostess. "Hi Opal! I am hoping we can get one of those two-wheeled taxis. One large enough for all our stuff. I do not want to be late for our boat."

"Of course, Sir Samuel." She moved toward a back doorway and called, "Hana, get loaded up please."

A biracial mix of Clan-Duin and Giant appeared.

After loading up all their belongings, and much explaining to the large and rather dim-witted man called Hana, he mounted a bike, and they bolted forward. Everyone's heads jerked this way and that with the swift movement of the rickshaw, front and back, with a snap of whiplash as the vehicle took off. They were perched among their bags and hanging on to each other. Hana was incredibly fast, but not very steady, around a few of the sharp corners. He giggled excitedly, peddling faster and faster, shouting, "Move!"

They sped through the city; those on the streets jumped aside. It didn't look like Hana would pause for anyone. A few locals stopped and cheered as he sped down one of the main avenues. "Go Hana go!"

They sped downhill, and after many city blocks, the rickshaw took a hard left. Yace leaned into Kipp, who was trying his best to keep them both steady on their seat. Now the rickshaw raced along a crowded boardwalk. Hana shouted at people to get out of the way, swerving toward seated patrons at outdoor restaurants; some braced tight against the boardwalk railing; some flew over the railing into the waters below.

Peering out the curtained windows, Irwin said, "He's fast!"

Still holding onto Yace, Kipp sputtered, "I'll never bad mouth a slow person again."

"Good. Because we all have our talents and our weaknesses, no one is ever better than anyone else."

Kipp looked at Irwin, his mouth open, and finally he said as they flew over a bump in the street, "Since when did you start talking like Dana?"

The rickshaw jolted to an abrupt stop. They had arrived at the entrance to the loading dock. Yace and Kipp were thrown forward and landed hard on the floorboards of the large rickshaw.

"We at dock!"

Rubbing his neck, Irwin pulled out two bananas, slightly smashed by Yace's fall. "Here you go Hana. Thank you for your promptness."

"Bananas!" Hana giggled and ate them whole, peals included.

The sailboat was at the dock and ready to leave. Irwin shouted at the captain, "Hey La, wait! We want a ride, please!"

The Erthin put his arms into the air, "It's good to see you, my friend. How are you tonight?"

"Good to see you too, La, we are good—especially now, having made your boat on time."

"Come on down, my friend, it's a good night for a sail."

They began to gather the bags.

"I see you have friends with you. Come-come, we will wait," La called out.

"Hello La," Kipp nodded and grabbed what he could. "Alright Yace, follow me."

Irwin carried most of their bags and supplies down the steep gangplank. It was low tide; the walk to the boat with heavy bags was precarious.

Kipp's baggage was easy to heft, but the angle was steep. He slipped a few times but kept his concentration on the boat. Yace was visibly scared, slipping and gripping onto Kipp, but then she stopped midway.

Kipp dropped the bags onto the dock and climbed up the wooden plank to her. He scooped Yace up and carried her to the boat's deck, putting her down on one of the wooden benches near the center of the boat.

"We good here?" La asked when Irwin was done organizing all the bags and baggage. Then he blew wind into the sails and the boat pitched forth across the calm waters.

Irwin gazed out across the glistening seawaters and audibly sighed—relieved to be leaving the buzzing city.

Yace sat still, her eyes unmoving. La noticed, "Ah, she gonna be alright?"

Irwin took a seat across from Yace and Kipp, "We are not sure."

"You didn't do this to her, did you? She looks drugged."

"No. We wish she was drugged."

La waved his hand across the front of her face; she did not blink—for the longest time. But once she did, her eyes tracked his hand, and she peered up at him with childlike innocence. Then her stoic blue-eyes settled on the watery horizon. Lights from the city and the moon and stars shimmered across the water.

"Do you know what happened to her?"

"She was taken by a Telepath."

"Oh no! You gotta be fooling me. I mean, I've heard of it happening, but I've never seen someone under their control."

"She is no longer under any telepathic control," Irwin said. "They just erased everything about her."

"Probably why Telepaths aren't allowed to live on this side of the wall. A few do, of course, but-but damn! That's no good."

"No, it is not."

"You find her like this?"

Irwin nodded, and La pressed, "Did you know that the Daos Prime side of Daos is a sanctuary city? Everyone who comes here, assuming they are not telepathic, can seek asylum—anyone! There are very few places on this side of Quetzal-seventeen that are accepting of all. And, except for doing work, those of us with Talents, we're not allowed to use our powers outside our job. That's not to say we don't in our homes when the curtains are drawn." His eyebrows moved up and down.

"In all my journeys around Daos Prime, I did not see any Psychic Attendants." Irwin pressed for information.

"You won't find but a few, and that's on the south side of town, down secret alleys. There are districts around the city where people prefer to congregate, not to say there isn't intermingling going on, but the Telepaths I've seen and met usually keep to themselves. It's rare to see them out during the daytime," said La. "They know they're not welcome in Daos Prime, if you know what I mean. Personally, I believe Telepaths are best suited to living with Mortals. That's who they want to control anyway."

"Telepaths wanna control everyone," Kipp growled.

"That is a broad generalization, Kipp."

"It's the truth."

They sailed on in silence for a while, and then La said, "So, you're saving the pretty lass?"

Irwin watched Kipp pull Yace's head toward his shoulder. Her eyes kept closing, the rocking motion of the boat summoning sleep. He watched how tender Kipp was with her, and said, "That is what we came here to do."

"Do you think she'll snap out of it?"

Irwin forced himself to look at La, "I hope she does."

"Luckily, it's dark, so you've got that to your advantage. I'd make sure that hood stays up, and maybe tuck in her hair; that way no one can see what she is. She's a lovely Telepath." He took a sip from a flask. "On that side of the wall, you can never be too sure who's lurking in the shadows. There are many fair-haired people over there."

Kipp whispered, "You wouldn't happen to know of any good Psychic Attendants?"

Irwin turned to him, "Now you want to talk to a Psychic Attendant?!"

"If you trust this guy, then maybe he knows of someone trustworthy."

"I know of an opium den. Halley Adtrib is the owner; she's part Daosian and trilingual. She should be able to help."

"It will be late when we arrive. Will her place be open?"

"She does her best business at night after everyone has earned a silver or two. Sometimes there're dancers with see-through dresses and bells around their ankles—fun to watch while smoking. They hypnotize you; I swear."

"How far is Halley Adtrib's place from Jetty Canal?"

"It's south of there by a few blocks." La looked around his empty boat. "If I pick up no one else, I can push this beast up the shore and drop you closer to the avenue where she lives. After that, it's about five streets down, midway off the intercepting avenue. There are a few non-thru streets you'll pass, but you've been down a few roads like that, huh?"

"And if you pick someone up?"

"It's Moon's Day. People usually take this day off—and Leaf's Day, too."

Kipp said, "Moon's Day? Leaf's Day?"

"Non-workdays."

"But you work them."

"Food is not free, nor is living in Daos Prime," said La. He had a lighthearted way about him. "Truth be told, I only work half days and switch shifts with two other blokes. So really, I don't work too hard for the tokens I earn. And I get to keep what I earn, so it's a win! Oh, by the way, none of you have paid for voyaging with me yet."

Irwin handed over twenty Rupees. "You're overpaying me." La tried to pass most of them back.

"If anyone comes asking about us, I need you to say that you never saw us."

"You in trouble? You're leaving Daos Prime, the best place to hide out on all Urthis! There are space-voyaging ships leaving all the time; you could be on another world in a moon's time."

"It sounds tempting, but we cannot leave Urthis, nor can we hide out in Daos Prime. We need a Psychic Attendant, and then we are leaving Daos Territory."

La raised one of his red eyebrows. "Did you steal her from one of those rich Capritians? I've heard they like to take beauties such as her and do with them as they wish."

"Yes. She was kidnapped—held against her will. We are sure she was mentally and physically tortured. We came here to save her." He watched Kipp lean his head against Yace's.

"Damn Capritians. There are a few families that live on the south harbor walls," La pointed. "Their houses face the city so they can listen in on all the happenings. It's creepy."

"How do you know all this?" Kipp asked, his eyes closed.

"Kipp."

"Irwin, I wouldn't buy into this Erthin's shit. He's a talker." He opened his eyes, sat up straight. Yace appeared to be sleeping against his shoulder. He glared at Irwin over her head.

"Kipp, you are tired—maybe you should rest."

"If you try your tricks on me again, Irwin, so help me. When Yace is better, I'll have her do something to you. You'll regret it!"

41

<u>Halley Adtrib</u>

They sailed on in silence until the boat neared the last port in Daos Prime. La waved to an old man standing on the dock. "Uh oh. That's Sir Alonnol Galispin, a real prick. He's one of those Capritians, the kind you never want to piss off."

Irwin asked, "Has that happened before?"

"Hey, Clan-Duin."

"Kipp."

"You'll want to disappear or turn into something else and hide."

"Why?"

"If you're getting off anywhere in northern Daos, Alonnol Galispin will, too. He'll follow you."

Kipp jumped to attention and eyed the dock up ahead. "We can't have a Telepath on this boat."

"I have to, company's motto. We don't discriminate."

"Do not worry Kipp."

"Dang me. What are we gonna do?"

"I will sit with Yace, and you will be next to me in dog form."

"Dog form?" Kipp looked at La. "Are dogs allowed on the boat?"

"We've ferried everything up to a small pony, and I do mean small."

Kipp was now in his four-legged canine form. Irwin picked up his clothes and shoved them into a bag. The boat slowed and nestled up to the dock. Irwin was now a shoulder for Yace to lean on. She sat erect after she felt Kipp leave.

"Yace, sleep." Irwin said as the boat was secured to the dock.

"I'll be back," La said. He hurried around Alonnol Galispin and raced up the main walkway. Irwin saw him go into one of the local businesses.

Wispy hair stuck out from around the elderly Telepath's ears, but there was none on top. His hat tried to float off his head, and he grabbed it and stuffed it back on tight. His piercing blue eyes studied Irwin, Yace, and the dog at their feet. He harrumphed as he boarded and took up a seat facing them.

Acting tired, Irwin closed his eyes tight and kept a close hold on Yace. He felt her move and opened his eyes to see her watching Alonnol.

Shit. What should I do? Should I kill the Telepath? No, he is linked. They all are. They are all linked in one way or another. I wonder if he knows what happened. How could he? Telepaths!

Alonnol's eyes never left Yace's.

Shit, does he recognize her?

He whimpered, "Please close your eyes, my sweet, rest."

Her forehead met the side of his neck, and Irwin summoned her unconscious. As Kipp laid his head across Irwin's feet, he did the same thing to him, putting him to sleep. He did not want the Telepath to probe, nor did he want his companions to think of anything that might compromise them from peacefully debarking at the northern docks.

Yace felt limper than before. He steadied her head and body and pretended to rest himself. They waited for a long time before La returned, hustling down the dock with heavy breath.

Stepping onto the boat, La asked, "You didn't touch them, did you, Mister Galispin, Sir?"

The old man's nose whistled. "They're all asleep, you twit. They were like that when I came onboard. Now get this boat moving! I haven't got all night!"

Tokens were tossed at La, and he caught them. Irwin felt the metal fly. The elderly Telepath had half a pound of coins on him. He felt the old man move. He had been looking at them, but now he gazed at the shoreline. Irwin kept one eye slightly open, watching Alonnol Galispin. But after a while of sitting in the rocking boat, Irwin fell asleep too.

The boat made its approach to Canal Jetty, and La woke Irwin. There was one lone light on the boardwalk. The boat slowed and La tossed a light to a lamp on the post at the end of the dock. The ropes were secured and Kipp, in his dog form, jumped ship and went to urinate on the green grass beyond the docks. Above and all around, bats chirped and skimmed across the water, catching mosquitoes.

"Here you go Sir, Mam." La helped Irwin and Yace up off their seat and off the boat. He helped Irwin hoist all the bags and boxes of food onto the dock.

La was readying to depart with only Alonnol in the boat. He looked at Irwin one last time, and said, "There are rickshaws on the south side of the canal. They'll be able to take you to your relatives." He shook Irwin's hand, sneakily handing off a piece of paper. "Good luck to you and your wife, sir."

"Thank you," Irwin nodded and helped La push the sailboat away from the dock.

He did not stay to watch the boat sail away, but Yace did. He lugged all their bags to the boardwalk and then retrieved Yace, keeping a tight hold on her until they were safely on the boardwalk. "Yace, I need you to stay here with our stuff. I am going to get us a rickshaw." She looked to have comprehended his words, though still standing statuesque. Irwin turned away and left Yace behind.

He felt comfortable leaving her for a few minutes. That was his first mistake. His second was dismissing Kipp's mad chirps, trying to get Irwin's attention. Yace had walked away. Leaving their belongings, she went down a dark alley. She sat in the shadows with closed eyes until Irwin found her. He knew she wanted to sleep, but he could not allow that.

"Kipp, stay with her please," he told the mouse, now on Yace's shoulder. She watched him move around her arm down to the palm of her hand. "Thank you for keeping her amused." He also gave Yace a thick metal bracelet to look at, wrapping it around her wrist. She sat down on a box and entertained herself with the mouse and the bracelet while Irwin found them a ride.

An eager taxi driver came to their aid. The prices for everything seemed to fluctuate if the natives thought they could hustle visitors. It worked most of the time. Irwin paid, and the taxi driver helped load and unload the hundred pounds of supplies. He paid another silver to have it brought inside the quiet opium den.

An old woman asked, "What are you doing?"

"Are you Halley Adtrib?"

"Yes." She watched as the boxes and bags were stacked next to her doorway. "You do not bring things into my home without asking my permission!"

"I will pay to store my belongings here." Irwin made three Rupees appear, handed them to Halley. "We do not plan on being here long."

She looked Yace up and down. "She does not look well. Is she why you are here?"

"Yes."

Irwin stepped close to Yace, further into the lit room. Halley gasped, "I have seen you before."

"You have?" His brow wrinkled.

"Come, let us sit. We have much to discuss," she insisted they follow. "You, Clan-Duin, come out and be with us, too." She seemed to know that Kipp was in the room. The woman locked the front door. "My place is lonely tonight. Your needs are great, and I am here to help."

Kipp was now in his two-legged form and pulled on a pair of pants. He looked at Irwin. "You came here before?"

"No."

Halley shook her head. "We have never met, but there is much to discuss."

Kipp leaned into his friend. "Irwin, I don't trust this lady."

"Shut up, Hauss," he chastised under his breath. "How do you know of us?"

"I have seen your faces. Your names I have heard. You are Samuel Irwin Miner."

"Fuk. This isn't good."

"Quiet, Hauss."

"His name is not Hauss," she said.

"Stop reading my mind, Telepath." Kipp said, nostrils flaring.

"She cannot." Irwin eyed the contact they were making, forearm against forearm. "How do you know of us?"

"Much is shared between here and there. Words are said and images spread." Halley motioned toward cushions as she sat in a rickety old bamboo rocking chair. Irwin and Yace settled in on the cushions, but Kipp sat upright. Halley continued, "There are men searching for you, Samuel Irwin Miner. I root for you. You have saved many today. I will let you use my psyche, and I'll keep quiet about you."

"What the fuk, Irwin?!"

"Hauss."

"Your name is not Hauss. You are Kipp Hauler, son of Jillian and Aneth Hauler."

Kipp tried to move forward toward the Psychic Attendant, but Irwin placed his hand on his friend's chest. He, too, felt troubled by Halley's knowledge of them. "How do you know about us?"

"I know you are deadly, Samuel Irwin Miner, and I like it." Her eyebrows wiggled with excitement, and she smiled, revealing only bottom teeth stained from smoking. She coughed several times. "They send images of what you are, what you can do. Images of what you've done. I sense that some fear you. They want you. They want to control or kill you. They say you're an abomination. You should be destroyed. Those are words that are meant to scare. I'm not scared of you. You are amazing, Samuel Irwin Miner. I am sure you will save us all."

Already rattled, Irwin didn't need any more of this kind of news.

"Do you know who sent images of me and my friend?"

Halley shook her head. "I know it came from the north. They spoke of you as a caution to others many moons ago. But then this morning, urgency was sent from Ishik Palace. Flashes of your destruction. They urged vengeance." Her smile grew. "We all know what you did this day: you destroyed the Ishik regime. Some of us support you; others will call you out if you stay in Daos City. Oh. And there are soldiers looking for you—the last loyal servants to the Ishik family. They want you dead, too. I know you can kill them. I'm not worried about you."

He sat back; Kipp was twitching—worried. "Dang me Irwin. She knows about us! What the fuk are we gonna do? We can't get out of Daos City alive if they know about us. They're hunting us!"

"Kipp, please stop!"

"They will hunt you both, but if you leave with the shadows and stay hidden, you shall not be seen. I foresee it; I see your future."

He nodded. "That is the plan."

"We can't trust her, Irwin!" Halley smirked at Kipp's outburst.

Irwin ignored his frantic friend. "We need to make contact with someone."

She studied them. "Who?"

"This is not a good idea, Irwin."

"Kipp, please hand over the talisman. We need to talk to Nonbry."

"Don't say his name! She doesn't need to know!"

"Halley will know, just like all the others. We know this," he said, trying to remain calm himself. "I will keep it quick, simple, and without much information."

"How are we gonna tell him what's going on if you speak riddles?"

"He is a Telepath." Irwin glared at Kipp. "Please hand over the talisman."

"If we are put to death because of this...." Kipp grumbled, pulling the talisman out of his tight pocket.

"Shut up, Kipp." Irwin did not have time for Kipp's fears, his rampant insecurities.

Halley looked at the wooden talisman and grasped it in her hands. Smacking her lips a few times, the Telepath hummed—pulling for Nonbry to enter her mind. Her eyes opened, showing only white iris. Nonbry grumbled, "What's your report?"

Irwin said, "Good evening, Sir."

"Kipp?" Nonbry snapped at the Clan-Duin.

Irwin said, "We have had a rough time Sir, but we have come far. Yace is finally with us, and we need a prompt return to you."

"Yace?" Nonbry looked at her. "What say you?" She did not reply, and Nonbry grumbled, "Miner, haven't you touched her yet?"

"I have, Sir, many times, but it has not been working, Sir."

"Enough with the Sirs!"

Breathe. Keep calm.

"We are as far south as we can be in Daos. Yace is with us, but not with us. She needs you. Where are you?"

"We are in no place to meet," Nonbry spat. "What in Holy Hakra have you been thinking, Miner?! I hear reports. People say you've killed hundreds if not thousands at this point. Decimated entire villages! Leading PCP on more chases! Is this true?"

"Yes." His throat went dry. "But ... But everything I have done, I have done to save Yace, Sir. You should not chide me for things that have happened because of that, and because of coincidence."

"COINCIDENCE! I told you to give your life for her, not go and do .... What you've done has ripple effects you cannot comprehend. This is exactly what Dephen wanted, all of it. Somehow, you fell under his spell. You were supposed to be immune to him. Had this Telepath more abilities, I'd turn you into an infant."

"Please do!" Kipp egged.

Irwin leaned forward. "But how? How was I manipulated?"

"Dephen's been working on this grand plan for decades. He's always wanted to be in control of Daos Territory. He believed he could do a better job ruling before I was even born. But moreover, he believed he could also rule Hakran society. ... do it better than Hakra and his PCP minions. His plan, all along, was to conquer Daos first. Then, somehow, the other territories would fall into his grasp. The thing is, he would always do it the telepathic way. Sure, he would tout that all people on Urthis would finally be seen as equals. No more telepathic tiered societal rule. But in the end, he would be the one to rule it all. Still a Telepath in control.

"Dephen wanted this to happen. I see it now. All of it as it is. He wanted to cripple the Hakran regime. And what better way than to create a Sleeper assassin? Have them kill hundreds of their most loyal yet powerful of subjects? Demonstrate to the commoner that even Hakra can't keep the ones with powers under control. Give them something more to fear about us. But then, once fear has taken over, he steps in to provide a safe society under the guise that devotion to him would create protection for all. And once the people devote themselves, given over their souls, he would have full control. Just like Hakra, but worse because they're fully dominated. No autonomy whatsoever. How obtuse! He's always wanted to be the ultimate being of power. Insert himself into that powerful position. Just like he did with Yace.

"Dephen said he would do whatever it took." Nonbry stared off for a moment, but blinked and returned to the room. "We believed you could thwart his power, Miner. That you would save Yace from Dephen. She was the perfect vessel for him. That is until he found you. Somehow. Somewhere. He got you under his power. Now all he must do is puppeteer."

42

LAND OF CANNIBALS

He recalled Emperor Ishik's telepathic voice. This memory echoed and sent a shiver down Irwin's spine. *'Nuaki Village. Ahradah. And to a lesser extent, Onj Raha. That was more you than us, but we knew what could happen.'*

This was the confirmation Irwin did not want to hear. Everything Nonbry had just said was true.

Oh, Kipp.

He was Irwin's best friend. He couldn't imagine his life without this person. Kipp was someone who accepted Irwin as he was. He was kind and competent at many things. He pushed Irwin to be a better person, encouraged him to grow up and discover the beautiful things Urthis offered. He had relished every moment with his fun-loving Clan-Duin friend.

It had been Kipp, and ultimately Dephen, through Yace, who manipulated Irwin's heartstrings.

Irwin was crushed.

This is all my fault. I should never have acted on impulse or acknowledged my feelings. Should have kept them bottled up. Used my wits. Ignored my heart. Damn you, Jorge.

It is not his fault. This is all my fault.

He was now afraid to see Kipp, eyes upon Halley's closed-toed sandals. He wanted to withdraw. But he couldn't. Too much was at stake.

Kipp balked. "Wait a moment. You're saying that Irwin was manipulated by Dephen? That's not true. Can't be! Irwin can only be influenced when directly touched by a Telepath." Kipp looked at him. "What did you say you were, Irwin? ... Impervious when you hold metal within, or something like that."

Irwin had no words. This was all very hard to digest.

Yace sat alongside Kipp, yawning and blinking.

"Irwin?" He could feel Kipp's eyes warming the side of his face. Irwin was afraid to look. Soon Kipp's attention reversed back to Yace and Nonbry.

"I have been called Sleeper Assassin by the PCP and Dephen." Irwin batted away tears and said, "This means I am compromised. That we are all compromised."

"Yes. Unfortunately." The Oracle's lips fell flat, firm. Nonbry seemed to be assessing all three of them. After several deep breaths, Nonbry spoke again through the Psychic Attendant. "We sail west from Arisham to Uer'Bin. A worthy port is Koumin, but not by foot. Be cautious when crossing the sea."

Kipp groaned, "Ugh, riddles."

All those names meant something to Irwin. He remembered seeing them on his Urthis map. "Yes, sir. We will see you in Uer'Bin."

"Wait a moment! Uer'Bin Territory?" Kipp squawked, "You're joking, right? Yace needs your help now, Nonbry. Yace isn't Yace!"

Nonbry appraised her. "She is fractured. Her memories have been altered. She doesn't remember her life as it was."

"You can see that?"

"This Oracle has Talent, but not enough mental spark to help Yace. And it would take days to train them."

Irwin pleaded, "Are there any here in Daos who can?"

Nonbry shook his head with a ferocity Irwin had not seen in him before. "You should not be where you are. Extreme caution needs to be exercised when speaking to, and thru, Oracles from now on."

"Are you positive there is no one around here who can help Yace?"

Nonbry grumbled, "In Daos there are those who have the power you seek, but not the want you crave—they will bring you down."

"Is there anywhere else between here and Koumin?"

"No. And all major cities should be avoided, like Ajihya."

Kipp's eyes grew wide. "Dang me, you're right. Irwin should not go to Ajihya."

"Why should I not go to—"

"You think Daos Prime turns you crazed?" Kipp sounded scared. "Everything in Ajihya is gold encased, and I mean everything!"

"I was referring to the Telepaths, you dimwit," Nonbry chided.

"From here to Koumin, we have to go through Ajihya," said Irwin.

"No, we don't," argued Kipp.

"You have not studied those maps like I have."

Kipp said, his voice softer, "I looked at them some."

"Sir, Nonbry, Yace needs you now. I cannot heal her; and I have tried."

"Your power should've worked on her." Nonbry sneered. "Perhaps you drained yourself after slaughtering all those PCP along the way?"

"My powers have worked all day, Sir." He felt like crying, and moistened his lips. "What I believe happened is that Yace arrived long before we did, and it did not go well. We found her in with the concubines. I sense that Yace has been mentally cleansed, cured of unwanted pests—so to speak—and left as a soft body for Ishik men to enjoy. I do not believe that Dephen is with her anymore. Yace is a clean page. No memories. Nothing."

The room went quiet—Nonbry deep in thought. "There is one place against the mountains before arriving in Tresdahla. If Kipp was paying attention during his lessons, he knows of it."

"Is it on the map?"

"No. It's hidden from maps."

"On my map, the road heads east of Tresdahla along the southern shores to the mountains. It looks like it could connect to Daos Territory. Is that where we need to go?"

Nonbry nodded.

Kipp asked again, meekly, "Wait. Is that the one refuge you told us about?"

Nonbry nodded again.

"Will they have what we are looking for?"

"Yes." Nonbry said, "But from where you are it'll be a trek by foot, and no ships port there."

"On my map, I do not see a road connecting Daos to Tresdahla."

"It doesn't."

"Then how do we get there?"

Nonbry's voice dropped. "There are old ways and old roads. Be cautious of cannibals."

None of that made sense to Irwin, but he nodded as though it did. "Thank you, Sir."

I think.

"I sense ... I sense this woman knows something about you." Nonbry paused, "You're truly a dumb child, Miner!" He glared at Irwin.

"Fuk, he knows what you did at the palace."

Irwin did not jump to conclusions, unlike Kipp. "Sir, is everything alright?"

"Hardly! What have you done?! You've changed the order of things on Urthis forever. This is exactly what Dephen wanted. The second block has been re-moved. Society as we know it will fall! You stupid child. I should let you be caught. Someone like you shouldn't … but then again … there's Yace. Be hasty with your flight from Daos City or be caught up in a whirlwind." Nonbry exited the Telepath, and she came back into awareness.

"We're as good as dead," Kipp muttered, eyes glistening. He was fearful about their outcome, just as Irwin was.

She smiled, seemingly happy to be back within her body; then her lips flattened. "Someone saw you this night."

Irwin started to say, "Alonnol Galis—"

She knew of the Telepath. "Alonnol Galispin is a despicable mongrel. He deserves death, but death does not want him—a scoundrel indeed. You leave now, out the back door."

"What about our belongings?"

"I'll hold them for you."

"Are there soldiers here?"

"No. I have customers outside. They wonder why my door is locked; usually it's open. They should not see you. Go. Out my secret door with you." She ushered them through a back door concealed by a tapestry.

"Fuk! This is bad," Kipp growled, and mutated into his owl form. Irwin grabbed his clothing.

Fuk indeed. We are all compromised. What do I do? Can I trust my own thoughts?

Can I trust Kipp?

What about Yace?

I cannot regret not surrendering to Emperor Ishik. But maybe I should have taken caution with their words. I should have asked more questions.

But he, they … they wanted my soul. They wanted to consume my power. Maybe Nonbry is right. Dephen wanted to be the next Hakra-like creature. But I killed him, and all those other Ishiks. That should mean we are safe.

Ha! Safety is a mental construct.

I am not safe. None of us are. Even if Dephen is dead, we are all compromised.

Kipp is correct. We are as good as dead!

He had to force down his frets and regrets. There were still remnants of a now fractured empire searching for him, hoping to kill the man who brought down the Ishik regime.

He contemplated his mountaintop.

Irwin pulled Yace along, making sure she stayed covered beneath her hood. They hustled down a narrow alley. He used his metal to find where his wagon was hidden. They would retrieve the donkeys and horses and escape Daos under the cover of darkness.

Yace made no sound other than heavy breathing; she held close to Irwin. She seemed to sense the urgency he felt and kept up with him. It was calming for Irwin to not have to keep Yace quiet. She was, for once, compliant with everything he asked.

The stables were quiet. Irwin's donkeys smelled him coming and bellowed as he opened the doors. Four other horses inside the elongated barn nickered or whinnied when Irwin and Yace entered the dark barnyard. "Shit, I need to pay in order for the wagon to stay," Irwin grumbled. To his side, Yace petted one of the friendlier animals. "That is Roper. You will ride him," he said. She petted Roper's gigantic head and touched noses with him.

Maybe there is hope.

He yanked both saddles from the wagon bed.

The old stable manager shouted in his native tongue, startling them. He strode through the shadows with a wooden mallet in his hand. "Oh, it be you, Samuel!"

"Good evening Ekaro. I am sorry it is so late. I have come to retrieve my animals. And I need to pay to keep my wagon here for a few more days. My friend who came here with me will be by to pick it up." He made up a satchel of Rupees.

"You take the horses, but leave the wagon?"

"Yes. My friends will be—"

"Yeah-yeah, I heard you say they be coming later for it. Well, you owe for tonight's feed."

"Thank you for taking such good care of my animals. I will recommend your stable to anyone who asks."

Ekaro noticed Yace in the shadows. "What a pretty little thing."

"This is my sister."

"She wasn't with you when you arrived. You had a male friend. Where's he?"

"Yes. He helped me sell my wares and find my sister. He will come and retrieve the wagon in a few days." He glanced at Yace. "She missed seeing our horses." He passed the sack of coins to Ekaro.

"You can stay anytime, my friend," said Ekaro, jubilant from the contents of the bag.

"Many thanks, Ekaro." Irwin returned to his task of tacking up the animals.

"Have a safe night." Ekaro left the barn.

Kipp waited for Ekaro to leave before changing into his human form. He helped wrestle saddles out of the back of the wagon—set panniers and packs next to the stalls. "How are we gonna get out of here, Irwin?"

"Do not worry about it."

"What about our stuff, all that food?"

"Do not worry about it." He didn't want to think of anything else than the task at hand. But his shoulders were heavy, burdened. He would miss his wagon, but they needed a swift escape. Even without it, he knew he could keep his friends safe and would kill people to do it. But he wanted to be done with the killing.

There was a sense of urgency, and the animals were getting agitated. He fumbled with leathers, making sure everything was tight for a quick getaway. After securing a donkey to each saddle, Irwin and Kipp helped Yace up onto her horse. She yawned several times and slumped forward in the saddle.

"Yace, stay awake," Kipp pleaded.

"I will ride with her." Irwin climbed on behind her. Kipp handed off Bodi's reins and mutated back into a rat, jumping from a fence post into a saddlebag.

Irwin ponied Bodi along Roper's side.

He wanted to retrieve their belongings and get out of Daos City before they were found. But there was no back route to Halley Adtrib's that the horses could navigate. They kept to the main roads—three blocks down and four over from the wide thoroughfare to the city center.

Irwin knew there were soldiers looking for him. He heard horses' hooves and felt heavy metal swords moving along the avenues.

Rounding the corner onto the street that led to the opium den, a pack of soldiers were entering Halley Adtrib's workshop. A cloud of smoke blasted the red-coated soldiers as they entered. He pulled his horse to a stop and whispered, "Kipp. Kipp, I need you. We need to ride out of here, now!"

Kipp was his two-legged self again and followed Irwin's line of vision. "What's the matter?"

"I need you to ride Bodi. We need to get out of here now."

"Were those soldiers?"

"Yes! And another block down and over is another brigade."

"You can feel them? Are they Talented?"

"Of course, I can feel them, but it is their swords. We need to leave!"

"What about my clothes?"

Irwin tossed Kipp his only pair of pants. Then passed over Bodi's reins. Kipp mounted the steed while pulling on his worn trousers.

Their horses' hooves echoed across the cobbles until they crossed a long bridge. Once on gravel and dirt, they sped through the darkened streets toward the outskirts of Daos City—toward the land of cannibals.

This is not how I wanted this to go.

At least we have Yace!

Irwin had been revealed as the "Sleeper Assassin" who brought down an empire—and now he can't even trust his won thoughts. Soldiers are hunting them through the streets and they're fleeing toward the deadliest place on Urthis. The land of cannibals awaits

Don't stop now—get Book 4: Land of Cannibals

If you enjoyed Sleeper Assassin, please leave a review.

Also By

<u>The Metalist's Journey</u>
0.25 ~ The Last Metalist
0.5 ~ The Metalist's Journey Prologue
1 ~ Secrets of Urthis
2 ~ Elements of Power
3 ~ Sleeper Assassin
4 ~ Land of Cannibals
4.5 ~ Bound by Iron & Blood
(+2 more at least!)

If you liked this book please leave a review!

Want more information about Irwin and the world of Urthis?
Join KD Lumsden's newsletter at https://www.kdlumsden.com/

The Unusual Creatures Mentioned

ANCIENT DWELLERS

APPEARANCE: Unknown

UNIQUE TRAITS: Deities who created the universes. They wanted life to happen; to experience love, hate, melancholy, triumph, and sorrow. Everything exists because of them.

CLAN-DUIN

APPEARANCE: brown skinned, black hair, hairy bodies, eye colors can be gray/ green/ brown/ amber

UNIQUE TRAITS: shapeshifters, can be feline, canine, raptor, bear, ape, and/or marine mammals. Are very loyal companions, prefer to live in packs, but can be loners. Linear thinkers, they can be stubborn and foolhardy.

COTERIE

APPEARANCE: pale-skinned, white to blonde hair, white to blue eyes, but can take on darker appearances if bred with other creatures, such as Clan-Duins or Erthins.

UNIQUE TRAITS: Blended children of the Guru, infused with Mortal DNA. Their abilities are similar to Guru, but can be limited by Mortal blood. They are considered bastard children of the Guru and are impure. Often arrogant and egocentric, they live anywhere/anytime.

ELEMENTALIST

APPEARANCE: grey to olive-skin color, auburn-orange to red hair, green-hazel eyes

UNIQUE TRAITS: can harness every element known to exist. They can create elements from within themselves, or through interaction with organic and inorganic life. They are known to have the ability to live out in space without oxygen or nutrients, they can oxygen exist inside their lungs without taking a breath. It is said they were the first beings created by the Ancient Dwellers, that they were necessary for creating the known universes.

ERTHIN
<u>APPEARANCE</u>: grey to olive-skin color, auburn-orange red hair, green-hazel eyes
<u>UNIQUE TRAITS</u>: hybrid Elementalist and Mortal. They can harness the five most powerful natural elements: Air, water, fire, earth, and spirit. They can be pure-bred and have all abilities, or part-breed and have abilities specific to person (ie. the ability to harness only one element).

GURU
<u>APPEARANCE</u>: white skinned, white-ashen hair, white-blue eyes.
<u>UNIQUE TRAITS</u>: Direct descendants of Ancient Dwellers. They have can use any type of power (teleporting, telepathy, shapeshifting). Considered living gods, they hide in plain sight and across all the universes. They can live everywhere/anywhere/anytime.

GYPSY
An enclave of like-minded people, usually Talented, who tour Urthis rescuing other Talented people. They often take the rescued to sanctuary cities.

HAKRA (Urthis's God)
<u>APPEARANCE</u>: black-skinned, blue-eyes, hairless.
<u>UNIQUE TRAITS</u>: considered a living god who resides in Akarah City, capitol of Urthis. Has lain the groundwork for Telepaths to shape Urthis into an interstellar hub; keeps the general population subdue through religion. Every few years produces a Tome for the people to follow, hypnotizes the masses through telepathic ideology; zealot followers are devout enough to turn in their brother or neighbor if they believe they are Talented. Every few years his followers take pilgrimages to Akarah to stand in Hakra's presence with hopes to be bestowed a gift.

ISHIK EMPIRE
Current rulers of Doas Territory, the Ishik Empire have been in control for the last thousand years. Believed to be the last full-blooded Coterie family, they claim

to be purebred; to couple with someone outside the family brings dishonor. They tout their land to be free of Talented people, yet employ Talented people to work at the palace. They maltreat their subjects, taking boys away from their families at 9-10, to work iron mines, daughters are married off by 8-9, families live in small dome-huts, and when compared to the rest of Urthis, Doas Territory is at least one hundred years behind in technological advancements.

METALIST

<u>APPEARANCE</u>: ashen skin color, gray hair, silvery-gray eyes

<u>UNIQUE TRAITS</u>: can harness all types of metal including, but not limited to; gold, silver, aluminum, nickel, iron, zinc, mercury, cadmium, cobalt, chromium, platinum, lead, etc. They can hold up to eight pounds of any given substance within their own flesh, flushed it under the skin to specific places. Their ability to manipulate metal starts with extraction, turning the metal into its liquid form, and integrating it back into its hard form, and can form anything imaginable with any amount of metal. They are known to give off a deathly scent when holding metal within. Direct descendants to Elementalist.

MORTAL

<u>APPEARANCE</u>: always pale-skinned, brown-eyed, hair light brown to dark-brown/black

<u>UNIQUE TRAITS</u>: Bipeds with no superhuman powers. One of the five eldest beings created by the Ancient Dwellers. They have been exported from their home world, brought to foreign worlds to repopulate but often exploited as cheap labor.

PLANETAIRY CONSTIBLE PATROL (PCP)

Comprised only of people with Talents. Telepaths are given powerful positions (Admiral, Captain, Colonel, Corporal, Sargent), Erthins can hold powerful positions (Lieutenant, Sargent), Clan-Duins are considered working soldiers or minions, but can be demoted and placed in a "court-yard sitter" position. Also called "Population Control Patrol". They usually patrol in groups of four and are seen riding large "warhorses".

SANCTUARY CITY

Not necessarily a city, but a place where people with Talents are safe from the PCP and Hakran ideology. Most don't allow Mortals to reside. Most require those looking for permanent residency to prove they are a positive influence, that they will help protect others with Talents, regardless of abilities, and not cause issue within the community. There are rules within each community to adhere, and if someone breaks that main rule they can be banished from one, or all sanctuary cities. (*Note: All Sanctuary cities are interconnected by Telepaths.)

SHAYOT

A truly talented child, usually male, but sometimes are females brought through the ranks. They are usually multi-cultural (Telepath and Clan-Duin, or Erthin and Telepath, or any unique mixture) and are trained by the worst of the worse in order to understand how to think like murders and rapest, thieves and mercenaries. As an adult they are highly regarded and given positions of power within the Hakra regime.

TALENT, PEOPLE OF (aka TALENTED)
Any being who possess supernatural powers.

TELECAPRITIAN
<u>APPEARANCE</u>: pale skinned, white to blue eyed, white to blonde hair
<u>UNIQUE TRAITS</u>: can use telekinesis and telepathy, can shapeshift appearance but only into same gender roles. One of the five eldest beings created by the Ancient Dwellers.

TELEPATH
<u>APPEARANCE</u>: pale skinned, white to blue eyed, white to blonde hair
<u>UNIQUE TRAITS</u>: hybrid of TeleCapritian & Mortal, they cannot yield telekinesis. There are many types of telepaths; dreaming (they see visions future or past based), some can hear thoughts, some can manipulate beings though 'telepathic' brain waves, others can only do this through physical touch.

TELEKINESIS
The ability to move objects at a distance by mental power or other nonphysical means.

URTHIS

Fourth planet from the sun in the Oska'al solar system and one of the many places in the known universe that hosts supernatural and natural powered creatures. It is the planet on which Samuel Irwin Miner lives.

VOLATILE

A derogatory word used against people of Talent. (see: Talent, people of)

WARDEN

<u>APPEARANCE</u>: enigmatic. They have the ability to become anyone of the same sex

<u>UNIQUE TRAITS</u>: a Warden is a breed of person (can be male or female—usually male) that is of Telepathic, Clan-Duin, and Elementalist descent. They are considered greatest of warriors and hunters, usually former *Shayot*, and work directly for Hakra and his minions. The only way to kill a Warden is to cut off their head.

About KD Lumsden

KD Lumsden was raised on a small farm where her youth was spent running away from angry bulls, riding horses, fishing, camping, and daydreaming about fantastic worlds. Born dyslexic, she has learned to use her neurodivergent mind for the good of mankind—creatures on other planets are another story. Though she's not a fast reader or writer, her mind flies with many stories, eagerly waiting to be told. Better with numbers and art, KD became an architectural designer long before it was cool to work from home, and has always enjoyed drawing, creating maps, laying out and designing buildings, and of course other worldly planets with amazing settings and diverse people. She lives on a farm outside Eugene, Oregon, with her supportive husband, imaginative son, and their many two and four-legged animals.

Get to know KD more by visiting her socials ....

https://www.facebook.com/KDLumsden/
https://www.instagram.com/kdlumsden_author/
https://bsky.app/profile/authorkdlumsden.bsky.social
https://twitter.com/KDLumsdenAuthor
https://www.amazon.com/author/kdlumsden
https://www.bookbub.com/profile/kd-lumsden
https://cravebooks.com/author/author-kdlumsden
https://www.goodreads.com/author/show/22489719.K_D_Lumsden

BLURB

Manipulation is palpable here. Blurred lines between friends and foes are everywhere. Trust in others must be earned, but at what cost?

Trapped in a sultry landscape brimming with Telepaths, Irwin and Kipp attempt to outsmart creatures that can read minds, plant seeds of doubt, and reap mental blows. Without Yace there to keep them safe, they are at the whim of merciless men, men who enjoy corrupting, who relish killing the innocent and guilty alike. This is what Yace's father, Lord and Master Dephen Ishik wanted—Irwin now knows this.

Fortunately, Irwin befriends an Empath named Jorge, who says he will help them escape the Telepathic clutches—only if he can journey with them. He is wary of extra companionship until the unthinkable happens to Kipp, and they are setback in their pursuit of Yace. Jorge has ulterior motives. Irwin's attention wanders. Kipp becomes jealous. Yace's future is more uncertain now than ever. But first, they must travel through inhospitable land and hope that fate does not intervene.

When Jorge goes missing, Irwin is forced to make a choice; save a man who loves and accepts him or continue to search for Yace. Time is ticking and telepaths enjoy controlling. Irwin must conjure the strength to destroy and rescue, and without prejudice. Can he do that without hurting Kipp and Yace? Can he maintain a relationship with a man who wants to stay in a place that will set his Metalistic powers off?